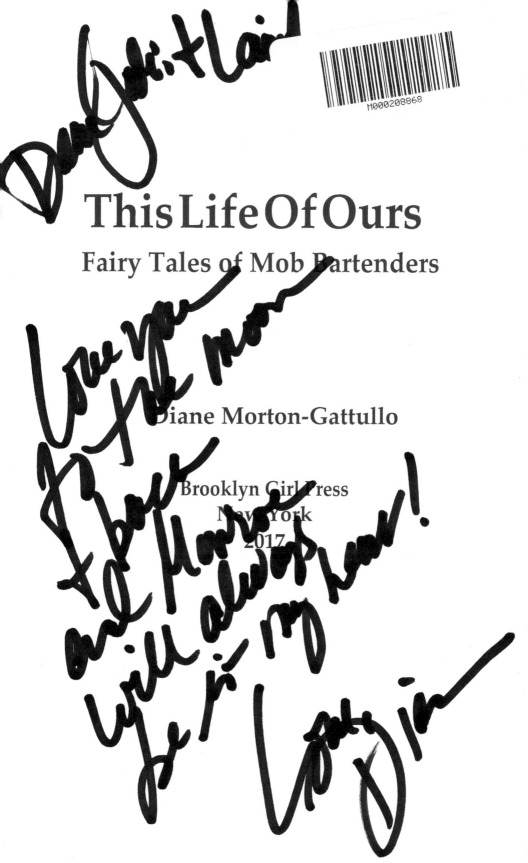

This Life Of Ours

Fairy Tales of Mob Bartenders

Diane Morton-Gattullo

Brooklyn Girl Press
New York
2017

This Life Of Ours

Fairy Tales Of Mob Bartenders

Brooklyn Girl Press, LLC

www.DianeMorton-Gattullo.com

ISBN: 978-0-692-60464-9

ISBN 13: 978-0-692-92440-2

Library of Congress Control Number: 2017949034

Editor: JMT Media

Cover Design: Panagiotis Lampridis, Okomota

Contents

Dedication

I'm proud to be from Brooklyn and dedicate this book to my family, friends, and to those who have passed through my life and are trapped in others. This novel will never be able to do our stories justice; we had more fun and our lives were crazier! The final chapter is still out there to experience!

Words cannot adequately describe the tremendous sense of loss and sadness I'm experiencing since the passing of my dear friend, Angela Raiola-Murphy. My world will never be the same, for I am crestfallen and deeply heartbroken. Angela was known for her larger than life and over the top persona, but I was fortunate enough to know the person behind the image for decades.

I dedicate this book to the woman who made people feel special, went out of her way to help others, and had a tremendous capacity to love wholeheartedly and without reserve! The world will never know how much fun we had, thank you for making nights brighter and days extraordinary! You passed too soon, but with such grace and dignity all during your battle with cancer. It was a privilege to be with you during the good times, and it was my honor to be there during the hard times up until the end. I know as you made your journey you felt our love thoroughly, and I believe you could hear what we said to you, the music we played by your bedside and feel my earrings in your ears. Thank you being my girl and making my life brighter! Pop a bottle at 3:01 because nothing fun happens before 3AM and save me a seat at the bar! Good night my friend!

Non-Negotiables

This is an invitation only club and if you're lucky you might be invited to the VIP section. This life is not for the faint of heart. Remember, you'll never know if you have a real friend once you enter our world. My name is Dannie and I will be your guide on the Crazy Train Express! We break for no one but stop at fuck me, feed me and paying my bills way, the fun house, mob dens, nightclubs and jail. Please don't sit near the windows; you could be shot in the head.

Ladies, these are the top 10 most important things to remember:

1. Live for the moment, no one can promise a better tomorrow.
2. Don't open your mouth, never repeat anything you see or hear, ever!
3. Save your money, because you're going to need it.
4. Don't cheat; you'll create bigger problems than you started with.
5. Don't steal; your guy is a big enough thief for both of you.

6. Look hot, stay hot, and most of all feel hot, because when you feel sexy, you are!

7. Party like a rock star, tip like a gangster, and dress to impress!

8. Walk with an air of self-confidence and never appear weak, because you are the strong girl everyone wishes they were.

9. Be loyal to your friends, but don't allow them to mistreat you. Friends never compete; talk negatively or deliberately hurt one another. When that happens, walk away; otherwise, they will confuse kindness with weakness. You can forgive, but never forget!

10. Have no regrets because you live more in one night than most people do in a lifetime!

I want you to understand our life is like standing on the edge of a cliff. You can choose to step back and not jump, but then you'll never know what I know...what we know, or you can take the leap because it's going to be one hell of a ride! Can you handle the rules? If so, strap yourself in for a wild fucking adventure!

When the veil is pulled back, this is the way it works...like any home; with many rooms our family had ours. The family room was the bar tucked away in a little corner of the world called Brooklyn. It was the neighborhood place where our memories were made. Once inside, you entered through a set of swinging doors that always made noise, a homemade alarm system of sorts. There was a long wooden bar with a jukebox, cocktail tables, and a small dance floor. Our home was far from ordinary. Deals were made; marriage vows were discussed, shattered, and repaired;

promotions and demotions in ranks were carried out, but most of all it was our safe haven or so I thought!

Little Italy was the kitchen, the heart of the house. The streets were filled with the most amazing aromas, laughter, and love. This was the place to be and be seen. Walking down the street, everyone would chat, say hello as they went about their business. Each place had its own personality, but it all blended in, like Sunday gravy. At times there were two alternative worlds and cultures colliding, but mostly we passed like shadows in the night. We lived, learned, and loved while the tourists and feds swirled around like annoying mosquito's nipping at our bare flesh.

The restaurant was the living room of the house where everyone would come together to kick back and have a good time. It sat on a street corner of Little Italy with floor to ceiling glass windows. The glass gave everyone a view of all the action and we were the action plain and simple. Girls like us didn't look anything like the pedestrians, but you should know anyone not in the life was considered a pedestrian. We created a floorshow never seen in any Broadway theater, by just being us. Where else could you see incredible looking women dressed to impress, dancing on tables and the bar like it was New Year's Eve on a Monday in March? That was an every night occurrence for us. There were about twenty tables, but rarely were there strangers sitting at them. How could there be when you needed a reservation six months in advance? This was our place to enjoy the art of food.

The bedroom belonged to the girls completely. Sex was, and always will be a huge part of the life. It was all in the hunt, being in a relationship with a wise guy is like none other. Having sex on a mink coat scattered with piles of cash is fucking amazing! There's a reason that guys lose their souls pursuing us. We're GOOD, and I mean real GOOD; we do shit most girls are too shy to even consider. That's why they spent anything to have us!

It starts with a look and the rest is history. When we walked by, we would turn heads. If we spotted it and liked who was looking at us, we gave the raised eyebrow glance, and it was all over from there. No man was safe; single, engaged, married, it didn't matter! If we wanted them we got them. I wasn't into married guys, like most girls, were, but I was a rare breed. We had no use for regular guys; they couldn't hold or control us that is where the boys came in. Only a real strong guy could get our attention and keep us satisfied.

The owners of the house were the boys; they ruled the streets and businesses. I call them the boys because it's the street term, but in my opinion, most should have been referred to as men. Each place had a crew of made guys who had their own crew of associates. They enforced the law of the street and collected all the money one-way or the other. The collections game would start early in the day and continue way into the night with paper bags being passed at every stop. Many local businesses paid tribute to be protected, and they paid dearly with cash, blood, sweat and many, many tears. Then there were the ones who owed because they were heavy gamblers or borrowed money and were now deeply indebted to the Shylocks for tons.

Their bar was where they would kick back, hang out and chase girls. Strangers were not welcomed if you get my drift, but there were always the few empty suits hanging around trying to look important without anything to offer. They would be the first ones to flip or run if the going got tough. Everyone knew you had to be prepared to defend yourself or your friends at any moment. If you hesitated, it was a sign of weakness called blinking. Weakness is the kiss of death and you could be banished, busted down in rank, or simply disappear. Funny how people just stopped existing in our world. Poof, you're gone! Those decisions were made in my favorite of all the places, the social club; their corporate headquarters. That's where they would do "things" enough said.

Friends are what made this experience extraordinary. My female friends all dated heavy hitters, came from "mobbed up" families, and were loyal as the day was long. We had a core group, but each one had tons of extended friends. We went out together, vacationed together, and talked constantly. When one of us had money, the ones who didn't were covered. Even the boyfriends were generous to the entire group. Our male friends were just as amazing. They had our backs and paid for everything whenever we went out.

I can't remember a single time; we ever had cross words with each other over guys, money or jobs. I could and sometimes would call any one of them at 5AM to bail me out of jams, and they dropped whatever or whoever they were doing to help. We only fought with outsiders, and usually over being disrespected, and when we did fight with each other, we still stood up for one another.

CHAPTER 1

Could've, Should've, Would've, If Only... Where Would We Be?

D annie is the face of the girl who struggled to try and make sense of a time and place in the underbelly world of the mafia. She is not a gum cracking, sleeping around pig, who vomits in the bushes from drinking too much kind of girl. She's bright, articulate, hardworking, and is a tough as nails woman who could feel at home on Park Ave. or in Brooklyn.

Babe is the best and worst of the boys and the life all combined into one character. Most girls who searched for guys like Babe did so because of their charismatic, intense and extreme personalities, but mostly for the sheer sexiness and clout of being with a gangster, which was the biggest thrill. We call them gangster cock chasers. Girls in the life, who actually knew a Babe, would fight tooth and nail to hold him because of the incredible person that lay deep down inside. Guys hung around a Babe trying to get noticed because a Babe was a mover and shaker who could make almost anything happen as he wished. Being a stand-up guy who was fucking tough, and sexy as hell only made the desire more intense. All in all, having a Babe in your life meant you would eventually deal with having your heart torn out and possibly your head blown off. How could you even think a normal life is possible? The bigger question is; are you willing to give up a Babe for a normal life or can you give up a normal life to have a Babe?

If you choose a Babe, be prepared to have tunnel vision; don't pay attention to the news and the outside world, reality is what you create in your head. You will feel the most intense pleasure of your life and may never want anything more. Great parties with lots of friends and children, amazing sex, and cash, cash, and even more cash! All of this will stop you from asking the simple questions ordinary couples ask each other. Please! Can you imagine asking your guy over dinner, "So, how was your day? Hard? Did anyone struggle much? Oh poor baby, here, have some more macaroni!" No, there are some things you never speak of, places you just don't go and how they earn their money is a big one. "Honey, can you work over time and bust a few more heads so we can go on vacation?" Ha, not gonna happen!

The worst part of a Babe is saying goodbye. After being loved that intensely, it is hard to imagine living without him. Saying goodbye could be for an hour or a lifetime either way, you won't be able to breathe, think or be the same ever again. Guys like a Babe are tough, sometimes cruel within their lifestyle, but when they love someone, it's wholehearted, intense and eternal. They may stand tall and emanate strength to the outside world, but they will bend down on their knees for the women they love and if you are that woman, not even God can help you when they leave. And when they do, you will struggle your whole life to move on.

These experiences will never be relived in this generation; the 80's and 90's were unique. Certain girls walked the walk, talked the talk, lived and loved on a completely different level while being surrounded by the most interesting and powerful men.

Loyalty should have been a given, especially in an environment that preached "live by the sword, die by the sword." The greatest misconception and shock of my life was how few people truly followed the code. If you are lucky enough to be on the outside, remember to help those who are still in. There is no greater crime than sitting home eating steak while someone is in the can eating bread, even when they make you crazy. I believe we should all do the right thing, I know I do.

I've often thought, the boys -our boys- were really smart, but just didn't know it. It takes a lot of effort and brains to constantly scheme and maintain the business of "things." If they had just put half the effort and time into having a legit career, they would have been successful. The earners were bright, they knew street math, money math, but were intimidated by school math.

The gravitational pull of the fast lane was just too strong to compete with boring old school. Why sit in a building filled with people telling you what to do and how to do it, when you could be out earning more in a month than your teachers made in a year? Funny the irony of that bothered me because I knew the outcome could be jail, where being told how and what to do doesn't end at 3PM, but is a 24/7 hell and that would suck. They may get away with low-level shit, but if they entered the big leagues all bets were off, and there was always a strong possibility they'd get pinched and do a long stretch in the joint.

As you will see this life of ours was really no life at all. My boys could have accomplished anything because they were bright and charismatic, they were driven, and they were hungry. They could have been legitimately successful if only someone would have persuaded them not to fall into the trap. They should have loved someone or even themselves enough to walk away, but they never did. The boys never realized that they would have still been funny, engaging and good-looking because they always thought it was the life that made them who they were. That wasn't really true because they made the life look so much better than it really was.

CHAPTER 2

Brooklyn Good Girl

My personality is very different from most girls, it's because I have a Brooklyn attitude and street smarts. Nothing rattles my cage; fear is not part of my vocabulary. Some girls are afraid to walk down the street alone, not me I own the fucking street! Others are afraid to go out alone, not me, everyone knows me. Funnier still, there are girls who shake in their shoes when they see "things" happen. Not me - most likely, I know the people involved. Oh, it's easy to live in fear, but living on the edge is a lot more fun. My life is never boring it changes on a dime. I'm like a duck; I let all the craziness roll off my back with my head held high while I swim in the shark tank. Most of the time they never nip at me, but when I swim too close I catch the eye of a great white and it's game on from there!

As I sat amongst the sharks on the front steps of the bar, my great white, Babe, toyed with me. He manipulated the conversation in a very methodical way, complimenting me, and joking around. I was comfortable around him, even though I knew wholeheartedly he was capable of extreme violence. Babe didn't toy with many people, he was known for being the ultimate predator, vicious and someone to fear, unless he liked you, then he could be charming and tons of fun to be around. Babe's stubbornness, exceptional sense of humor, and sex appeal made it easy to overlook his sharp teeth, and turn a blind eye to the little bite marks that would eventually come.

Gazing up at the sun, I thought about how much I enjoyed being around the boys, but it was in this moment that Babe started nibbling at my soul. "What are you doing after work?"

"Going out with my girls. Why?"

"No reason just wanted to know, that's all," he said lighting a cigarette. Clearly, he could see I was waiting for him to ask me out and of course he wasn't going to do it just to burn my ass. Babe wanted me to know he was hanging out, but without committing to anything. My smirk taunted him. He reacted the only way he knew how- by moving away from his car advancing towards me, grinning. "You think you're so funny, don't you?"

I playfully slapped his arm, as he got closer. "I'm fucking hilarious, I crack myself up, Babe! And evidently you're amused or you wouldn't be here."

He grabbed me giving me a huge bear hug and before I knew it, he threw me over his shoulder. As he popped open the trunk of his car, I didn't bat an eyelash as he tossed me inside and slammed it shut, laughing. "So where did you say you were going?"

Babe, you must have thought I'm some wimpy pedestrian chick! Wrong! I lit a cigarette to illuminate my surroundings. Smiling I blew smoke so it would come out of the sides as I counted how many I had left. Ten, perfect I had enough to make him nuts. He thought I would freak out. I've been tossed playfully in a few trunks before, and you don't frighten me!

Sitting on the trunk, Babe noticed the smoke seeping out. "What the fuck? Are you smoking in my trunk?"

I started to laugh, as I called out "Yup, what else am I supposed to do?"

"Hey Fats, don't smoke in there! I'm gonna get good coin selling it, but not if you ruin the carpet." Muttering curses, he popped the trunk to find me lying back grinning like the Cheshire cat. He bent down kissing me and picked me up and out. "You know, nobody but you gets out of my trunk smiling! Fucking nut!" I didn't say a word or look back; I just concentrated on walking up the stairs shaking my ass like I was a stripper, as he walked away laughing to himself. I knew it wouldn't be long before he was back. Babe always came back.

It was one of those cold, crisp November nights; the kind that keeps people home in their warm houses, instead of on the Avenue. I looked out of the bar window, watching the snow teem past the street lamp, laughing to myself about Babe's trunk. Pretty little ice crystals floated in the air, swirling around covering the street in a blanket of beautiful virgin snow. I was alone, but not for long. The card club around the corner would let out soon and the boys would swing by to check on me like they did every Thursday night. Most people would be scared of being alone at night in a bar, but this was my Brooklyn and I wasn't scared. Why should I be? I was a bartender working for the boys. At different points in my life, they would become as close as brothers, husbands, and fathers. Everyone knew me, where I worked, and what type of place it was; it wasn't a secret. Our bar was off limits to anyone who wasn't one of us.

I was passing the time, watching the snow, when out of nowhere a guy sprinted up the front stairs of the bar. He was wearing a shear-ling jacket with the collar up and hat low. Smoking a God awful cigar, he sat in the back of the bar at a table. I didn't think I'd seen him before, but it didn't matter. I asked what I could get him, and he asked for a glass of water.

Geez, I hate water drinkers! I sat down at the bar, and said, "Did you see your name on the canopy outside? This isn't your house; this is a bar. So what are you drinking?"

He was puffing on his smelly cigar and asked for an espresso and water, shooting me a cold hard look. Serving him a single espresso, complete with the lemon peel, and a side bottle of water, I patiently waited to be paid. But he didn't make a move, instead he asked me to put it on his tab.

I had to laugh at him. TAB? "Cash only my friend, it's $10 please." Now I saw his eyes for the first time as he looked up at me with a questioning expression. His eyes were as cold as ice, I've seen eyes like that a few times but that's another story. "$2.50 for the espresso, $2.50 for the water, and $5.00 for me, officer." He started to laugh, but didn't put his money on the table, so I said, "It's going to be $20 soon if you don't pay up." I smiled the whole time, but I held my ground. The last thing I wanted was to entertain an undercover cop who was going to ask me questions I wouldn't answer.

Just at that moment, the boys started piling into the bar. Each one called out to me, "What's up Fats? Have fresh espresso?"

Followed by a million of the same questions they always asked me. Finally, Babe came in with that swagger only the boys have, and grabbed me around my waist, hoisting me up in the air, beaming like a king. Playfully, Babe kissed me hard and gently nibbling on my dimple while my feet dangled in the air. He wasn't hurting me, but I was happily and helplessly trapped in his vice grip as he introduced me, "I want you to meet a friend of ours, Phil." I knew then that I was meeting his boss.

Babe gently lowered me to the floor, but keeping his arm firmly in place. It just hit me the water drinker was Big Phil. He stood up, extended his hand to meet me while kissing my cheek. Shaking his hand, I realized we never officially met before; he was one of the few stone cold gangsters I didn't know personally. I wasn't about to apologize or change my behavior, because then he would think I was impressed or intimidated. That would mean I blinked, and then Phil and the boys would take advantage of me. I liked the way thing were between us now and didn't want anything to change.

Not all of the boys treated women as well as these guys. I've had the displeasure of seeing girls used and abused so badly I would question their sanity. Many guys in the life were heavy handed with their woman, which was a turn off for me. A real man never hits a girl; only a coward would beat the potential mother of his children. Some girls had such low self-esteem, that any attention was considered better than none at all, so they tolerated getting cracked. Any weaknesses including falling in love with any of them, was not in my game plan. Like sharks, if they smelled fear, they would attack.

As Phil took off his jacket and hat, I was able to see he was extremely handsome, standing around 6 feet tall, in fantastic physical shape with salt & pepper hair, neatly brushed back in a DA, aka the Brooklyn Italian look. He had an amazing smile and beautiful eyes, even though they looked as cold as ice. I remember thinking he smiled with his eyes. Funny how handsome the guys in this particular crew were most were gorgeous, and he was no exception. Handsome or not, he had a reputation for being extremely ruthless. He handed me a $100 bill and told me to keep the change. I was beginning to like him!

After all the kisses and hugs, everyone started to relax, that's when Phil started making small talk. "So you like working here Dannie?"

"Sure, it's all good and I love the guys."

"That's what I like to hear. Now you understand we've had a change in management around here?"

"Hey I worked for Andrew yesterday, who I just love and trust like a brother! I don't want you to misunderstand me, he's a good friend, but today I work for you and who knows who'll I'll work for tomorrow. It's the way it is. If he thought I shouldn't be here anymore he would have told me to leave and he didn't so here I am!" I said as I wiped the bar around him.

Flashing his pearly whites, he laughed slightly. "So you love him, huh? Well, let's see how you feel about me after a while."

I stopped wiping and looked him dead in the eye. "You keep tipping me a 'C' note and I'll love you too. Even though I love and respect certain people, this is your world and theirs, not mine. Everything changes on a dime, I just roll with it all."

"Good to know! Things have changed, and if you play by my rules, we'll get along just fine! Understand?" Phil said sending me a silent message not to repeat anything to Andrew about what's said in the bar.

"I'm all good! Phil, be good to me, I'll be good to you. Simple really, if not I'll leave and work somewhere else." *I could land another gig by the end of our conversation, so I'm not worried if this doesn't work out!*

"That's no problem, I'm a gentleman and so are my guys, so we're all going to get along, right? And if they're not, you tell me and I'll take care of it."

Returning to my smart-ass style I said, "The guys are like the brothers I never wanted but I love them!" One rolled up a bunch of cocktail napkins and tossed them one at a time at my head laughing at what I had said. I stood there very composed totally ignoring getting pelted by the napkins. After a minute I excused myself and turned around nonchalantly. They knew I was up to something so they started to grab the ashtrays thinking I would toss one at them, but instead I picked up the soda gun, putting my right index finger over the water hole and pressed the button as I aimed it right at his forehead. Bam I hit my target right between his eyes! The room exploded into laughter. Turning back to Phil I continued, "I'm sorry, where were we?"

Phil laughed at the whole exchange. "I can see you can handle yourself!"

Grinning, I looked back at Sammy who was wiping his face off from all the water and said, "I NEVER miss, never! They all know it too, whether its glasses, ashtrays, bottles or water I nail my target!"

"I can see that, remind me never to get on your bad side," he said continuing to laugh.

I smiled at Phil; for being one of them, he had a great personality with a perfect combination of humor and confidence.

CHAPTER 3

....

New Broom In An Old Room

We talked throughout the evening, and I explained how I covered for another girl a year earlier so she could go to a wedding, and I never left. However, I also worked in Little Italy at a restaurant, the Slime Lite, and bounced around covering for friends too. Phil wanted me to know he was the new sheriff in town, you know "the guy." I'm not stupid; I knew who he was, and what he was. Also, I was aware there was something going on the last few months, the beginnings of a "situation." Wars and beefs are their business, I'm a girl and not involved in any of that. I paid my taxes, and lived a somewhat regular life, except I worked in the bar and nightclub business.

Babe stared at me as he spoke with Phil. It was obvious they had a great relationship; it was more than being assigned to someone's crew, they actually enjoyed each other's company; their facial expressions spoke volumes. Later on, I would find out that Phil was grilling Babe about me.

Phil called out, "Hey Dannie, so I hear you're responsible for making Babe late last night."

I said jokingly, "Me? Hardly, it must have been one of the girls in his fan club! If it wasn't snowing out, they would be here!"

Phil slapped Babe's back laughing! "Oh, you're the man!"

Red-faced Babe played stupid, which was one thing he wasn't. "I have no idea what she's talking about. You know she's crazy!"

I cut in, "Hey, Mr. Cranky, you do know I'm not deaf...right?"

Phil continued teasing him because he was one of the few people who could. "She's got claws in you, I can see it."

Turning, I faced him with my hand up. "Phil, the only claws in Babe are from one of his fans. We're just friends!" I tried to keep a straight face, because as much as I pushed him off, I loved his attention. It never hurt to have the hottest guy only have eyes for you.

"Phil, you got her all wrong! Dannie is so ugly no one would go out with her unless they're blind? The guy would have to own a stick!"

Shooting him a look, I waved my finger laughing at him. "Give me a stick so I can hit you with it you, prick!"

Continuing the torture, he said, "Prick? Stop asking to see my prick already will ya, it's getting embarrassing, but that's the nicest thing you've called me so far!"

Laughing, I straightened my spine and gave Babe a sly smile. "Don't get used to me being nice, I'm just showing Phil how much I love you!"

"You love me, because I feed your fat ass! I think we might have to expand the bar too, just so you could fit behind it."

"Come close to me, I don't need a stick!" I joked with him.

"Come on, we feel sorry for you, that's why you work here." Babe was laughing at his own jokes, thoroughly enjoying teasing me.

I shot him a raised eyebrow, grinning. "Hey watch it! Don't go too far or you'll be buying me lobster for a month!"

"Oh yeah, just to watch you eat it with someone else! Thanks! That was cute, very cute." Babe let his guard down enough to let me know he was annoyed, and secretly I was glad.

Phil roared laughing as he slapped the bar. "I knew it! That's what the smell was in the car last night! That's why you were late?"

Babe threw his hands up in the air as if surrendering. "Fats over here wanted lobster, so I drove to Sheepshead Bay to pick it up, but it took longer than I thought. I dropped it off figuring she would wait for me to eat later, but no, not this one!"

Phil continued to laugh, "You should have told me you were busy with this beautiful girl, I would've understood."

"Oh right that would have gone over big time with you," Babe said, giving Phil a sideways glance.

Smiling at Phil, I said, "Well thanks Phil! You're the only one here with 20/20 vision!"

Babe smirked at me, tilting his head. "Tell him what you did with the lobster; go ahead big shot!"

Beaming with pride I shrugged off his teasing. "No problem! I ate it!"

"What's wrong with that?" Phil asked confused.

"No, not that she ate it. Ask her who with, because it wasn't with me, even though I paid for it!" Babe said trying to act wounded.

"That's right not you! Tough guy, you were too busy and I couldn't let it go to waste so I ate it with that cute kid, Michael. By the way, how do you know?"

"See? I'm such a nice guy, look at this abuse I have to go through," he said, laughing at me while talking to Phil as he put his hand on his heart. Swinging his head around to give me the eye he asked, "Cute?"

Breaking out laughing and trying hard to bust his chops, I said defiantly, "Yes, cute! He's a younger version of you! So Phil now you know the claw marks couldn't belong to me, they must belong to another girl he delivers lobster to. And answer my question!"

"Because I drove by and saw him from the window eating my fucking lobster, you're lucky I like that kid, otherwise that would have been his last fucking meal! Fugeddaboudit!"

Phil put his hand on mine playfully trying to be the peacemaker. "Sweetheart, you have more than hooks in this guy! Don't be so rough on my good friend here; he's a little out of practice!"

I beamed at his admission, but challenged it. "Hardly! I don't know what line of shit he's giving you, but his fan club tells me different. You should see them all hanging out to get a look at him. Please!" I countered as Babe shook his head in denial. He jumped up, grabbed me and buried his face in my neck almost knocking me on the floor.

All the guys laughed along with Babe as Phil said, "Oh Babe, you're hooked pal! Dannie did I see you at a wedding recently?"

I playfully held onto Babe wondering why he asked. "Yup, I went to Gerard's wedding."

"Weren't you with Kid?"

"Yup, I went with Kid as a friend, and before you ask, I went because he asked me and your friend here didn't!" I said pointing at Babe.

"I didn't take anyone!" Babe said shaking his head.

Laughing Phil asked, "Dannie, why didn't you go alone?"

"Why should I? Just because he didn't ask me, doesn't mean I should stay home. I was invited, but I couldn't go alone or people would talk." Is this guy out of his mind? Alone, why should I?

Babe laughed smugly, "Dannie, people were talking anyway about you following me there. Let's not even get into the fact the fucking guy had to buy your dress for you to go with him and after you two walked in, you dumped him!"

"And how would you know Babe? Hmm?"

"Because he was crying at the bar all fucking night about it! You know he thought he won the number walking in with you!"

I started to laugh covering my face. "Kid's nice, but he's just a friend."

"You better be just friends!"

"Oh please! Listen to me, I'm a free agent, I'll go anywhere I want, with whoever I want! And one more thing! Me follow you? You must have me confused with YOUR brain dead fans!"

Cracking up, Babe gave me a mischievous look. "The only place you'll be going is my trunk again, if you don't smarten up!"

I slapped the bar, laughing. "Again? Come up with something new already!" He kissed my neck hard laughing with me. This was the beginning of many nights of good-natured teasing between all of us. Phil would become a good friend for many years, not as close as Babe, but still someone I would love and respect. He was a family man; spoke with pride about his children and wife. Babe would become the closest to me out of all the boys, but it was hard, I'd become super tight with a few of them.

Babe was tall with dark brown hair, deep brown eyes and completely ripped. You know the kind of ripped, that says you just got out of jail and have been lifting weights for ten years ripped. He stood out from the crowd of the boys, because he was so good looking, in a quiet self confident, I could kick your ass way. With a dry sense of humor, bordering on being a major ball buster, you either loved or hated him, there was no in between. As I watched them talk, I giggled remembering meeting Babe after he came home from the joint. Sometimes you just know when you meet someone and there is an instant connection, and that they will be with you forever one way or the other; well that was Babe.

In fact, the first time we met, I didn't know it, but he had just come home from a long stretch in jail. Andrew came in to check on everything. As always, Andrew called out, "What's up Fats? All good?"

"Hi Boss!" I walked over to kiss him hello, and spotted his friend. I shook Babe's hand as Andrew introduced me. *Oh he's a cutie!* I waited on the side of the bar until Andrew collected his mail and checked the register. Andrew couldn't pass me even though I was rail thin, because he was a little stocky. If he was a pervert, he would have tried to rub up against me to get behind the bar, but he never did. That's how the "Fats" nickname was born; outside of that bar I was called "Ohhh Dannie." I'm not sure I ever met another guy in that life as decent and straight up as Andrew. He never treated anyone badly in front of me or acted inappropriately ever; he was a major street guy, but he was a class act, and a true man in every sense of the word. As the afternoon passed, Babe called me "Fats" over and over again. I shot him a look to kill, in other words cut it out. It's funny the first forty times, but after a while I turned around and said, "Really? Excuse you!"

Laughing, Babe challenged me more, "What's the problem Fats?"

"Shut up, you're not fucking funny." *Are you kidding me?*

Andrew knew me well and could joke around all he wanted, but Babe didn't. I could see he was taking a wait-and-see approach, hoping I wasn't going to lose my patience and fight with his friend. Not that I would ever disrespect Andrew by fighting with his friend, but there is only so much abuse I would take from a complete stranger! I walked out from behind the bar right over to Babe, who was sitting on the barstool. I had my hands on my hips, standing between his legs when I put my face up against his, nose to nose and told him in a lowered voice, "I don't know you, stop calling me fat! I respect you! You respect me! Unless you just graduated from college, there's no excuse for your behavior." College is their term for prison. It sounds better to say Daddy went to college for years instead of Daddy's been in prison.

He looked me dead in the eye, grinning, like he'd just won the war. "It's your lucky day, I just graduated! Fats you're some welcome home present!" Then he kissed me hard on the lips. *Oh my god he was an amazing kisser, but what were the odds he just got out of the can today? With luck like this, I should head right over to the track!* Andrew looked as if he was going to have a heart attack on the spot from laughing so hard. After he released me from the kiss, I didn't move. I just stood there staring into his eyes thinking don't blink; don't let him see he got to you. If you look at someone deep in their eyes and show them that didn't freak you out, they feel it in their bones and usually, in other words they'll blink and back off first.

Biting my lips, trying to make myself as sexy looking as possible, I smiled and said, "Not bad, for someone who's been out of practice for a while!" At that moment I knew by the look in his eyes he willingly jumped on the hook, ate the bait, and would go out of his way to make me crazy. I pulled Andrew into the kitchen when I walked away from the bar, busting out laughing, and asked him to make his pain in the ass friend stop calling me fat. He apologized and palmed me a $50 bill, explaining that Babe had just been released after 10 years. He said they were close friends since they were kids, a standup guy who wouldn't hurt me. I thought I'd let him get away with a little horseplay since he was newly released.

I snapped out of reminiscing as I noticed our meeting and all of our brief history being retold to Phil in bits and pieces. I could tell he was sizing me up. Leaving a little after midnight to go meet up with his boss. This, I soon found out, would become his routine. Funny, some guys were just like the stereotypical wise guys, married with a girlfriend. Some would parade them around me, but he never did. There wasn't a moment he wasn't in absolute control and respectful. Phil, Andrew and Babe were very similar in how they conducted themselves publicly. They always set the example of how to behave. There was no denying they were all easily lovable, gregarious, outgoing and larger than life kind of men. The more time you spend with guys like them, it's easier to overlook the issues from the life, especially when you're just a friend.

That night turned out to be fun, all the boys were in a good mood; it was infectious. Every song was something we all loved and sang along with. I danced and poured my way through the night, and soon everyone was getting down grooving too. Babe was feeling happy, but in total control as he was keeping one eye on me the whole night smiling over the rim of his glass. That night was one of the ones that you just know you will remember for a long time.

Babe stayed with me as I closed the bar up. I knew he was about to make his move; he was giving me the signals and I was enjoying his attention. I wouldn't have allowed myself to be left alone if I weren't interested. He came up behind me, put his hands on my waist, and started to kiss the back of my neck. Whew, it was like a jolt of electricity running through my body. I almost dropped the glasses, because my knees were buckling.

He read my body signals right on cue and gripped me tighter to support me. Slowly turning me around he started to kiss me gently. For a guy who's been away for so long, he had the absolute best moves. As much as I was enjoying the moment, and I mean really enjoying the moment, I was so confused. Stepping back, he looked at me while he took the glasses out of my hands and kissed the palms of each one. My skin instantly tingled when his lips touched them. Then he gripped my hips again holding me close while he looked down and kissed me.

As soon as I responded, it was like unlocking Pandora's box; he put his arm around my neck and the other hand was holding the small of my back right above my ass. This kiss was right out of the movies; you know the type...when you forget your name kind of kiss! Babe was giving me a generous sample of the pleasures that lay ahead if I continued. I have no idea how long it lasted, the music went on from song to song and I just swooned. This was a monster make out session, like none other!

His lips were soft, and so perfect! Babe was an excellent kisser, just the right amount of everything, including eye contact. Definitely a man in total control at that moment! He didn't rush through trying to get any further; he just enjoyed me for the longest time. There isn't a girl in the world that doesn't love to have the right guy just kiss them; it's a soul searching experience.

When he started caressing me; I knew I had to make a decision soon before it got out of hand. *I want to make out with you, but I'm not sleeping with you! Why should I give myself easily without being in a relationship? My heart and snatch are the few things I'm never cavalier with. Anyone who gives me grief over it doesn't really care for me anyway.*

His body was pressed up against mine; I could feel his ripped arms enveloping me. In the back of my head, my silent alarm was screaming, *STOP!* I slid my hands down from his neck to his chest, which almost silenced everything completely, and then Babe backed me into the wall, kissing me. His hands were everywhere as he nibbled on my ear and neck, unbuttoning my shirt and in a flash it floated off me, landing on the floor.

Making his way down, he tried sliding the straps off my shoulders as I was up against the wall running my hands through his hair, chewing my lip barely able to control myself. Holding his head in my hands, I was getting lost as he deftly kissed my skin, whispering how beautiful I was. *STOP! STOP NOW!*

My Brooklyn good girl sensibility kept hammering away at me. I couldn't sleep with him in the bar; if I gave in, he would never have any respect for me. We weren't in a real relationship; he never even really asked me out, and if I slept with him, he never would. I would die if I thought he looked at me like one of those girls. So far, he'd only joked around, and teased me, but it wasn't the way it was supposed to be.

He knew I was holding out for the old fashioned way of asking me out, because I was worth the wait and I was going to make him work for it. It wasn't about the words as much as making someone earn the right to be with you. There were a lot of guys who would promise girls the moon to get down their pants and after they did, they'd walk right by them as if they didn't exist.

No way would I ever be that girl; plus, he just came home from prison. What was I thinking? I couldn't go with him! No sloppy seconds for me. Every girl from 10th Ave. to Ave. U loved him, and were all trying to hook up with him. I was going to keep my eyes open to see what kind of a man Babe really was, before I gave in so easily. My girlfriends and I had been watching him out in the clubs ever since the day we met, and he had no shortage of admirers. I had to stop this until I could figure out what I wanted. Sliding his hand down my back, I started to pull away and said in a ragged breath, "I can't, you have to stop."

He did for a second then he gave me the mother of all kisses. Babe kissed me intensely for an hour, making my head spin more every second. Nibbling on my bottom lip he moaned, "Do you still really want me to stop?"

Screaming to myself to hold my ground I whispered, "Yes."

"I don't believe you! Something tells me otherwise." He said as he pressed up against me while still holding me. "Why do you want me to stop?"

Panting shirtless I moaned, "Because I'm not sleeping with you in a bar! Babe, I'm not that kind of girl."

"I don't care where we are and you know I don't think of you like that," he said as he bent down and kissed me again stronger then before.

"And you never will if I have anything to do with it. You have to do it the right way," I said as a tear started to spill down my face.

"Don't cry." He said as he kissed my tear. "What's the right way? Am I doing something wrong here?" he asked, crushing me in his embrace. After a moment he stepped back and I bent down to pick up my shirt. Turning to pull up my straps, Babe grabbed my shoulders and started to kiss my neck. I reached up and held his head as he bit my ear. He was breathing hard in my hair, while he slid his hand down my stomach to the tip of my pants and I froze. Feeling my body tense up, he stopped. "I want you to tell me if I can go any further." Babe was old fashioned to the core; he wasn't about to go anywhere he wasn't clearly invited.

I panted, "I can't." Like a complete gentleman, he stopped. Babe straightened my clothes and hair and kissed me gently on the lips again. Soon I was standing on my own reeling from the experience. Babe didn't skip a beat; he helped me finish cleaning up so we could leave while making small talk and joking around.

As we were about to walk out he turned grabbing my hand and said, "All kidding aside you need to know I don't want to just sleep with anyone! You're definitely not just any girl to me either. Understand?" I nodded and locked the bar door.

The official cat and mouse game began. Just who the cat was, I wasn't exactly sure anymore.

CHAPTER 4

....

Glitter Goddess

Most people cover up and dress conservatively before entering a church...umm not me, because my church was a nightclub! I loved getting lost in my world at the Slime! My customers were a mix of hedge fund and investment bankers, wise guys, celebrities, and movers and shakers! A lot of my Brooklyn boys flocked there, because of the non-stop excitement of being in the middle of Sodom and Gomorrah on ecstasy!

Not that my boys were high, but the rest of the club was, so it was an interesting mix. Reality was warped and redefined; nothing was, as it appeared to be. Hot girls were really club kids in drag. The altar was the bar, the choir loft was the DJ booth, the library was a hedonistic playground, and the sacristy was home to lesbian only parties! Forget the bathrooms, oh my God, it was a freak fest! None of this ever changed, night after night was and is like being on a wild acid trip.

Being a true New Yorker, I can't pass up a visit to a good hot dog cart, and the one outside of the Slime, rocked. Like clockwork, I would hit the cart at 4AM, and watch the tourists being forced out of the exits like a colorful movie being played out in front of me. Just as I was chilling, I spotted Babe's work truck pass; I pretended not to notice when he made a U-turn and pulled up in front. He rolled his window down, and whistled for me. *What am I fucking cab driver? Whistle? You got the wrong girl, buddy!*

I just stood there smirking while I munched. Babe spoke first, "Slime Lite, huh? You hang out in some classy joints Fats!"

Babe could always make me smile with his sense of humor. I walked over to his window, grinning as I offered him a bite. "Oh please, I work here on and off. It's not so bad, I love the music, and the night goes by fast. I just realized I forgot to eat, so I ran out for a hot dog."

"How many jobs do you have? Mama Mia! You're all over the place!"

I punched his arm giggling and leaned up to kiss his cheek. "Are you kidding me, I love what I do! Plus, it keeps me out of trouble! Gotta run!" I turned and started to go back inside the club.

Babe shouted after me, "What time do you get out?"

I never turned, but shouted back as I weaved through the crowd, "Its hide-and-seek time Babes. If you want to know, you'll have to work for it! Later gator!" and with that, I disappeared into the crowd of freaks.

The end of the night is never the end of my night, but it's when the staff gets to kick back and have fun while we close up the bars. I turned in my cash drawers with all the thousands I rang, and loaded my tips in my bag. After I sat on the bar drinking a bottle talking to my hedge guys while the bar-back finished cleaning.

The last person I ever expected to see in here was Babe, but there he was coming straight towards me. His eyes were locked on mine as he walked right through the crowd and picked me up off the bar. I didn't put up a struggle, I just giggled as I called out like a wise ass over his shoulder, "Bye guys! See you next week! Thanks John! Thanks Ron..." I would have continued, but he cut me off by covering my mouth with his hand!

YES, he came back for me! How hot is this guy! I put my head on his shoulder as he opened the car door. He sniffed me asking, "Hey Fats, have you been drinking?" I looked up, but didn't answer. Babe gently lowered me into my car, and closed the door. Right before he was about to take off, he asked again. "So Fats, are you tanked? Where's your car?"

I put my head back on his arm smiling. "No, I'm not whacked, I had two drinks and WAS drinking a bottle until you came in."

"Yeah I saw the bottle. Nice big shot drinking champagne on the bar."

I grinned as I teased, "Oh, you noticed?"

"How much did you drink tonight?"

Smirking, I tried to minimize his question. I really don't like being questioned! "It takes more than that bottle, which I didn't get to finish, I have a high tolerance. I'm just tired, but I'll get my second wind. Where's your truck?"

"I just got off of work. Where's your car?" he asked.

"In the lot around the corner," I said. "Thanks, you can drop me there."

"How about I drive you home, and you leave your car until tomorrow?"

"Nah, I need to get to the club to setup the food so I'll need to have a set of wheels."

"Solved, I'll drive you home and get you to the club since I'm going there too. I'll have someone drive your car back for you, okay?" I narrowed my eyes while I thought about it. When I hesitated he added, "I'll cover the lot."

Now I smiled, "Okay, sounds like a plan. Where do you want to go?"

Babe gently laughed as he narrowed his eyes. "You want to go out? You look beat!"

"Are you kidding me, why waste the buzz, lets go!" I said, enthusiastically.

"Where do you want to go?"

"Somewhere I can get to know another side of you, and by the way, I don't mean a hotel!" I said grinning! "You pick it!"

"Anywhere? Are you sure?" Babe grinned like he was contemplating taking me to hell and back.

"You don't frighten me! I don't care if we go to have breakfast, a club, after hours, sit on a bench or in the car." I grinned like the cat that ate the canary. While he was thinking, I asked, "Are you embarrassed to be seen with me looking like this?" I really did look off the wall dressed in a cut off skin tight tank top and hot shorts and combat boots with crazy writing all over my arms and legs. There weren't many places he could take me looking like this, and I had glitter all over my body to boot!

"Me? Nah, you look cute!" He said smiling as he picked a piece of sparkly glitter off my eyelash.

I raised my eyebrow. "Hmmm cute? Okay, I'll take it."

"What do you want me to say, you're fucking hot? Because you know you are!" He gave me a smirk as he continued, "Stop thinking so much of yourself, will ya!"

Waving my hands above my head, I joked with him. "Oh, you're bringing down my head! I've been worshipped like a goddess all night long and now you're telling me not to feel like one? I'm on an adrenaline rush, from dancing for eight-hours."

He cut in, "Dancing? You bartended right? Don't tell me you strip."

I roared laughing cutting him off! "Are you kidding me? I make more money than any stripper I know, by keeping my clothes on! And the Slime isn't a strip club."

Babe dismissed my comment as if he actually knew what I made. "Come on, stop it, you're lying. I can see you do all right, but strippers make the big bucks."

I had my back up against the passenger car door, and was facing him smoking a cigarette out of the window behind me. I titled my head just staring at him. The cigarette stayed put hanging out of my mouth, as I grabbed my bag opening it. Out flew rubber band piles of cash. "See this...this is what I can make in one night. AND I would never let guys stick their dirty hands inside my clothes for tips, AND I do make more then anyone swinging on a pole, because I don't have to pay back a percentage to the house, DJ and pimp. I only tip out my bar-back."

He eyeballed the piles, all broken up into bundles of hundreds, fifties, twenties, and tens. I had at least four-thousand dollars! *Hey Baby I'm a moneymaker.*

"Not bad, Fats! Look at you...you're making some serious coin. He touched my calf gently, as he started to ask about the big elephant in the room. What's up with this? Why are there phone numbers on your legs?"

I flashed him a wicked smile. "You've never seen me work here, have you?" He shook his head no, but kept his hand holding my calf next to a scribbled message from a Patrick claiming to love me with his phone number! "Well, I work the main bar with three thousand people and body surf the crowd to serve drinks to my high rollers. If they write on me, and by the way only respectful comments are allowed, they have to tip me $100 each time! If by chance it's not respectful, they're punished! Severely!

No cutting the line to get in, they have to wait like all the other pedestrians and pay, they won't have a spot at the bar, in fact I won't even serve or acknowledge them! That's social suicide! Believe me, nobody wants to be demoted, so they all follow the rules! The glitter comes from the house boys, they bomb me when I'm surfing."

Babe's eyes darken, betraying his emotions. "So strangers touch you is what you're saying?"

He doesn't get it! This scene is all too new for him! I smirked shaking my head. "Don't take this the wrong way, but you've been away. Surfing the crowds, whether to serve or to dance is all the rage! They aren't groping me, but handing me off over their heads, believe it or not it's a ton of fun!"

He shook his head, because he just didn't like it. "It's none of my business, but I don't like it, and this writing's bullshit! It's fucking wrong!"

"Well, the writing, the drinking out of my shoes, getting glitter bombed, and the body surfing is all part of the show I put on here. But make no mistake I don't do this at the other places I work at. This is the land of Oz! Everyone is dancing around half baked, almost naked, or dressed like ducks.

What you think is a girl, is really a boy, and what you think is a boy is a butchie girl; you're only seeing me dressed on a main club night, but when I work the library for private parties or the sanctuary for the lesbian parties, I look very different. I change my look for everything."

He cut right in, tightening his grip on my leg. "What do you look like then?"

I had to laugh. "Listen, don't be an uptight wise guy. I put on a show and create a fantasy for the price of a drink. When you come to see me, you can find me looking like your deepest fantasy; a hot teacher, a cowgirl, a club kid, an elegant old Hollywood starlet, a grunge Goth, and sometimes, even in regular clothes, but I'm never the same, never. If guys wanted to see the same thing, they'd stay home and stare at their wives! And before you find out and blow up, sometimes, I bartend in a bikini!"

He took his hand right off me as he blurted out "Get the fuck out of here!"

I moved my leg away, as I scowled at him. "Yup, I've been known to be in a bikini with a cowboy hat and boots. Always around the first of the month, holidays, and Wall Street bonus time! Like it or hate it, it's what I do. I support myself and do a damn good job of it. Babe, I answer to no one!" Without waiting for his response, I started putting everything back in my bag. *Is he kidding me?*

He cleared his throat, getting aggravated. "Just tell me one thing. Do you go with any of these guys or girls?"

I burned red, annoyed. "I'm not gay, I've never been with a girl, but I don't judge anyone. People should be able to love whomever they want, I'm not into the Brooklyn homo-hating shit! I don't sleep around, but if you have to ask me that, we have nothing more to talk about!" In a flash, I opened my door and got out, slamming it behind. I couldn't walk away without letting him know how I felt so I bent in the window. "Babe, things have changed out here, and frankly, how can you judge me, when you make your money in a very fucked up way?"

I turned and walked away, without waiting for a response. I fell in line laughing and smoking with the crowd that was still hanging around outside as Babe watched from the car. *Now there's a problem, after seeing me outside of Brooklyn? Oh please! I have a great life, so many other girls wish they could do half of what I do!*

My drunken Wall Street guys were still all over the place. As I stood there sipping a bottle of water, one guy dropped down on his knee begging me to go away with him! *Patrick's really cute, rich and educated, but a big drinker and cokehead...major turn off!* I smiled at him thinking of course I treat you like a king, because you tip like one! He liked all the attention I gave him in front of his friends, so he would go over board hitting on me! He was making a big show, holding his hand over his heart, slurring devotions, as I looked right at Babe and smiled a fuck you smile, but he gave me the same look as he drove away. He made it to the corner, and popped a U-turn and came back the wrong way.

He left the car running and walked over to me handing me my beeper. "You dropped this in my car." Without another word, he walked back to his car.

Oh he really isn't such a bad guy, just new to this scene! I sauntered over, no longer as tipsy, just playful. "Thanks hey wait up! Friends?" I turned my head sideways as I smiled and continued, "Listen, I think you have the wrong impression of me. If you're not too embarrassed to be seen with me dressed like this, do you wanna grab a cup of coffee?" He shook his head for me to jump in, but I cleared my throat with my hands on my hips waiting in front of the door. He doubled back and opened it, and I grinned jumping in.

Babe pulled up to a little coffee shop and returned a few minutes later carrying two cups, but must have thought I was asleep. He got in quietly, as I whispered; "I'm not sleeping, just resting my eyes after a long day."

"Are you tired? You wanna go home?"

I groaned with pleasure sipping as I flashed him a wicked smile. "NO WAY!"

"Fucking nut! What am I going to do with you? Hey, are you sure you don't have plans with the drunk jerk off?" Babe laughed at my eagerness. He had a great laugh hearty, full of strength and life.

I playfully punched his arm. "Who Patrick? He has more money than God, and is in love with me, he's a worshipper, Babe!" I cracked up laughing at the whole situation.

"Fuck him!" He smirked at me.

"Nah, he's been asking for about a year, but I'm not interested." He gave me a sideways look, but saw I was playing around and laughed with me.

We cruised aimlessly until he pulled over at the Fish Market. I never said a word, but looked around in amusement. I got out grinning, because a regular guy would have taken me somewhere boring, but not Babe. Prostitutes and drunks surrounded the Market, so I'm sure I fit right in looking like a nut. We walked around the stalls goofing and laughing, ignoring all the looks we were getting. We heard someone call my name out and I turned to find my friend Mark, beaming. I hugged him hard, rocking back and forth and turned to introduce him, "Babe, this is Mark, Mark, this is Babe."

Babe eyed him as they shook hands. I squealed with delight as I saw Mark's father. When Babe turned, his expression changed from annoyed to sincerely happy when seeing his old friend, Marco. Marco grabbed Babe, hugging him like a bear, as he called out over his shoulder. "Hey guys! Come here, look Babe's home! Wow...wow...oh my God you look great!" I beamed at Babe, happy to see him welcomed so warmly.

As soon as Marco pulled away, he introduced Babe to his son. "Mark, this is my very good friend, Babe. Babe, this is my son, Mark, you remember him, he was the little boy running around driving me crazy back then." He shook Mark's hand again much friendlier this time, as Marco broke in, "Dannie I'm mad, you don't visit us enough!"

I smiled and kissed his cheek hard. I loved him so much; he was like a second father to me! "I know, I'm terrible, don't hate me! I'm always working, in fact, I just got out."

I shivered a little with the early morning breeze off the water, so Babe put his arm around me and instinctively I snuggled into him. As he rubbed my arms, warming me up, Mark gave me a white fish coat to put on. Now I really was a sight, a glittery fishmonger with graffitied legs. As Mark helped me into the coat, Babe stepped away to talk to Marco.

Mark and I made small talk, mostly about all the places I worked that he never visited. "So when are you going to come visit me?"

"Oh please! I work every fucking day!"

"That's no excuse! Remember you're only young once, and you know I'll make sure you have a great time, so you better come soon! You might actually like being around girls that don't smell like dirty snatch!" As we broke out laughing, I heard Babe ask Marco how he knew me.

"Babe, she's been in my house since Marie was in first grade, they went to school together. You've seen her there, I'm sure. Mark, Marie and Dannie running in and out of the pool during the barbecues. She's like another daughter to me."

That's a good reference; I must have a plus in that column!

Babe looked at me shaking his head, "I don't know, maybe I do and just don't recognize her. Anyway, I just wanted to stop and say hello, I just realized you guys know each other. Lets talk more in a few days."

"You got it! Hey how's your Ma doing?" Marco asked.

Babe smiled as they walked back over to us. "She's great! You know her, she's my best girl!"

Marco waved his hands in every direction shouting orders to his workers. "Mark, get the guys to put together some boxes of lobsters for Babe to take home and give this skinny kid some too. Dannie you better eat a meal soon, before you blow away! Come over Sunday for dinner. Call Marie tomorrow! What am I saying you two still yack it up everyday!"

We all laughed and within minutes we were back in the packed car. Babe leaned over, kissing me softly looking genuinely at ease and amused. "So everyone knows you, even the workers came out to say bye! This is going to be interesting!" His forehead rested against mine. "I don't think I can take you anywhere else, because of the lobsters. You okay with that?"

"Absolutely! I had fun, thanks!" *You have no idea Babe!*

He threw the car in gear and we were off. As soon as I felt his hand on my headrest playing with my hair, my eyes got so heavy I dozed. So much for being a party princess! I felt my hair moving and opened my eyes to find Babe whispering to wake up. Yawning I mumbled, "I'm sorry I fell asleep. I think you put me in a trance when you started playing with my hair."

"Its fine Fats! Let me get you home to bed."

"I had a good time, thanks!" I kept my eyes closed for a few more minutes.

Babe gently felt my forehead. "I'm glad, I had a good time too. Bet you never went to the fish market on a date huh?"

"Date? I don't remember you asking me out."

"Why, is that stuff important to you?"

I grinned, slowly taking his hand from my head and moved it in front of my lips. He thought I was going to kiss it, but instead I shook it like a class A ballbuster. "I think this is the start of a great friendship, it was nice getting to know a different side of you."

"Listen Fats, I think we've moved past friendship a long time ago, so stop busting!"

Ummm no! Just because I make out with you doesn't make you my boyfriend! "Until I hear what I wanna hear, we're special friends."

Roaring laughing at me, he gently smacked my head. "Go fuck yourself, with this!"

"If I could, I'd never leave the house!" I joked as we grabbed a few lobster boxes carrying them into my apartment.

He sat on the couch as I emptied my bag of cash and organized my piles counting quickly what my night yielded. I discarded all the phone numbers in the trash as he watched from the corner of his eye relaxing once they hit the pail. When I joined him, I was more than tired, but not ready to end my night. I didn't want him to leave, truth be told I wanted to slip into twilight wrapped in his arms. I sunk lower and lower into the couch until I curled up with my toes buried in his lap. The moment felt peaceful, comfortable in a way that made my stomach flutter.

Soon, he was nodding off. A few hours later I woke up startled, feeling Babe move; somehow we became intertwined sleeping head to toe. We tumbled off the couch trying to figure out what had happened.

Babe mumbled as he tried to pull me up. "Hey baby, are you okay?"

Smiling, I said, "Yeah, I'm good, I'm sorry I fell asleep! Hang on I have to run to the bathroom." I ran inside, and when I returned I looked better with a washed face, and brushed hair. I was still a glitter queen, but smelled fresh, like toothpaste and soap instead of vodka and olives.

Babe's smile spoke volumes as we passed in the hallway on his way going to my bathroom; he liked the cleaner version of me. I was sitting in a tracksuit with my hair up in a ponytail beaming when he returned. His eyes immediately zeroed in on my chest, realizing I was now braless. I blushed folding my arms to hide while I giggled.

Laughing, he said, "I better go, you must have things to do."

No! "Actually I have nothing to do for hours, except rest before I go to the club. If you don't have anywhere to be, you can stay Pal!"

"Pal?" He shot back.

"Of course, we're friends. You can stay, if you don't have anywhere else to be that is."

"Sure it makes sense, since I'm driving you to the club anyway. But don't you need to sleep more?"

"Maybe, but I feel pretty good, and I'm not working crazy hours today anyway." *You better get the hint!*

"You're off tonight? Do you want to have an early dinner?"

YES! "Hmmm that sounds like fun, I just have to setup at the club at four and place the order for tomorrow, so I'll be free after six. But we really need to do something with the lobsters, so they don't go to waste."

"From the looks of them, you're going to have enough lobster for months!"

I scratched my head, revealing more then I should have, again. And when I noticed his eyes focused on my chest, I just broke out laughing, "Listen, look up and stop staring at my chest! Friends don't gawk!"

He was sleepy and playful, laughing in a deep voice, "I can't help it, they're like there!"

"I'm a girl, I have boobs, and everything else I'm supposed to have. I must say, I'm pretty proud that they are all in pristine condition and hardly used, but if we're going to hangout you have to get over all my...my accessories." I said as I playfully slapped his arm.

He grabbed my hand as I connected, pulling me close, "Listen Rocky, why are you trying so hard to keep me as just a friend?" He didn't give me a chance to answer, choosing instead to kiss me passionately. A soft, personal, intimate kiss that made my eyes flutter closed. When he was done, he stayed lip to lip staring into my eyes. "So what were you going to say?"

He bit my lower lip as I answered in a breathy voice, "I was going to say because you're my friend until you become more or aren't at all, but you have to be my friend first!" He kissed me again harder, pulling me closer until every inch of his body was pressed up against me. I moaned slightly making him crazier.

Again, I pulled back slightly as he whispered, "More!"

I whispered back, "No." as I closed my eyes waiting for Babe to kiss me again, and boy did he.

We kissed GOOD for some time as I reached up running my fingers through his hair, which made me moan just as much as he did. Babe started to lift me off the ground, pressing me intensely close to him as he carried me to the couch. After God knows how long, he slid his hand inside my track jacket, and just as casually I held it. I didn't pull it away, but didn't let it wander either.

Babe pulled back and asked, "What gives?"

He bit my lip as I spoke softly, "Babe, listen, we're definitely not having sex. I honestly don't sleep around casually."

"Then what are we doing here?"

I smiled softly, "We're getting to know each other, because you said more, and because I want to, but that doesn't mean full speed ahead."

Trying to joke around, he asked playfully, "Okay, how about if I say more again, will that work?"

I smirked giggling, "Nope, but I like the sound of it, so I hope you keep kissing me, but you can't pass go! Understand?"

After a while, I think he reached his making out limit and was about to come in his pants like a high school boy, so he pulled back. I watched him intently as he straightened my hair and caressed my face. My lips were pouty and I know the look on my face was saying something very different from what was coming out of my mouth. Whispering, "Babe, come close for a moment, just take it slow and enjoy the moment."

He leaned back close with my arms on the side of my head staring into my eyes as he asked, "Yes?"

I didn't say a word, but just closed my eyes kissing him. So far I was a willing participant, but now I was the aggressor for a few minutes. As I ended it, sucking his bottom lip until it was raw, I finally opened my eyes. "If I ever sleep with you, it's going to be because you're in love with me, so until then, thank you for being a gentleman." *Yes, yes I did, I said the horrible LOVE word, but now you know! Sex equals love for me, plain and simple!*

"Look where being a gentlemen gets me, I have a raging hard-on, and I'm only allowed to kiss you." He joked as he rolled over onto his back, giving me a smirk.

I looked up at the ceiling and blew out a breath, "Well, that's the way it is until we're in a relationship."

"Relationship?" He laughed without thinking how I would react.

I bolted up shooting him a fucking look to kill before running into the bathroom, slamming the door behind me. *The word love didn't freak you out, but relationship did? This is exactly why I don't sleep around!* After a few minutes, he started gently knocking on the door, but I just wouldn't answer him. I turned on the shower and ignored him as I washed off the disgust of the experience. When I was done he was too, because I was alone. I locked up and went to sleep for a few hours. I woke up with a vengeance, annoyed that my car was still in the city! *What a pain in the ass!*

I called one of the valet's from work and asked if he would grab my car and drive it back for me, and of course he did. I tried to give a hundred dollar tip, but he wouldn't take it, I guess it was his way of thanking me for allowing his friends in and hooking them up at the bar. By the time I was dressed, my car was right in front of my house, and he was the extra set of hands I needed to help me load the stupid lobsters in my car.

A few stops later, and bags upon bags of stuff, I descended on the club like Martha Stewart. Within a few hours I turned the backyard into a welcome home party for Babe. Even though he's been out, it will be months before he sees all the people he knows again, so we will be doing this party thing for a while, but today I was going to kill him with kindness! As I hung a banner and put out festive tablecloths a few guys volunteered to fill the mesh bags with the lobsters, corn and clams. They've all been in the can and love to cook in a group setting, and thoroughly enjoyed doing it. Bobby was the first guy to see Babe outside the club, and he was happy as a pig in shit as he called out, "Babe, go out back, and grab a lobster, before they're all gone. Dannie has a big pot of them!"

He walked back to find me dancing to Stevie Wonder's Uptight blaring on the stereo. Once I spotted him, I glided over, grabbing his hand and trying to get me to dance with me. He waved no, so I tried again but stopped when I saw the annoyed gangster expression. Trying to snap him out of his mood, I smiled brightly. "Oh stop being so uptight! I saved the biggest lobster for you!"

Annoyed, he said, "Yeah, you did, why, did you spit in it?"

I stopped dead in my tracks still smiling. "Hold up Babe, can I talk to you for a minute in private?"

"Nah, I'm good. I don't want anything from you."

"What? What are you talking about it?" I asked. *Why would you speak to me like that you, ungrateful prick?*

"Nothing, listen go back to whatever you were doing," Babe snarled.

My hand was on my hip as I tilted my head eyeing him, "Excuse me?"

"What are you deaf? You heard me, I don't want anything from you!" he snapped.

"Really? You seemed to want a lot from me before, and now you can see why you didn't get it! Go fuck yourself and by the way welcome home!" I stormed out so hurt; all the guys turned their heads in confusion.

I could hear Vinnie call out as I grabbed my bag, storming past everyone. "Hey Babe, what did you go and do that for? You made her fucking cry, and all she did was throw a welcome home party for you!"

Babe gave some lame excuse so I could hear, "I don't know why she's crying, she must be pissy! I didn't do anything!"

I sat in my car, fixing my makeup sniffling when he knocked on my passenger door to make me unlock it. He slid in and turned to say, "Listen, I didn't mean to get you upset..."

I put up my hand cutting in, "Babe listen, I was going to tell you that no matter what happened earlier today, I hope we're still friends. That's all!" He tried to break in, but I shushed him, "We're both looking for very different things and I get it, really I do, but that doesn't mean we have to be enemies."

He broke in annoyed, "How do you know what I'm looking for?"

I raised my eyebrow, "Really? You're looking to get laid and I'm looking for a relationship. But now that I know the score, I can put this morning behind me."

"Yeah okay, I'm just looking to just laid?" Babe acted all confused, as if this conversation wasn't going according to his plans.

"Well, if I'm wrong, let me know. But I'll tell you this now PLEASE don't treat me disrespectfully, especially in public. I won't stand for it and don't deserve it." I finished my sentence whispering. I was a hundred percent certain Babe has never had a girl say no to him, call him out on his behavior or be nice to him just as a friend. In fact I'm not sure if you know how to be friends with a girl! *You want to see me cry, throw a fit and beg, because that's what you're used to...stalking love-sick broads!*

Babe was working out the course of events and trying to make sense of it all in his head as he said, "I didn't mean to leave like that, and have all this happen. I like you, so let's start again."

I sucked in my breath, turning to look at him, "Listen, let's work on being friends first." I leaned over and kissed his cheek.

"We're already friends, okay?" Babe said almost confused at feeling bad and even more shocked at the words coming out of his own mouth.

Good, feel bad! Can't you see how much I like you? I smiled. "Great! Listen, I'm going to take off, you go and enjoy and by the way I didn't spit on your lobster so eat it!"

He laughed as he dismissed my joke. "Where are you going?"

I broke eye contact looking away, "I made plans to go out, so I'm going to get my hair done." *I guess you forgot you asked me to have dinner with you.*

He stuck his hand in his pants grabbing his money. "Okay have fun, be safe and I'm sorry I forgot about your car, but it looks like you had that under control. I promised to pay for your lot, so here's a hundred dollars, that should cover it."

But before he finished the sentence, I stopped him short, "Stop, it's okay. I didn't pay for it anyway. Save your money."

"Really? Who paid for it then?" He demanded.

"Excuse you, really?"

Babe didn't wait for my explanation, he tossed the money at me and walked out of the car and not too fast because I peeled away like a bat out of hell. *How's it feel to know I won't fuck you, and you can't fuck me over, but better yet who else is trying to fuck me? Hmm if I didn't pay, why? Better yet, who did? Hope you feel like a dick when you see your name on the sign, cake and cover on your lobster that I threatened every guy so they wouldn't eat it on you! Why can't you just be nice, you know I like you! I almost cancelled my weekly dinner to hangout with you!*

The rest of my afternoon flew by, leaving little time to dwell on his stupidity. Like clockwork, T picked me up. Same time, same night, same restaurant, and table! We never ordered off the menus, we always ate the same meal. The valets knew to hold his spot, because T would never allow anyone to hold his car keys. Our routine was set in stone, along with most of the other guests around us. My time with T was always crazy; trouble seemed to find me whenever we were together!

As I sipped my champagne, I spotted Babe at the bar with Vinnie, but they weren't alone for long. Soon they walked right passed me with two girls. *Really? Asshole!* I wouldn't give him the satisfaction of seeing me upset, even though I was pissed. Babe never looked in my direction and I didn't go out of my way either. Soon enough, he would know I was there.

T wasn't the type of guy to get up and go over to anyone, but he liked Babe and sent over a bottle with the waiter. I saw them all smile and look around to toast a thank you to us. I huddled close to T and told him what was going on, he tapped my arm smiling as he said not to worry my pretty little head over any of it!

Babe walked over carrying his glass smiling, but as he got closer he finally realized that it was me sitting there. They shook hands and hugged as he said, "Hey T, so good to see you!"

"Welcome home Babe! Dannie was just telling me about the party today. Still out celebrating?" T said busting a little bit for my sake as he returned to his seat.

Babe smiled, leaning over to kiss me hello. "Yeah, something like that. Hi Dannie, thanks for going out of your way."

I waved my hand, "Oh please, it was the least I could do for you, I'm glad you enjoyed it!" The place was so crowded he couldn't stand there very long, so he made his goodbyes and returned to the fucking idiot girls and Vinnie.

Through the meal, my stomach burned as I could see the girl slipping her hand on his lap, but he kept moving it off. *I hate girls!* Just when I felt like flinging my knife across the dinning room, I excused myself to use the bathroom. As I walked through the crowd, a drunken customer grabbed my arm. I pushed him off as I shouted, "Don't you ever fucking touch me jerk off!"

He slurred at me, "Come on remember when you used to like me?"

"I was working, I like everyone who tips me asshole!"

He got up and put his finger on my chest, "Yeah, you do? Huh, what else do you do for money bitch?"

What a dick! Infuriated, I smacked him across the face. Just then Babe came up behind me. "Hey Rocky, you okay?" His eyes moved from mine to the guy as he almost went through me to get at him "Hey did you call my friend here something? Tell me exactly what you said so I can rip your fucking tongue out!"

I pushed back against his chest, begging him not do anything. "NO, NO, NO don't do anything, PLEASE DON'T!" Babe was reaching around me grabbing at the guy to rip him apart limb by limb. We were in the tight space, and I tried to prevent him as best I could because I just didn't want him to get locked up!

T cut in, "Everything okay over here?"

I turned red, "Yes, thanks! He's an asshole that I barred for being a bad drunk. I was on my way to the bathroom and he just started acting stupid!" Knowing Babe didn't need one ounce of encouragement to fight, I turned, putting my hand on his chest again shaking my head no. This went against his whole code of ethics, but I quickly feigned fear, burying my face in his chest. "Oh please Babe I'm really scared, can you walk me all the way to the bathroom?" We all knew I wasn't frightened, but he had no choice but to follow because I had asked. T's guys were already in action dragging the drunk out by his neck to teach him some manners.

Babe turned his attention towards me as I opened the bathroom door. "Just give me a minute, I'll be right out okay?" He didn't let me finish when he pushed me in and locked it behind him. He didn't say a word as he kissing me hard against the tile wall. He was about to run his hands all over me, but stopped right above my breast as I pushed him off. I started to panic when someone knocked on the door. "I'll be right out." I turned to Babe whispering, "Now what am I going to do, I have to pee!"

He shrugged, "So pee."

Turning purple I blurted out, "I can't pee in front of you!"

Babe smirked, "Do you realize where I've been for ten years? Come on, I'll turn on the tap so you can pee okay?"

"Turn your back too! I can't believe I'm going to do this!"

He turned around and held the tap open, but I knew he was watching from the mirror as I pull up my dress revealing I wasn't wearing underwear. *GOD HELP ME!* When I was done and washing my hands, he leaned in kissing my neck whispering, "Commando? Nice!"

I turned redder than a fire engine and bolted past him opening the door to get away, but we both walked right out to find his idiot dinner date standing there with her friend. The girl went nuts screaming and swinging at us as Babe reached over pulling the door closed in their faces. I fumed, as they cursed and pounded on the door. I started to flip-out, "You're ruining my reputation! These broads are going to tell everyone, I'm fucking you in the bathroom!"

Being a ball-buster, he asked, "So?"

"I'm not the type of girl to get laid in a scurvy bathroom EVER! I'm getting out of here!"

"Stop! I'll tell everyone that I didn't fuck you! Is that what you want?" Babe grinned, absolutely enjoying making me crazy.

I'm going to kill you! I blew my top! "Oh great, now I'm not even good enough to get fucked by YOU in the bathroom? Are you kidding me? Get out of my way! DON'T SAY ANOTHER FUCKING WORD!" I pushed the door open hitting them right away, then I grabbed the girls dragging them into the bathroom as we jumped out. I slammed the door on them and put a chair under the handle so they couldn't get out. We walked back to the dinning room as if nothing had happened.

Thank God, T walked over. Tilting his head, he started to hustle me away. "Come on Dannie we have to leave before the cops come. Babe it was good to see you!" He grabbed my elbow escorting me away from the mess as I glared at Babe.

We took off to go to Vibes with Babe and Vinnie right up our ass. We all got out of our cars and walked in to shouts from the DJ calling out over the mic, "Ohhh Dannie's in the house! Let me hear some noise!" I took off leaving all of them in the dust, as I stormed the dance floor. Let them talk; let them do whatever they want!

T leaned over to Babe, as I hit the dance floor. "She's a wild child, don't try and understand any of it! But she's good people, you know!" They casually walked like kings of the jungle to the VIP lounge.

Babe and T were on their third drink when I made my way up there, and was warmly welcomed by Brianna shouting, "Oh shit here comes Ohhh Dannie!" I leaned over the bar kissing her, as she popped open a bottle of champagne. "Dannie this is on Tough Guy, your next is with Jerry, and the next is with Big Mike. You have four more after that so far!"

I turned to kiss all the guys and thank them for the bottles, as Toni Girl came over with a huge basket of roses! She said they were from my close friend Mikey Champagne with love! I just adore Michael! Snatching a rose, I ran over to hug him while the basket was removed. Within minutes all my girls came out of the woodwork, joining in the fun. We shared my bottles, getting loud and rowdy bouncing around talking with everyone. The VIP room banquet booths were jammed packed with girls in tiny dresses sitting on the boys' laps, guys hung over each other smoking and laughing in their leisure suits, all while others surrounded the bar calling out their orders. Somehow, Brianna managed to keep everyone's drink full, tabs paid, and people happy.

She was loved by everyone because she was the conductor of the party crowd symphony! The girls roared laughing with their group of guys throwing back shots of tequila, while Dana sat with Big Mike and his suit-and-tie crew, drinking scotch. The rest were with us at the bar, occupying my attention, so I didn't have time to talk to Babe, even though he never took his eyes off me. T slapped his back a few times joking that my ass was going to catch fire if he kept staring at it! *Love you T!*

I only returned to refill my glass because he was immersed in multiple conversations with so many guys. Every few minutes I heard another guy call out, "Holy shit Babe, welcome home! Bri, buy the bar a round!" Babe was getting hugged, slapped and kissed so much it would make anyone's head spin! Just when it couldn't get any better, it did; The Power by Snap came on and my girls jumped up on the tables, seats, and bar dancing! Babe's eyes popped out of his head watching the place erupt into organized chaos!

The guys loved the show, cheering us all on. Fat Franco had his cigar hanging out the corner of his mouth while he jumped up and started tossing bills at all of us laughing. I could see Vinnie and T howling with laughter as James danced in front of me while I was on the table with my girls as I held a champagne bottle in one hand and glass in the other, dancing as if it were our last night on earth.

As the words rang out "I've got the power" we sang it into the bottle like a microphone and pointed at him. Now other guys were trying to join in and tried to dance with all the girls. They didn't know Babe liked me, all they knew was we all hung out together, so no one was prepared when Babe grabbed one guy by his neck picking him off his feet when his face was too close to my legs. I kept going, making more of a show, while his eyes narrowed, giving me a look to kill. Vinnie leaned in pointing at me, "Babe ease up, they do this every fucking night! I swear to God, every fucking night! He don't mean no harm, let him go!"

T just slapped his back, "I pity anyone who tries to tame Dannie, or any of the girls, and it's never ever going to happen! She loves life my friend, and look at the bottles and roses! Life loves her right back!"

He stood there taking it all in. A few songs later, I jumped down and danced right in front of him with James. When I thought my heels would break right off, I took a break to refill my glass. Leaning over his shoulder, I whispered in his ear, "Babe life's too short, smile and just enjoy the moment!" Before he could respond, I licked his ear intimately and moved away quickly to dance again.

Now he had a smile permanently affixed to his face, he finally figured it out. I was just being me, I wasn't out to make him jealous, and I didn't need his attention, because I had plenty! As James danced while drinking, Babe walked over to him putting his arm around his shoulder catching him mid sip. Before he could say anything I heard James say, "Babe, I gotta say, Dannie and me are good friends, we hangout all the time. And before you take it the wrong way, she's like a sister to me! Swear to God!"

It's funny that we were all trained to hear the tiniest of whispers in a loud nightclub! I could hear Babe mumble to James that they would talk later before they hugged and continued to drink. I saw Brianna pop another bottle and extend her arm to me to take the whole thing, which I gladly did.

Now some of the young thugs made their way up to the VIP lounge, I toned down my antics, because they were well known for being troublemakers, and I had enough of that for one night. I stood by the wall, talking to my boy Michael as Babe watched us like a hawk until another song I liked started playing. As I started to dance, I felt his hand on my shoulder, turning me to face him as I continued to dance, now making a show of it for him. He leaned into my ear, "Nice swing Rocky!"

You want my attention, okay now I'll give it to you! His arm was above my head leaning on the wall, as I moved close up against him to put my arms around his neck, "Yeah, and don't you ever forget it! You're not the only tough one!"

He nodded, "I can see that! Remind me to never get on your bad side!"

"I never hit a friend, except for an occasional punch in the arm. But I got your back, don't worry I won't let anyone hurt you!"

He pulled me close, "Yeah, you gonna protect me Dannie? And what's with this Ohhh Dannie stuff?"

"Yeah, I'll protect ya!" I giggled, before answering. "That's my nickname! Did you really think people call me Fats except for you guys?"

He pulled me even closer, "Glad to know, I'd hate to have people think I was with a fat girl!"

"Don't worry, I won't ruin your reputation if I'm not with you!" I squirmed out of his arms to walk back to the bar only to find a guy standing in my spot. I titled my head towards him and said, "Excuse me."

He grinned a jerk off smile, "You're excused!"

Ugh! "Sorry, I meant excuse you, because you're in my way."

He opened his arms playfully inviting me to join him. "There's room enough for both of us if you're with me!"

Now I was done being nice. "Thanks, but no thanks!"

"Suit yourself!" He reached over and tipped over my champagne bucket all over the floor just grinning at me.

I jumped back, getting splashed with the ice water as the bottle foamed out all over me. "You fucking jerk off! You owe me $250 for that bottle you just knocked over!"

He started to laugh, but the grin quickly disappeared when I saw T grab the back of his head slamming it into the bar. In a split second all the guys were up out of their seats to see what happened when the ice bucket hit the floor, as Babe was trying to rip him out of T's hands. They were both playing tug of war with this guy's head, Babe had his face in his hands, while T had the back of his head. They both just slammed him over and over again against the bar so fast it looked like a movie.

The bouncers pried the guy out of their grip and carried him out the side door as they regained control of themselves. The waitress was helping me dry off with a bar rag as they both came over to see if I was all right.

Before anyone said a word, Henry the bouncer bent over the rail, handing me a wad of cash, "Hey, here's your money and a little extra!"

I leaned over grabbed his face kissing his cheek. "You're the best, but keep it! Thanks for watching out for me!"

"Thanks, baby! We got your back!" He winked tucking the cash inside his suit jacket, before disappearing into the crowd below.

T and Babe broke out laughing as I turned to them and hugged and kissed them both in one big embrace. "I love you both, thank you so much!" It was so special to have them both hold me and kiss each side of my head that I just laughed in their arms, beaming at them. T backed off first, allowing Babe to swing me around in the air above his head until he slowly lowered me to meet his eyes. For a split second it became too intimate, too serious for such a public place. Biting my lip I stared at him while he blinked realizing the same thing I did.

Like the flick of a switch, he went right back to being a ball-buster, lowering me to the floor. "Ouffa Fats, you're a trouble maker! You're gonna ruin my alter boy reputation!" We all drank together, joking around and before I knew it, the night was ending. Babe was in rare form, I don't think he built up his drinking stamina yet, but he wasn't bad enough for anyone but me to notice.

"I'm taking off. How are you getting home?"

"Vinnie's driving me, but I think he should take me to your house." He pulled me close. "Come on say yes, and then you can tell me what you're taking off."

Semi-drunk and exhausted, I turned him down nicely, "My door is always open to you as a friend, but tonight I think you should go home. I had enough excitement." I gently removed myself from his grasp and leaned in kissing his cheek. He tried to turn his head to catch my lips, but I was too fast for him. *I know that trick!*

T said his goodbyes, promising to get me home in one piece. I was showered and about to go to bed, when my doorman rang to tell me Babe and Vinnie were in my lobby. I let them come up and met them at my door holding my robe closed. Babe was grinning while Vinnie looked stressed.

Vinnie said hi first, "What's up Dannie?"

"Not much, what's up with you guys? Do you want anything to drink?"

Babe sat down on my couch looking tired and drunk, as he closed his eyes. I turned to Vinnie, "It's okay Vin go home, he can stay here."

"Are you sure? I don't want to leave if you feel uncomfortable."

"No, it's okay, we're friends, I trust him."

Babe shouted, "DON'T TRUST ME!"

I slapped his head, "Stop that! I do trust you, so you can stay Buster!"

As he slid lower until he was lying on the couch, he mumbled, "I'm telling you, don't trust me!"

Vinnie gave me a sideways look, "Maybe I should stay too?"

"You're always welcome Vin, but I really don't think he'll give me a hard time, BECAUSE BABE KNOWS I TRUST HIM!" I said shouting over his head.

"Okay, I'm going to get going. Let him know I have his car, and to call me when he needs to get picked up. Dannie he has to get up early, or should I say soon to check-in at the half way house, don't let him forget it." He kissed my cheek before leaving.

Creeping around, I shut off all the lights, and was just about to put a blanket on him when Babe called out, "Dannie come here."

Bending down, I gently moved his hair and touched his face whispering, "What is it Babe? What's wrong?"

Babe held my hand to his lips, "Just listen to me. I want to sleep with you." I started to pull back, but he held on, "No not for that...not sex, I just want to be loved tonight. Can you do that for me?"

Oh I think I love you already! I knew want he meant, his heart hurt, he was lonely and tonight was a lot for him after being locked away for so long! I gently whispered, "Okay Babe I get it, come with me." I had to help him up and practically carry him into my bedroom onto my bed. I slipped his shoes off, hesitating at his pants. "Do you wear underwear?"

"Hey Fats for the first time I wished I didn't!"

"Okay, then help me take your pants off." He had to pick his butt up so I could unbutton his pants, before I slid them off. He fell back into a cloud from heaven; my goose down feather bed was all soft and fluffy. I'm sure my silky sheets must have felt so good after so many years of sleeping on a crap cot. Ever so gently I helped him pull his shirt over his head; and when he was finally free of his clothes, the noise of the club, the people and yes, prison, he pulled me down to lay next to him, mumbling, "Just love me tonight."

I slipped in next to him, snuggling close, rubbing his chest to soothe his soul. He must have felt some sense of peace, because he drifted off almost immediately, holding me tightly.

CHAPTER 5

....

Just Friends

Why is something moving next to me? Oh my God, what the hell is going on? I jumped up and fell out of bed. Blinking a million times, I focused on a strange body next to me. Burying my face in my arms, trying to figure out what was happening as Babe kneeled next to me, cradling my whole body. "Hey, it's okay." Babe picked me up in one swoop, placing me in the middle of the bed. Like a child, I peeked over my arms at him, as he brushed the stray hair away from my eyes and slowly moved my face up. "Hey, don't cry, I would never hurt you."

Slowly, my fear subsided, and I started to straighten my spine to sit up while I wiped my tears away on my sleeve. "Oh I'm so embarrassed, I can't believe this!" I stuttered a bit, completely flustered. "I had such a bad dream, and when I felt you touch me I freaked out. I'm so sorry!"

"It's okay, really it is! What did you dream about?"

My dreams are not up for discussion! I cleared my gravely voice and I said, "Geez I don't remember."

"Really? That was pretty intense not to remember it."

"I'm telling you, I don't remember, because I don't. Just drop it please."

Babe looked unsure of what to do, but I guess going to the bathroom won out. He stood up saying, "Okay, I have to pee, I'll be right back."

I must have made him so nervous he never realized he was standing in his briefs with a raging hard on right in my face! His innocence and obvious affliction snapped me of freaking out. I pointed to the bathroom waving him in the direction as I tried not to laugh out loud. "It's okay. In fact, really, go ahead, I'm fine." As soon as he left, I jumped up and quickly changed into a tracksuit, and made my bed. He returned with my towel wrapped around his waist, pretending as if nothing was amiss. Now it was my turn to use the bathroom, and when I came back he was completely dressed in my living room.

Thank God! "Good morning Babe!"

"Hey good morning to you too! Listen, I'm sorry I barged in last night, I was pretty drunk."

I smiled as I walked to the kitchen to put on a pot of coffee. "It's okay, in fact I'm glad to know you're not a psycho drunk."

"Yeah? That's good to hear." He chuckled.

"Are you hungry?" I asked as I looked in the fridge.

"No, I'm good with just coffee. I like it black."

"I think I know how you like your coffee by now," I giggled because now I knew he was nervous too.

As I poured two cups and handed him one he broke the awkward silence, "Listen sit for a second." I could feel my face flash red as I sat at the dinning room table with my legs pulled up to my chest, resting my feet on the seat. "I hope I didn't do anything to make you get upset this morning, but when I woke up and saw you sleeping I just moved some of your hair away from your face, that's all, I swear!"

I put up my hand, minimizing the situation, while I dropped my eyes. "Don't worry about it, I just had some freaky dream that I don't remember. Crazy, but I guess I just was in such a deep sleep and got startled."

"Okay, again I'm sorry...sorry about all of it. But I had a good time last night Rocky!" He slapped my leg trying to make me smile.

"Oh brother! What a fucking fiasco with those broads! But I had a GREAT time at Vibes! You on the other hand...hmmmm."

"I almost tore some guy's head off for you and you wouldn't let me get to the other one, so I think I was pretty good!" Babe smirked at me.

"Oh, that's not what I mean, but thank you for sticking up for me! No way did I want you to get involved and locked up! But don't minimize the bathroom incident, it was all your fault!"

He laughed while he sipped, "You asked me to take you to the bathroom, because you were scared, so I thought I should go in with you that's all!"

I turned my head sideways, raising my eyebrow, "Really?"

"Yeah really!"

"Okay, whatever you say! The bathroom was a nightmare! I was referring to the fact you never danced with me once!" I said, smirking.

"No, I didn't, but that didn't stop you! How can you do that for hours? Holy shit!" he said laughing.

"I love to dance, and I do it all night when I work AND I don't care if I dance alone, I just do what I want when I want."

"Oh that's what you meant in front of the Slime!" He said visibly relieved, and letting me know he was still processing everything he knew about me. "Hey, it looks like you forgot all your roses too."

I turned redder if that's possible. "Are you kidding me, what the hell would I do with all those flowers? Please, I thank everyone and then send them to the back so she can resell them. She makes money, my customers and friends enjoy giving them, and I'm flattered in the process! But don't tell anyone, it's our secret!" I said, winking.

He laughed his true laugh that made my stomach tingle. "What a racket you got going! You don't do too bad either, in the bottle department."

I guess its time to explain a little! "Listen, I only drink champagne, and I don't mind paying my own freight, so when guys buy me a drink, they know its an expensive one! I give away as much as I drink, so everybody's happy!"

"That's a lot of guys."

"Oh please, between my customers, and friends its all good. I never say yes to anyone I don't know and like. I've turned away a ton of offers, because I don't want them to think they're getting anything for the price of a shit bottle!"

"It seems we have a lot of mutual friends, and they all really like you. I think Vinnie was pissed I came here."

"Yup, and I'm sure so many more we don't realize yet. And Vinnie is a doll, I love him!"

"Yeah, you love him like how?" Babe asked with a raised eyebrow.

"Oh please, like a brother and James too while we're talking about this. I hang out with all of them, more James, but all of the guys a couple nights a week."

"I gotta ask seriously, are you dating anyone, because last night I talked with T about his relationship with you. I don't want to step on anyone's toes if you're involved. I've asked you this before, but now I want a straight answer."

I narrowed my eyes, and asked, "YOU asked him what?"

"I asked him, man to man if you guys were more than friends. After all, you were having dinner with him. You can't blame me for doing the right thing."

"T and I have dinner once a week, same table, same meal, and same bat channel! But I see him several times a week in the clubs. WE ARE JUST FRIENDS!"

"Okay, so you and T are just friends, but what about anyone else? Because there has to be a reason you keep turning me away when we're alone even though I know you like me."

My cheeks burned as I broke eye contact to take a nervous sip of my coffee. "I turn you down when it comes to sleeping with you, not anything else!" *Of course I have dates, but nobody I really like at the moment. If I say yes, you'll walk, if I say no, you'll think I'm a loser!*

"I know that, but we're not strangers." Babe said, amused that he was making me blush.

I squirmed, answering, "I date when I want to, I don't have a boyfriend at the moment, and most of all I don't randomly fuck people if that's what you want to know. But I gotta ask why did you come here last night?"

"Because I guess I wanted to be with you. Are you mad?" He took another deep sip of his coffee measuring my reaction to his questions.

"No, it's okay I'm not mad, but what about your girlfriend? Isn't she going to be pissed?"

"I don't have a girlfriend," He answered a little too quickly.

I cut in, "I don't know if I believe you, but if you say so! Who was your dinner date last night?"

"They were some girls I picked up at the bar, because...because I really don't know why."

I dropped my head lowering my voice as I said; "You randomly picked up two girls, not one, to have dinner with?"

"I only picked up one..."

I slapped the table laughing as I cut him off, "Strike one, don't lie to me, because I saw you walk in Vinnie and he has a girlfriend and doesn't fool around. So you were saying, continue!"

"Okay, I picked up two girls, it's not a big deal!"

"It is when you're asking me about my social life," I said raising my eyebrow challenging him. *Oh you are just so cute right now!*

He grinned at me. "I have a right to ask, because if you're dating someone I know, there could be a problem."

I grinned right back at him! "You were thinking about that last night when you came here...hmm? What would have happened if I was with someone?"

"DO YOU bring guys home?"

"Answer my question first!"

"I don't know maybe I would have left, or beat the piss out of him, depending on who it was."

"Hmmm, well yes I bring people because this is where I live! BUT they're only friends at the moment. James is here a lot, and he sleeps on the couch before you get crazy. And frankly, my girlfriends crash here all the time too. Oh remember, I'm not a dike!"

Babe's face flashed dark for a second. "So let's get this straight, you and James are just friends?"

"We are not fucking around, we never have fucked around and have no plans to. James is too young for me I like older guys, but I genuinely love him like a brother, so don't give him a hard time!"

"Since you mentioned fucking, who are you sleeping with?"

"That's just none of your business, but let me ask you, where were you yesterday? Who were you fucking?"

Babe face flashed a look like I was crazy as he responded with the typical gangster answer. "Me? I don't know what you're talking about."

"It's an easy question, who were you fucking yesterday? Because I know you did, you mumbled in your sleep."

He shot back, "You're lying!"

"Why would I? You held me tightly until you snored like a truck, then you tossed and turned, trashing like a shark mumbling 'oh yeah, I like that, come on baby' and moaning. At one point your hands were all over me, almost choking the shit out of me."

"That never happened!" He snapped!

I know my face turned so red, I could feel the flash. "Yeah it never happened? Well, you tried to jam your fingers into my vagina and look at this." I stood up and unzipped my jogging suit jacket all the way and exposed myself. There were bite marks, bruises and scratches over my neck, chest and breasts.

He ran his fingers through his hair as I turned and zipped up. "I don't remember any of it! I wasn't with anyone; it must have been just a dream." He lied because he lost his self-confidence momentarily and fumbled for a cigarette. "And about my hands and your...I'm sorry. Why didn't you hit me? Wake me or something?"

It's too early for a complicated conversation! "Because I understood you were just lonely, plus you were drunk and if I hit you, you might have woken up and killed me. But I did get you to stop and no you didn't get any farther than groping me roughly."

Now it was his turn to be embarrassed, he cleared his throat. "I don't know what to say."

"Why don't you start with who you were dreaming about, because it wasn't me?"

Babe looked at his watch trying to avoid this completely. "I told ya, I wasn't with anybody."

"Okay, if that's your story, but let's make this crystal clear. First, we're friends and if we are to remain that way you need to understand, there's a chance you may run into me on an actual date, so don't make a scene. Second, I'm pretty cool, but I have zero tolerance for bullshitters, so if you're telling me the truth, I'll take you at your word, but if you're lying you're out. Third, I'm a brawler, so if you're dates get disrespectful with me; I'll knock 'em out. We good on that score?" I asked extending my hand.

He took it trying to kiss it, but I shook his instead. Smiling, he said, "Deal, but the same goes for me. Don't lie to me either, and if your dates are disrespectful be prepared, but that won't happen because, like I always say, where you gonna find a blind guy to date Fats?" He stood up pulling me, wrapping his arms around me, crushing my body into his. "Now I have to call Vinnie to get me, unless you want to drive me."

"How about you take my car and leave it by the club or bar, since you live a few blocks away. Put the keys in the register for me."

"How do you know where I live and how you gonna get there?"

Winking, I boasted, "I know everything, just remember that! I'll get a ride or call a cab, don't worry I know you're in a hurry. Don't you have to go the half way house today?"

"Yeah, I do, did I tell you that too?" Babe asked, giving me a questionable look.

"No, Vinnie told me before he left to make sure you didn't run late." He kissed the top of my head before walking to open the door. "Hang on, I have to shut off the alarm."

As he pulled his money out of his pocket, he looked at all of the locks on my door. "Wow, you got more locks than Fort Knox! Listen, take this for a cab." Babe palmed me fifty bucks for the eight-dollar ride, before vanishing like a dream.

CHAPTER 6

Trick Bag

A day, a month, a year, it didn't matter; we were developing a routine that felt like it was a hundred years old. I always liked working, but now it was different, work was an adventure. Word traveled fast, I became an attraction that guys would come into look at. Who was the girl that had captured Babe's attention? Without meaning to be in this position, I was. At work, I was becoming Babe's girl; all the guys just assumed I was his. He hung very close to me whenever possible, but without showing up unannounced at my house. I know that wherever I went, he would get a phone call about it, he was tracking my moves without invading my space too much. After the impromptu sleepover, Babe was crazy busy working, going to the half way house and probably chasing girls to get what he could from them, because I wasn't giving him anything. Going out, I was still my own person, but the lines were quickly intersecting.

Being an attraction wasn't anything new to my girlfriends and me. In our line of work, it was common; in fact it built up our earning potential. Everyone wanted to be part of the in crowd. Kind of like the allure of the boys, only we sold a fantasy with a drink. I worked all over Brooklyn, New York and even LA, sometimes in more than one place at a time. It was all about supply and demand, and where the money was. *The life was amazing!*

We lived and loved in the greatest bars and clubs in Brooklyn and New York City. We went where we wanted, when we wanted, and we were never told there wasn't a table or a parking spot just for us. Life was like the lyrics to a song and we sang it with every action and move we made, because we were the rat pack of the nightclubs. People on the outside either despised or envied us, but we never noticed them. If they weren't part of our world, we didn't care. Life was fast and furious; we loved and played hard, it was the big car and big cigar days, dripping with diamonds and furs.

My haunts were the hottest clubs; my girls and I hit them almost every night. Club lines were a part of a pedestrian's everyday life, but not for us. Other people waited on lines; we were offered them. No bouncer ever stood in our way, unless it was to get his kiss on the cheek. Stopping to pay admission was an absurd concept; the clubs should have paid us to be there. We brought the party with us and collected souls along the way. No velvet rope ever barred us, but we surrounded ourselves with them. We spent like rock stars, tipped like gangsters, drove hot sports cars, and dressed to kill. Pulling up to a club, we tossed our keys and walked past all the amateurs waiting in line. Truly, we were living the life people couldn't even imagine it was fun being us! Once inside the real party would begin. My customers would hangout in the same places I did, and we would all party together.

Having Babe's eye on me only increased my street stock. I had a strict rule, that I didn't date my customers. I worked in multiple locations and depending on where I was, I was asked out and pursued relentlessly. If I had dated around, a lot the money would have dried up. The more you say no, the more they ask and the more they spend. My customers were split amongst the group that were just my friends, the ones who wanted to date me, and the group that wanted me to keep their secrets. I had a steady, loyal group that would follow me from place to place.

There were the wise guys that would come in, most would leave the wives with me pretending to have a meeting, but really go bang their girlfriends. It was always the same routine, I would be entrusted with the task of keeping the wife occupied and amused while he screwed some twenty-one year olds brains out near by! The wife would grill me about his activities, adding how much she loved her husband and their kids! I felt sorry for her, but could never do more than nod in agreement that he was such a great guy. Occasionally, one particular guy would make me babysit his girlfriend, Tina so he could take his wife out without running into his goumada. She would get so drunk, threatening to tell his wife about their relationship, I would always try to put out the fire by distracting her.

After work one night, I was forced to take Tina out with me at the end of my shift or, she would have hunted him down and created a problem. The night quickly spiraled out of control because she partied way too much. All coked up and drunk, Tina was beyond embarrassing, so I valeted her in my car while I stayed in the club, which I did often with drunken girls! Once I returned, I found her laid out not moving, foaming from the mouth. Panicking, I felt for a pulse, but couldn't find one. I shook Tina like a rag doll, but still nothing.

Good grief, I couldn't have a wise guy's girl die in my car! Finally, I pulled out my makeup mirror and put it under her nose, and thank god there was a slight haze in the mirror. I called out to the valet kid to get me a bucket of ice while I started to pound on Tina's chest. Within minutes, he returned and I tossed the whole bucket of ice on her. She jumped with a start cursing me. So grateful this trash bag lived through the night, I drove her home and deposited Tina in her bed. The next day her boyfriend stopped by and gave me a bonus on top of my babysitting fee because he heard from the club bouncers what I went through. Sweet, a quick $500!

There were always the guys that copped an attitude if I said no to their advances, getting mad and becoming a torch because they wanted to know if I thought I was too good to go out with them. Most of the time I was pleasant, but it was time consuming and exhausting. I was notorious for turning most admirers into good friends, in order to keep their money close and not bruise their egos. It's a fine line for a girl to walk between wanting to earn without being taken advantage of.

Up until Babe, close friends, friend's dads, my smart mouth, quick wit and my right hook protected me. I was thinking I might be ready and happy to give up and let Babe take over, and he definitely was tough enough to make all the crazies back off.

Babe didn't seem to mind the loons and never mentioned them to me. I'm sure if he knew about all the off the wall moments I had with so many people he knew, he wouldn't have been pleased to say the least. Working at the bar, I developed a close bond with so many more guys than girls, not counting the ones I already knew since childhood. There was this one night when I bumped into this guy, Matt, who was a well-known relative of a boss from one of the five families, and friends with all the players. He was, of course, married with a steady girlfriend, but didn't hangout in the bar, and normally was in complete control, never really allowing himself to be seen whacked.

Frankly, he was always, and I mean always, one of the best behaved and nicest guys around. As luck would have it, I was out at Vibes wearing a micro black dress, with stockings and heels when we ran into each other. We happily talked and drank together in a group for most of the night, and I could see Matt was getting trashed.

He asked me if I wanted to go to after hours to continue to party, but I declined because after hours would always lead to a problem, unless it was with the right crowd. As I started to say goodnight, Matt grabbed my wrist and pulled me back to talk to him playfully. Repeatedly telling him to stop only made him wilder, until he did something so out of character I was floored. Bending down, Matty put his hand up my dress, ripped my stockings off from my crotch and proceeded to tie them around his head like bunny ears!

Everyone in the VIP section froze and then burst out laughing at the absurd scene unfolding in front them. I stood stock still as it happened, thinking did this guy actually just put his hand up my dress?

Turning to face the bar, he picked up his glass and toasted me wearing my stockings around his head! My face turned completely red! If I allowed him to get away with it, even though we had known each other since I was five years old, then every guy would think they could touch me. I slapped Matty across the face right before one of his friends or cousins could stop me. One guy, Neil, grabbed my arm and whispered a warning to me about who he was. I didn't care, he wasn't one of the big wise guy's to me; he was just a regular old drunk guy now who crossed the line.

Time stood still for a moment as everyone froze waiting to see his reaction. The VIP section was no ordinary place! This is where all the big guys hung out and there was a strict rule not to fight, because it was too small a space, and if there were shots fired, a lot of people could get hit. The higher rank the guy was, the more he had to lose for a stupid incident.

Funny what a slap will do to a guy; it either makes them enraged or snaps them back into reality. In this case, Matt realized he was acting like a lunatic and ripped the stockings off his head, profusely apologizing as his cousins burst out laughing. They loved me, because I regularly got them out of trouble in the strip clubs for getting out of line with the dancers. I couldn't be appeased; I walked out pissed and embarrassed. The next night, a huge floral arrangement, like the ones at a wake, was delivered to my job with a note asking for forgiveness. I threw the note in my bag just in case I needed it for future use, and had the busboy carry the flowers to my car.

I drove like the wind until I reached his social club and threw the flowers out on the sidewalk. Without a word, I drove back to work furious. A short time later, Matt sheepishly walked in to apologize. He had no idea why he did what he did and kept asking me to please let him make it up to me. I finally relented, because he really wasn't a bad guy, just momentarily stupid.

We made plans to meet in the city for drinks that night, since the club was slow. Millie and I jumped in my car and quickly caught up with him on the FDR. I spotted Mattie's red Lincoln ahead of me as I drove and high beamed him. I could see his hand wave out the window, acknowledging me, but as I stepped on the brakes before we approached 34th street I realized something was very wrong. My car wouldn't slow down, no matter how hard I hit the break pedal. He must have been looking at me from the rear view mirror, and sensed there was a problem because he was slowing down. But I needed him to get the hell out of my way, so I wouldn't hit him!

We were about to die on the FDR! My options were slim; I could either throw it in park or pull the emergency brake, but either way it was going to be bad. I chose to throw it in park and as I predicted it was rough, but I had to ride it out and steer us out of a crash if at all possible. The grinding sounds were horrific until I ground to a halt.

Matt dragged us away in total disbelief at the whole situation. A tow truck showed up and we jumped in his car; but instead of going home we went out drinking. Recounting the incident all night long, we drank as if it were our last night on the face of the earth. The next day he called to let me know my brakes were cut and that he would have my car fixed.

Cut? Good grief! It took about a week to find out who did it, but after the guy was tracked down it was ugly to say the least. The brakes were only one small moment from pre-Babe days that I know would make him crazy!

Whenever Babe would come in, my foot fetish crazed Marines would all say hello to him. They would drink out of my shoes; actually out of new shoe stash that I hid under the bar. Somehow that became a craze, and even when I was out, guys would take my shoes, forcing me to keep spares in my trunk. Somehow Babe never mentioned anything about it, I guess he was either very secure or more used to deviant freaky people than me.

God knows what he must have seen in and out of prison. Knowing that those places were filled with mental patients mingled in with gang-bangers, rapists, murderers, pedophiles, and white collar along with RICO criminals, only made me more amazed that he was as normal as he was.

It wasn't like the movies where the boys serve their time in a country club environment. The boys went to hard-core prison for long stretches where they faced time in the hole; which is complete isolation from everyone and everything for extremely long periods of time. Being deprived of real food, adequate medical attention, and basic dignity could turn some people into depraved shadows of themselves, but as I would find out, thank God, not my Babe.

I've known hard, really tough standup guys that totally changed once inside the joint. One guy very close to me explained in a rare personal moment, "People change when they're alone for a long time, they just do." Some change more than others for various reasons, and under extreme circumstances. Losing their sense of balance and humanity while they experienced dark times, you could tell it was happening even if they couldn't by the way they behaved and what they said.

The saddest case was a cute neighborhood kid, JP, who did his time in a dormitory style state facility only to be raped every night. I heard he cried himself to sleep nightly, eventually losing his mind. His crime was nothing so severe to deserve five years of nightly rape.

Not that Brooklyn was 'Crooklyn,' but so many of our guys from every type of family, rich or poor, had someone who went to prison. We didn't like it, didn't want it, but accepted it as a fact of life, because it was what it was. Everyone grew up on the same block with a fireman, politician, gangster and priest all co-existing nicely.

There were the ones who turned to drugs to escape their environment. Once hooked, they would sell themselves to get their fix. Truly fucking sad! You can see it in their eyes if they got hooked on the junk. It's ironic how they lived like tough guys outside only to become someone's bitch inside and for what? Drugs! The root of all evil has always been drugs. It can make a stand up guy get down on his knees and suck someone's dick just to get high. Nothing is worse than watching that total descent into hell, because they're not gay, just willing to swallow for a fix.

Finally there are the ones who do their time, without the time doing them; leaving it behind when they re-entered society. They would die first before being a snitch or a switch hitter. They went in straight and left straight. The stigma of being in the mafia makes you feared in the can, but also a target for the yahoo's who want to earn a name by taking out a tough guy. To survive you have to be heavy-handed and take no shit. Fighting to keep what's yours and keep the animals away is just a fact of life. Banging heads when you have to and even when you don't need to, sends a message "Don't fuck with me!"

Never did I see any of the facilities that are mentioned on TV and the movies, where the inmates are in a country club setting, playing golf and tennis all day, eating contraband lobster. Don't get me wrong, they do get little creature comforts, but they pay fucking exorbitant amounts of money for a frigging smuggled in espresso. The posh joints don't exist. It's a lonely, cold, 8x8 filthy box in which you are trapped for most of your time without any means of being rehabilitated and no sense of dignity- the system treats inmates worse than dogs in a kennel.

CHAPTER 7

Poison

I always owned a car; a hot sports car in fact, and was the driver out of my group of friends, but now I stopped driving to work in Brooklyn regularly, because of rising tensions in the street. There was a rumble going on in the jungle that I wanted no part of. Babe would find a way to be there to pick me up and drive me everywhere I wanted to go. Even though we flirted with each other, made out, and he'd seen more of me than he should have, we were still not officially in a relationship. I kept the chase game going, pushing him away until I could make sure he was single and available. This gave me enough time to think things through and decide if I wanted to be his girl and deal with everything that came along with that title. He drove a black convertible turbo Porsche and was a crazy driver. His looks, charm, and humor were more than intoxicating, so being in the same car with him, it became an adventure.

Like clockwork, at 6PM Babe pulled up to take me to work. He looked great smiling with a giant grin and sparkly eyes, wearing a white t-shirt and jeans. We flew out of Bay Ridge, cruising the streets heading towards Dyker Heights. The weather was amazing, just cool enough for long sleeves, but warm enough to have the top down. As we passed the golf course, Babe pulled into a spot with a clear view of the park. Putting his arm around me, I leaned back and put my head on his arm and we just sat there staring at the sky.

"So you still date that blind guy?" Babe asked. Leaning closer, he nuzzled my hair and took a deep breath. "You smell delicious. Do you know that? Really I love the smell of your hair. Come closer."

You finally noticed enough to say something! You should only know my perfume is called Poison! Giggling I said, "I can't get any closer; I'm already leaning on your arm."

"I repeat are you still dating that blind guy? You didn't answer."

I tried to joke my way out of this conversation, "Maybe baby, why? You don't want a girlfriend anyway, if I told you I was really single you wouldn't be interested and you know it. You just like playing this game with me."

He turned to face me and I could feel his breath on my face and lips. Staring seriously into my eyes he didn't say a word for a long time, he just stared. Finally I broke the silence pointing to my lap and said with a smart-ass attitude "See this? This is where I won't let YOU IN; so don't worry about being out! It's locked up like Fort Knox! You don't have a shot even though you've seen me naked!"

Laughing, he grabbed me and said, "Really? Well, I've been known to be a bank robber, so don't be so sure and don't be a fucking tease. I get what I want; it's as simple as that."

"How do I get what I want?" I continued to tease trying to get under his skin.

"What do you want honey?" He said tickling my side.

Squealing as he increased the pressure, "For you to go away! Stop tickling me!" Babe knew I was lying; I didn't want him to go anywhere.

"You know I'm not going anywhere, I'll be here waiting until you give in." He stopped and tried to kiss me again.

"Seriously, you go with a different girl every night after being in the can for ten years, so I'm not running fast into anything just to be cheated on. I like the ways things are between us now."

"I have no idea what you're talking about," he said laughing. "There's only one girl that I love more than anyone, she's called my mother."

"Not your mother, the others!"

"Did you ever see me with anyone since the restaurant?"

"No, but do you think I don't know what you guys are like? I'm sure when you went away, you had two girls on a string waiting in the wings just in case you beat the wrap. What happened? Did they move on, or just get older?"

"That was a long time ago, I don't remember," he said relaxing in total control and enjoying teasing me.

"I'm sure the day I show you real interest you'll be kicking me to the curb, but I'm enjoying the ride while you're around. You're a prick though because now you have me worrying about you all the time! No matter what I love you, you're my friend, so don't forget that."

Babe leaned over and opened the glove box exposing his rolls of cash stacked neatly. He placed a roll of twenties on my lap. Hmm that's one of the biggest attractions of the boys, they always spread their cash around and are very generous to the girls they have their eyes on. I grew up with money, so as much as I found it flattering, I wasn't swayed by it. I didn't touch it; I didn't want any more of it. *I've already taken too much from you.* "I like the sound of that! You care, nice! Listen go get your hair and nails done, buy a new outfit and heels. I may want to take you to dinner this week."

Laughing I turned to him and asked, "Are you asking me out?"

He smirked, "No, but I might. So get ready!"

Being from Brooklyn I talk with my hands. Laughing, I waved my well manicured fingers in his face "Well, I'm not available!"

Grinning big, Babe asked, "Really?"

"You've got the wrong girl, if you think I'm sitting around waiting for you to just show up and run into me at a restaurant. I'm no last minute Lucy; you have to ask in advance, AND by the way I'm booked for the next six months!"

"Too bad, because I might be lonely this month," he said playing along.

"We're both always joking around, but seriously I don't need your money." If I continued to let him give me big money, he would think I only liked him for it, and that was the farthest thing from the truth. I liked Babe, I really was falling for him fast and hard, and it had nothing to do with the flash and cash. It was him- the real him- that made me melt every time I looked at him. But if I gave in too easily, he would own me, and that wasn't going to happen! I would own his heart, before he possessed my snatch!

"Don't mistake kindness for weakness. I know how I want you to look, so take the money and go shopping, get yourself all dolled up for me."

"I look just fine, in fact, I always look good otherwise you wouldn't have noticed me."

"You're beautiful, but that doesn't mean you can't get dressed up for me!"

"You only want to see me naked who you kidding? Listen I gotta get to work, so put your ass in gear." I rolled the cash off my lap and let it land on the floor. Neither one of us reached for it, it just sat there as a reminder. *The more I say no, the more you wanna give it to me but I don't want you getting jammed up!* Pedestrian girls not "in the know" never knew how to handle one of the boys. Forget Jersey girls completely, they're fast and are known for sleeping with guys on the first date, and were, therefore, relegated to the last choice on the hook-up list. They gave in way too quickly, but not girls like us.

This is how it goes...if one of the boys chased you, you would hold out until your last breath. Saying yes the first month means you're easy, and going with them right away meant you're a pig. It's all about the chase. No one wants anyone that's easy, the harder the better. By the time any one of the boys got the girl, who was in the know, he would be drooling, and by that time, a girl had a pretty strong indication of what kind of person he was. Everyone appears to be great when you first meet them; only time gives clarity to rose colored glasses.

If the guy couldn't keep up with the chase, he wasn't worth it. Those were the worst guys of all, because they would lie about being turned down. That kind of talk would ruin a girl's reputation and chances of finding a husband. No matter how much a girl would try to deny it, the majority of people didn't believe her. The girl would have to be really well liked and tough to survive that kind of character assassination. You can't imagine how many guys lied about sleeping with girls! If they got laid half as much as they claimed, they wouldn't have enough time to eat. Thank God my Babe wasn't like that.

Pulling out of the spot, he drove slowly towards the bar. Babe kept his hand on the back of my seat and gently twirled my hair, releasing more perfume. "Listen, I want to make a stop before we get to the bar." He pulled in front of a storefront that obviously wasn't a regular store. It was a private social club, and there were guys all over the street doing the walk and talk. As we pulled up, they all waved and some walked over to the car. Everyone spotted the wad of cash, but nobody mentioned it rolling around on the floor. He was still twirling my hair, while he spoke. I knew exactly what he was doing; staking his claim to me, so that no one would ask me out.

Ha game on! He wasn't the first to try this! Instead of sitting silently in the car, waiting for Babe to be done, I turned the tables on him. Without a word I climbed out of the car and walked into the club to say hello to the guys I knew. I knew most of them; they were from the neighborhood and knew me from childhood. I was welcomed with open arms and huge kisses. Babe was now waiting for me. After twenty minutes, I figured he had enough punishment; I climbed back in the car. I waved goodbye, blew kisses and shouted to give my love to their families. Turning to Babe I smiled, and told him I was ready to go.

Babe beamed at me with his brilliant smile, leaned over and kissed me on my forehead saying, "You think you're funny? It doesn't matter, they all know now if they didn't already. Now let's get you to work before you get fired for being late and I have to take care of you." We rode in silence the rest of the way to the bar each planning our next move.

He never banked on me being so stubborn; Babe didn't understand I was well aware of what my life could be if only I said yes. Being one of the "it girls" I had the world at my fingertips and really wasn't looking for a mobbed up boyfriend. Friends were one thing, but I didn't want to get serious with any of them ever again or ever be a sidepiece of ass.

Once bitten twice shy was my motto, but in my case, my past relationships were more like going ten rounds with a pit bull biting my ass. I've served the wives on Saturday, and the girlfriends on Friday, with the late night hookups at 4AM. After becoming jaded from it, being in it and watching the humiliation, I decided I was never going to be one of them again.

Visiting my husband in prison with our kids by day, and crying myself to sleep alone at night would be too much to bear, because I'm one hundred percent sure I would find out he had another family completely, and that they visited on the alternative days. I could do the wait, if only I knew I was the only one waiting. But that's the funny thing in this life; you never really know anything, its all a leap of faith. There was one big problem with my plan;

I hated regular guys because they bored me to tears. So far I couldn't find one that held my attention. I tried, I really did!

I firmly believed regular guys were as interesting as watching paint dry, but I craved their continuity and security. Really, the downside of the boy's life was not the life I wanted. I might never find my husband, but if I did, he was going to be a great lover, my best friend, able to take care of me, definitely not be a slouch, and be able to defend me. He would also be handsome, confident, smart witted, successful, and always make me feel like I was the only one. He was going to be the father of my many kids. Basically, I was looking for a needle in a haystack; no matter how daunting the search was, I kept looking.

One of the winners, during the pre-Babe days, was named Joe. He owned a bar, was outgoing, and everyone loved him, maybe a little too much for his own good. He cheated on me from the moment we started dating, until the night I finally reached my boiling point. Joe was a schmoozer and girls ate up his line of bullshit like bread and gravy.

One girl actually slit her wrists and smeared blood all over his door while we were inside. I found her and called the ambulance, hoping she wasn't going to die in front of me. Joe's lies were so good; he convinced me she was a nut case, because, really, who would do such a thing. So I forgave him and took him back, again. Why? I have no idea; I didn't like his family, his living arrangements, or him after I really got to know him. I just liked his bar and life style. Joe dated me because I was arm candy, but mostly, because I came from a lot of money. He just didn't know he was never going to get any of it.

Joe's family owned an apartment building and the WHOLE family lived there. There was absolutely no privacy. His apartment was across from his parents'. Everyone kept the doors open until I starting dating him. I remember the first time he took me home. His mother was sitting in her housedress at the kitchen table; she turned and looked at me like I was the devil. She was an overprotective Italian mother- enough said. I was definitely not what she thought her son should be dating. Americano!

Sipping red wine from a glass jelly jar, she eyed me like I was completely evil when he introduced me. I hated her from the first moment we set eyes on each other. Every time I came over, I closed the apartment door so she couldn't sit at her table and stare at us. Eventually, she would close her door when she saw me too, because her wandering-eyed husband loved to get up and make a show of kissing me hello.

I think Joe secretly enjoyed making her crazy, because he dragged me there all the time. His problem was that his mother was overbearing and allowed her own husband to treat her badly; therefore, she condoned and encouraged her son to treat his girlfriends just as horrendously. His father was a lowlife and cheater; it seemed to be a genetic trait he inherited.

The night I reached my limit, we were attending a wedding at Back on the Bay. I overheard two waitresses talking in the restroom about the guests at the wedding. One told the other she met a hot guy named Joe who owned a bar, and was going to go out with him after work, but first he had to drop off his stupid girlfriend. Now I was thinking, what are the odds there are two Joes who both own bars here at the same wedding let alone with a stupid girlfriend. None!

It had to be my two timing jerk, and I must have been the idiot she was referring to. So I decided to leave Joe and that relationship behind at that moment before I became the nut case slitting her wrists, or the beady eye old hag wife, drinking out of glass jelly jars.

I stumbled head first to the point of no return, and along the way I found my pride and dignity again. I walked out of the catering hall and took his car out of valet, because I had his ticket in my purse. I drove his Corvette to Pennsylvania Avenue and parked it with the windows down and T-tops off next to the projects and left the keys in the car. I simply walked away; I wasn't a half a block when the car was being stripped down to the frame right on the spot. As they hustled, stripping at remarkable speed, the guys cat called how hot I was and one walked up along side of me, calling me fine white chocolate!

I gave my sly, seductive look with my raised eyebrow to make him crazy as I said, "Heads up my friend, you can strip the car, but not me! I'm a look, but don't touch broad! Think 'Danger Will Robinson' and it's all good." He doubled over laughing as he adjusted his head rag, in a strange attempt to look more presentable.

The beautiful custom sculpted Italian leather seats were being hoisted above and passed back through the crowd like a trophy. The Benzie Box was jacked and I could hear their screams of delight over the fact it was a German radio. I stood waiting at the bus stop, dressed to kill from the wedding, smiling from ear to ear watching the melee. It was like a Christmas free-for-all for these guys stripping the Vet. Somehow, I felt the nut case girl was smiling somewhere too.

I looked in my bag, and realized I didn't have change to catch a bus, and had to walk back to the melee. They gave me a snarling look, hoping I wasn't going to try and get the car back, not that there was much left of it. I explained I didn't have any change, and that they could keep the ride, but I needed whatever was in between the seats to get back home. That seemed to be a good swap, so they scrounged around until they found enough. To my surprise they hung out and waited with me until the bus arrived. We laughed, and bonded street style sitting on over turned garbage cans talking about Joe.

The general consensus was, Joe had to be a major dick for cheating on me, because they felt I was a fine piece of ass! Once the bus pulled up they gave me all the gang hand symbols, and invited me back anytime. People on the bus just looked at me like I was from Mars, dressed to the nine's hugging gang bangers goodbye. Oh well, it couldn't hurt to be on their good side just in case I was ever stuck in the hood, or needed to ditch a car. Two hours later I was home, exhausted, and single, but liberated.

Joe pursued me for a while after, but I think it was just to get close to me again, and probably pay me back for his car. I heard he went to a couple of guys to have a sit down but they wouldn't get involved. Joe was told basically if his girlfriend made a tool of him, he must have deserved it and be happy he had insurance. The boys rarely get involved in girl drama or in between girlfriends and boyfriends, so he was out of luck. Before I was truly done with him, I laid a shovel across the windshield of his replacement car as a gift of sorts with my red lipstick print on the handle. Feeling satisfied, I decided to kick him to the curb and move on.

After that night, he was dead to me; I rarely had a civil word or gave him the time of day. That wasn't enough to make him walk away though; Joe would torture me occasionally by calling my phone while he had sex with other girls so I could hear him. As soon as I would answer, I would be greeted with screams and howls of a girl getting banged as he laughed in the background. What a jerk off! He's my only ex that I loathed completely with every fiber of my being, because of the way he publicly cheated on me.

CHAPTER 8

Big Little Italy

I worked in Little Italy, which was like a second home to me. I worked for another family all together, separate from my Brooklyn gig. When times are good everyone gets along and the money flows, and even when they're bad, it's still a party. Days and nights were always exciting and seemed to run into one another as they flew by. This was just as much my home as the people who lived on Mulberry Street. I had explored every nook and cranny long before working there.

The place I worked had a grand opening a few months earlier and it was a who's who of the boys. It was like a red carpet runway, because of the flashy clothing. The girls were all decked out in diamonds, killer heels and furs; the boys were in three grand suits with manicured nails and meticulously haircuts. I made thousands that night. Millie and I were raking in the dough ever since. I loved working there, but only for Pino. His partner wasn't very nice to me and I let it be known I liked him even less. It didn't matter; I was an earner, so he liked me as long as I brought in the cash. And I was the cashqueen.

Very few girls were real workers; normally they sat back and just collected the tips. But not me or my girls- we earned every penny. Earners with off the wall, killer personalities; triple threats! I had another talent that was very useful and helped me earn extra money. I was a counter: and very accurate, up to thirty grand at a clip, right to the dollar. Counting machines were so expensive, it was cheaper to pay me to come in earlier in the day and count all the money from the restaurants and bars in the areas. You have to be respected and trusted to sit in a room with a guy reading the racing form with a piece on the table, as you count cash over and over again.

I loved working for Pino. He was a larger than life guy who was the worker out of the partnership. Like so many of the boys, his major flaw was gambling. He'd bet on a cockroach crossing the street if someone were to take the action. Even though he was married, (maybe on paper only, who knows) we never saw her. Pino, Millie and I would hit the track, casino or hottest club at least once a week after work. He loved having each one of us on his arm; a hot blonde and brunette boosted his image. It didn't hurt mine either, I sat back and enjoyed the moment for however long it was going to last.

Later in life he would be shot in the head playing cards; I was devastated. We were great friends, but nothing more. He wouldn't be the only person to be killed because of this life of ours. Wakes were a constant event; I lived in black clothing, and still do.

Certain things separate us from regular people; like seeing someone shot in front of you and having their blood spray your face, sleeping during the mornings, eating out almost every night, dressing in outrageous clothing, paying with cash for everything, and never talking to outsiders and cops. It's much more than working in a bar; it's a lifestyle. Our rules were different and we held ourselves to a different set of standards. Each one of us had a nickname and was known for something. Being a standup person meant you were honorable and trustworthy; it was a badge of honor. It was the only badge we could get as women. The guys could be made and earn their button.

There were different card games going on all the time, creating a buzz. After 47th street's diamond district, there wasn't another neighborhood in the city that had more fire power then Little Italy. It was a densely populated place filled with cafés, and restaurants. To the outsiders it was a tourist spot, to anyone in the know; it was the epicenter of the life. What most outsiders didn't realize was that even though a guy was with a particular crew and family, they actually were close friends with different family members. They didn't stay exclusively insulated in their crime families. Every family was represented, and you could visit all five, simply by having drinks at five different restaurants. It was definitely a man's world, but some women, only the respected ones, were revered and allowed in.

The day I started to work at the restaurant, waiters placed bets on whether I was actually running the place or not. Up until then, no girl had run a restaurant whose dad didn't actually own the place; I was something of a novelty. I got a kick watching the guys spit, shout and pay each other out right in the window after asking Pino what exactly I was doing there.

The main attraction of a place like this restaurant needed to be established from the beginning; I felt strongly that the bar was the heart, and the food was the soul. The bar being so important had to be just right to attract the clientele I wanted. I always kept it immaculate, because the boys liked it clean. There are no dirty gangsters, they smell good, dress well and get manicures.

I surrounded myself with the dads of my childhood friends because they were powerful men, and amazingly big spenders. While in eighth grade, a regular friend's dad drove me home after a sleep over only to make a stop by the local school to attack me. I was just a kid; I even had my sleeping bag and Teen Beat magazines with me. I jumped out of the car window before he could actually rape me and ran to a friend's house and her parents took me in. They treated me with extreme kindness; the whole situation left a huge impression on me and shaped how and who I surrounded myself with for the rest of my life.

I never wanted to be that person anyone could take advantage of again, so I worked around people who insulated me. That bastard almost robbed me of all the teenage milestones I was supposed to have. Word traveled like lightning, and most of the other dads from the life took a shine to me. What he tried to take away was replaced by much more by the extended families I gained.

Now all the brothers and cousins were growing up and becoming the rising stars in their crews. They were the hottest guys around and created a ton of action, all while hitting on my girlfriends. I was having the time of my life surrounded by all of them. The financial lean years ended, and now it was Fat Tuesday everyday. One of the few guys who came to every place I ever worked, no matter what family ran it was James. He got along with everyone, and hung out with many different crowds, plus he loved my girlfriends.

Millie was the closest to me, like the sister I always wanted. We met when we were sixteen and remained tight for most of our lives. Tall, blonde, with crystal blue eyes and a body to die for; she had the biggest heart of gold or so I thought! Always up for an adventure, she was the dancing queen with high standards and principles. Every wise guy around loved her and asked her out, but she actually dated very little, trying to hold out for the right one.

There were other girlfriends, who were all bartenders, and they also lived large and in charge, loved deeply, while having a killer adventure! The restaurant and club scene were like the Wild West fraught with danger, but no matter how many off the wall things that happened. I couldn't image working in any other industry.

We would bounce from the Japan Club on Monday nights, to Holler's and Strings on Thursday's and hit the Slime and Surf & Turf Club on Sunday's. Not to mention the hottest restaurants where pedestrians needed a month or more advance reservation, but not us. We ate when and where we wanted. New York was our playground to do as we wished. Each place had at least one of the boys that looked out for us while watching over their various schemes. It was particularly interesting to see them after they were drinking and how overprotective they became. If I thought Babe was nuts, it was magnified a thousand percent being with a crew that thought they had to watch over you as a favor.

One late night, I ran into a regular guy, Christopher that   I grew up with. We chatted for a while at an Upper West Side bar. He excused himself to the restroom and never came back. I wouldn't have thought much, except he left his beeper at the bar.

Feeling uncomfortable about leaving to go to another place with his beeper still on the bar, I decided to look for him. I walked to the men's room and asked a waiter to go in and look around for him. When the waiter gave me the wide-eyed, terrified look I knew something was up. Knocking on the bathroom door, I heard a muffled scream. Knocking harder, I announced I was coming in. Pushing the door open, I found Christopher suspended in the air by his tie surrounded by a bunch of guys. And there was T right in the middle!

"Jesus Christ T! What are you doing?"

"I just want to see who you're with, that's all!" He said smirking.

"Let him go! He's from my neighborhood, a friend, not a date! This is Christopher." I walked in between them and made them lower him to the ground. The poor guy was purple and embarrassed, but grateful for my intervention. He clung to me like a life preserver on the Titanic!

T walked over straightening out his jacket and said, "Let me make this up to you kid!"

Stuttering, Christopher replied, "NO! I mean no, that's okay." Trying to edge his way out of the bathroom, he realized he wasn't in any position to say no and had better go with the flow.

I gave him a squeeze of the hand to let him know he should follow my lead. "Let's go back to the bar and talk about this. This room is making me nauseous!" Grabbing his arm, I pushed him past all the boys. Once we walked back to the bar, I leaned in and whispered, "I won't leave you alone, just go along with whatever I say. They're all whacked. Don't drink too much either, I can't go with you to pee." The guy's face was white; he didn't know if he should run, or trust me. We had another drink at the bar and then were invited to go to a private club. *I love private clubs!* We jumped in a waiting car outside and drove to a dilapidated building with a rusty door. Once we walked inside, we found it was a gambling club as posh as can be.

This poor guy was about to throw up with fear when he realized where we were. Again I reassured him to follow my lead. We had a few drinks, which I tossed in the plant when no one was looking. Walking around a bit, I stopped to say hello and brought luck to a guy who hit playing Blackjack. I cornered Christopher and whispered, I'm giving you a $100 bill, give it to the bartender when I give you the look that we're leaving and I'm going to get us out of here. Slipping the bill in his pocket, I gave him a squeeze on the arm and walked him back to the bar. I loved T; he was great fun from the first time we met. Talking with him tonight, I realized he was more outgoing then normal. In all the years we were friends, I never saw T out of control, high or drunk, but tonight he was in a vicious pleasant mood if you could imagine, almost as if he was toying with his prey.

"T, listen, I'm tired, we're gonna go. Christopher here is going to propose to my girlfriend Dina and we were out discussing the details. If I don't get him home soon, she's gonna think I stole him for myself!"

"Nah! Stay for one more!" He said with a deep smile tilting his head.

"I can't, but how about dinner tomorrow night? Brooklyn or the city, it's my treat"

"You never pay while I'm around! Forget that! Let's go to a Thai place in the lower east side that I like, six good?"

"Perfect! You'll drop me off at work after?" I asked as I leaned in and kissed him.

"Don't I always? Get home safe!" He turned his attention to Christopher and held his arm poking him in his chest. And just like a real predator he growled in his face. "If this fucking girl goes home with any hair on her body touched, I'm going to find you! There isn't a place you could hide, you understand me?"

Looking visibly shaken, Christopher stammered, "I, I understand...sir. It was nice to meet you, thank you!" I gave him the look and he took out the hundred-dollar bill out and placed it on the bar and put his glass on top.

T seemed to like the gesture and slapped him on the back hard. "Nice, that's nice kid. Good luck on getting married!" With that we walked towards the door. Once outside, Christopher started to shake while I hailed a cab.

I noticed he was crying. *Crying! A guy crying and no one died?* "What's wrong with you? Are you crying?" I had to ask in total disbelief.

"I thought he was going to kill me all night long. That one guy is crazy! Did you see him, all of them? They kept asking me questions about you in the bathroom," he cried, totally freaked out.

"So what? T's not crazy, just a little over protective. You could have relaxed after I took you out of the bathroom." I said, trying to be nonchalant.

"So what? Those guys are in the mafia, that's what!" He shouted at me.

Shocked I shot back, "What's your fucking problem?"

Practically spitting at me, "How could you be friends with people like that? You're a lowlife!"

Fucking angry at his stupidity I shouted back, "Lowlife? You can't shine their shoes asshole! Oh what's your head made of wood, what do you think your family is you idiot? Wake up!"

Looking at me like I was a liar, he shouted, "My dad's not like that!"

"Really! You're a fucking tool!" I said giving him a slap of reality. *Why did all the kids find this to be shocking? Didn't they ever wonder how their parents afforded the big houses and flashy cars? Certainly not from slicing off bologna by the pound!*

Choking on his tears, he said, "Leave me alone!"

"No problem! But oh, stop crying, you big fucking baby! I left my friends to take care of you and now I'm stuck here and all you can do is whine and CRY? If you were tougher they couldn't have taken advantage of you like that to begin with. You're lucky I saved you in the men's room."

"You call this lucky? Get two cabs, I'm not going anywhere with you!"

I stared at him in total disbelief and when the first cab stopped I got in and spit at him, "I should've let them roll you! Get your own fucking cab jerk off! By the way you owe me $100, send it to the bar by Friday or you'll owe me two bills by Saturday!" I slammed the door, and secretly hoped one the guys would see him on the street corner and have some fun with him. *So much for regular guys! I needed to go find Babe and get away from these crybabies!*

CHAPTER 9

....

Boundaries Are Made To Be Broken

Bouncing back home in the neighborhood was becoming less of a priority, because I felt I was making it too easy for Babe to keep tabs on me. Ever since he slept over, I tried keeping a lower profile, but he knew every time I saw him, I was excited; my huge smile gave me up right up! Babe would come in and act as if nothing was different. He was a complete gentleman in that way, even as he called out teasing, "What are you doing Fats?" Each time he smiled more with that deep, I got you smile! One day he sat at the end of the bar and drank a soda. Playing with the ice, he jokingly asked, "How was Rio's last night?"

"Awesome, just like it always is!" *Oh no, he knows I was out last night!* My date was one for the record books! The idiot tried to show off and took me to a hot spot, and after he drank way too much he tried to push my head in his lap as he attempted to kiss me in the car. I cracked him, jumped out, and hailed a cab to hightail it out of there. I bounced around mingling with my club friends trying to forget the embarrassment of being treated like a pig.

Babe gave me a cross-eyed look. "We just missed each other, you left right before I showed up."

"I went over to the Surf & Turf club. Did you stay at Rio's all night?" *No way am I telling you about my awful date!*

Babe lowered his head, eying me. "No, I went to the Surf too, but I didn't see you there."

Oh I wish you would've found me! "That's because I went to the Japan Club after Surf's."

He laughed slightly. "You go anywhere else in one night?"

Here we go again! I started to laugh, trying to avoid answering. "No place interesting. Tell me what you did, I'm sure it was more fun." I poured him a drink that he didn't ask for, hoping he would relax enough to explain why he knew where I was last night.

"Me? Not much, I had dinner and then went out for a few drinks. I didn't stay out late, how about you?"

I laughed, turning pink and looked at my other customers to see if they needed refills. Thank God a few did. I walked away hoping he would change his line of questioning, by the time I returned. Babe's eyes never left me; I felt them burn into me until I finally walked back. His drink was low, but he put his hand over the top so I couldn't freshen it up. "So you were saying."

I titled my head grinning. "What were we talking about?"

"I asked if you stayed out late."

"Oh I don't remember. Why?"

He leaned in slightly saying, "You don't remember what time you went home?"

Jesus, Mary and Joseph! "What's the big deal?" I asked more amused, than annoyed.

His eyes narrowed, but he maintained a friendly smile. "You have something to hide Fats?"

"Maybe I do! I'm sure you have lots of girlfriends and dates since I haven't seen that much of you, someone must be occupying your time!" I saw the twinkle in his eye as he pondered his next verbal chess move.

He continued to twirl his ice until he said, "Me? You must be out of your bread box!"

"Oh yeah, I'm so sure of that!" I laughed, because we both knew he had tons of girls chasing him all fucking nightlong.

"So how about you?"

"Hmm maybe I happened to meet a guy that doesn't find me so ugly!"

"I guess he must be gay or blind! When you're ready to date a straight guy with good vision, you let me know." Babe lowered his voice, so no one else could hear us. "By the way, your date went back to Rio's and drank himself sick!"

I grabbed the remote and started to search for another ball game to watch as I mumbled, "I don't know what you're talking about."

Babe reached over and took the remote out of my hand, and held my wrist making me look at him. "Don't go out with him again, he wasn't very respectful at the bar, but I'm glad to know you wouldn't blow him in the car!" He rubbed my hand gently pausing. "Needless to say he got the message loud and clear that he's no longer welcomed at the restaurant."

I wanted to cry, but I tried not to, instead I just laughed nervously. "Hmm I have no idea what you're talking about." As I removed myself from his grip, I couldn't hold back my tears any longer. Clearing my throat I excused myself to go outside and smoke as they slid down my cheeks. I burned with embarrassment, taking back-to-back drags, kicking myself for even saying yes to that idiot to begin with! I composed myself and walked back inside to where he was sitting. Babe was looking at the TV when I whispered his name making him turn to look at me. Cupping both of his cheeks in my hands, I stared into his eyes before I kissed him passionately. When I pulled back I whispered thank you. I cleared my throat, walking back behind the bar and dropped the embarrassing conversation.

I guess Babe understood that although he wasn't taking me out, I wasn't just sitting home waiting and after that conversation he started sticking closer to me. He hoped to wear me down and win me over with his wit, but never went the extra mile to move the relationship along. Even though he wouldn't give me exactly what I wanted, I welcomed his protective presence, because there were a lot of strange things going on.

Rumors were wild that all the guys were fighting, and two sides had formed. One family was splitting between two groups, vying for control. Life long friendships ceased to exist in the blink of an eye, war was officially declared. Everyone was affected; the situation brought more heat than anyone ever realized it would, because bodies were piling up everywhere. When people disappear in the night never to be seen again, that's one thing, but when they are tossed out on the sidewalk and shot in the face in broad daylight to send a message to their family, people notice.

Now everyone had to look around before walking outside, and just standing next to someone could get people shot. It was all over the news and when that happened, the Mayor on down has to show they're doing something about the spike in the crime. War was declared on the mafia and the boys were under the magnifying glass. This wasn't like an episode of Law and Order; it was real and far dirtier than a TV drama. These guys had families that were tied together and now couldn't go near each.

Guys I was used to seeing daily just disappeared, and new ones popped up. Andrew was no longer around; he was MIA. That threw me for a loop; he was one of the good guys in my opinion, and I had a hard time adjusting. A lot of the others didn't really matter as much. I didn't care how the deck was being reshuffled; I never understood the stupidity of being tied to a group forever. Sounded like the makings of a bad marriage. Suppose you don't like all of them, or they don't all pull their weight? Suppose your boss gets promoted and you're reassigned to another guy who's a complete douche bag, you should be able to quit. Needless to say, I didn't see the situation the same way everyone else did. All I knew is that life changed dramatically. Almost all of them were stand up guys, but a few were pure evil, they just hid it well. I could write volumes on those types I've known, who were neither wise nor real men.

By the time I met Phil, everyone knew Babe had a thing for me. This was no ordinary guy taking a shine to me; Babe was one of the most feared and respected street guys around. Had the books not been closed, he would have been made years before, and promoted from there. The combination of being that tough and crazy made even his close friends afraid of him. Many of them would whisper a warning to me to be careful because he's a dangerous guy, but I never cared, I trusted him from the start more than most of them!

Babe had his little fan club of female friends that followed him around, hoping he would give one of them a tumble. He never did in front of me; his eyes were always locked in my direction. More than once, I encountered girls sneering at me across the bar. There were three in particular that would come in and always talk about him in front of me, but never actually to me. I would roll my eyes and just ignore them as they drank.

Giggling and talking about how cute he was and that they saw him here, there and everywhere, but never with a girl, they were always trying to provoke me. They went right to the edge without putting their toe over the line, knowing all too well I would have ripped their heads off and pissed down their throats if they said anything I deemed out of bounds. I've always been fiercely protective of my friends, I still have zero tolerance for anyone trash talking.

As soon as Babe would walk in with that gangster swagger, and with his friends trailing behind, the trio would become gaggling fools. They not only hated me because I was on a different level, but also because he wanted me, and not them. Whenever they went on the porch, I could hear them talk. "What does he see in her?" They were lucky I never put my cigarette out on their foreheads, because I tried to keep my temper under check. Not because I didn't want to kick their asses, but because Babe would have had a field day torturing me in front of all the guys. I put his haters on the pay no mind list; trying not to lower myself by engaging in a conversation with them, but there were a few times I had to express myself.

Weeknights were the most fruitful when hunting down a guy and in particular a wise guy. One late night, there were a bunch of single girls, including the three gagglers hanging out trolling for gangsters. They were flirting, and dancing around in front of Babe. He seemed to be enjoying himself a little too much. My eyes were zeroed in on him, and the hair on the back of my neck started to stand up. I just felt itchy, fully aware that this was going in a bad direction. Some of the boys responded to the trollers and were pairing up.

One new straggler was making eyes at Babe and he started drinking more martinis than normal, so his inhibitions were coming down. I saw him grooving to the music and making polite conversation with her. And then she made her bold move, the bitch put her hand on his arm. At that moment I knew I was going to rip her fucking arm off and beat her with the bloody stump. Babe saw my face and walked away from her to the bathroom grinning in satisfaction. A second later I stared stunned at the brazen chic following him. Oh no way was this going to happen!

I bolted over the bar, and found her chatting him up at the men's room door. Cunt! Whether he would have gone with her or turned her down, I'll never know, because I was hell bent on killing her. No conversations, no excuses, no nothing! I punched her square in the face. She fell back against the door and I was on her like white on rice! She never had the opportunity to get her bearings because I held her firmly by her hair, low so she was bent over, as I punched her in the face over and over again. I tossed her a fucking beating and a half to teach her and the any others in the crowd not to fuck with me again.

Babe stepped back out of the way, and after a minute or so, peeled me off this bleeding mess of a broad. He picked me up and carried me, still swinging back inside the bar, and tried in vain to calm me down. But I was grabbing everything within my reach flinging it across the room at her hoping to split her head open until one of the guys swept the bar clean.

Babe firmly held me fearing I was planning on a round two, while her friends carried her out. I screamed over his shoulder at the girl promising her another beating if she ever showed up in the bar, or any bar I was ever in again. That was it, the abuse started because I blinked. So far I'd been able to brush off and minimize our conversations, but now he knew I was more than interested.

No matter how he felt, and what I was starting to feel, I still didn't know him well enough to know if he was trying to take advantage of me, so I kept my emotional distance, because we still weren't in a real relationship. We started getting to know each other by joking around and small talk, but inevitably each time our conversations stretched until we would be engrossed for hours. He tried to fuck me, drove me everywhere, followed me like a hawk, and knew my every move, but we weren't at that level...yet. I really, really, really liked him, and unfortunately now he knew it!

Babe and I were finally alone after everyone left, and my hands were shaking and my stomach was flipping because I had tipped my hand in the relationship card game. He walked behind the bar and poured two Frangelico's and handed me one. I drained the first and he quickly refilled it, but I downed that one too. I looked at the empty glass shaking my head that I wanted a real drink as I asked for Jack Daniels. But he only poured another bullshit drink, shaking his head no. Tapping my glass, I lit a cigarette waiting for him to start in on me.

Babe wet a towel and wiped my fingers as he smugly asked, "So, how's your hand Rocky?"

"My knuckles are bleeding, but I'll be fine. They're not broken," I said trying to minimize the situation.

"That girl's gonna have some face tomorrow!" He said taking a sip grinning over the rim. "What did you hit her for?"

Squirming I blurted out, "Because she was disrespectful and overstepped herself." I hated being in the hot seat and questioned.

"What did you think was gonna happen?"

Completely pink I snapped. "Please! Are you fucking kidding me?"

Tossing his head back he roared, gloating! "You're beat! You want me, otherwise you wouldn't have hit her."

Taking a big sip, I bluffed. "Yes, I would!"

"Hot shot, you never beat up the girls James goes with!"

"Shut up, if that bitch would have stayed in her fucking lane I wouldn't have hit her!" Inwardly, my blood boiled but I just smirked at him over my glass. I held my tongue because I really wanted to yell at him, but I had no right. "Plus he doesn't get head in the bathroom."

"First we're talking about James here, he gets head everywhere. Second, how do you know that's what was going to happen?" Moving in a little closer he smoothly added, "I could've said no."

"You didn't look like it, so I made up your mind for you."

"You'll never know now." He put our glasses down leaning down and kissed me. Every kiss was always deliberate and intense. "How's that feel? To never really know? Now go crazy thinking about that!"

My ego was bruised because he had me between a rock and hard place. "Would you actually 'go' with a stranger in the bathroom?"

Tapping his lip with his finger he wanted to make me squirm, as he made fun of me. "If we're talking about someone I know, then that's a different answer, but a stranger? Hmm I have to think about that." Laughing at me, he picked up his glass and took long and deliberately slow another sip.

My body still shook with rage and I was dangerously close ripping his beautiful eyes out and eating them like olives. His delayed response ate at my core. "Think a little faster before I rip the bottle out of your hands!" *I hate you but could fuck you right now!*

Babe's involuntary giggle broke the ice. He lowered his glass revealing his killer smile. "Sweetheart calm down! Come on, I'm not into pigs. I'm a guy with morals and a sister. What do you think?"

"I didn't think so, but I was making sure your moral compass was sober." I didn't even want to hear who was on the list of people he knew, and would take into the bathroom!

"Did you ever see an oak tree?"

His question melted my anger. I batted my eyelashes tilting my head down as I asked, "Sure, why?"

He placed his glass down and gently tipped my chin up forcing me to look at him. "They're strong, really strong, but when they crack and break it's not pretty," he said moving in again to kiss me. "I'm like an oak tree, think about it."

His lips were wondrously delicious and made me blush. I understood what he was trying to tell me. When he falls for someone it's hard and strong, but when he gets hurt, he splits like an oak. If you've ever seen an oak, you will understand what I mean. When they crack they're left with a brutal scar. I'd felt like that before, I knew his pain well. We finished our drinks and closed up.

Babe took me home, passing the doorman that quickly gave a fearful and respectful good evening sir greeting while lowering his head. Looking like he owned the place and me, Babe escorted me to my apartment like a perfect gentleman. He kissed me intensely against my door, messing my hair up and leaving me with pouty lips and unstable as a bowl of jello. Saying goodbye was getting harder to do, but I kept my game up.

I knew I was going to get teased relentlessly at work, so I was mentally ready for the abuse. Babe drove me to work and walked me in the next day, and of course the guys started in right away. First, Jerry started humming the theme to the movie Rocky, and then Paul started to ask Babe if he went to the bathroom recently. It went on and on with each one having more fun teasing me.

Eyeing me, Paul joked, "Hey Jer, you want the girl's number? Maybe she can meet you in the bathroom tonight."

Jerry was trying to get under my skin when he pointed to Babe, "Oh no, she's Babe's friend. Thanks anyway."

I growled clearly getting annoyed, "Shut the fuck up, she's not his friend, and I won't be yours much longer if you keep breaking my chops!"

Babe started to laugh, "Don't I have any say in this at all?"

I jumped right in, spinning my head around to stare him down, waving my index finger "No! No, you don't!" I knew he gave me the liberty to speak like this to him; he could've stopped me in my tracks a long time ago, but he found me amusing. It's rare that wise guys let anyone get away with talking to them that way, even close friendships can dissolve in a moment. They can start shooting each other over a perceived disrespectful comment. Girls seem to have more leeway, but only if the guy is taken with them.

Babe gave a little wave of his hand and his friends fell away quickly so that in a flash we were all alone. Everyone was outside on the front steps pretending nothing was going on. I sat on the beer box clearly annoyed, when he grabbed my hand, and held it tight without hurting me. He could have snapped me in half like a twig, yet he always held me like I was a Fabergé egg-soft, caring and gentle. He looked into my eyes and said, "Don't go out tonight."

"But I have plans with friends."

"What friends?"

"Well, friends!" I said nervously tucking my hair behind my ear.

"Where are you going?"

"Out!"

Babe stared very seriously as he pressured me. "Stay home!"

"No! Are you staying home?" *You must be kidding me!*

"I can't, I have some things to do, but I want you to go home!"

"Why, so you don't have to worry about running into me? Please, you stay home, because I'm going out! But don't stress over running into me, I'm not going to any of my regular haunts!" I responded completely pissed.

Babe narrowed his eyes and asked me straight out. "Are you just playing hard to get with me, because if you are, don't. I'm done playing games, I want to know now if you and me got a thing, plain and simple."

How was I supposed to answer? I mean on one hand, he was one of the hottest guys I'd ever seen. Every time he touched me in any way, my heart skipped a beat. He had me big time...hook, line and sinker! But he just didn't know what to do with me yet. On the other hand, he was one of them. I know it was mean of me, but I said it anyway, "Babe, seriously, if you want me to be your girlfriend, just fucking ask! But I'm telling you now if you think you're just going to come over, bang me, then go out whoring around while I'm stuck home, your wrong! Please! I know you're probably married, with a few girlfriends on the side to boot. Lets call a spade a spade, you're just playing me to get in my pants and that's NEVER GOING TO HAPPEN. You should know that by now, since you've tried so many times already!" *Why do you keep asking me about all of this, if you're not going to take me out?*

Babe was a felon and did a long bid already when I met him, but never mentioned his marital status. He didn't wear a ring, but most of them never do, and I never heard him talk about a wife, but seriously how could this type of guy not be taken? He had a reputation for being a real tough guy; in fact, I didn't know anyone who would go up against him. No matter what he was like in that world, he was a complete gem with me, even when he made me nuts! And that made it harder to say no every single day, except for the fact I didn't know the answer to the married issue.

His tough guy exterior wasn't what was alluring. When I looked into his eyes I saw his soul and it captivated me completely. Our time together was becoming so intensely private and intimately personal, that our souls were becoming bound together. I was a moth drawn to his flame, just hoping not to get burnt.

Every guy who comes home hops from girl to girl, and I absolutely wasn't going to let him hop on and then over me! He looked like I stabbed him in the heart, and I guess I did. Dejected and slightly insulted, Babe said coldly "Why do you fight me all the fucking time? Why won't you just do what I tell you to do? I don't know what kind of guys you're used too, but I'm a standup guy and I would think you know that by now. I treat you right, that should mean something."

I never pulled my hand away I just looked at him, really looked, at him and said, "Really? Listen I've had the absolute worst relationships in the past. Most guys are liars and cheats..."

Breaking in, he barked, "I'm not anyone from your past! Don't compare me to the jerk off guys you've dated."

"You're a knock around guy; I know that and everything that comes along with it."

"Any other girl would jump if I paid this much attention to them, and they do except for you. I could've gone in the bathroom, but I didn't."

"REMEMBER I didn't give you the chance!" I spit out sarcastically, "I'll never be just the girlfriend, and not the wife. Plus I'm the marrying kind of girl, so just know now you can't take me out on wife night, and lock me up on girlfriend night, thinking I won't have a clue you're cheating, because I'm well aware of that routine."

Babe's mood changed for a split second, and he laughed at me, breaking the tension. "I didn't even take you out yet, but you have me convicted of cheating. Funny you're the wife already too, huh? Where's that girl's number? I'm gonna call her!"

"Go for it, just remember I'm not that easy going; we would all have a BIG problem." Digging my nails in his palm I continued, "plus don't ask me about my life when you're one of them."

I worked long enough for the boys to know very well that they all cheated. Multiple girlfriends, plus a wife was the norm in that world, not the exception. What I found most baffling was that the wives were all beautiful in the beginning. After they were married and had kids, they fell apart! One fatter than the next, almost inviting their husbands to go get a girlfriend. I mean if my husband wielded that kind of power and respect, I would live in the gym. Looking fine and being dressed to the nines would be my number one job to keep his eyes on my ass only; sadly enough I never met one wife that followed my philosophy.

Note to self, success does not equal a fat ass. During the many trials I would attend throughout my life, the wives always looked like stuffed sausages; overweight in ill-fitting clothes. While girls like me wore skintight black pencil skirts, tight white blouses, killer heels and big black glasses with designer handbags.

Babe reached over and kissed me with his eyes open just staring into mine, lip to lip. When someone with their eyes open kisses you they're serious, they mean business. As he stared at me, I could feel his breath on my lips and tears were forming in my eyes. Some amazing people have kissed me, but he was the most intense ever.

Still, I felt a stab of pain because I knew he wasn't good for me, but I really wanted to make him be the guy of my dreams. I wasn't looking for anyone like Babe, but somehow I found him and was starting to feel very confused. I kept reminding myself every moment that I would be better off just being his friend and nothing more. Seeing his expression and feeling his eyes on me, I knew deep down inside there was no way I could stop this train wreck from happening. Finally he got up and walked out to talk with the boys, but not before he turned and pointed at me. "You're fucked up! You know that?"

He left me clearly exasperated, but I went back to work, not exactly knowing what to say or do next. Some of Babe's friends started to wander back in, all waiting for a moment to slip in a comment. James was the most vocal, because we were the closest platonic friends. Young, tall, handsome and truly a standup guy, James knew damn well I would listen to him more than anyone else, because I loved him wholeheartedly. Sitting at the end of the bar flipping through the paper he finally said, "Listen Babe is a good guy, he really is!"

I said holding up my hand. "Ah, don't!"

Grinning, he said, "You should just give in already and go out with him!"

"If you like him, you go out with him!"

Holding out his hand to me, James tried to be sincere, "I'm talking to you like my sister."

I snapped! "And I love you for that but ah, no!"

Giving me that cutie pie face he tried to wear me down. "I've known him a long time and he's a stand up guy."

Shaking my head no, I wasn't going to fall for his big smile routine. "No doubt, he's all that and more!"

Laughing at me, he blurted out the obvious. "I gotcha! I get it, but excuse me; look where you work. Come on, really?"

"You don't know what you're talking about. Babe didn't ask me out, he just wants to fuck me."

"We all know he likes you! You know it too! What more do you want?"

"Again! He's just trying to sleep with me. You know the routine, if I wasn't behind the bar, he wouldn't even notice me. Being back here, I become more attractive, and alluring."

"You girls are meant for us! That's why you're here."

"No! I'm here to take all your money!"

"You want everyone to think you're so tough, but you're a piece of bread! You're not a money hungry bitch. You're one of us!"

Holding up my hand I told him the truth. "Shut, enough! Please I've met a lot of Babes, they all move on after being home for a while. I prefer to be the friend; it lasts longer than the first home coming girl that gets kicked to the curb."

"Friends, huh? So why did ya punch that girl out?"

"I was waiting for that!" I turned around and grabbed a cigarette before blurting out, "I punched her because she overstepped her bounds here!"

"By hitting on him?"

"Yes, she didn't know if I was with Babe or not, but she made a play for him in front of me. I don't fucking think so!"

"I heard you japped her out good by the bathroom!" James snickered, completely amused at the whole situation.

"Yes, I did! She was going to give him head!"

Smirking he asked, "So you like him?"

"No, that's between him and me anyway."

Shaking his head looking at me with veiled eyes, he went on making fun of me, "So you don't like him?"

"I didn't say that!" I snapped a little too quickly, essentially blinking. "He's a knock around guy, and you know how I feel about that."

"So you might like him, if he wasn't a street guy, but you don't date regular guys because you like street guys, and to top it off, you won't let him go with anyone else?"

"Yes! Exactly!" Smiling from ear to ear I exhaled and tucked my hair behind my ears. "Listen I promised myself I would never go out with that type of guy again after the last two."

"I'm telling you he's not like that. I know you like him, I can see it in the way you tease him and stuff. Otherwise you'd talk to him the way you talk to me. Come on."

Holding my ground I shouted, "No!"

James grinned, "Just think about it."

"No!" I grinned back!

"So let me ask ya, why do you make out with him if you don't like him?" James grinned big, as he picked at my scab!

My face flashed scarlet, because I hadn't realized people saw me with him like that. "You don't know what you're talking about!"

"Oh pal, I think I know what making out is! Don't even deny it! Everyone in Vibes saw you," he broke out laughing and started to pound the bar. "In fact, do you think you two are the only one's by the golf course? I pass his car all the time with you sucking his face!"

Oh Jesus Christ! "Shut up! You have no idea what I want and what I do!" I had to laugh, because he wasn't teasing me in a bad way, he was just busting!

Waving his finger at me, he said, "Really he's one of us. Come on you know you want to."

"Stop! I'm not taking advice from you of all people. You've slept your way through almost all of my friends," I said shaking my head.

"Hey!" He shouted laughing at me.

Cutting him off, I had to tease a little. "Ah really! Do you have to do it in my elevator of all places? My neighbors stare at me and shake their heads whenever you're around."

Grinning he snapped, "Because its fun and I can!"

"Oh geez! I have to ask, did you ever get it in the bar bathroom?" I said remembering I wanted a guy's opinion on that hot button issue.

Slapping the bar, he roared, "Oh yeah!"

"You're an ass! Oh how come I didn't know that?" I asked shocked.

"I don't hide it! I just like your elevator better!" Laughing while he turned the page.

"Well stop doing it, your big smile only goes so far in my building," I said as I playfully slapped him on the arm.

"You know your friend Rotten is my favorite. You girls going out tonight?"

"Probably, but I have to go home first after working all day. Hey, stop calling her Rotten, people are going to think she smells you idiot!"

"Sorry but she's the hottest girl around, blonde and blue eyes. There is no way anyone is ever going to think she smells. I just like to freak everyone out by saying it. Anyway, maybe I'll meet you guys in the city later. Babe has to work tonight SO you 'should' be free."

"See you at the bar," I said as I leaned over to kiss him goodbye. Brooklyn people are big kissers; we kiss hello, goodbye, and everything in between.

CHAPTER 10

Mob Den

As I wandered into the club to check on the food, I spotted Babe playing cards. His eyes gave him away; I knew he was pleased to see me. "Hey Fats, what are you doing?"

I leaned in to kiss him hello. "Just checking in before I head home to change to go into the city."

"Yeah, you have a big night planned?"

"Just the usual; dinner with the girls before I go to work."

"I'm sure I don't have to tell you to have a good time!" Babe laughed as he stared at his hand.

I smirked at him. "You got that right!"

He tossed a card down before he was dealt another. "So where are you working tonight?"

"At the Slime, why?"

"No reason, just making conversation." His eyes never left his cards; he was as cool as a cucumber.

Why don't you just ask me out already? "Hey Babe, why don't you come to the Slime tonight? I'll hook you and your friends up."

He laughed at the idea! "Nah thanks! I don't think it's my speed."

James broke in, looking mischievous. "Babe, you don't know what you're missing! Fucking place is insane!"

I shook my head laughing, because James was right. "Suit yourself Babe, but you're missing out; I'm going to be in a bikini."

James was about to say something, but shut his mouth right away. Babe's eyes shifted for the first time in my direction, giving me a look to kill. "What's your rent due?"

I laughed hard along with the other guys, because he was right! "Yup! Tomorrow's the first of the month, so it's bikini night!" *You blinked! It bothers you!*

"Now I definitely won't go. You know Fats, I like my vision."

I put my hand on his shoulder grinning. "Very funny! Don't sweat it, I'll be so busy surfing the crowd making everyone else blind."

He looked up at me, letting me get a view of his hand, before he spoke. "Nice, maybe you'll find a date by the end of the night."

I put my hand on his shoulder grinning. "Maybe I will, but I think the only loving girl you'll find tonight is the queen of hearts in you hand!"

I cracked up as he looked at his cards frowning. "Oh was that nice?"

Leaning in, I kissed his cheek. "Oh don't be mad, maybe you'll ask the queen out considering she's so pretty sitting there waiting to be put away for the night! Later Babes!" I walked out laughing and waving to the guys as he groaned. Babe had a good sense of humor; he could take a joke just as good as he could dish it out.

My grin was enormous as I drove away, because I could bet my last dollar I was going to see Babe tonight! Somehow, someway he would be somewhere I would be. This thought was a major factor in my choice of what to wear to dinner and work. I slipped on a little dress with killer heels over my bathing suit and packed a pair of shorts, cowboy boots, and a hat. I picked a little black halter-top with fringe two-piece because when I dance the fringe sways seductively. *If you come in, you're gonna cringe!*

I didn't mention anything later on when I met up with the girls and soon we were laughing, eating, and drinking at Kantellas. Our group swelled into a small mob with all the guys we attracted. The waiter basically never left our table, and if I was him I wouldn't have wanted to either because the cash was flowing like the Nile River. Angelo, the chef, sat down with us for a while thoroughly enjoying all the mania. What a fucking funny guy! He was a genius in the kitchen, but an over the top wild man when he stepped off the line. I kept checking my watch, and before I knew it I was turning into a pumpkin and had to go to work.

I made my reluctant goodbyes and started to walk out, but one of the guys, Jeff, jumped up. "Hey! Wait up, I'll walk you out!"

"That's okay, I'm just running to work." I smiled knowing fully well where this was going. Jeff's really cute, a Financial Analyst, and a lot of fun.

"Let me get the door for you."

"Thank you!" I said as I pulled a cigarette out and stopped in the doorway to light up. I looked up and saw Babe and Vinnie standing by my car smoking. I focused on Jeff instead of making eye contact with Babe while I walked towards them.

Jeff didn't even notice them as he made his move. "Listen Dannie, we've run into each other a lot the last couple of months, and I've never seen you with a man. I'm assuming you don't have a boyfriend, and if you're free I'd like to take you out for dinner."

Hmmm interesting! I kept smiling and listening to him as I walked towards my car. When I couldn't avoid Babe anymore I stopped to kiss them hello. "Oh hey Babe! Hi Vinnie!"

Vinnie grinned looking like he wanted to crack up but didn't. "Hi Dannie!"

Babe gave me a sideways smile. "What's up Dannie? Who's your friend?"

You're jealous! I turned to Jeff, and waved my hand. "Jeff, this is Babe, and this is Vinnie. Guys, this is Jeff."

They shook his hand with the biggest grins spread across their faces; they seemed to enjoy the introduction and trying to make me squirm. I continued towards my car as if nothing was happening. "I'm sorry Jeff. What were you saying?" *You better ask me soon, or I'll go out with him!*

Jeff opened my car door, and leaned on it, looking really cute, trying to be charming, but Babe and Vinnie walked right over to the passenger door as if they were apart of the conversation. Jeff looked at them and back to me; I had the top down exposing us as if we were in a big fish bowl leaving him no choice but to talk to me in front of them.

Babe relished the uncomfortable situation, and thought he'd break my balls. "Go ahead Jeffrey, don't let us stop you. You were saying."

Jeff's expression was priceless, but he went for it. "As I was saying I'd like to take you to dinner. Can I have your number?"

Bingo! This couldn't get any better! Someone's asking me out in front of you, and I'm ready with my number on a cocktail napkin. I opened my bag and pulled out the napkin handing it to Jeff. "Sounds like fun, here's my number."

He smiled like he won lotto and handed me his business card. Jeff put all his chips on the line when he leaned in kissing my cheek in front of them! "Okay, I'll give you a call."

I smiled putting the car in gear and directed my comments to all of them as if this was all so normal. "Great! See you guys!" I drove the few blocks to work with the biggest shit-eating grin I ever had in my entire life!

I ran into the Slime chasing the clock, pulling off my dress, and heels while slipping on my shorts and boots. Dressing and running is a difficult task, but even more so when the doors are opening with a couple of thousand people waiting to get in. Sliding over the bar, I hopped into the pit to my waiting bar-back, holding my cash draw. Lights started to swirl around the church, the fog machines blew out pink smoke, the music started to blare, and I readied myself for the staring role of the nightly show.

The hours flew by like minutes because song after song was a monster hit. The DJ seemed to get off on making the crowds cheer and go crazy. James and a few guys walked over to the bar and took up their spots. I started popping their bottles, and it became infectious. Everyone around them started ordering bottles too; my ring was going to be insanely high tonight. I couldn't hand off a bottle to a group of guys who weren't lucky enough to score a spot at the bar, so I jumped up on top of it. Immediately the roars started and I just fell back into the waiting hands that would pass me off until I reached my destination. How my cowboy hat didn't fall off was a miracle. The trek was an experience, because I was getting slammed with glitter from every direction, while a few guys stopped to write love notes on my legs all while the crowd cheered.

No one ever complained as they waited for their delivery, because they loved being the cause of the sideshow. Once I finally made it to my Wall Streeters, I handed off the bottle of DP and glasses. I was rewarded with a $100 tip on top of the $250 for the bottle! The crowd passed me back over to the bar and once I was standing again, I thought I'd reward them with a little personal attention. My bar-back knew my routine and handed me the soda gun while I stood on the bar. I pointed it up towards the ceiling as I partially covered the hole while hitting the water button. The water shot out like a gentle rain all over the packed cheering crowd. I loved doing that, it was so much fun and my crowd expected and paid handsomely for the experience. Once I was done, I jumped back into the pit and the first face I saw was Babe's. He was standing with James, looking at me like I was a lunatic! I guess I was compared to what he was used to!

Yes, you got to see a little bit of my act! I'm so glad I put my shorts on over my bikini bottoms! Before he could say a word I pushed myself up and partially over the bar to kiss him and Vinnie, while James just laughed at me. He knew both sides of this, I always put on a show, but I was enjoying having Babe jealously watch me as I welcomed the money and attention I was getting.

"BABE! I'm so happy you finally came to visit me like a real customer!" I beamed at him as I showered his face with kisses.

I didn't give him time to respond, I slid back into the pit and set him up quickly as I took multiple orders from the crowd. He never said a word to me, but then again I really couldn't talk either. Babe stayed by the bar talking to his friends as the cash rained down on me along with phone numbers until the night ended. I kept his glass filled, but had to do my thing, because the Slime wasn't anything like the bar in Brooklyn, this was hedonism at its extreme! Once it was 4AM, I pulled the cash drawers and started my routine of closing down and putting everything in locked bags and signing off on the receipts.

The customers in the main room were being chased out, but the other rooms remained quietly open. I waved security away from my group, as I counted and piled my tips into my bags. The bar-back was always so grateful that I tipped him out at a much higher percentage than was the norm. That was something all my girlfriends did, our bar-backs were the most important part of what made us successful!

Jumping up on the bar, I sat smirking and swinging my legs as I took a sip out of my bottle of champagne all decked out in my outfit. "So Babe did you have a good time tonight?"

He gave me a half-assed smile. "It's been an enlightening experience to say the least!"

I spread my arms wide laughing. "Oh come on Mr. Grumpy, admit it, it's so much fun here!"

"Certainly looks like you enjoy it!"

I grinned at him, loving the attention. "Okay, who's hungry? I wanna go to WoHip!"

James was the first one to chime in. "Good call, Fats! Let's go!"

I slid down and pulled Babe's hand along with me. "Come on big guy you're coming!"

As we made our way out, I shouted goodbye to everyone and stopped to kiss all the glitter boys and promoters who were still milling around outside. Babe never said a word, just watched it all with eagle eyes. Babe and the guys stuck out like sore thumbs, because they were the only ones not dressed like club kids. When we arrived at Wo Hip it was the same thing, a complete freak fest. We ate and laughed all through the meal and before we knew it the sun was coming up and it was time to leave.

Babe pulled my arm holding me back from the guys. "Hey, let me take you home."

"I have my car, I can't leave it here." I have to put up a little resistance!

Babe made up his mind. "It's already settled, give Vinnie your keys. You're going in my car."

Giggling, I walked over and palmed Vinnie my keys as I kissed him and all the guys' goodbye. Babe was waiting for me, holding his car door open. "Shake some the crap off, before you get in." Turning over I shook my hair out making the glitter fly around.

When I was done, Babe tried slipping a track jacket on me, but I pushed it off. "Oh this doesn't match my outfit! Don't you like my fringe top?"

"That's underwear, not a top!"

I giggled as I started shaking my fringe to make it dance sideways. "Oh Babe, this is a bathing suit that I could easily wear as a top! Don't be so old fashioned!"

Narrowing his eyes Babe snapped at me. "Stop that!"

I did it more teasing him. "Why?"

He growled at me, playfully annoyed. "Get in the car!"

I jumped in pulling my hat on firmly so it wouldn't fly off with the top down, grinning as Babe took off. We made small talk during the ride, until we reached my house. Babe opened my door and groaned as I got of the car leaving glitter all over his leather seats. We walked into my building looking like two very mismatched people. Once we entered my apartment, Babe made a quick call while I cleaned up and changed. The look of approval was stamped all over his face.

I giggled as I sat down waiting for him to start in. And he didn't disappoint me in the least. "So that was a regular night at the Slime huh?"

"Yup! Did you have a good time?"

"A fucking blast! Your outfit was a hit, Fats!"

"I know I made tons of money!" My grin let him know I was thrilled he noticed.

"I saw the looks on the guys faces as they held you up serving the crowd!"

"Oh, did you now? You could have joined in any time, but you'd have to beat them off with a stick to get that spot!" I said giggling.

"Hmm I can see that! Oh before I forget, Jeff won't be calling so don't get your hopes up!"

I laughed outright, because he was just too cute. "Really, why won't Jeff be calling me?"

Babe reached into his pocket and pulled out my napkin with my phone number tossing it at me. "Jeff and I had a conversation, and I assure you he won't be calling!"

I didn't play into his jealousy. "Oh please he visits me at the Slime, so I'm sure he'll ask again."

"I don't think so, I think he's giving up the club scene for a while. It's a healthier choice for him."

I frowned at his choice of words. "Don't go beating any of my admires up Babe, that's not nice! It's not like he tried to follow me into a bathroom for a blowjob." I laughed so hard I snorted before continuing. "He didn't do anything, but have to the balls to ask me out, unlike some people I know!"

"You're a funny girl! Balls? Hmm we'll see who has balls Fats! I gotta go you need your rest. I'll be by to pick you up for work tomorrow."

I smirked walking him to the door. Babe punished me by giving me a peck on my cheek, but I'm sure he went home wishing it were more.

CHAPTER 11

....

What Were You Thinking?

I was constantly busy, but now all I could think about was HIM! I must have been preoccupied as I walked into my building, because as I opened the first set of doors and was about to put the key in the inner doors, someone suddenly shoved me. I felt a hand on my upper back, pushing me forward, while the other hand shoved something into my lower back. I don't know if it was actually a gun, but I didn't put up a fight. Growling, the guy demanded that I give him "the bag."

Jesus fucking Christ, he knows about the bag! Money is replaceable I'm not. I quickly dropped the paper bag between my legs. At the same time, I hit the bell panel with my palm ringing every apartment in the building. Hearing the buzzers the guy grabbed the cash and took off running.

Where's my doorman? Fucking guy was nowhere to be found, the desk was empty and the double doors locked. I was robbed because I had to stop to use the key to get in! Totally freaked out, I stabbed the key into the door and ran up the stairs into my apartment. My hands were shaking so badly, I had to redial Babe's number a few times before I got it right. He quickly returned my call, and I begged him to come to my house, that it was an emergency. Poor guy had just gone to bed, but he came. As soon as he rang my bell, I buzzed him in right away, and ran down the stairs to meet him half way. As I threw my arms around him, I started to cry hard. Babe picked me up and carried me into the apartment.

"Hey, what's wrong?" He said as he locked my door.

"I was robbed!" I sobbed, "Some guy shoved me and stuck something in my back. I'm not sure if it was a gun, but I didn't want to find out."

As calm as could be he sat me down asking, "Did you see him?"

"No, I didn't try either. He knew I had a bag of money, because he said, 'Give me the bag.' He knew I had cash!" I cried hard trying to catch my breath as I spit out my fears. "It was in a bag. So that means he knows me!"

As he pet my hair trying to calm me down he spoke gently, "Not necessarily."

Falling back into the couch, I was lost for an explanation and just wanted to cry like a little girl. "This has never happened to me before, what am I gonna do? I can't replace that kind of money! I'm in trouble, I'm gonna have a big problem."

Now Babe was the confused one, he very patiently asked, "What kind of money are you talking about?"

I shook my head, because I knew I had to tell him, but I kind of thought he knew already. "The money...the money I count for everyone. Don't you know?"

He shook his head as I unfolded the details of how I earned extra money counting for the mob. I had a steady list of customers; I would count undeclared cash from their restaurants, clubs and bars. I even counted for car dealerships and card games. My skills earned me a nice stash of cash. When I was done, he had a strange smile on his face, as if to say, you're not as squeaky clean as you pretend to be. And I guess I wasn't.

"I'm here, don't worry. Go inside, do something 'cause I need to use your phone. Listen go take a shower, get cleaned up, you'll feel better after," he said as he continued to pet my hair and kiss my forehead. I did exactly what he suggested, because I trusted him. Walking out of my bathroom a half an hour later, wrapped in a robe and towel drying my hair, I found Babe on my couch sleeping with his beeper and my cordless phone on his chest. Poor guy, he looked so tired. When I put a blanket over him, he woke up. He sat up, yawning, "Sorry! I fell asleep, I'm tired."

Feeling alarmed that he might leave; I sat next to him and held his arm. "You're not leaving me, are you?"

"Honey, I'm beat. I'll close my eyes in the car in the front of your house for a few hours and come back."

I shocked myself as I blurted out, "Stay here, I didn't go to sleep yet either."

He started to laugh, "Are you asking me to sleep with you?"

Flushed with embarrassment, I stumbled on my words, "Not the way you think! No, I want you to stay and sleep, but not with me exactly." I said slapping his arm. "You're making me fucking stutter!" I grabbed his hand and walked him into my bedroom. Following without saying a word, he looked happy when he undressed and kicked off his shoes and started to lie down on top of the comforter. As I was about to walk away, he held my hand and kissed it.

"Don't go, stay with me again." He gently pulled me closer. "I know you're scared, I'll be a perfect gentleman with you, I promise." I crawled next to him and cuddled on his arm leaning on his chest. He pulled the throw blanket on us and kissed the top of my head. Within a few minutes he started to breathe deeply, falling asleep as he held me. It was such a comforting feeling; I felt so safe that I fell asleep too.

Mentally and physically exhausted, I slept for a long time. I felt Babe move next to me, but it wasn't enough to bring me out of my coma. He left the room and returned a few minutes later; I could hear him quietly walking around. I felt my hair move as he whispered my name. I opened my eyes to him kneeling beside me, trying to wake me up.

"Hey, good morning." He whispered.

Holding my hand out to touch the side of his face, I asked, "What time is it?"

Grinning looking very sexy he softly said, "One in the afternoon."

"One? Oh my god, I can't believe I slept so long!" I leaned up on my elbow, trying to shake the cobwebs from my head. He started to straighten my robe collar, pulling it closed; I imagine it must have opened while I slept, and without realizing it, I was flashing him.

Joking with me he said, "I'd like to say that I wore you out that's why you slept so long, but I'm a gentleman. Even though you've been sleeping with your robe open. By the way you look good baby, real good!" He was laughing at me as I turned beet red! "Okay, last night is over. I'll take care of everything. Don't think about it or talk to anyone. From now on, someone will bring you home every night after work."

I sat quietly, listening, feeling frightened. "Should I be afraid? Is someone after me?"

"I wouldn't say that, but you should be more aware of your surroundings, and keep an eye out." He held my hand seriously, trying not to frighten me. "Get dressed, I want you to show me the building unless you wanna show me anything else? Hmm?" Using one finger to pull the top of my robe he opened it a bit to peek in. "Baby you're healthy and all real!"

Flaming red, unsure of what to say, I just giggled. "Okay, you want the tour now?"

"Unless you have something else you want me to do?" He said leaning in and kissing my forehead.

Once again, he reduced me to stuttering, "Um, um just give me a few minutes." What was I doing stuttering? Oh my god! He knew he had me. If I didn't get robbed, I wouldn't have blinked so fast.

Grinning wildly, he got up and said, "Unless you want me to stay here with you and without your robe, I'm going to use your phone inside. Okay?"

"Absolutely! Help yourself to anything-um not anything-but you know what I mean!" He knew I meant anything, just not me. Stumbling worse than a high school kid, I tried to get out of the embarrassing situation. "I'm sorry, I didn't even offer you anything to drink, I'm just all out of whack!" *Stop acting like a schoolgirl idiot! Be yourself!*

Opening the fridge was even more embarrassing; I had olives, cheese, and bottles of wine, champagne, and water. Turning around to him clearly dying, I said, "I seem to only have water, unless you would like wine or champagne this early."

"You're a real Susie Home Maker huh? No, water's fine. Come on, I'll take you to breakfast when you're ready." I grinned and poured him a glass of water in a crystal wine glass as he said, "Fancy!" Leaning in he kissed me, then with the same finger he pulled my robe open and took a step back eyeing me up and down slowly. "I don't care if you can boil water honey!"

Feeling a little playful I didn't cover up, I just let him get a good look and when he looked hungry enough I replied, "I don't believe in waiting for tomorrow, it may never come. I use everything now; I drink out of crystal and eat off of china. I like fine things, only the best! If you're done, I'm going to change." Letting the robe slip from my shoulders to the floor I walked away naked leaving him dumbstruck holding the glass, hoping he wasn't going to drop my Waterford crystal. When I closed the bathroom door I stared at myself in the mirror while I put on my makeup and styled my hair. *Where was this going? My life was a roller coaster, way too many twists and turns. Could I be happy with him? What was I doing?*

All my dormant fears resurfaced and I became conflicted. I walked from the bathroom to my bedroom deliberately avoiding making eye contact but naked. He watched me close my bedroom door like a hawk as he spoke on the phone. Twenty minutes later I was done, and walked into the living room to find Babe looking at my photographs framed all over the house.

"I like this one." He said pointing to a picture of me behind the bar in a costume. "That's some outfit, what were you dressed like?"

"Oh, I worked a Halloween costume party, I went as a famous singer."

"Oh, no wonder, I was away; must have missed that."

"I'm so sorry! How long were you away again?" I asked as I grabbed his hand.

"Ten years."

Holding his hand tighter, I leaned up and kissed his cheek tenderly. "Well, that's all in the past. Thanks for everything!"

Looking sad, he said, "You're welcome. Anyway, you ready?"

Taking the frame from his hands, I opened it up, removed the picture, and slid it into his shirt pocket. "Take it, so you don't forget what I look like."

"Yeah? You trying to make me blind?" Laughing, he pushed the photo down securely into the vault. "Come on honey, you ready?"

I grabbed my bag, and entered the alarm code, while opening the door. When we entered the elevator, Babe looked around and said, "So this is the famed elevator I was hearing about last night? I've been in it before and I just don't see it!"

"Please, you can't imagine! I think it's about doing my friends in an elevator. James is very freaky you know!" I said laughing as I hit the button to the basement.

Babe surveyed my whole building before we went to the lobby. I held his arm tightly, still reeling from the experience, until he made a move to talk to my doorman, who was MIA during the whole incident. He went over and spoke to him about the hours that the desk was manned and whether there were cameras in the lobby. I guess he was satisfied, because he walked me outside and we casually drove to the diner.

And as we ate and talked, a group of guys came in and sat at the counter. I knew them well and waved hello, but they returned the wave coldly. The guys weren't as friendly to me as they normally were; I realized it was because I was with him.

"So you know everyone? Regular fucking mayor!" He remarked as he sipped his coffee.

Giggling, I tried to be funny. "Not everyone, maybe there's one or two I don't. Don't you know them too?"

Ignoring my question, he growled, "You done? I have to run." I felt his mood sour, and he had returned to being an uptight gangster. Babe tensely and silently drove me home, doubled parked and walked me to my door. "So, I'll pick you up later and take you to work."

"Really? You're picking me up too?" I asked, surprised.

"If I'm driving you home after work, wouldn't I take you there too? Dense! All kidding aside, you're not going anywhere alone for a while."

Putting one hand above my head resting on the door, he kissed me goodbye just as my neighbor, Justin, opened his door. Clearing his throat, he mumbled hello while Babe glared at him. I could easily see that Justin was nervous, because Babe looked like the king of the jungle guarding me. Just as he entered the elevator, Babe kissed me goodbye again as he called out for Justin to hold the door. He jumped in with him at the last second. Good God, poor Justin!

With that, we started an unofficial escort routine. Most days, he would pick me up and it was like going on a date driving to work. I gave him a key to the first set of doors in my building, but not my apartment, and I told the doorman to him give entry up to my floor. Babe would ring my bell and walk me out of the building with his arms wrapped around me, almost covering me.

Every night he took me home, it was the same protective routine. I thought he was just being gangster possessive, but soon enough I found out that there was a car stationed outside with guys from the other side waiting to shoot him. They never had a clear shot, because he was wrapped around me. What a fucking slap in the face of reality to think he could have been shot in my arms, or worse! I could have died, just walking in and out of my building! There was a bounty on his head, and I could have been collateral damage, like so many other girls who dated guys like him. Babe never told me, because it wasn't his way to talk out of school with anyone not in the life, but he was always prepared for anything.

Once we were in the car, we would talk, joke around, and stop to grab a bite to eat like any other couple; only we weren't, yet. I found myself spending more time getting ready for work than before. I made sure my makeup was just right, my hair was perfectly sprayed with perfume, so that when it moved he would get a hint of my favorite scent; Poison. I made sure I leaned on him at least once so it would stay on his body.

When Babe least expected it, he would get a fragrant reminder of me, and somehow I would be on his mind longer than he had planned. I always wore the same perfume, so that he would associate that smell with me. I wanted him to be intoxicated by it, so I used it to make a fragrant imprint on him. Every time Babe kissed me, he became fixated with smelling my hair.

After about a week of my being escorted like the crown jewels, we were walking up to the front door when I stopped and faced him. He looked so handsome in the moonlight and I was slightly tipsy from having a couple of drinks with him as I closed up. I leaned up and surprised him with a deep kiss. As I wrapped my arms around his neck, he grabbed my waist and pulled me close almost eating me alive on the spot.

Lost in his arms, I never heard the car pull up, but he did. In a blink of an eye, he picked me up and ran with me as I heard a popping sound. I gave his pursuers a clear view of his back, because I stopped to kiss him. Breathless and shocked I clung to him as he protected me from the dark unknown. Just as quickly as it happened, it was over. Once we were both in my building, he carried me right into my apartment.

"Quick, turn around, are you okay?" I cried as I tried to check him for any bloodstains. Wiping away my tears, I patted him down like an idiot.

"I'M FINE, STOP!" he yelled looking very angry and uptight. Rightfully so, he was almost whacked a minute ago, because I was stupid enough to be impetuous. "Lock your door and don't fucking answer it for anyone! Understand? NO ONE!"

"No one, I get it. I promise!" Looking at him, pale and alert, I promised him what he wanted to hear. Grabbing a key from the bowl by the door I pressed it into his palm. "Here take a key to my apartment. If I don't answer when you come back, you'll need it to get in."

He held the key and looked at me with eyes of steel. "If you don't let anyone in, then I have nothing to worry about, but I'll keep the key just in case I wanna wake you up!" He turned, on a dime, back into the sexy animal that made me weak in the knees. Babe kissed me hard and unlocked the door. Turning he asked, "What's your code? I don't want to set off any alarms unless they're the ones in your pants!"

Turning red, I whispered, "I change it every month, but right now it's your birthday."

He grinned radiantly. "My birthday? If I didn't have to run I'd rip your clothes off right here at the door!"

I grabbed his arm clinging to him and said while I choked back my tears, "I'm so sorry, I really am, I didn't know. I wouldn't have kissed you, if I knew they were out there."

"No more tears, I know you didn't, but now you do." With that, he kissed me once more and disappeared like a thief into the night. I looked out the window, trying to spot him to make sure he got in his car safely, but he was too fast. All I saw was his car peel away. I lay on my bed, reeling from the whole experience, thinking about all the past times he took me home and wrapped his arm protectively around me, holding me like I was worth a million dollars, risking his life each and every time. Now I knew why Babe didn't let anyone near me as he walked me right to my front door.

Funny, he never pushed himself totally on me, but would definitely leave me ravished looking after his goodbye kiss. Babe would only leave after he heard me double lock the door, and put the alarm on. There were times I would listen at the door as he walked away, because I wasn't sure if I really wanted him to go. I often wondered if he did the same. Every thing had changed now that I had given him a key. He was in my life faster than I would have let him had he not been a gangster on the fast track.

But what is Babe to me? A boyfriend, a friend, could I really give him my heart and soul and risk everything? Things were going too fast for me and I still didn't know what I really was to him. He could be married for all I knew, that was it I really didn't know anything intimate about him, and I didn't dig into this life, because anyone I would ask could repeat our conversations to him. I held my insecurities and questions very close to my vest.

I was so confused. Were we both so stubborn, wanting the other to give in first before we told our dark secrets to each other? Or deep down inside, were we both so apprehensive and leery of getting hurt again? I knew I was afraid to love him. The relationship was new and cloaked in all the excitement that goes with that, but the reality was that he was a wise guy, and could disappear tomorrow and I would be left heartbroken.

Had I really understood, and had he really opened up to me, maybe I would have moved faster and more aggressively-but he didn't-so we wandered through, taking our time. Time was never our friend, though; it flew by too quickly. It had an uncomfortable way of sneaking up on us. As the days ran into each other, I found I worried more and more about the possibility of losing him. Before I realized, I was completely dependent on him for protection.

Early in the morning, I woke up to go to the bathroom and was totally shocked to find Babe sleeping on my couch with his piece on his chest. He snuck in and stayed there, maybe to protect me, maybe to hide. I'll never really know. I didn't want to walk past and startle him, because he could shoot me. I went to the bathroom and went to bed, slipping back to sleep. When I woke up, he was gone. I found a note on my dinning room table from him.

"D-

I stopped by to check on you. I have to go to work, but I'll be back to take you to the bar. Stay home today, lay low.

–B"

That day was so long, one of the longest of my life. It's one thing when you want to stay home, but it's another when you have to. I cleaned the already clean apartment, and didn't answer my phone or beeper for anyone. When it was time to be picked up, I sat on the couch, waiting on pins and needles as the clock ticked away. Soon, there was a gentle rap on my door, as the tumbler turned. Babe walked through my door, shut off my alarm looking so tired, but looking hotter than hot and I started to cry. Holding my face in my hands, I just cried, because I was so worried all day that who ever tried to kill him the night before had found him.

Babe held my hands and gently pulled them away revealing my tear-stained face. "Hey why all the tears, am I that ugly?"

I threw my arms around him and pulled him to his knees as I sobbed in neck. "I was so worried something happened to you!"

"You care!" he said, trying to joke around.

Smirking and crying, I joked back. "Yes, but no, I mean no I don't but you did almost get shot in my arms so I guess I feel responsible."

"Hard ass!" He said as he rolled me onto my back and lay on top of me. Babe kissed me like he hadn't seen me in a year. His lips were soft as he moved to my neck, biting me and licking my skin, setting me on fire. He started to grind me as he wrapped his fingers in my hair. After a moment- or a year, who knows- he looked at me and asked, "How about now?"

Being coy, I grinned and said, "Maybe a little!"

With that he started to ravish me, but his beeper went off snapping him back to reality; we had places to be and people to see. Before he got up, he kissed my eyelids and whispered, "You're saved by the beeper! Let's go, we're both late." He got up and held his hand out to help me up. As I freshened up, he made a call and soon after we made a mad dash to his double-parked car. He pulled up in front of the bar, grabbing my hand before he opened the door and asked, "Hey, are you in or out?"

I was startled, forgetting all about what he said earlier. "We have to talk more, I don't know. I need to know a few things first before I answer you." I saw the look in his eyes and felt terrible. What a long night I have ahead!

Being "in" meant I would walk into the gates of hell, of my own accord, and put my life and heart on the line without ever really knowing what was going on, because of love. Being "out" meant I would have to walk away. Babe would be forever lost to me. Unanswered questions swirled through my mind; was I willing to lose myself to have him? Did I love him or was it lust? Why couldn't he give me more time? Why was I being forced so soon? If I said yes, would I really have him anyway? Wasn't I already in anyway? Was I a normal everyday person now or ever? No! Taking a breath, I took one step closer towards the cliff wondering if I was going to jump or be pushed over the edge.

CHAPTER 12

You Can't Punish Me

What a night! The stress of the last few days was too much! One drink led to another and before long, I was whacked with my whole bar crowd. Whacked wise guys are either hilarious or dangerous, but tonight I was in luck. By midnight, I was getting hundred dollar tips and slurred appreciation for having my girlfriends in the bar. We could sit in a car and turn it into a party. I could see Babe's expression change every time I was tipped big, and fawned over. The icing on the cake was when Mario announced everyone-including myself- was going to Atlantic City.

Yes! Oh I want go to AC...but...but the strange look on Babe's face is telling me to pass. I walked over to him at the end of the bar to feel him out. "So, are you having fun?"

"A ball! I'm taking off, since you're going to AC!"

I put my hand on his arm, pleading, "Why don't you come?"

He shook his head, "I can't, but don't let that stop you from having fun."

Jesus Christ! I can go and ignore his situation, or I could skip one night of fun. I tilted my head towards the crowd as I said, "I think I'm going to pass on AC anyway, I'm tired."

Babe gave me a sideways smile. "You? You're tired? Go ahead, go with your friends, it's okay."

Waving no while I made a drink, I smirked at him. "Nah, I wanna go home, but you don't have to hang around to drive me if you have something to do. Anyone here will give me a ride later." I knew throwing that in would make him crazy. *Stay on your toes, Babe!*

He narrowed his eyes, "If you're not going, I'll drive you home. They're all drunk!"

I smiled as I danced by the register, because I knew he was burning a hole in my pants staring. I called over my shoulder, "Great, thanks!"

As everyone settled up and started to leave, my girls kept teasing me for staying behind. I turned them all down, trying not to make Babe feel bad. They pulled me out from behind the bar into the back. We all piled into the bathroom, so I could take home their cash, before they spent it at the tables. After all, they were going to get all they would need and more to play with from the guys, so why lose their own? When I returned to kiss the guys goodbye, Babe watched their hands and lips very closely. Good!

He locked the door for me, turning around he caught me lifting my shirt to empty all my money on the bar. "What the fuck are you doing? There's a window here you know!"

I grinned as I pulled my bra up letting more trapped money float out. "Who's looking in with you guarding me? Come over here and help me so I don't lose my cash." When I was satisfied my shirt was empty, I starting pulling more out of my pants as he scooped it up into piles. Unfortunately, I forgot about the notes mixed in. Ignoring all of it, I opened my bag and dumped it all in as if it was all so normal-and it was, for me. He never mentioned anything, and I didn't offer an explanation, as we closed up and drove home.

Babe walked me into my apartment, kissed me goodnight, and left, all with a slightly annoyed attitude, but never mentioning anything. Exhausted and buzzed, I crawled into my bed after getting cleaned up. I almost fell asleep by the time I heard the tumbler and alarm code, but I willed myself to get up to see what was going on. I knew it was him- I could tell by his footsteps. *You just drove me home and you're back again?* Babe had crept into my apartment, but he didn't come into my bedroom. I dragged my ass out of bed and walked into my living room to find him listening to my answering machine messages.

I cleared my throat to get his attention, but he never flinched, instead he glared at me. "Who the fuck is hanging up on your answering machine? Are you kidding me?" Babe looked up with an expression that was meant to stop me in my tracks, but it didn't. He wants to be a tough guy, we'll see about that.

"I'm not a frigging psychic, I have no idea and nor do I care. But it's not okay to listen to my private messages!" Shifting my weight onto my other foot, I pointed at him. "Listen, stay if you want, or go, but I'm too tired for this."

His expression was hard and never wavered. Something must have happened and he was taking out his frustrations on me, but I knew he wasn't about to tell me what it was; Babe was all gangster at the moment. I had a strange feeling he was contemplating ripping my answering machine out of the wall as I walked over to move the base out from under his hand.

"Tired, huh? Go to bed! I'm leaving!" He shouted at me as if I were a child, before walking out without an explanation or a goodbye.

I'm wide awake now and pissed! *What the fuck was that about? Why am I home, when the world is still out? No, this isn't right at all! I should have gone to AC! Fuck this!* I changed my clothes, grabbed my keys and took off to go to after hours. There were several hot places to go to, and normally it wasn't my thing, but when I was in a mood I would always chose wisely, because most of them were drug dens.

My car was on autopilot right to Bundles, my regular haunt that stayed open late, but wasn't exclusively an after hours joint. The sun hadn't fully risen yet, so it wasn't too weird walking into a club. Once through the door, the owner welcomed me with open arms. No matter where I went, there was a good chance I would wind up behind the bar, and this was no different. Bartending whacked is an experience in itself; the music just carries you through the motions, you don't have to think if you know the drinks by heart already.

My mood was wild; I had a crazy night, and no way did I want to be punished by Babe and sent home. He wasn't really my boyfriend, and his crazy ass life was truly taking a toll on me. As my friend Rudy walked towards the bathroom, I followed, because he was a local dealer. I never pay for much in the nightlife and restaurant world, let alone for a few lines, so he was more than willing to toss me a package.

Partying isn't my thing, but every once in a while I indulged. Twirling a dollar bill into a makeshift straw- one, two, three-I blasted through a package. My eyes must have looked like two black disks when I walked back outside to dance. The booze, drugs, and music kept me in my own world, and all I wanted to right now was to get lost in my own head.

When the room became brighter, I sat down at the bar to attempt to have a crippling conversation with the owner, Jimmy. As I moved my feet, I kicked something by accident. When I bent down I found a Louis Vuitton bag. I had to think for a second, but than I realized I didn't even have a bag, and it wasn't mine, so I unzipped it to find a license. To my surprise, the bag was filled with cash. *Okay, I'm sober now!*

I tapped Jimmy and flashed him the bag. His eyes opened wide and motioned for me to follow him. Once he closed the door in his office, I was already turning the bag over on his desk. *Good God.* There was ten grand all neat in cashier wrappers and a wallet. Jimmy's eyes were huge, as he just looked back and forth between the cash and me. "Dannie, where the fuck did you find this?"

"Jimmy, it was on the floor, under the bar. I kicked it by accident!"

Shaking his head, he was shocked staring at the piles. "Do you know who it belongs to? That's too much money for someone to forget about!"

"I know, turn on your cameras, so it's all recorded, just in case the owner says some of it's missing, and I'll try to find a number to call."

"My cameras are always on, I got everything don't you worry about that. Do what you have to do, I gotta check on the bar."

As I looked inside the wallet for a clue, I could hear commotion outside. Jimmy was already walking outside to see if the club was getting raided. There was a little phone book amongst the makeup and crap. I looked and right inside the cover I found a name and number with the word boyfriend written with hearts. I called the number and tried my best to sound sane and sober.

When a girl answered, she was obviously upset and freaking out that I called her house in the wee hours in the morning, but when I said I had just found her bag, she dropped the phone. A guy picked it up and I explained to him what had happened. He thanked me profusely and asked for my name. All I would say was that I would be waiting in the office of the bar they lost it in and hung up. I didn't want to give my name for some reason, just in case this became an issue. No way was I leaving that kind of cash unattended, so I just sat there. I didn't have to wait long, about twenty minutes passed, Jimmy opened the door with two guys and a girl following him in.

The girl was bleary eyed, and the guy was in shock as they counted it, and put it back in the bag while they thanked me over and over again for returning it. The second guy with them extended his hand and introduced himself while he peeled off a thousand dollars to give me. No way, I can't take it. I could have easily lost my bag and I would hope someone would return it if the shoe were on the other foot.

One of the two guys stood back a bit as the couple walked out of the office. "My name is Carl. Hey, don't I know you?"

I shook his hand, laughing. "Hey Carl, nice to meet you. Who knows, maybe we met somewhere, but it doesn't matter. Just be happy it was me, and I was in Jimmy's place, because we're both fucking honest."

"You're right, thank you! But I didn't catch your name."

Tilting my head, I smiled as I tried to say as little as possible. "That's because I didn't say it." I extended my arm motioning for him to exit first. After I closed the office door, I tapped his arm saying goodbye and walked away to say goodbye to Jimmy before I bolted to the door.

Carl called out to me, "Hey, can I get your name and number? I'd like to take you out."

Great, just what I need another street guy chasing my ass! Was he shocked I just gave ten G's back without taking a finder's fee or was it my cute little jogging suit, zipped low, and my wild hair? I just waved over my shoulder walking out, without turning around and eagerly jumped in my car, peeling out of the spot. I whipped a U-turn and drove off, but before long I had company. Sirens blared as the cops pulled me over.

Drunk and high, great! This is what I get for being a nice person, a potential night in the Brooklyn Tombs. I pulled out my PBA, and Secret Service courtesy shields and cards, along with my license and registration, as the officer approached. Thank god it was a neighborhood cop that knew me!

He laughed, walking over to rest his arm on my windshield frame. "What's the rush Dannie? You in trouble?"

I shook my head no, "No, I'm good Larry. Thanks!"

A Benz pulled up along side with the window down, so I could see Carl's concerned face. "Hey, I'm gonna call you Lucky, because of tonight! You okay?"

I waved smiling. "Yup! Thanks I'm all good!"

Larry turned smiling. "Dannie's fine, I didn't know it was her when I pulled her over."

Carl was ballsy, and certainly not intimidated by the cop, because he wouldn't drive away. "Oh Lucky, you have a name! So how about breakfast now that we know each other?"

Jesus Christ! "No, I think I've had enough excitement for one night, but thanks Carl!" I turned to Larry. "So, Larry, are we all good here?"

He backed up smiling. "Sure doll! Just be careful getting home, do you need me to follow you to Shore Road?"

Great, now my new admirer knows my name and where I live because Larry wants to show off! "No, I'm good Larry, but thanks! See you soon." I turned to look at Carl and waved. "Good night, thanks for checking on me, I appreciate it!" I didn't wait for a response, but took off zipping down a side street to get them both off my tail.

At the light I spotted Babe's car in a parking spot with the top up. After I circled twice, I pulled over a half block away to think. I went around the block again to see his car again. *Could this get any better? What was he doing here? Should I play Mannix and sit here to see what he's up to? Do I really want to know? Yes, yes I do!* I put my top up and sat there, low in my seat, with my lights off. After half an hour, I had to go to the bathroom. *Do I stay and bust a kidney, or do I go home?*

As I smoked my last cigarette, I gave up stalking. I kept my lights off as I pulled away, but a car behind me that wasn't his flashed its high beams, letting me know I was spotted. *Fuck! Who was that? I should have stayed home; this was the night of almost all the way around. Almost got locked up, almost made a grand, and almost got away without being noticed!*

By the grace of God, my spot was still there. I wanted nothing more than to go to bed, because Babe's car was gnawing on my last nerve. My apartment welcomed me with open arms, and I ran into it, before any more craziness found me. Ripping my clothes off, I jumped into bed, until I heard the alarm chimes again. *Fuck! I'm home for no more than ten minutes, and he knew!* Grabbing my bat, I headed for the door naked, and low and behold I ran right into Babe looking like a lunatic. His clothes were a mess; if I didn't have my own shit to hide I would be all over him about why he looked the way he did. He took the bat away, and just stared at me, seething, while he stalked through all my rooms to see if someone was with me. "Where the fuck did you go?"

I hated being questioned about my behavior. I tapped the counter, trying very hard not to scratch my nose, which is sure sign that I was partying. I'd rather he thought I was bombed, not high. I turned my head slowly and played the balls to the wall card. "I could ask you the same thing, but I'm not. Nor am I flipping that you keep walking into my fucking apartment!" I walked to the fridge, and pretended to look for something. *Food, yuck!*

Babe looked like he was about to snap. "Are you kidding me?"

"Nope! You hungry?" I asked as I searched for something to munch on. If I keep my answers to one or two words and eat, he'll never think I did a few lines. All I had was leftover Chinese food from the bar, so I pulled it out and handed him one carton and a fork while I took the other. Leaning on the wall, I picked on it watching him stare because I wasn't scared or kissing his ass. "So, why are you here Babe?"

"Because I dropped you off a few hours ago, and now I find you've been out staking out my car!"

I raised my eyebrow, because he was guilty. Of what I had no idea, but he was guilty, and he didn't know what I did or did not see. "So, I could say the same thing! You made me go home only to go out yourself! Then you sneak in and listen to my answering machine to boot! So, did you have a good time?"

"Its none of your fucking business!" He was spitting mad, holding the Chinese container as I stood still with one leg crossed in front of the other, smirking at him.

"Well, it's none of your business either, so we're at a stale mate! Why don't you take a shower and get cleaned up, you'll feel better. You can stay if you want, but I'm going to lay down. I'm tired!" I sincerely doubt any girl ever spoke to him like this; he was in total shock. I was dismissive, but not argumentative, and that made him crazy.

He shouted at me in total frustration. "AND WHY THE FUCK ARE YOU NAKED?"

The moment was broken when my phone rang. I moved for it, but he dove ripping the receiver off the base. Babe barked into the phone, "HELLO! HELLO? HEY, FUCK HEAD WHO'S THIS?"

Really! What the fuck? I took the phone out of his hand and held it while I looked at him. "Are you kidding me, Babe? How dare you!" I placed the phone down on the base, hanging up on the caller, hoping they wouldn't call back.

He scratched his head in total confusion. "I left you sleeping, and everything was good! I went to do a few things and I'm hearing more shit about you and your crazy fucking friends! I come back home and you have hang ups on your machine! I leave again thinking you're going to bed, but no! Not you, you fucking went out to follow me!"

I slammed the container down. "HEY! I DIDN'T FUCKING FOLLOW YOU! DON'T FLATTER YOURSELF! I drove past your car on my way home! And I sleep naked all the time!"

"Yeah, home from where? Where were you?" He shouted, trying to intimidate me.

"Where were you? Hmmm, Babe?" I walked around him calmly to put away the container, relishing having the upper hand. I had to choke down the food, because I just didn't have an appetite, but I kept the pretense going.

He put the other container down and grabbed my arm pulling me right up against his face. I swear he was sniffing me, but then again I was paranoid. His eyes were cold, and deadly. "Where were you?"

I smiled, softening my eyes, trying to pull back, but he held me in place with his steel grip. "Babe, you need to stop, you're going to hurt me. I'm a big girl, I go where I want, when I want. I'm never going to be that obedient Stepford bitch who stays put, twiddling my thumbs while you're out doing God knows what with God knows who. But if you need to hear this, I'll say it. I wasn't with a guy, I wasn't out doing anything like what you think, but mostly, I didn't follow you." He tried to interrupt, but I kept going. "If I think I have to follow you, and that I can't trust you and we shouldn't be with each other."

He leaned in to kiss me, but I pulled back, because I didn't want him to taste the blow. I shook my head, acting repulsed. "Don't kiss me after God knows what who you were with! Why don't you calm down and take a shower. Okay?"

Releasing my arm, he turned and walked to my bathroom. Once he closed the door, I grabbed my beeper and cleared the memory, just in case he checks it, and looked on my caller ID to see who called me as I silenced the ringer. I knew the number it was Jimmy. Thank fucking God he was smart enough not to say anything when Babe answered. When I cleared the memory, I turned to find Babe standing there watching me.

"So you ran to the phone to see who called?"

Thinking fast on my feet, I said, "Yes I want to know who I have to apologize to tomorrow, because you were an animal answering my phone! I didn't do anything wrong, but I know you'll never believe me!"

Narrowing his eyes, he went back to grilling me. "So who was it?"

"I don't recognize the number, but I'm sure I'll hear all about it in a few hours. So when I find out, I'll let you know so you can apologize! Would you like to tell me who lives in the house you were parked in front of? Because I will find out, this is my neighborhood, not yours!" Without waiting for a response, I walked into my bedroom, because he wasn't going to tell me anything anyway.

Why do you have to be the last standup gangster, that doesn't talk out of school? As I turned on the TV, I thought if he leaves well then it's his choice, but either way he's the one with something bigger to hide. I drifted off to sleep alone, but when I awoke he was sleeping on my couch. As I walked out of the bathroom, finally wearing clothes, I found Babe ready to leave. He was still in a suspicious mood, avoiding eye contact, but analyzing my every move.

As I handed him coffee, he took one sip, announcing that he had to go. "I'll see you later when I get you for work."

I was as natural as always, putting his cup in the sink. "Okay, thanks! I'll be ready when you get here." I held his arm for a second, looking sad because I didn't want to fight with him, but I just knew if he was worried that I saw him do something, it had to be about another girl. And then, I was even sadder; because I had hoped he wasn't going to be a piece of shit like all the rest of them. Instinctively, I wrapped my arms around him and put my head on his heart, holding him for a minute. "Don't hurt me, I need you do right by me."

That broke the ice. Babe kissed the top of my hair as he held me tighter. "Come on, don't do that." His words trailed off making me feel even more vulnerable. When he broke away, he saw the sadness in my eyes, and touched my face gently. Before he left, he became Babe the ball breaker again. "I hope you know what a pain in the ass you are!"

I giggled, because I guess he was right- then again, so was he. "Funny, you're no walk in the park either my friend! Let me go down with you, I have to go to the mailbox."

We rode down in the elevator together and kissed goodbye before I turned to the alcove where the mailboxes were. I was about to go back up when the doorman called me over to pickup a delivery of flowers. They were beautiful, a dozen long stem roses in a vase. A stapled note said, "Lucky, you're quite the lady!" *Oh my god, Carl found out where I live! I mean there are nothing but buildings all along Shore Road, and this guy found mine. This is not good, not good at all!*

Lost in thought, I never heard Babe walk up behind me. He must have been watching me from the door. "So, what's this?"

Now I know I looked guilty as hell, but I wasn't going to admit to shit, because I didn't do anything wrong. It wasn't my fault I acquired a new fan. "What are you talking about?"

He fingered the card, looking right at me. "This! Who sent you flowers?"

I looked at the card, with a questioning look. "What are you talking about? These are for someone named Lucky, not me. I just came over to see if I had any packages. I'm waiting for a box from Bloomingdales."

He couldn't prove anything and he knew it! Frustration and distrust filled his body, I could see he was getting enraged, but couldn't prove me wrong. He touched the tip of my nose, eyeing me before walking away. I never spoke to the doorman or acknowledged any of it. For all I know, he gave them to his girlfriend. I walked away fingering through my bills.

I walked back in and tossed the mail on the table. I needed a shower, I felt grimy from last night. As the suds ran down my body, I held the wall, relaxing, loving the hot water.

I was exhausted and had every intention of going back to sleep when I was done. You know when you can feel someone watching you? The hair on the back of my neck suddenly stood up and I freaked out! Slowly, I turned to see Babe watching me in the doorway. I screamed so hard, you would think I was being stabbed. Defensively, I threw my hands out to keep him away, pushing the shower doors off the track making them crash. Protective glass doesn't mean shatterproof. Little jagged glass rocks sprayed the room.

Babe lunged forward as I screamed incoherently hitting him over and over again. He grabbed my swinging arms and pulled me right out of the shower roaring for me to stop screaming. But I didn't, I couldn't stop myself! I sunk low and got my arms free, starting on him again but now I was connecting. How he didn't defensively beat the shit out of me, I don't know. In the whirlwind of fury, he managed to get my slippery wet body up against the wall. Heaving, and crying I was panic stricken as he pushed up against me pinning me in place whispered in my hair. "Shush, calm down...shush...shush."

My heart was jumping through my chest, I thought I was having a heart attack, because I couldn't calm down, and it was actually getting worse. "Oh my god...oh...I can't breath."

Babe's face went white, "Calm down, come on breath, come on." But that wasn't working, the room was spinning, a sudden intense pressure in my chest was only overshadowed by huge waves of nausea. I felt all free will leave my body as I slid down the wall right out of his arms. Now everything sounded strange; I couldn't keep my eyes open. Then there was nothing.

I felt my hair move, and something was in my nose irritating the hell out of me! I tried to swat it away, but my arm burned as I moved. As I fluttered my eyes open, there were strange things around me. Startled I tried to sit up, but felt hands pushing me back down. *Where the fuck am I? What is that sound?* A constant beeping and alarm rang out piercing my ears. I felt my heart race as I realized I was in a hospital bed with an IV in my arm and an oxygen tube up my nose.

Babe, with a faint black eye, stood over me, stroking my forehead looking worried as he stroked my arm. "Honey stop you're in the emergency room. I'm sorry, I'm so sorry!" My teeth started to chatter; I was absolutely freezing as I shook uncontrollably locking eyes with him. Babe barked so loud I jumped even more. "Hey I need a doctor over here! NOW! HEY NOW!"

I felt the room spin again. *Good god!* Closing my eyes tightly, I held the sheets under me as I prayed it would all stop. A mask replaced the tube; I could feel blankets being placed on me. When I felt steadier, and the shaking stopped I heard the doctor speaking to Babe in a hushed voice, "Maybe you should wait outside, until we get her calmer." He looked torn between staying by me, and doing what he was told. I didn't want to be alone here of all places, even though I was mad at him. Memorial Hospital was a death trap, anything over a sprain should be treated somewhere else. Babe's hands were gripping the handrail tightly; his knuckles were completely white. As he released one hand turning to leave, I reached out and grabbed his wrist, pulling him.

I moved my mask, and spit out, "Don't you dare leave me here to die!"

His eyes glimmered with amusement and relief washed over his face. He looked at the doctor, grinning. "Hey Doc, I think she's going to be just fine. She's back to being feisty!" He closed the curtain giving us privacy, lowered the bedrail and sat down close to me. "How do you feel?"

My eyes should have told him that I was going to kill him, once I could get up. I kept the mask by my chin, so I could speak. "Terrible and it's all your fault!"

Babe ran his hand through his hair, looking very upset. "Baby, I didn't mean to scare you."

"Scare me? You left, I was alone taking a shower! Why would you do that to me?" I knew the answer, but had to ask just to make him feel like shit!

His face turned dark, he was jealous and didn't want to admit it. "I forgot something and when I came back I wanted to ask you a question, but you turned around freaking out." He was lying like a fucking rug,

"What did you want to ask me, Babe?"

"It doesn't matter, all that matters is that you're okay."

"You're lying! You came up because you thought I was doing something!" I could feel my blood pressure go up, as I got excited. The monitor confirmed it, and Babe looked between the machine and my face.

He took a deep breath, and sat back. "I can't get over the look on your face when you were screaming. Baby, are you afraid of me?"

I turned my eyes to the wall and thought about my answer, and when I looked back his face was so hurt. "I'm afraid of anyone who is watching me in the shower when I don't know about it."

"That's not an answer."

"No, I'm not. I don't think you'll ever hit me, let alone kill me. Maybe I'm wrong." I moved my hand to the edge of the bed and raised my fingers for him to hold my hand. His big hands were rough and calloused, but felt strangely soothing. "Babe, if it comes down to a situation like that, there's no coming back."

"There's no coming back from a lot more than that. I need to know, were you with someone or just following me?" His hands turned to steel, cold and firm.

"I went out, because I wanted to and got pulled over for making a U-turn like an asshole, and then I found your car. I did pull over to see what you were doing, but it was a random thing. I smoked all my cigarettes and had to pee, so I drove home, and you know the rest."

His eyes looked satisfied, he flipped my hand over to expose my palm. Gently he trailed my lifeline, digesting what I said.

It was the truth, minus a few details. "You know I know you're lying! If you didn't do anything wrong, why aren't you telling me everything?"

Fumbling for the bed remote, I struggled to sit up before I answered. Now I was upright looking at him in the face. "Babe what were you doing when I found your car?"

"Who high beamed you when you left?"

I frowned, because I thought it was him or one of his friends. "I thought it was you!"

"No, it wasn't, so who was it in a new Benz with tinted windows?"

No way am I telling him anything! Deny, deny, deny! "I have no idea."

"Who called you?"

"I don't know yet, I haven't been home to find out...thanks to you!"

"Who sent you flowers?"

"They weren't for me! But if someone, anyone, sends me flowers, you better not grill me like this over it. I can't help what other people do."

He narrowed his eyes, but remained calm. "Okay, I'm going to drop this for now, but I know more happened then you're admitting to." Babe was fishing. If he knew anything, he would be mentioning details, but so far I know he's just trying to intimidate me.

"So when can I get out of here?"

He moved into the chair pulling a bunch of folded of papers out of his jacket pocket, and started to unfold them. "Well, let's see what your file has to say...hmm very interesting!"

I ripped the papers out of his hands. Sure as shit, he had photocopies of my file, including everything in the system about me. "How the fuck did you get these?"

He turned his head sideways smirking at me. "Really?"

"Yes, really! They're personal, you're not my next of kin!"

Grinning like a champ, he started to tease me. "I am now! I took the liberty of filling out your forms and listed myself as your husband! So I get to see everything! Glad to know you don't have any diseases, aren't pregnant, but it looks like you have an ulcer, again!"

I read everything and he was right. My past hospital history was listed, and in the spouse section there it was in black and white, his name and number. "I can't believe you! I want to go home!"

"I'll get the doctor, but make no mistake, I'm going to finish reading that report. And don't be a baby and rip it up, I'll only get another. I have friends here!" He winked at me before he pushed himself up out of the chair and walked out.

I kept reading, and found the blood report listing that cocaine was found. *Jesus Christ!* If he saw this already, he wouldn't be here right now. As the doctor and Babe spoke, they both looked at me like I was a naughty child interrupting an adult conversation as I read through the papers muttering that I wanted to go home.

The doctor started reminding me that I needed to have more iron in my system, cut out fatty food, and to see a nutritionist for my ulcer. I was throwing him daggers, as he went on, and when I thought he would say something about the blow, I interrupted, "STOP, I just want to be discharged NOW! Where do I sign myself out?"

Babe looked like the most caring husband as he asked, "Danielle sweetheart, don't you want to know what happened? Why you passed out?"

I ripped the mask off and IV out of my arm, and stood up. "I know why I'm here! Where are my clothes?"

The doctor looked at me, and back to Babe confused. "But you really should stay until the IV drip is finished. There's more for us to talk about. Let me see your arm."

"No! We have nothing more to talk about. I'm not sick, I'm not pregnant and I don't have a communicable disease. So there's nothing more to discuss!" I walked over to the chair where my clothes were all folded and started to pull on my sweat pants under my gown. Since they weren't leaving, I dropped my gown and pulled on my sweat jacket zipping it up. "Now where do I sign?"

He handed me a pen and release form. "But I have to tell you that you came in here with very high blood pressure and you seem to be having a panic attack. I can prescribe something for that..."

Babe interrupted, waving his hand. "NO! My wife doesn't need any of that stuff, no medication that she can get hooked on! I'll make sure she rests."

I shoved the paper at the doctor and grabbed Babe's hand, pulling him out of the room. He walked slower just to bust my balls so I had to yank him a few times. When we passed the nurses desk, they all called out saying goodbye to him. *Fuck! I just hate everyone!*

I stopped short and shouted, "Stop talking to my husband!"

His eyes opened wide while he roared laughing, putting his arm around my neck, pulling me close to kiss my hair. "Okay, wifey, take it easy!" Without warning he scooped me up and carried me out like he was crossing the threshold.

Fucking guy, you will be the death of me! I didn't say a word during the drive; I could hear my heart pounding in my chest as the minutes ticked by. Babe just grinned sideways at me, taking the turns nice and gentle until we pulled up in front of my apartment. I turned, seething from the whole experience. "You have some fucking balls! You make ME go home, then go out yourself! I find YOUR car parked in MY neighborhood, you accuse ME of stalking you, while you were probably fucking someone! Then you storm into MY house, answer MY phone like an animal!" I took a deep breath before continuing. "Then you pretend to leave, but you're really watching MY every move and then you come back accusing ME of getting flowers, and you leave again. But no, you don't really leave; you sneak into MY house and bathroom to watch ME take a shower! You scared the shit out of me! And to top it off my shower doors are destroyed and I'm left with a big fucking mess! Let's not forget you got copies of MY medical history, pretended to be MY husband and flirted with the nurses to get what you wanted! AND I'M NOT EVEN FUCKING YOU YET!" I grabbed the door handle and got out, but before I slammed the door, I screamed, "Who the fuck do you think you are?"

I slammed the door with every ounce of strength I had I stormed into my apartment and I cried in bed, flicking through the TV channels with the phone off the hook. I didn't want to talk to anyone, let alone him. My head and arm hurt, and I was exhausted to the core. I drifted off, dreaming of smacking his smug but hot face.

My mood was no better when I woke up, because I walked into my bathroom that was in complete shambles. *Fuck this!* I dressed and left without waiting for Babe to pick me up. Tonight I had to work in the city, and I drove with a vengeance. I couldn't help but seethe over the incident, and as I closed up I knew I had to go home. If I stayed out, no good would come from it. I turned down a dozen invitations to go clubbing and eating. I parked and walked into my building, avoiding speaking with the doorman, because I didn't want to be asked anything. Not about how I felt, not about the flowers- nothing. As I put the key in the door, I could hear a drilling noise coming from inside.

It's one in the morning, what the fuck? Should I go in? Should I run? Listening from the hallway, I could hear the radio playing music. Confused, I opened the door and peered in to find tools and metal on the floor. I tiptoed in, following the music and there was Babe in the bathroom installing shower doors. He knew I was there, but didn't turn around, instead he just yelled over his shoulder, "Oh, good your home, hand me the wrench."

His toolbox was open, so I reached in for it. I extended my arm and handed it to him while I scanned the bathroom. I had a new shower head, tub nozzle, handle and shower doors. Babe was moving onto my sink, changing the hardware to match everything he just installed. As pissed, as I was earlier, I had to admit, this was very cute. He broke my trance, "If you're hungry, go inside, there's gravy on the stove."

Without a word I walked into the kitchen to find macaroni, gravy and meatballs. Babe was a very good cook. I made a plate, poured a glass of wine and returned to the hallway. I sat on the floor leaning on the wall eating as he made small talk, but I never answered with more than a few words. The last thing I remember was Babe saying he was changing the toilet handle, before I fell asleep on the floor. When I woke up, he was gone and I was tucked into my bed, but I had a completely upgraded bathroom.

CHAPTER 13

....

Gone and Forgotten

My phone rang, as I was about to walk out the door for work. I almost didn't answer, but I recognized Brianna's number and grabbed it. "Hey, what's up?"

"Can you get off for a few days?" she asked.

"Sure, why?"

"Because Mario's sending me away for the weekend, and he said I can invite you guys! I want to go out tonight, bouncing in the city, so pack before you go to work. We leave early tomorrow morning!"

I lit up like a Christmas tree. "Awesome, thank you! I'm working the day shift, so meet me at the restaurant, we'll go out from there!"

"We won't be sleeping tonight so get ready!"

I hung up, grinning like I hit the number. My Louis Vuitton bag was always ready for any impromptu adventure, so I didn't have to do much before going out. I drove away stoked, ready for a fun night. A few hours after I was settled into work, Babe beeped me to check in, but I couldn't speak for more than a moment. We were packed; I had a waiting list for tables from the moment we opened until the girls arrived that night.

The crowd decided to leave with us, so I was able to close and go out. Our first stop was Café Social, where we were always treated like royalty and tonight was no different. Bottles started to pop, and we whipped up the crowd, drinking and laughing. After an hour, we moved on to eat at Mama's where we feasted like Roman soldiers, and finally ended up at Regina's.

At this point we were cabbing it, because we were drinking heavily. Thank God some of the guys took our cars back to Brooklyn for us, so we were free to party on. Around two in the morning, we barreled through the front doors all dressed to the nines, and feeling no pain. I spotted Babe right away, but didn't try to look too excited, even though I was. All my friends had their steady boyfriends there, except me. Babe was about as close to a boyfriend as I had at the moment, and after the shower incident, I wasn't even sure about him anymore. Respectfully, I went over to Babe first, and loved seeing the look on his face as he stared at me. His table was mixed, between his pointed collar friends and assorted girls. I couldn't care less; there are always girls around guys like them. As long as when I show up, I'm not second fiddle, it's all-good! I'm number one or I'm not interested. And right now, at this moment, I'm very interested, even though I want to kill him!

"Hi Babe! You look cute!" I winked at him, and before he could say anything, I moved on, kissing everyone at his table hello. Then I made my way through the room, kissing everyone and finally made my way back to him, my stomach filled with butterflies and booze. He looked smoking hot, and I wanted to be with him at his table, even though I was invited to join each group. The champagne started to pop, and Barry White came on to welcome Bri. She was the ringleader, and this was her hangout more than anyone else's; it didn't hurt that she was a former model, and a VIP bartender. Her blonde hair, blue eyes and huge chest made everyone stop and stare.

Big Mike was up and out of his banquet and walking over to Dana, who was fucking striking, drop dead gorgeous. Tall, with short, blonde hair, she had a rocking body and walked like a cat. Everything about her was sexy, and none of it was lost on Mike. His eyes never left her, from the moment she walked in. He quickly and proudly escorted her to his table like the Hope diamond.

As I sipped the glass of champagne from Big Mike, Babe asked, "So, you decide who you want to sit with yet?"

"Nope, not yet, I'm keeping my options open!"

"What options are we talking about?"

I smiled, turning my head sideways smirking at him with one finger on my lip, holding the glass in the other. "I love everyone! How can I pick one table over the other?" Nervously, I finished the glass and immediately the waiter came over with another. I smiled, thanking him, when I heard a song I liked I asked, "Oh, Babe dance with me!"

"Why don't you come over to my table first? You really should take it easy, wifey!"

"But I don't want to sit like an old person watching the fun, I'm young, I want to be part of the entertainment!" I giggled with my arms around his neck trying to make him dance. Babe swayed putting his hands around my waist, as I looked down towards the floor getting into the song. When I looked up, I gave him a seductive look. "I'll take it easy when I'm old, but right now I'm prime so I want to party!"

He laughed at me. "Prime? You certainly are, but don't get a big head!"

I stuck my tongue out at him giggling. "I am prime, and I hope it gives you a big head!" I leaned up to kiss him playfully.

He laughed pulling me closer. "You're a fucking nut, you know that! So, are you following me again?"

Excuse you, what? Me follow you? This is what I get showing you attention, a big kick in the ass! I smirked, but didn't answer as I held out my hand holding the now empty glass. I never had to wait long, a few seconds later the waiter came running over with a fresh glass. The music changed and Babe took the opportunity to escort me off the floor towards his table. All the guys were happy to see me, but the looks already started from the girls. Babe held me close right next to him. He had a way of making me comfortable and I guess I fell in the trap, because I loved being with him. Impulsively, I rested my head on his shoulder, because he had his arm around my shoulder and it felt so good. I couldn't help but smile up at him, but I fought the urge to kiss him as much as I wanted to.

"What's with the big smile?" Babe asked.

Pushing my lips together, puckering, I purred, "Maybe it's because you look cute all dressed up. Nice collar, big shot!"

Babe grinned, pulling me closer. "Well, thank you! You look absolutely beautiful too! Every time you say something like that to me, you've been drinking. So, how much did you have tonight?"

I frowned. "Stop treating me like a child! I'm a grown ass woman. How much did you drink tonight?"

He tilted his head giving me the look. "So how was your night so far?"

Without skipping a beat, I beamed. "Great! I had so much fun! How's yours?"

"Not bad. So you must have heard I was here, tell me is that why you're here?"

Ugh you're a dick! I put my glass down and calmly said, "I came here, because I always stop by, but I think its time for me to go." Without saying another word to him I got up and walked away leaving him staring. *You big jerk! I always come here, but it was a bonus that I happen to run into you!* I wandered, talking to different people, hiding my hurt feelings. To make matters worse, none of my friends wanted to leave. Before the night was through, they were going to get their spending cash for the trip and weren't about to leave until they did. I couldn't stay, even if I had to leave and take a cab by myself, but Pino saw my face and waved me over.

He held my arm pulling me close asking, "Hey baby, why the long face?"

I had to fight back the tears threatening to spill down my cheeks. "I'm an ass that what's wrong!"

"Oh stop, come sit with me. Forget whatever it is. Come on."

"Nah, but thanks! I gotta go." A tear slipped down my cheek; I kept looking up to stop the rest from ruining my makeup.

"Oh, no crying! You really wanna go?"

"Yes!"

"You got it! Let me take care of the check first." Pino stood up calling over the waiter and settled up. He wrapped me in his protective arms walking me out without looking back. Once we were in his car driving away, I told him what happened and he shook his head. "He was probably kidding, you know we all say stupid shit. Don't worry your head over it and get rid of that faccia, you're too good looking to walk around with that mug on!"

I hugged his arm harder kissing it. "No! I know he's a good guy, but he makes me feel stupid when he jokes around. I'm not into the big shot shit."

Pino gave me a sideways look; "You're fucking kidding me right?"

I had to laugh, because I knew what he was referring to. I really meant it, but in a different way. "Yeah, yeah but you know what I mean. I'm not a gangster cock chaser, so I don't like being treated like one. Fuck-head asked if I went there because I knew he was there! Really!"

Pino grinned, "He's into you, you know that, right?"

Now, I was interested. "Yeah, is that what you think?"

"Listen, we're all dicks when we drink, but he wouldn't have you at his table if he didn't like you. There are more than enough broads hanging around. Got it?"

"Hmm maybe, but he's still a dick tonight! Where are we going? Wanna go see T?"

"You read my mind! So, I forgot to tell you, someone's been asking about you."

"Good grief, who now?"

"Carl, do you know him?"

"Umm not really." The conversation was interrupted because we pulled up to T's club in Hell's Kitchen. I made a mental note to ask him about Carl later. Once we walked in, T happily greeted us and quickly we got sidetracked in different conversations. Pino gravitated towards a card table with a fist full of hundreds; he was never able to fight the urge to gamble. I floated around, but mostly hung around the bar talking to a bunch of girls I've had the pleasure of babysitting.

My head was swimming, but I never lost my balance on my heels. Thank God Pino hit, because he could walk away instead of camping out, trying to win it all back. We made our way through the crowd saying goodbye, because I had a flight to catch and he had his winnings. I couldn't stop laughing at nothing as I held onto Pino dancing while I walked, until I saw his face. Babe was walking in as we were walking out. Talk about bringing my head down Jeez!

It took some effort to speak without completely slurring, but I tried to flub my way through saying hello. "Hey Babe! Now what are you doing here?"

"Visiting a friend, how about you?" He said, giving Pino a look to kill.

"Having fun, see ya!" I mumbled trying to walk past him. *Okay whatever, yada, yada, yada!*

Pino stopped, giving Babe a kiss and hug. "How are you Babe?"

"How do you think I am? I'm always good!" Babe barked, obviously annoyed.

Pino didn't back down, they were equals in their world. "Oooh hey what's the problem?"

Babe looked like he was ready for a fight as he barked. "I don't have a problem. Do you have a problem?"

"I never have problems Babe, never. But if you do, come by and see me tomorrow."

"Why wait for tomorrow? Let's talk now."

What? Oh no, I couldn't get Pino in a jam especially with Babe for just being a good friend. I broke in, "Hey, hey, hey stop this both of you!" I released Pino's arm to hold onto the wall to steady myself. "Listen, Pino is my good fucking friend for a long time. And you're special to me; everyone knows it, so stop acting like this! End of story!"

Babe snapped at me. "Hey, was I talking to you? I'm talking to him, so mind your business!"

Pino stepped up to Babe's face, eye balling him. "Good idea, let's talk now! Come on let's go inside."

"No, let's talk here!" Babe turned to me growling, "Go back inside NOW!"

I threw my hands up in the air. "Are you kidding me? You have a problem with me, not him so stop this now!"

Pino and Babe were now squaring off eye to eye as I stormed off inside. Not another word was said until I was gone, I guess they were going to head to head and I couldn't do a thing about it.

T looked at me confused and walked over. "What's going on, I thought you were leaving?"

I shook my head in disgust. "Oh please, Babe just showed up! He's flexing his balls with Pino, because I guess he noticed I left Regina's with him."

T looked concerned, but stayed with me. It was a one on one issue and as long as it didn't become a shoot-out it would stay between the both of them. We made small talk, waiting them out until they finally walked in looking stressed but okay. Babe walked over to T, shaking his hand and kissing him hello, before he turned to me. "So, big shot your night's over. Let's go!"

Confused, I asked, "Why, are you driving me to the airport?"

His head turned around like the exorcist, but he spoke calmly. "We'll talk in the car, let's go!"

I leaned in and kissed T, then my Pino. I straightened his tie looking up at him, and said, "Pino, I'm sorry if I caused you any problems!"

Pino looked at me and than back to Babe, "It's all good! I'm always here for you kid!"

I whispered, "You're the best and I love you! I really am sorry! Do you want me to stay instead?"

He tapped my back, shaking his head, "No, there are a few girls here who can't wait to keep me company! Go! Have a safe trip!"

Babe and I said goodbye to everyone while he pulled my hand into his arm walking out. He didn't say a word until we were in his car. "So what airport? Where do you think you're going?"

I tucked my stray hairs behind my ear, realizing I never told him I was going away. "I'm going to an island for the weekend with the girls."

"Are you, now? And when were you going to mention this?"

"Well, I would have tonight, since we just made the plans, but you acted like a dick, so I thought you'd figure it out when I wasn't around."

Babe narrowed his eyes as he shouted, "DICK?"

I shouted right back! "Yeah, DICK!"

"Listen to me, I'm no dick! I was only playing around with you before, I had no idea you were gonna get bent out of shape and take off!"

"You embarrassed me! Just because you just came home, doesn't mean I did! I go out all the time, and we WILL run into each other, because we all have mutual friends!"

"I was kidding around, you didn't have to make a federal case out of it!"

"Look who's talking? You made a case out of me being with Pino! How embarrassing!"

"Yeah, let me ask you a serious question. You have something going on with him?"

I wrinkled my face as I pouted. "NO! Pino is my friend! Plus he's married!"

"Well, you spend a lot of time with him! You got him to leave the club!"

"Oh my god! I work for him! I hang out with him and his friends!"

"Why did you leave?"

I kept playing with my hair, because he was making me fucking squirm. "Because you made me cry, and I didn't want anyone to see."

"Oh stop, nothing I said could make you cry. What is that time of month?"

Oh my God, really? What is wrong with you? What world are you living in? I was beet red. He was right, but it still had nothing to do with making me feel like an idiot earlier! Babe put his arm around me, pulling me close. "Okay, okay, I get it. Don't get upset. You look mighty fine tonight, and I AM HAPPY TO SEE YOU!"

I smiled, even though I was still embarrassed, but grateful the conversation was ending. "I have to get home soon, before the limo is there."

"Fucking nut, you're taking a limo? I'll drive you to the airport."

"No, it's all arranged already. Mario is treating all of us to a weekend away and the limo will be at my house in two hours." I said, trying not to sound like it was a bigger deal than it was.

"Mario is going with you girls?" He asked looking at me sideways.

I shook my head, waving my finger, "No! He paid for all the tickets, and hotel, but it's just the girls!"

"Nice, that's very generous of him."

"Oh Babe, Mario is so good to all of us because of Bri!"

He reached over and opened his glove box and took out a wad. "Here, put this in your bag. You have your own money; you don't need nobody to take care of you down there. Understand?" I shook my head chewing on my lips, deciding if I should take it. Pino already gave me five hundred, fun money, so this was an added bonus! "Stop just take it. I don't want you running out of money."

I leaned over pulling his cheek closer, kissing it. "Thanks Babe! But you know you don't have to."

"Stop telling me what I can and can't do! I want you to have spare money, so take it!"

Throwing money doesn't work with me! He was right though, I couldn't tell him anything. The more I did, the more he pushed back, so I didn't put up an argument and just stuffed the cash in my bag. Funny, I always stashed his money away and used my own, but it made me feel special that he wanted to give it. I stayed as close as I could during the whole ride back to Brooklyn; almost wishing I wasn't going away.

We beat the limo with time to spare. As luck would have it, he found a parking spot. I could see his eye gravitate to my LV duffle bag all packed and waiting. I had to jump in the shower so I could hit the sand looking good. We were going to be on a secluded resort, so I could go topless and have even tan lines. I quickly dressed in a comfy jogging suit, minus the bra, just to make him jealous. Babe's eyes never left my cleavage, peeking through the open zipper. *Good, you big jerk!*

When the bell rang, he reluctantly walked me to the limo, carrying my bag and mink. As the driver put the bag in the car, Babe opened the door to find all the girls wrapped in their mink coats, smashed, drinking tequila and passing the bottle around. They roared with laughter, seeing Babe shocked. I threw my arms around his neck making out with him. He smelled so fucking good I could have banged him on the hood of the limo.

I was definitely showing off in front of the girls, because he looked hotter than hell. I got over being mad because I was completely whacked, and didn't give a fig what I was doing, as long as it was with him. They started catcalling me, even bribing me with the bottle to get in the limo, but I hung on to his neck, kissing him madly. Brianna leaned out pulling on my pants; since they were sweats, they started to slide down. Babe caught them going down my thighs, and pulled them up laughing. "Oooh, wait a second! You better go before you lose more than your pants!" He sucked my lip and finally let me go. "Get in the car, before you miss your flight. Hey call me when you get settled." Just as he was going to close the door, he stopped. "Oh, when are you coming home?"

I already had the bottle in my hand and paused in mid sip, "I left the itinerary on my bed. I'll call my number if you're staying here and I'll leave a message on my machine if you're not there."

"Okay, but beep me so I know when you land. Have fun, hey, not too much fun big shot!" Laughing, he closed the door.

We drank all the way to the airport, in the airport, and on the plane. We were completely annihilated when we disembarked in Aruba. I snoozed all the way to the resort, but when we checked in it was game on. God only knows how we were able to make it to the beach. We had a cute, young waiter assigned to us, but we turned him into our bitch. After our first round arrived, he had to apply sun tan oil to all of us. This poor kid, was the luckiest kid on the island.

Every few hours we were surprised with compliments from someone's boyfriend. First, the trip was on Brianna's Mario, including airfare and the all-inclusive resort, then the round trip limos to the airport and on the island all were thanks to Lester. The rest came as a surprise, spoiling us rotten each time. Our dinner cruise the night we arrived and boat tour the next day, complete with a full staff cooking and serving, were a gift from Dana's Big Mike, and the daily massages and mani's and pedi's were from Tony. It just never ended; we had no idea why the guys gave us money, but we didn't pay for a fucking thing.

I was drunk from the moment we landed; I didn't remember to call or beep Babe until after we spent the day on the beach and was ready to go out for the night. I ran to beeped him and waited for him to call as it dawned on me that I left him alone in my house with access to my answering machine, phone book and all my little secret things. *Good God what was I thinking!* I left a slurring message on my answering machine to cover my ass and beeped him again. A few minutes later Babe called back, sounding just as cute he was when I left and I had to tell him.

"Hey baby did you get settled in okay?"

"Yezz, we're all good! But I'm a little in need at the moment." I said giggling nonstop.

"In need? In need of what?"

I moaned, "You know, in need!"

"Oh! In need, well if you were here I'd help you out!"

"Well, what can you do for me over da phone?"

Babe's laugh was deep like a growl; he was getting a kick out of me being playful. "I wish I could help, but you're the one who wanted go to away, big shot! If you were home, I'd make you eat your words right now!"

I giggled, "Yeah, I might make you eat something too!"

"Now settle down there, Fats! It sounds like you're in good shape! Be careful and slow down."

"Heehee, are you kidding me? I'm whecked!"

"Do you mean wrecked?"

"And that too. Hmm I'm having fun, but I wish."

"Yeah what do you wish?"

"I can't say."

Babe's voice fell deeper, and was so smooth, "You can tell me anything, go ahead say it."

"I witch, no I mean I WISH you were here with me."

"Yeah you do? I like that! What else do you wish?"

"Stop prying everything out of me! So, what are you wearing?"

He laughed gently. "Why, Fats, what are you thinking of?"

I moaned into the phone, "Because you looked so fucking good when I left, crazy fucking hot!"

"Damn, what are you drinking? I'm gonna buy it by the case!" He laughed playfully.

"Stop, you're making fun of me, and all I'm doing is telling you how you make me feel."

"No baby, the booze is making you say things you're gonna regret when you sober up, but I'm LOVING IT!"

"Noooo! You really looked, you know...arrrr, so tell me something."

His voice was deep and sexy as he growled, "If you were here I'd show you."

"Well if I take off my bathing suit I could tell you."

"Stop right there! I'm with some of the guys."

"Yeah? Well that's too bad for you because it would have been good! I have to go before I'm late for dinner." I giggled rolling around on the bed.

"Stay with your friends and don't leave the resort. I can't come and get you if you get lost." Babe said as he cleared his throat.

"I'm fine, just having a good time. But wait...hmmm fly out and meet me, I want you!"

"Oh sweetheart, I can't leave the state let alone the country, but if I could I'd be there tonight! I'll see you in a few days and when I do, you're going to be sorry you said all this to me."

I moaned, "But I want you now!" Giggling I whispered, "I wanted to drag you into the limo or maybe on top of it!"

He laughed amused at my confessions. "You want nothing to do with me, big shot, remember?"

"Hmmm not at the moment! I want a lot to do with you!"

His voice dropped lower. "Fuck my friends! Tell me like what? What do you want to do to me?"

"Noooo, its want I want you to do."

"Get the next flight out, I'll pick you up!"

I let out a deep breath laughing, "I can't, but I guess I'll have to just think about you while I'm out!"

"Hey, listen to me you better stop drinking before you get in trouble! Where are you guys going?" He kept me on the line and secretly I didn't want to hang up.

"I don't know it's all taken care of. The guys planned things for us; it's all a surprise. Anyway, I just wanted you to know...umm I love, no I miss you."

"I wish I could tape this call! Well, I better let you go, beep me if you need anything. I don't give a fuck where you are, I'll call back."

"Okay, later Babe!" I hung up feeling like I should have jumped through the phone to attack him on the spot.

That night was a blur, and the next morning was hazy. As soon as we woke up, we crawled into our bathing suits and hit the beach. The only way to get over a hangover is to have another, so we started with Bloody Mary's to ease our way back into a new day. By lunchtime, it was time to upgrade and kick it up a notch with Captain Morgan Pina Coladas with a float of 151 Bacardi. Our little chippie assistant escorted a group of island boys carrying tables to our section.

They setup massage beds on the beach with three-sided tents for privacy. We stripped down and laid out facing the beach with gorgeous men rubbing oil all over us. What a sight we were, all lined up. Getting our rub on! A loud voice broke our trance. Our video store clerk, Reggie! What were the odds? His beaming face spoke volumes of what we looked like. Once he found us, he never left and we didn't care. What was one more person on our adventure?

Even though we were exhausted from the sun and drinking, we still got up to go out. No excuses for staying in on an island vacation. We hit a local club by ten, and were surprised to find it looked like Vibes, right down to the colors. Now we felt like we were home. The owner couldn't be nicer, he knew we were coming and put us in a makeshift VIP section. Waitresses carrying trays of tequila shots ran back and forth, while we popped bottles of champagne, settling into the scene. The DJ switched to NY club music and we broke out dancing.

As the local guys started to dance with us, a group of local girls got pissed and started shouting that we should back off their guys. One word led to another and a full fucking brawl broke out. Brianna and I were standing back to back just punching every girl that came our way, while Madelyn kept downing the shots off the waitresses' abandoned trays.

All the other girls joined in as we fought our way out of the middle of the room, while Dana rounded up a car for our escape. By the time we all made it outside, our drivers were all lined up, but the girls ran out as we drove away. How could this happen again? Every island we vacationed on, the local girls were jealous loons! It's not like any of us were there to take them, or even borrow them for the night! We left Aruba with huge hangovers and even bigger sunglasses.

As we flew home, a stewardess approached me demanding that I make my friends stop drinking out of our smuggled tequila bottles and settle down. She got upset when I told her that was what she got paid for. My eyes closed while I turned up my headphones and covered my head with hood. *I'm off duty! Not my circus, not my monkeys!*

How did my bag become so heavy? Ugh! I barely made it through my door before collapsing. My bed called to me. I was snoring from exhaustion when my phone rang. "H e l l o."

"Hey, welcome home! Did you have fun?"

"Shush, not so loud!"

Of course, he spoke louder. "Oh, really big shot, does your head hurt?"

"Ohhhh, yes!"

"Go to sleep, I'll wake you up soon!"

"Mmmm, later Babe!" I barely hung up before I drifted back to sleep. When I finally woke up, my nose followed the smell of something delicious. Babe was in my kitchen, cooking.

"Hey, welcome home! How's your head?"

"Not bad, just foggy. I'm so tired from drinking, I could sleep for a week." I said as I curled up with a bowl of escarole and beans on the couch. I wasn't going to tell him a thing. *What happens on vacation stays on vacation!*

"That's it? I know you had a blast, but did anything happen that I should know about?" He sat next to me and chuckled as I dug my toes under his ass. Babe asked me a million questions, but already knew the answers.

"We drank, ate, got into a brawl and got kicked off the island. So nope, nothing much happened!" I grinned while wiggled my toes.

"Okay so you're not gonna to tell me. I'm sure you were all just tanked the whole time."

I giggled and winked because I knew it sounded too far-fetched. "Why don't you tell me what you did while I was gone?" The warm food made me sleepy, but I wanted to hear anything he was willing to tell me.

"I'm not that interesting, tell me again how much you missed me?" Babe took my bowl and carried me to bed.

"I have no idea what you're talking about." I giggled holding onto his neck.

He lowered me onto the comforter and climbed on top of me holding my face. "What was it you wanted to do to me in the limo?"

"What I really wanted to do was on the limo, not in it!"

"I'll have one here in ten minutes, just to help you out 'cause I'm such a nice guy!" He kissed me gently, playfully, and genuinely. As he pulled back, he played with my hair, staring at me. "So do you have an even tan?" He peaked inside my top to check my tan, and made a disapproving sound. Then he moved on to my pants and when he saw the bikini line, he smiled. "That must have been one tiny bathing suit, your line looks like dental floss!"

I giggled, snuggling into him. "Yup, and it was a hit!"

"I'm sure, you fucking nut! I'm glad you were on the rag for this trip!"

I bit his arm jokingly. "You're like a little old man, a real grease ball! Having my period should have nothing to do with anything. It doesn't stop me from doing anything."

His face wrinkled. "Yeah, I'm a grease ball and your period will stop me from a lot of things, believe me."

I laughed at him. "Oh so I could beg you to make love to me, and you would turn me down because of it?"

"Afraid so!"

"Good grief! Well, I'm not begging, and yes I still have my period. So I guess I'm saved!"

"For now!" He giggled and held me tighter kissing my head.

Smiling, I curled into his arms. After a few minutes he rolled onto his side and settled into watching TV and cuddling until I was out cold keeping my adventures to myself!

CHAPTER 14

....

Train Surfing

Since coming home from vacation, I heard things and now, every moment, I was aware of the strangers and recently lost friends around me. I had walked into a few heated exchanges and turned my head when I saw people carrying guns around. Even when I hugged Babe I could feel he was always packing now. I never really cared before, but now I studied everyone's face, and read their body language. Was the person in front of me an actual stranger, a Fed or a flipper?

Everyone was now suspect, so better safe than sorry. While working one afternoon, a private detective came in, snooping. I wouldn't get up from the side chair at the end of the bar, because I just had a feeling. As he sat amongst the locals-who kept their heads down and didn't say a word- he asked me a lot of questions, including if I worked there. I said no, because I didn't know who he was or what he wanted. He pretended to be confused by my actions, he asked to buy a cup of coffee and I told him he would have to wait until the bartender came back. I beeped Babe unsure of what to do, being very wary of strangers.

He walked in from around the corner and went right over to him. Within a few seconds, Babe knew the guy was no good too and dragged him outside to the train tracks, kicking and screaming. The look of terror on the guy's face was plain for anyone to see. He screamed loudly, but no one stopped to help. People crossed the street and turned their heads, pretending they didn't see this guy get tossed over a chain link fence by his neck, up and over by his throat. He screamed and cried like a girl for a moment. Hanging him over the fence in broad daylight was a real ballsy move but hen Babe upped the ante and shook him by his ankles over the moving trains below.

"Who the fuck are you?" Babe roared at him.

He screamed, "I just wanted a cup of coffee!"

"Nobody drinks coffee in a bar jerk off! Who are you?" Babe roared louder.

"I told you." He howled completely terrified.

"I know what you told me, but I don't believe you. Say something, anything, before you're surfing the top of the trains." He continued to shake him back and forth until he was so sick and scared he puked.

Crying louder, "I'm a private investigator. Don't kill me!"

Pulling him back up, Babe took his wallet and pocketed his license. In a very up close and personal way Babe explained strongly, "You're not welcome here! Do you understand? DON'T ever come back, and DON'T EVER talk to that girl again! Got it?"

Without saying a word, he shook his head, crying and pissing his pants, leaving a puddle on the floor. He ran away as soon as Babe let go of him, like his ass was on fire. I never saw him again. The avenue went back to normal, people walked past us as if it was just a regular day.

Babe turned to me, asking, "Dannie, you okay?"

"I'm better than he is!" I laughed; pointing in the direction the guy ran in.

He held my arm and asked, "Don't sweat it baby, get off the street. Go inside. If anyone else comes by call me, got it?"

"Sure thing! Thanks, love you!" I said without thinking, as I quickly turned red.

Grinning, Babe kissed me he and slapped my ass propelling me forward a few steps. "You got some ass, Fats!" He went back to the club like the king of the jungle once more!

I couldn't imagine not having Babe there to look after me; it was a big turn on to see him in action defending me. I was getting sucked in, moment by moment, and enjoyed his animalistic, protective nature. Returning to the bar, the customers shot me looks because my face was so red. I acted as if nothing was different and went about my business like normal. A few hours later, Babe came back and sat down at the end of the bar.

"What's going on?" He said protectively, as he eyed the crowd.

"Hmm, nothing just same old, same old. How about you?" I said, nervously.

"Nothing, I just wanted to see what time you want to go home." He pressed me, because I said I loved him.

"I think I want to go out tonight after work. It's Wednesday, and I usually have dinner with T."

He dropped his head and stared at me. "How long is this going to continue?"

"Oh come on, we're GOOD friends, but not at all like what's going through your dirty mind!"

Aggressively, he fired back. "Well, then cancel! He'll understand."

Annoyed and flattered, I asked, "Why should I?"

I set off that gangster flame in him, because he changed into tough guy mode. "Listen to me NOW I said CANCEL YOUR PLANS!"

"Why should I? Are you taking me out?" I grinned, putting him on the spot.

"No, I can't, I have things to do later."

"Well, then, I'm going out with T like I always do!"

He slapped the bar hard. "I'll call and cancel for you!"

"Ouff, relax Capone! You can talk to T all you want about whatever you want, but unless you CANCEL your plans and take me somewhere other than my apartment, I'm going out with him!" I said, annoyed with his attitude. I started to light a cigarette but looked up pointing right at him. "And another thing, I'm always well behaved and when I'm not, it's on purpose. Understand that?"

Babe stood up, tossed his chair across the bar and walked out, almost reducing the wooden swinging doors to splinters, cursing under his breath. I looked at him like he had three heads. A few hours ago, he was prefect, now he was a lunatic. What Babe didn't know was that I needed to talk to T about the Carl thing, because I was getting messages from people that he was asking about me.

About an hour after he stormed out, T walked in. I was surprised, because he never came into this bar before. I quickly walked over and kissed him. "Hey T! What a surprise!"

"Yeah, I hear you need a ride to dinner so here I am. You ready?" He said, smiling tensely.

"I can only imagine what else you heard!" I flashed red at the thought.

"Come on let's get out of here, we'll talk later." He said, clearly uncomfortable. I grabbed my cash and bag walking out with him as the next bartender came on duty. As we walked onto the porch, he grabbed my arm and pulled me back in the doorway and looked around before we made a mad dash for his car. I don't know if I was more nervous at the thought of being a target in front of the bar, or getting in his car that could blow up any moment. After all, he was a well-known exterminator. But I followed his lead, and as I jumped in the car I could see some familiar faces on the corner watching me like a hawk.

Ten minutes later, we were back in the Ridge. The looks started as soon as we sat down, the pedestrians stared curiously at us. After my first glass of wine, I quietly told him everything.

He mulled my story over in his head before he responded, as I sat waiting for him to impart his wisdom upon me.

"I know Carl for a long time. He's from Long Island, a standup guy."

"Well, that's good, but chances are he knows Babe, and I don't want to create a problem."

"Do you want me to speak to him for you?"

"Maybe, I don't know. I mean I like Babe, you know I really like him! But I wanna see where things go. I really don't want to be the one saying I have a thing going with him, when I don't. So I guess I should stay mum, just in case it doesn't work out, I don't wanna look like a J-O!" I took a sip of my champagne thinking about Babe. "Plus I'm going to keep my options open until I actually have a date with Babe. And I don't mean driving me home trying to fuck me either. It's either a real date or nothing!" Carl wasn't bothering me! In fact it's flattering that he likes me, so I won't put a stop to it just yet!

T laughed to himself. "You would have made one hell of a fucking guy!"

I tapped his arm, grinning. "Oh, can you imagine how bad I would be? Oh my God!" We started to eat and moved past Carl and Babe and talked about everything and nothing at all. Before we knew it, we were leaving to go to Vibes. We parked in front and walked past the line, waiting to get in. When the velvet ropes opened for us, some of them barked at the bouncers, but we happily ignored the complaining pedestrians until I could hear a girl yell out, "Oh yeah, she gets to cut the line because she's with one of them!"

My head turned to find the face that went with that voice. She was cheesy looking, ill dressed, and an unattractive girl. I shouted at her, "No! I go in because of who I AM, and you're not ME, so you might as well go home!"

We laughed as we started the hello tour of all our friends. Making our way in, we stopped to say hello to every bartender along the way to hangout with Brianna. It was packed the music was slamming. Within moments in the VIP room, our bottle was chilled and we were toasting each other and all the friends around us. Millie and Lori were already there and joined us for a drink. Surely all the girls would come trickling in eventually, and then we would truly be like our own mob. Judy Torres came on, followed by Lime; their music was like ringing the dinner bell, as we all stormed the dance floor. We took it over and had all the guys around us doing their best moves. As I went off, I saw T watching me along with his crew of guys. I motioned for them to join us.

One pedestrian moved too close, and Billy quickly moved in between us. The stupid guy didn't understand, so he mouthed off to Billy, telling him he was there first making his moves on me, and to beat it. The idiot got smacked for the attitude. I guess his girlfriend didn't like her guy trying to dance with me, let alone getting smacked around so she shoved me. I turned just as she swung at me, and caught her hand mid-air, forcing her back with my weight. She grabbed for my hair, but I tossed her.

What I didn't realize was that she wasn't alone. Her girlfriends jumped me, and then some of mine soon followed suit, causing a full-blown brawl to erupt. It didn't last very long; the guys picked them off, kicking and screaming, but in the midst of the commotion the first girl dropped her bag, and was dragged off the dance floor. Feeling bad, I bent down to pick it up and everything fell out. I did the right thing, collecting what I could, and then followed the bouncers. As I approached, the girl was flipping out that I stole her bag.

Annoyed, I held up her handbag and shouted, "Hey, stop screaming, I didn't steal your bag, asshole, I'm giving it to you! You dropped it!" But she wouldn't listen. She swung at me again so I turned her bag upside down and dumped it all over the floor and walked away.

Returning to the bar, T was laughing at me. "I thought you were going to keep a low profile! Any lower you'd be on the fucking wanted posters in the post office!"

Laughing at the absurdity of the whole situation, I shouted over the music, "Can you believe this shit? Really unbelievable!" His guys joined us, and we all shook our heads as we continued to drink, but that was about to change quickly. Someone tapped my shoulder; I turned to find it was Larry the cop in his uniform.

"I'm really sorry, Dannie, but this girl said you robbed and beat her up. You have to come with me," he said as he put his hand firmly on my forearm.

"Larry you have to be kidding me? Robbed her? Beat her up? She looks bad to begin with, but if I beat her up she'd look a lot worse and you know it!" I said, annoyed.

"I know that, but she's filing a complaint. You have to come with me, please."

"Go fuck yourself, Larry! I'm not going, and I don't think you have the balls to cuff me and take me out. Do you?"

"I do, but I really don't want to so just walk with me." He said grabbing my elbow.

I quickly snatched it back and stood my ground, "Larry, you're barking up the wrong tree, I'm not going to go easily." T leaned in and advised me to go and he'd come outside to talk this through. I shot him a look like he was nuts and shook my head. "Sorry, no can do!"

Larry grabbed my wrist cuffing me and started to drag me through the crowd. All the while, I kept spitting at him and pulled back causing him to use his muscles to get me out. As he paraded me out, I taunted him. "Larry you know the only way I'll go anywhere with you is if you have me in cuffs, you prick! Are these real or just your kinky sex toys? I hope you washed them after the last girl!"

He never responded, but moved me through the crowd as it parted, shocked at sight of me in cuffs. Once we were outside, I could see that the crazy girl was pointing and screaming at me. I stood there, still fucking restrained, shouting over her that I was pressing charges for battery too, but I needed an ambulance from being jumped by her.

A car pulled up and more of my girlfriends got out laughing, stopping in their tracks when they spotted me. They swarmed us and started to go after the girl. She realized she was going to get arrested too and saw who my friends were, and knew she would get a beat down the next time she showed her face, she blinked.

Within seconds she dropped the charges and the cuffs were off, while Larry was blasting me.

Seething, he said, "You know I had to do it, so why did you give me such a hard time? You spit at me? We've been friends for a long time, I should arrest you for that!"

Laughing, Madelyn called out, "Hey I see you're having fun Dannie? Did we miss the party?"

Shaking my head in disbelief, I smiled at everyone, shrugging my shoulders. Turning I hugged him, whispering in his ear. "Shut up Larry! You can't take me out without a fight, you know that, plus, you need me! You know why, so don't forget it! I'll see you at the bar when you meet my married girlfriend for a late night date if you're lucky! You know it's very unhealthy to fuck someone's wife in our world! Sleep tight my friend!" I backed off and kissed him closed mouth right on his lips, and then I turned around and walked past T and the guys and back into the club.

As I approached the bar, I could see someone was in my spot, but I couldn't tell who it was from behind. Once I got closer I found out it was Babe, I contemplated turning and leaving but there was no use in running away. I walked up and pinched his ass; he flew around like a rocket to face me. "What the fuck are you doing?" He shouted.

"Pinching your ass, that's what. You have a problem with that?" I asked now in a mood that could turn either vicious or humorous.

He was so red, but I wasn't sure if it was the pinch or the anger making him look like a cherry tomato. Just then, another song came on that I liked and, feeling more in a trouble-making mood than before, I grabbed the bottle of champagne and drank right out of it while I danced. My girls all joined as Madelyn was calling out, "What the fuck now I'm sorry we took so long to get here!"

The VIP lounge was now a mini go-go bar. The crowd was going crazy, because we could all dance better than any stripper around. Girls on the pole know how to take off their clothes, but not necessarily how to dance. We knew how to do both, even though none of us were ever strippers. I saw Babe turn purple, but T was howling. He put his arm around Babe and spoke in his ear. I have no idea what he said, but Babe's normal color returned and he started to smile. Now I was facing him dancing on the table waving my finger at him to come closer, while my little dress got shorter with every move. Holding his glass, he approached and stood in front of me. I may have had clothes on, but I was doing a virtual strip tease for him.

As "Bust A Move" raged on, I turned shaking my hips like maracas and all of the sudden I felt someone bite my ass. Looking over my shoulder I saw Babe's face crushed up against my dress, pulling it lower with his teeth. Playfully I ran my fingers through his hair grabbing the top, as I swung around to shimmy down to face him. After taking a sip, I kissed him hard, and passed the champagne into his mouth. He put his arm around my waist lowering me to the floor, when the crowd erupted in applause.

"So this is a nice normal night out for you?" he asked, grinning and being a ball buster.

Keeping pace with him, I answered like a smart ass. "Pretty much! What can I say? This is my form of excitement; you have yours, I have mine! What's up?"

"I came out with my friends, I didn't know you were going to be here," he said trying to make this look like it was a coincidence, which we both knew was not true.

Moments later, a group of very large guys strolled in wearing shark skinned suits clearing a path for the big boss, Jimmy, and his entourage. They took over half of the VIP lounge. Everyone was kissing and hugging Jimmy. He was always so much fun to be out with. Jimmy bought the whole section a drink and joined right in, laughing and joking around with my girlfriends.

He especially loved Brianna, and would go to the corner and talk with her. Jimmy joked that if Bri were a guy, she would have been a boss, because no girl was tougher. As I drank, talking with T and Babe, I saw Harry the Mute stumbled up, and just as he reached Jimmy he tripped and tossed his whole drink on his suit. We all stood like mutes ourselves, in total disbelief at what had happened. Harry mumbled something as the human refrigerators grabbed him and dragged him out the side door.

If you knew Jimmy, you know he was immaculate; he fumed that he was wet. The only saving grace was that it was a clear drink. As Jimmy wiped his shirt, he walked towards the exit to go outside and stop the beating. He brought Harry, looking all disheveled, back in and bought him a drink because he felt sorry for him. Jimmy never ordered the beating and didn't like abusing pets, children or handicapped people. He was strictly a stand-up and tough guy, a man's man, and never an asshole. *What a night this was turning out to be!*

As 4AM approached Babe put his arm around my waist and asked, "You ready to go home yet?"

Now I was feeling no pain from all the champagne. "Why? Do I turn into a pumpkin soon?"

"I have to go, so I think I should take you home," he said strongly.

"I'm with T tonight, he's got my back. Can't I stay longer?" I asked imploring him while I ran my fingers over his shirt dancing by the bar.

"I'm not sure T deserves to have you throw up in his car, you're too whacked! No seriously, I told him I would take you home so it's all worked out already. Let's say goodbye."

"So you're busted pal! This was no coincidence, you came here to see me!" I said hanging on his neck, grinning. *I could ask you if you're following me, but I'm not!*

"Yeah, yeah I'm busted. I have a feeling you're going to be a handful, you girls are a little wilder than I expected," he said while holding me close.

I said playfully, "I'm more than you can handle, just admit it!"

"I never admit anything, you should know that by now. Come on, let's go." I let him lead me as we made our rounds, kissing everyone goodbye. As we approached T and Jimmy, I dropped Babe's hand and gave them huge hugs before Babe did and I thanked Tom for the night.

"T, thank you for everything! Dinner was great!"

"No problem, baby! And we're on for next week! Remember if you need a ride let me know. Next time try not to get locked up!"

Jimmy looked puzzled, "Locked up? What happened?"

T started laughing, "Some guy tried to make a move on her on the dance floor, and his girlfriend went after Dannie. You missed it, the girls were brawling; all they needed was some oil! It was some fucking show! Tell me you didn't know these girls are tougher than us?"

"Really! I love when the girls break loose; I knew I should have come earlier! Dannie, I may have to give you my list of enemies!" Jimmy roared.

"The cops came and cuffed her! Some jerk off cop dragged Dannie out while she was spitting on him! You should have seen it, too fucking funny!" T was now holding Babe's arm laughing. "Babe, you got a real tiger here, these girls are the sixth crew! You know that, right?"

Babe shook his head laughing, "I see that, this had been a real education! Thanks again for looking out for her."

Now the girls heard our tag name and came over with their hands up dancing, "That's right baby, we're the sixth family! You got that!"

We all laughed kissing goodbye. Babe put his arm around my waist, escorting me through the club surrounded by his guys. I threw kisses to everyone while I danced towards the door, even though I was in a vice grip, just to annoy the shit out of him. Once we were in the car, he turned to me and just stared. I got nervous maybe he was mad; I wasn't sure how to read him. Finally, he turned the key and took off. We pulled up in front of my house with two other cars in front and behind us filled with his guys just in case there was trouble. Some of them got out and stood watch with their pieces clearly visible in their hands. Babe helped me out of the car and picked me up in the air, carrying me as he hustled me into the building. Once we were in the elevator, he gently let me down.

I held on even though I was standing, and asked playfully, "What was that for?"

"Can you imagine being shot at with a drunk girl? It's easier just to carry you and get it over with fast," he said as the doors opened to my floor.

Following him out of the doorway, I laughed, "Nothing is going to be easy with me just so you know, just like you're not easy either. It's no walk in the park being shot at for me either!" I looked around, shocked to see more guys standing at my door, waiting for us. They were in my building, guarding my door. I muttered hello and thank you as Babe pulled out my key and opened my door, quickly closing it behind me. He turned on the lights and walked through each room as I just stood there watching him in full gangster mode. Once he was satisfied, he returned and took my hand walking me into my bedroom. My heart was racing, not sure what he planned on doing to or with me.

"Okay, you're going to bed, I have to leave."

"Where are you going? I'm not tired yet!" I said playfully as I took off my clothes and pulled on my robe.

"You're done, you've had enough excitement for one night! Plus, if I stay here any longer, I'm not leaving, understand?" He held my waist looking down at me and kissed me in the way only a guy like him knows how.

I moaned as he ravished my lips, and let him lead me to the bed. When I came up for air I whispered, "Are you coming back?"

"Why, are you going to invite someone else here?" he said as he held my face in his hands.

"No! I don't put out until my guy is thoroughly broken in. I like them humble and grateful!" I teased him, kissing his neck.

"You're so fucked up, but I like that!" Babe opened my bed guiding me to lie down. He didn't cover me up past my knees; in fact he opened my robe and took a long look at me naked. Bending down he gently kissed my lips and moved slowly down kissing a line right down to my cleavage. He took a deep breath and returned to my lips, looking right into my eyes. "I'll be back to take you to work tomorrow, beep me if you need anything. Night!"

I whispered, "Okay, Babe be safe!" He shut the lights off and left. I had already fallen asleep by the time I heard the tumbler.

CHAPTER 15

....

Fun House

I was tired of being constantly escorted I needed to just be me. As much as Babe wanted to escort me, I went out every chance I could. One night as I was driving past a hot strip club in Staten Island, I spotted Babe's car. *Looky, looky, who do I see, a man in a place I'm not supposed to see!* Truth be told, I had every intention of searching for him, but I didn't expect to find him so early in the night. It's no secret that guys, especially wise guys, like strip clubs, and that most of the dancers are whack jobs. I say mostly because there were some legitimate ones that stripped for a higher purpose, quick cash to pay their college tuition and bills, and I've even met some that were working their way through medical school. The high-end strip club circuit was relatively new and small in the city and outer boroughs. Pedestrians thought they were dingy smoke filled hovels full of skelly dancers and perverted men. That was somewhat true, but the reality was the dancers provided a provocative, and mind blowing experience that normal girls just couldn't or wouldn't do for their men, so they went elsewhere for it.

What I found mind-boggling was that the strippers could roll around on the stage, simulating sex acts, swing on a pole like champs, but couldn't really dance. You would have thought they could have taken a class or two. Some had set routines and stage personas, like female construction workers or the hot teacher look. They were entertaining, but one girl stood out the most because she made me puke; in my opinion, was less than attractive, but could swallow whole foot-long hot dogs and shot glasses. I remember tossing my cookies after witnessing her act.

Jesus Christ, I know she was pretending to give a blowjob, which was fine and dandy if she wasn't downing slimy hot dogs. God, it was disgusting. The guys I was drinking with didn't agree, and relentlessly teased me all night long. I get it, really I do; guys like ladies on their arms, but whores in bed. When a stripper is staring into a guy's face pretending to blow something as if it's them, they're in heaven. Most regular girls want the lights off, to be on the bottom, have unshaved legs, don't wax consistently and rarely talk dirty while they please their man. Actually, most regular girls don't know how to please a man to begin with. Yes, they like being on top and in control, but they fantasize about having their girl on them screaming his name out and how good he is. And strippers fill that fantasy,

Most of the strippers knew me, and we had a decent relationship because we all knew our place. Dance, make your money, do what ever the fuck you want, except steal from me, or fuck my guy. They were pretty simple matter-of-fact rules. This worked well most of the time; fighting only interrupts the flow of money and that was bad all the way around, but there was always one that created more drama than it was worth.

In the NYC area, clubs that served alcohol required the dancers to cover their tits and snatch, but they slid the outfits sideways to flash their moneymakers for a big enough tip. There was one dancer, Darcy, who was a black haired, Puerto Rican and Italian beauty. She was one of the few who could dance like J-Lo. That girl made thousands a night. Darcy liked me, and nicknamed me, "Brooklyn." No one really ever used their real names; nicknames were the rule, not the exception. She was my go-to girl when I was in need of a stripper for a party. Darcy never disappointed, or copped an attitude and did almost everything the guys wanted. Almost meant she would do anything short of fucking them. She made tons of cash in that grey area of do's and don't. The grey area was the border between crazy, fucked up things and downright prostitution. Whatever floats their boat, who am I judge? So, after I picked Millie and Lana up, I circled back around to spy on Babe and found his car still in the lot. Now I was more than curious to see if he was one of the degenerates or a cool, laid back customer.

Lana spoke up first, "Hey, isn't that Babe's car?"

Smirking, I turned to face them. "Yup, you wanna go in so I can see what he's doing?"

Millie laughed, "I feel another Mannix moment coming! But what are you going to do if you find him acting like a dick?"

That was a good question, what would I do? But I was pretty sure by now or hoped at least he wasn't a dick, because that would be a huge turn off. "I guess there's only one way to find out. Come on let's go in, we know everyone in there." They were almost out of the car before I turned off the engine, itching to be in a room filled with men. The doorman, Adam, knew all of us well and welcomed us with open arms. Instead of going directly to the bar, we went right for the ladies room, because behind the stalls was the entrance to the dancers dressing room. It was one big room with rows of vanity mirrors and long counter tops. As soon as I walked through the arch, the hooting and hollering started.

I introduced my girlfriends to the strippers and we sat down to bullshit for a few minutes. Then I heard the music change, and the DJ announce the next dancer in the line up. As Lovely Lynn walked out of the room, I followed her to peek out at the crowd. I scanned the guys, seeing many familiar faces, but not Babe's. I could spot him in a room of hundreds, but I didn't. Then I heard the alternative beat coming from the private lounge, so I turned to ask what was going on. One of the girls said there was group of guys having a welcome home party. Another welcome home party? It had to be for Babe. He deserved all of them, after all the years he was away.

Now that I found him, I had to figure out what to do with him. My girlfriends got antsy and walked to the bar. Our friends were hysterical when they saw real girls they could actually hangout with, and the drinks started to flow. As they were absorbed into the crowd, I went to the back entrance of the private room and walked in. It was like seeing my bar crowd, but just in another place. All of the usual suspects were in there drinking with almost-naked girls hanging on them. I spotted the back of Babe's head as he was getting a lap dance. The dancer saw me as I smiled and put my finger to my lip signaling for her to be silent. She went on with her routine, and Babe looked pretty happy from behind. The smoke was rising from his cigar as the girl grinded him.

I walked slowly into the room and stood behind him peering over his shoulder and ran my nails through his hair softly. He didn't flinch, but leaned back looking up. The last face Babe ever expected to see was mine; he almost fell off the chair and instinctively grabbed the girl to make sure she didn't fall. Ha, at least he was a gentleman!

Joking, he laughed, "Well, look what the cat dragged in!"

Grinning at him, I joked back. "Nobody dragged me Babe, I walked in to see my friends and happened to find you here." As I said that, the dancers all came over kissing me hello. I had to tease further, so I asked, "What's up girls? Are you all taking care of my friend here?"

Each one looked at him and started to cover their assets with their hands. Then Darcy walked in from the main room, shouting, and "I hear BROOKLYN's in the HOUSE!" She gave me the biggest hug as Babe just grinned his million-dollar smile and all of his friends laughed, calling out hello to me.

I gave her a huge hug and stood with my arm around her neck facing him. "Darcy, I hope the fellas are tipping big. Take all their fucking cash, all of it! Especially this one!" I said as I pointed to Babe.

She laughed and asked, "What makes this one so special? Is Babe your man?"

My face turned pink, but I laughed it off. "Just go to town and give him his money's worth. I'm going to the bar."

Babe stood up and wrapped his arms around me. "What the fuck are you doing in a strip club?"

I smiled up at him, teasing Babe with every word. "You don't know me well enough! You have no idea where I go and what I do! I have friends everywhere!"

"Yeah, you do. Well, are you gonna be my friend tonight?" He asked playfully.

"I think you have your hands full, and when I found out you were in here I wanted to stop by and say hello. Now go back to your party!" I kissed him on the lips staring right into his eyes and put my hands up on his chest to move away, but he only held me tighter.

Babe turned his head calling to his friends, "Go outside to the bar, give me a few minutes." As soon as they walked out, he turned to me, whispering with a huge grin on his face, "What will it take to have you dance for me? Tell me and we'll leave now!"

I swayed sideways running my fingers through his hair, guiding him to the chair. Once Babe was there I gently pushed him back into the seat and walked around the chair teasing him. I touched his face as I looked over him and bent down to meet his lips, then pulled back. I swung around dancing until I faced him and started to provocatively dance over him and then put one leg over until I straddled him. Babe was holding my hips, staring intensely as I lowered myself on to him. My ass was propped up, my hands were tightly wound into his hair and I was licking his ear whispering, "I'm not YOUR stripper baby." After that, I pushed back and kissed my fingertip I put it to his lips, and took his finger gently licking it for a second then pulled it out sucking the tip as I stood up. "But if I was, you'd be a brokester!"

Babe narrowed his eyes as his mood changed. "Dannie go home, I don't want you here!"

"Don't worry, I didn't plan on hanging out with you while you do your thing." I pulled away and opened the door where Darcy was waiting. I took a hundred dollar bill out of my bra, and held it to between my fingers sliding it into her G-string. "Hey girlfriend put a smile on his face for me. Show my friend what a Brooklyn babe can do." Then I turned to his friends and blew them kisses as they hollered asking if I was going to pay for their lap dances too. Laughing and shaking my head, I walked out to the main room as his friends walked back in the party room knowing fully well he was burning a hole in my ass, staring at me, floored I didn't go crazy finding him getting a lap dance like any pedestrian chick would.

I found Millie and Lana sitting with more of our guys, laughing and drinking. I ordered one and joined in the conversation, pretending to forget all about Babe. The dancers went through their routines, and stopped by to collect their tips at the end of each song. They all leaned over, kissing me hello, trying to tease the guys with the idea of some les-be-friends action. I laughed them off, knowing they were out of luck.

The mood was fun and easy but the moment Babe came out, all the boys stiffened up around me, but I wouldn't turn around. Darcy walked on stage and the crazy house music started, as she pounded the hell out of the stage, running her hands up and down her body and slamming her knees on the floor, as she swung her hair wildly around. She jumped up and ran towards the pole, jumping up and swinging around it, creating a frenzy. The crowd cheered as she did upside down sit-ups, suspended by her legs that wrapped around the pole. She motioned for me to join her just as I felt Babe's hand on my arm. I turned to see his face, but jumped up and over the bar to make him crazy. The cheers were now roars and money floated all over the place.

I leapt onto the other pole swinging around it a few times with one leg wrapped around it, and one arm holding myself up. No way was I able to do the shit she did; I didn't even try, but I was having fun. I could easily have been a first-rate stripper, because I could do the moves, swing, and dance, but Darcy was in a league all in her own. That girl could fly from pole to pole, hit the swing, and split like she was made of rubber. As I climbed off, I saw Babe grilling me with his eyes, completely crazed that I was onstage. Grinning, I went to the edge of the stage, and had a dance off with Darcy as the guys made it rain cash on us, which I let her keep. I unbuttoned my shirt dangerously low and played with the button of my jeans as I locked eyes with him, and then leaned forward balancing my feet while still on the stage, but rested my hands on the bar. I extended myself on the toes of my killer heels and leaned in and kissed his lips. He quickly grabbed me and dragged me right over the bar.

Once I was standing on the customer's side, he lifted me off my feet to meet my eyes, breathing heavily on me. As soon as I smelled the scotch, I knew this could become an issue. Being his bartender, I knew how certain liquors affected his mood, and this mood I knew intimately well. I did what I always did, I joked around. "Hey, big guy, did you like your lap dance?"

Even though Babe was smiling, more so for the crowd, it was clear he was pissed. "Don't ever get on that stage again!"

I wrapped my legs around his waist and arms around his neck grinning. "But why, I thought you liked strippers!"

He raised his eyebrow. "Are you a stripper?"

I matched his eyebrow. "Never, at least not in public!"

He backed me up against the wall holding me up by my ass. "What the fuck does that mean?"

Now I had him on the ropes a little and felt like I should put him out of his misery a bit. "Are you kidding me? Just because I have skills doesn't mean I use them in public!"

He pushed me harder against the wall on purpose to make a point. "Then who do you use them with?"

I bit my lip, giving him my pouty face as I licked his lip. "No one."

"No one? You looked way too fucking comfortable up there, somehow I don't believe you."

I licked his scotch lips again as he gently kissed me back, more because I wanted to, rather than to make him nuts. Babe had luscious lips! "Believe what you want, I don't have to lie. You either do or you don't. And just so you know, I used to bartend here, everyone knows me, so calm down!"

He shot back annoyed, "Are you fucking kidding me?"

"Nope! Your friends loved coming here, I treated them like kings!"

"I fucking bet!"

"Stop, it's no big deal!"

His eyebrow relaxed slightly, as he leaned in to kiss me. He pulled back and gently put me down, but put his hands over my head, locking me in place against the wall. Leaning in, Babe kept kissing me. This was very strange in a way, because I was never into public displays of affection, and very rarely let someone kiss me in front of my customers. But what the hell, the whole night was strange, so I went with it.

While kissing me, he asked, "Come home with me?"

Feeling flushed, I continued to play with him. "I can't, I have a few more sets..." I couldn't finish the sentence, because he smothered me by wrapping his arms completely around my body. Once he came up for air, I joked with him more, "Hey, you didn't even tip me, and you're getting near the cookie jar!"

Without breaking his stride, he reached in his pocket and pulled out a wad of cash and slipped it into the middle of my bra and returned to kissing me. Without breaking the kiss I slid my hand up and removed the cash and slid it into the front of his pants, right past his belt down to his package. I whispered, "How about you dance for me?"

Babe's response was a combination between growling and laughing. "Let's leave now and I will."

I put him on the spot just to see how much scotch he drank. "Are you asking me out?"

"Nope!" Babe growled as he kissed me. *Fucking guy was still sober!*

He jumped back a little, because I bit his lip hard to teach him a lesson. "Then no, I'm not going with you. Maybe you better grab a dancer!"

Playing me like I was playing him, he asked, "And what are you going to do, watch?"

"I'm not into comedy shows, I like action flicks, so no, I won't be watching." Abruptly, I bent down and walked out from under his arms back to the bar pissed.

Arrrr, again I let him get the best of the situation! I jumped back into drinking with our friends, as he went to the corner of the bar. He ordered a round and started to toss money at the dancers, just to irritate me. They gladly hoed it up for him, and I could see a deviant smile simmering over the rim of his glass. Then, somehow, I got distracted and when I looked back, he was gone. *Really, what the fuck?* I picked up my glass and walked around the bar, thinking maybe he was sitting down and I couldn't see him in the crowd, but he wasn't there. Then I checked the parking lot and found his car, and just then I got that sick feeling right in the pit of my stomach. Babe was with a stripper. Like a rocket, I shot back into the club past all of his friends, right into the party room and there he was in a club chair with Jackie, a dancer, all by themselves. This was not just hanging in a group with a stripper, playing around and mentally masturbating; this was intimate. She turned her head and smiled at me as she slid her G-string sideways rubbing her snatch on him. He sat like a king with a scotch in one hand and a cigar in the other grinning at me.

I blinked; my jealous side came out in full force as I called out. "Hey blowjob, get off him!"

Jackie laughed at me. "No, I don't think so. Wait your turn Brooklyn!"

That's it. I snapped. I took my glass and smashed her right on the side of her head, knocking her off his lap. "I don't wait for nobody, douche bag, and I don't ask twice!" Then I smacked him right across the face. I knew he let me; he could have caught my hand in time. Babe just laughed as he grabbed my arm, pulling me onto his lap.

"Jealous?" Babe joked; as he pulled me close to kiss my chest, as it was clearly right in his face.

I pulled myself up and stalked away without a word to him, but I did turn to Jackie to spit at her. "Jackie, you and me have a big fucking problem! This is not over!" She continued to cry holding her face as I left without waiting for a reply.

The bar called out to me, and I embraced it with every fiber of my being. I never saw him come out, and I fumed thinking he was getting head in the back room. At the end of the night, I walked out alone to go to my car. Earlier, my girlfriends headed out to after hours with the guys to continue the party. I now faced fifty lesbian bikers in the parking lot, waiting to kick my ass. I'm a fighter, but not stupid, I couldn't fight that many girls, and walk away without being beaten to a pulp. I turned around and went right back in to figure out what the hell I was going to do. *Call the cops? Nope!* Not even five minutes went by, and Babe walked in obliviously, finally hammered from the night.

"Hey Tyson, how come you're not outside?" Babe cracked up, enjoying making fun of me!

"Stupid, I'm not! Those girls will kill me, they look tougher than you!" I smirked.

"Yeah I think your right Dannie. Come on, I'll take you home."

"No! I have my car and I was thinking about sleeping on the bar until they leave anyway. It wouldn't be the first time!"

"Suit yourself, but you should know your car is back in Brooklyn. I had one of the guys drive it back for you. I did you a favor so you don't get nailed for DWI."

"You robbed my car?"

Babe roared laughing at me as he grabbed my waist trying to nuzzle up against me. "Call the cops if you don't like it!"

Narrowing my eyes, I grilled him and pushed away, because I was so pissed. "Ewww, don't touch me after having that skank blow you!"

He had both arms wrapped around me, and was enjoying laughing at my expense. "I DID NOT get head from Jackie, she fucked me!"

"You are totally disgusting! Get away from me!" I picked up my hand to smack him again.

Like lighting, he caught my wrist. Babe leaned in and whispered in my ear. "Oh no, you won't get away with that again! The staff is here, you're not cracking me in front of them!"

"You're disgusting, get away from me!" I whispered as I pushed away, but it was no use, Babe's chest was like a brick wall.

"Relax! I didn't so anything with that girl!" He pulled me into a complete bear hug trying to act all serious.

"You're an ass!" I said as I relaxed in his arms.

He kissed the top of my head and started to guide me towards the door. "Hold my hand and don't become a fucking boxer with these broads. Got it?" I shook my head and walked along side of him out the front door.

They were still there, and started right in on me. "Hey tough girl, we wanna talk to you!" Collectively, they sneered at me while they railed insults, but never touched me.

I ignored them and walked with Babe to his car and got in without answering, but I burned inside, feeling like a fucking coward- a living coward, but a coward nonetheless.

He threw the car in gear and pulled out, shaking his head over the whole situation. In a matter of a few minutes we were pulling up to my apartment. He parked, opened my door, and proceeded to walk me into my building. Once the elevator door closed, he started to maul me. When the door opened I looked a lot different. My heart was pounding as we walked to my door. He took my key and opened the door, but grabbed me and went right back to aggressively kissing. Within sixty-seconds the beeping started, then the ear-bursting alarm went off. I pounded the keypad to shut it off, as he was pulling at my shirt. When I finally turned around, I could see he was a man on a mission. Babe was just too perfect, he made every part of me tingle. I kept trying to whisper in between kisses when he advanced to my neck. "Babe, I'm not fucking you."

He whispered back, "No problem, because I'm going to fuck you, but first I'm going to strip you naked and you're going to let me, because you want me...tell me."

He was blowing my mind! Every part of me wanted every part of him, but there was that one little thing about being in a relationship. "What if I say no?"

"You won't!" With those two little words, he stuck his hands down my pants. I shivered and climaxed right on the spot. Babe growled with satisfaction. "That's why you won't say no."

Should I just say fuck it to being a good girl? If the Nuns saw me now, I would have to do a shit load of Hail Mary's! I was about to make up my mind when his beeper went off. Babe's hand froze and gently he pulled it out, and looked at the number. We locked eyes and he truly looked sorry as he kissed me and turned to leave without a word. I stood there stunned as he closed the door and vanished like a thief in the night.

CHAPTER 16

Jungle Drums

My whole shift I thought of Babe and Jackie. He was right about one thing, I was jealous. As my night was ending, I cleaned the cocktail tables, and then there was a rap at the window. I looked over and saw the faces of a few guys from another crew that didn't hang out at my bar. They started to bang on the glass with more force than what was friendly. *What the hell is going on?* I almost opened the door, because I was so taken aback, but my gut told me to hide, so I did. These guys were out for no good. They were banging on the door pretty hard and screaming, while they peered in through the window.

I wasn't sure how long it would take them to get inside, so I had to act fast. I hugged the wall and made it to the back where the pay phone was and beeped Baabe. He called right back, I told him what was happening and that I was trapped. He was in the city working and told me to hang up and wait for his call back. I did as he said, hoping the front door would hold up against their pounding fists. They were kicking the door now with tremendous force, ranting and raving "Come out, come out where ever you are! Open the fucking door! We can see you, come on honey open the door."

What seemed like hours were actually only a minute or two as I sweated it out for Babe to call back. His call was a Godsend. "Listen for a garbage truck and as soon as you hear it, run out the side door and jump in."

I cried into the phone, "Are you kidding me? I can't open the door; there may be more of them at the side door! What am I going to do if they catch me?"

Lying to make me feel better, he coached me along. "Listen, just do it. I'm sure the neighbor's called the police and they'll be there soon, but now just run. You can do it! Do you hear the truck yet?" He yelled.

I tried to tune out the yelling, banging, and my own internal screaming until I finally heard a rattling garbage truck. I screamed, "Yes, I think I hear it. Oh my God, oh my God, why is this happening to me?"

"Run now! Go, drop the phone, don't hang up, and just run!"

"Okay, I'm going to go..." my voice trailing off as I dropped the handset and ran out the side door. Just as Babe had said, the truck was there and I jumped in. The guys saw me just as I was closing the truck door. Screaming, they tried to run up along the side, but Allen was driving and he took off like a rocket. They would have to be absolutely insane or out for a hit to shoot at a private sanitation truck!

I was shaking like a leaf, crying. "Allen what the fuck just happened?"

"Dannie, I don't know anything! Babe asked me to come and get you and that's what I did, and at the looks of it, just at the right time. You can't go back tonight, where can I take you?"

My brains were scrambling to figure out what to do, so I had Allen take me to my girlfriend Millie's. I thanked him and jumped out of his truck running into her house. As soon as I got in, I beeped Babe and within seconds, he called me back I then explained what had happened. Waiting for him to get off of work was one of the longest and worst nights of my life. I must have fallen asleep on Millie's couch, because I woke up with Babe leaning over me stroking my hair. It was daylight and the sun was pouring into the window. I could see his face; he was clearly beside himself with grief. I just started to cry uncontrollably as he cradled me "Shush, stop crying."

"I was so scared!" I whispered through my tears.

"Shush, I know, but you're okay now." Babe said, as kind as could be. He knew I was more upset than he's ever seen me before.

"What's going on? What were they doing?" I asked, knowing fully he couldn't and wouldn't tell me. My mind knew the reality, but my fear was asking the questions.

Rocking me, he whispered, "Shush, calm down. I don't know."

"You're a wise guy, what do you mean you don't know?" I choked out.

"DON'T SAY SHIT LIKE THAT!" Babe lowered his voice trying to make me calmer. "Things are crazy now. I don't want to talk here! You're okay, that's all that matters to me right now!

Everything else you're asking about is just stupid shit," Babe said as sincerely as possible under the circumstances.

Crying through my words, I blurted out "Maybe they're the guys who tried to shoot you!"

Frustrated, he said, "Stop. I said THINGS are crazy now."

"That's not good enough! What were they after? Me? Were they going to rob me or rape me?"

Trying to be funny and to break the tension he said, "Hey, no one's getting there before me so stop crying! Come here sit on my lap." I crawled deeper into him, just letting him hold me until I was done. Cradling my head, he gently kissed my cheeks, on each tearstained line running down my face and stopped on my lips. Slowly, he lowered me onto the chair as he went down on his knees and took my face in his hands pulling me close. It seemed like an eternity; he was staring into my eyes, resting his lips on mine. Babe whispered, "I will never let anyone hurt you ever! I will take care of this! Let me take you out of here, I gotta leave." I had this street guy who was known for being a lunatic, but as kind and sweet as can be with me. Babe gave me a chaste, closed-mouth kiss and held me tightly, sending with it a million silent messages.

Yup, this is what its like to be with a street guy; tears and fears! He will get on his knees to be with me in one breath and in the next breath make someone else beg on their knees for their life. Crazy! I jumped up, whispering, "I can't do this!" What I wanted to say was that I was falling for him hard, but was afraid of him. Instead I babbled like an idiot about things that didn't really matter at the moment. "I don't really know you! You just came home after ten years! How many girls have you had so far?"

Babe started pacing around spitting his words at me. "What? You don't know me? Girls?"

Continuing my meltdown, I cried more. "No, I don't! Not really! And yes how many girls?"

Now he was hurt and it came out. "I don't fucking know you either then, but you called me and I'm here! I don't see anyone else here helping!"

"I'm sorry! I don't mean it like that!" I wasn't looking to hurt him, but I was so freaked out.

Putting his hand on his chest, he asked. "What do you exactly mean, then? What's the problem with me?"

"Please! You're too wrapped up in this life; I can't. I just can't fall for you and handle you not loving me enough! You know what I mean, Babe? Then, God forbid something happens to you! I just can't do this." I said letting him know my innermost fears, finally.

Exasperated, he spit out his words with a pained look. "I don't know what to say, I can't promise you anything, but you know I care. You know it; don't act like I haven't showed you. You knew what I was and seemed to enjoy it. So what the fuck? What do you want?"

Going in for the kill, I asked, "Are you in love with me?" *Why can't you see I love you and need you to love me back?* He didn't answer, but stared at me looking completely naked, raw and transparent as if he had given me a window into his soul. I asked the second most pressing question on my mind. "Are you guys... what is fucking going on?"

"STOP!" He shouted.

"I can't stop, you're all friends! My friends! What the fuck is happening?" Losing it more, I cried harder.

Trying to get me to stop my interrogation, he shouted, "Stop now! I'm not going to tell you again, we are not having this conversation!"

"Okay how about this one? Can you leave all this for me? Don't answer, because I know it already!" My tears were uncontrollable. "I'm in the middle of something. I don't understand, because of you and I don't even know if you're married!"

Babe exploded, running his fingers through his hair, clearly enraged. "Are you fucking kidding me? I'm not married and haven't been with anyone! I'm with you every day, when I'm not at the half way house or working, I'm with you!"

"Oh please, how do I know that? Me, only me? How many keys do you hold?"

"Yes, you! There are only so many hours in the day; I spend most of them with you! You don't let me near you, no matter how much I try. You're like a nun, none of this and none of that! I only have your key that you can have back any time you want!"

"I'm not the kind of girl that fucks anyone, especially without a commitment!" My words trailed off as I cried.

"This is not the time or place for this! I don't know what else you want from me, but you know I care for you!"

"No, I don't! Your silence is deafening!" I said, crying so hard I almost threw up. "I don't really know what you think of me; you assume I know, but unless you actually say something, I have no idea how you feel or what you're thinking! You throw dirty paper at me, scare away anyone who looks at me, and I know you like to hangout and try and fuck me, but that's it! I need words and a commitment from you!"

"Dirty paper! That's fucking hard earned cash! Are you blind? I show you more attention than I've ever showed anyone else. Everyone else can see it but you!" He said, as he ran his hands through his hair, clearly frustrated. "What do you want from me? I live like a fucking monk! What? Do I need to be seen out with some broad and then you'll want me more? Listen, I'm not going to keep going round and round, I'm no beggar!"

"I would never look at you again if I saw you with someone else!" I screamed knowing I would hate him forever if he made that choice. Babe would become a Joe!

"Liar, who are you kidding? You're not going to let me go with anyone else and let me be seen with them. So stop this game, you're a fucking tease!"

"Fuck you! I hate you!" I lied just to hurt him as I crumbled to the floor, crying.

He bent down and started to rub my hair, trying to calm me down. "Stop! Calm down, I'm sorry all this happened, I didn't mean anything I said. I don't want you to cry or be scared! I promise, I'll take care of you if you just let me!" Babe looked like he just let me see into the door of his soul for a second, but just as quickly, the door closed. "Come on, get cleaned up, we have to get your bag from the bar."

"I'm afraid of the bar; I don't wanna go back there now," I said choking through the tears.

Babe bent down even further and picked me up. Wiping away my tears, he said, "Whether you want to realize it or not, you're part of this world, because of where you work and who you surround yourself with. Everyone knows you belong to me, but you have to figure out what you want once and for all. If you can't handle this, you should find a regular guy and get married. If you don't want that, then you need to tough it out. You can cry with me, but never and I mean NEVER let anyone see you cry! Come on, I'm taking you back to get your bag. I'm walking in with you, and I won't leave you alone. Get cleaned up now!"

As I brushed my hair in the mirror I was watching him, thinking he was right, and I knew it. *Babe was always a gentleman with me; he never overstepped himself. In the midst of all the craziness, he made me feel safe. Babe was the first person I would call without even a thought about anyone else. I do talk the talk every day, so I guess it's time to walk the walk. But I still think I might want what I wanted; a straight guy that would love me and never leave at 3AM to answer to the boys, or have a wife or girlfriend in the wings that I didn't know about. But how could I give Babe up? I just wasn't ready to make that choice. Why should I have to? Who makes the rules? Me, that's who, so I go on.*

If you didn't see my clothes the day before, you would never know I had slept in them, crying most of the night. We pulled up to the bar and the cleaning guy was outside sitting on the steps. He saw me and jumped up. "Dannie I was so worried when I came in, and the doors were unlocked. I found your bag, but not you. I thought something terrible happened." He grabbed me giving me a big hug, and then quickly dropped his hands saying, "Sorry Babe, I was just concerned and all. I hope you don't mind?"

"No problem! Looks like we're all cursed. It's okay." Babe slapped his back and walked in the bar looking around. Everything looked normal.

He blurted out nervously, "I didn't touch anything. I just walked around looking for Dannie and when I realized she wasn't here, I sat outside waiting for someone to come, because I didn't know what to do."

Nothing looked different from last night. If they came in through the side door after I left, they didn't touch anything. My bag, the night's deposit and the cash register banks were all intact. I thought this was more upsetting than finding a trashed bar. Now I knew for sure it was me they were after. I was the target, just to get to him.

"Okay pal, please clean up, another person will come in to work the bar today, just stay until they get here. Thanks!" Babe said, slicing off a fifty-dollar bill, and tossing it to him as a bonus. He grabbed my hand and hustled me into the car.

"Wait! I have to work today!" I said, surprising him-and myself for that matter.

"Not today, you're not!" He looked at me like I was crazy. "A little while ago, you said you were afraid, now you're not?"

Now that I could think clearly, made up my mind to stay. I can't let anyone make me afraid. If I run now, I'll never come back.

Defiantly, with my balls to the wall mindset, I held my ground. "No, I am, but I have to. I changed my mind, I'm working the day, otherwise whoever they are will think I'm afraid. You know, get back up on the horse when you fall thing? I have to do it, or I'll never go back."

"Then switch with someone and work tonight. I'll be around the corner if you need me," he said tapping my leg not waiting for my response.

"No!" I shook my head stubbornly. My afternoon flew by, before I knew it, it was the early evening. The guys were in and out. Babe stayed at the end of the bar most of the time, busting my chops. His teasing kept going farther and farther, because I think he was still sore about our previous conversation. It didn't help that I was overly sensitive too; this turned out to be a bad combination.

I was starting to crack under his pressure, repeatedly yelling at him to cut it out because he wasn't funny anymore, I didn't think he was going to feel satisfied until he hurt me as much as he thought I hurt him. He went way over the top teasing to the point that I ran out of the bar, crying. As I ran, I grabbed a random jacket off the hook by the door and put it on while I ran across the street. At that moment I heard an SUV engine roar, I turned and saw it heading towards me, hopping the curb at a high speed with its high beams on. It chased me onto the sidewalk until I made it to the corner, and made a right turn.

Before I knew it, I was running for my life. The truck had to slow down to make the turn, giving me enough time to make it to the club. I never tried to open the door; I just kicked it open and went flying in. The social club was filled with the guys playing cards and eating. They jumped up and cards went flying along with drinks and dishes; they all pulled their guns out. I had a maniac behind me and twenty guys with guns ahead of me. I was beyond hysterical. A few guys ran outside while Tommy Pizza brought me to a table and tried to get me to tell him what happened.

All of the noise of the chase alerted the crowd at my bar, and they came flying out. I was still wildly crying when Babe showed up, he pulled me to him tightly trying to calm me down, comforting me. He did a double take as he looked at the jacket I was wearing and hugged me.

Shaking, I choked, "What?"

Looking controlled, but upset he mumbled low, "They must have thought you were someone else with this fucking jacket on."

"Who?" I said bewildered.

"Never mind, just take it fucking off and throw it out," he said as he started to remove the jacket.

Confused and freaked out, I didn't understand what a stupid jacket had to do with almost getting killed. "What are you talking about?"

"Do as I say for once! Throw out that fucking jacket, it belongs to someone else!" Grabbing my arm and making me look at him, he roared. "That's it, I had enough! Time to go home!"

I didn't argue I really was done! As I returned, everyone had a good laugh at my expense and ribbed me about kicking the door in. I never knew who was behind the wheel for sure, but I had my own list of suspects. Grabbing my purse and money, I jumped in his car. He peeled away and was now driving with a vengeance. I could feel his anger boiling up like a volcano. I had no idea where he was going, but I sat in silence. We left the neighborhood, jumped on the highway and traveled towards Long Island. He surprised me and veered off towards Breezy Point. Babe pulled up to a block barred by gates and he whipped out a plastic card, swiped it across a little pad and the gates opened to a private community. Within a few seconds, we were parked and walking into a beautiful beachfront house. It was at the end of the secluded gated community.

Babe grabbed a phone and walked into another room, leaving me standing in the middle of a large family room and kitchen. I walked over to the windows and stared out to the ocean. The view was amazing! The house was small, but truly my dream home, with a big fireplace, kitchen, huge comfy couches, high ceilings, floor to ceiling windows and all hardwood floors. Babe walked over, holding the phone. "Listen, I think you have to stay here for a day or two until I can figure out what's going on. Can you handle being here without telling anyone where you are?"

"Sure, I guess for a day or two, but more than that might be hard," I mumbled.

The volcano started to erupt inside of him as he looked at me with a different set of eyes and said, "You're gonna fight me on this too? Every fucking thing you challenge! So tell me why can't you just stay here? Is it because of one of your boyfriends? Is he going to worry about you, or is it just me that gets that privilege? He gets to fuck you and I get to hide you!"

Boyfriend? What boyfriend? I lunged forward as I pointed my long nails at him. "That's it, I've had enough! I didn't do anything wrong, except maybe work for you guys! You've seen me out; you're always stalking me when you're not with someone else so you know I don't have a boyfriend!"

Turning purple, he shot back. "I didn't say you did anything wrong! Why can't you shut the fuck up?" Seething he continued, "Stalking? You got some set of balls to say that!"

"You're accusing me of being with guys, when you know I'm not, or at least haven't been since Rio's! How could I be with anyone, you're always there! How could I meet anyone anyway with the way you behave?" I stood up straighter, trying to make a point even though my head was spinning. "You need to tell me what the fuck is going on. Why is this happening to me?"

Cold as ice, he spat out, "It's just one of those things."

"Things? What kind of answer is that? Things!"

Lost for answers he said, "It's the best I can do."

"I have no idea what those guys wanted from me, if I'm who they wanted to begin with! I think they wanted to send a message through me to one of you guys. Maybe even rape me to deliver it; did you notice the cash was still in the bar?"

I looked around for the door and started walking towards it when he called out in a sarcastic tone "You're at the end of the earth sweetheart, you can't walk anywhere. Sit down, be quiet, and just stop fucking driving me crazy! Please just stop!"

My jaw dropped open. After a minute, I turned around, fighting back tears and quietly said, "Thank you for bringing me here to protect me, and really I'm so grateful you check on me. Just let me know when I can go home. I have enough cash to take a cab." He just stood there, staring at me, fuming. I tossed my bag down on the couch and walked outside.

I sat on the beach smoking for what seemed like an eternity. Watching the waves roll up, getting closer each time comforted me as I cried. My tears flowed like the foam trail left behind in the water's wake. Weighing all my options, which I realized weren't many; I was going to have to trust Babe's instincts and follow his lead. As it was getting dark and cold outside, I decided to put my big girl panties on and face what was happening around me. Slowly, I walked back into the house shivering from the cold beach. Nothing looked better to me than the couch; I was mentally exhausted and wanted to sleep my problems away. Curling up, I crashed for an hour. At one point, I started to smell the most delicious aromas; I woke up to find Babe in the kitchen, cooking. I was starving, and rose with a fierce appetite. I didn't want to presume he made anything for me, so I stayed quiet. The table was set for two, and I watched him cook silently knowing fully that he knew I was awake.

Pointing towards the cabinets with a wooden spoon next to the sink he said, "Can you make a salad? Everything is in the refrigerator and you'll find a bowl over there." I quickly figured out where everything was and made a pretty decent salad to accompany his pork chops. As soon as we started to eat, the pressure melted away and we began to enjoy ourselves. He served and I poured the wine. "Pick up your glass. Too bad you didn't buy that new dress; I told you we were having dinner soon." he clinked my glass and winked with a smile.

Smiling, I said, "Jerk off."

Grinning, he said, "Thanks to you, yes, I have been. Enjoying your meal?"

Shoving his arm, I teased, "Ugh, is that what the special sauce is? You know this isn't a date."

Smirking, he winked at me again. "Don't hold your breath, you don't deserve me! Plus you're always so fucking pleasant; you're killing me with kindness."

"Hmm, we'll see, but I bet you'll ask soon and eventually you'll ask me to marry you too! So, on a lighter note, do you have spare blankets for me so I can sleep on the couch?"

Laughing at me, he said, "Marry you? That would really be a fucking life sentence! Smile, I'm joking. You're not sleeping on my couch you can take the bed. I have to go to work anyway so you will be alone."

Alarmed, I looked around at the complete darkness that surrounds his house. "Alone? Out here? It's a little scary in the dark on the beach. Can't you stay home with me?"

Touching my face, he looked me in the eyes. "No, I gotta go."

Trying to get him to change his mind, I pushed, "Oh come on, call out sick. I don't want to stay alone here after everything that's happened."

"You're gonna be fine. I can't call out sick ever, or I'll violate my parole," Babe said trying to get me to ease up.

"Really?" I asked.

"You got a lot to learn, don't worry I'll school ya!" He said, laughing at me. Babe put his hand on my arm and turned very serious, "Listen, you can't open the door to anyone. You have to stay inside while I'm gone and most of all, don't answer the phone. If I want you, I'll beep you first and then ring the phone."

"Why, is a girl going to call looking for you?" I asked coyly, as I bit my bottom lip. I was emboldened by all of the wine I drank and I was trying to figure out if I wanted to say what was in my head.

Not giving me any play, he said, "No, it might be business. Don't answer it. Understand?"

"Geez, don't get so uptight! Don't worry, I won't. I couldn't care less who calls you, but what if I need to make a call?" I was so annoyed he didn't offer up any more information about his personal status. He's not a regular guy so we need to have a real heart to heart conversation, before I believe him. *Haven't you figured it out yet? I won't give in if you're married, no matter how much I love you! I really hope you told me the truth!*

He wouldn't budge on his conditions. "Nope, don't use the phone."

"Oh come on, suppose I get beeped?" I asked playfully.

"Ignore it," he grinned.

"I can't," I said pouting.

"YES, you can."

Looking him dead in the eyes, I raised my eyebrow. "I bet you wouldn't if one of your little friends were looking for you?"

Babe's face turned beet red. He got up to clear the table. "I don't have any little friends! Oh boy, you're starting to get whacked!

Come on, time to watch TV and settle in, I have to get ready for work."

I let him lead me to the bedroom, but I wouldn't give up my glass of wine or the bottle. *They're both coming to bed with me tonight, maybe if I drink it all I might invite someone else to join.* Oh my god, the bed was tremendous and so luxurious; it was snow white and fluffy, he had pillows everywhere. *There's definitely a girl's touch here.* I walked into his bathroom and closed the door behind me to peek inside the shower to see what type of shampoo and body wash he had, but it was all manly stuff, so I move onto the medicine cabinet and there wasn't anything feminine in there either. I almost finger-brushed my teeth, but I saw his toothbrush. *I've already made out with him so why not use it?*

I returned to the bedroom. Babe was sitting on the edge of the bed and asked, "Snooper, are you done?"

Trying to bluff my way out of it, I smirked. "I wasn't snooping! I had to go to the bathroom."

"Really? You didn't flush. Plus I heard you opened my cabinets. I'm telling you, you won't find anything. I'm a monk! Come on change into this while I take a shower." He chuckled handing me a button down white shirt and a set of boxer shorts. "Wait until I go inside, I'm not a full monk just yet!"

I was so confused; I could've had some fun with this if only I wasn't such a good girl! "Okay, I'll wait. Get going before you're late." I turned my back and started to kick off my shoes, and then I unbuttoned my jeans. I could hear Babe as he turned on the shower and took off his clothes. I turned around a little earlier than I promised just as he stepped into the shower to catch a peek.

I wondered what he looked like naked. I wasn't really surprised, I knew he would have a rocking body, but holy smoke he was hot! The water was cascading down his muscular back, drenching the firmest body I'd ever seen.

What was I doing? I couldn't do this, could I? I clicked the TV on and started aimlessly flicking through the channels; I slipped on his shirt and boxers and climbed into the bed. Babe took a fast shower, but he was facing the wall the whole time, I wondered if he knew that I was watching him. Nervously, I turned my attention to the TV, trying not to be a Peeping Tom. Babe stepped out of the shower and wrapped a towel around his waist. While he dried his hair, I pretended not to notice him, but I was straining to see his tattoos; they were mostly the green jailhouse type. I've never really noticed anything but his face before, and now I couldn't take my eyes off him. I was secretly disappointed when he put on a clean pair of jeans and a black t-shirt.

Sip your wine Dannie stop being a pervert! I'm a terrible poker player! My face was red; I was a total bumbling idiot at the moment. Babe sat on the edge of the bed and slapped my leg, "Hey Peeper, listen I have to go to work. Stay in bed and watch TV, remember the rules and be good. Can you handle that?"

My face flashed red; he knew I was looking at him. Staring with my big eyes while chewing on my lip, I said, "I'll try, but I wish you could stay here with me."

"I know, me too, but I can't," Babe said, as he moved a strand of stray hair away from my face. "Hey I hope you didn't strain yourself before, did you get a good view?" Laughing, he kissed my forehead. Babe tapped my leg before getting up and walking over to a panel on the wall in the living room to set the alarm.

Before he slipped out of the door, I yelled, "I didn't see much, you poor guy! Later gator." After about a half an hour, I figured Babe was long gone, so I got up to snoop around. I looked in the closets, there wasn't anything unusual, clothes, shoes all the normal stuff. In fact there wasn't anything anywhere that wasn't normal guy stuff. I couldn't find a lip-gloss, a tampon, or pair of panties. *Is this guy really alone, could he be telling me the truth?* I decided to settle back in and watch a movie; just as I was getting comfortable the phone rang. I jumped as the answering machine picked up. Clear as bell, it was a girl's voice, wanting to know if he's going to stop by and see her. *What?*

Babe was married, had a girlfriend or both! God, she was calling looking for him. What a fool I was, am, and will be if I stick around! I knew it, just knew he was like all the rest...a fucking player, a liar...a Joe! How could I stay here, what can I do, what a mess I got myself into. I have no choice I have to stay.

I was so hurt I decided to drink with a vengeance. Ripping mad, I rummaged through every cabinet and closet searching for whatever he stashed. I found wine, a good start, but certainly not enough to appease my mood. I finished the bottle, and opened another. Two bottles down, I moved onto a bottle of vodka all while chain smoking. I'm not a vodka drinker, but I figured it out quickly. The room was spinning and I was in rough shape, crying and very drunk. It was a very stressful twenty-four hours and I couldn't handle the pressure. So totally unable to come to terms with this revelation, I started to sink deeper and deeper into despair as the hours passed. Asking myself why he would pursue me like a madman only to add me to his collection of girls; I just couldn't come up with a valid explanation for it. *Why? Why me? Was I that terrible, I couldn't get and hold my own guy?*

I heard the door open and the chimes of an alarm vaguely in the background. His voice was very loud, in fact too loud for my very drunk head!

"Geez what's that smell?" He spotted me and looked incredulous. "You're drunk and you reek! Holy shit, what's going on?"

I was curled up on the floor with the comforter; I think I fell off the bed at one point and couldn't get up. My voice was raspy and I shrieked, "Check you're answering machine, scumbag! Your fucking girlfriend called looking for you. Or maybe it's your wife. I knew you were just too good to be true! LIAR, just like all the rest of them. I knew it, I knew it, I knew it! Too good..." My slurring voice trailed off as I choked on my tears.

"You don't know anything! I'm not married anymore; we divorced while I was away."

"Really, who was that on the machine?" I asked not believing one word of his bullshit story!

"My daughter, she beeped me when I didn't pick up here. She lives with her mother."

Raising my eyebrow I asked, "Your daughter?"

"Yes, my daughter! Why are you crying over me?" he said calmly standing by the answering machine, and stopped to play the machine. It turned out the girl's voice belonged to his daughter. After listening to the message, he picked up the phone and walked in the other room. Returning, he bent down to pick me up, because I was still on the floor drunk, and crying unable to get up on my own. "Okay its shower time for you, you smell!"

Grinning, Babe grabbed my arms, hoisted me off the floor, and carried me into the bathroom. "Listen, stop crying. Boy if I knew you cared this much and would get so upset, I would have paid someone to call you before." He turned on the shower and started to peel off my clothes. "Am I really too good to be true?"

"Shut up, you're not funny." I mumbled.

"I think its pretty funny, you're drunk, and I won't even mention you calling me a scumbag! Why did you get so upset?"

Feeling stupid, because I never thought about Babe having a daughter, I whispered, "Because I didn't know about your daughter, I thought she was a girl."

Laughing at me, he busted my chops. "She is a girl."

"You know what I mean. A girl, girl!" I couldn't stand up on my own; he had to hold me up. *Wow, this is too close for comfort.* He wasn't struggling at all; I appeared to be as light as a feather as he slipped my boxer shorts off and unbuttoned my shirt. I held my breath, because I was stark naked in the shower with him fully clothed as he held me under the water. My arms were around his neck and I had my head up against the tile wall just watching him. *Mama Mia, this was a very intense sensual experience having him wash me all over!*

"This isn't what I thought I would be doing tonight...washing you," he said as he stopped to look into my eyes. He leaned in and kissed me. Pulling back, leaving me dazed, he was somehow able to wash my whole body, face and moved onto shampooing my hair. He was making me moan as he gently massaged my scalp. There were suds everywhere, all over me and I was starting to pant heavily, because I couldn't help but react from the physical contact. My head was spinning; I was thinking I'm going to lose control as the water washed my face. As much I didn't want him to know what he was doing to me, I couldn't help but drench his leg as he supported me. Moaning, I leaned into him, it was strange to feel his shirt instead of his skin.

His face darkened as he kissed me. "Was that good Peeper? I saw the whites of your eyes."

I groaned opening my eyes, "Mmm yes. Babe take off your shirt, I want to feel your skin."

Babe whispered in my hair. "You're drunk and I'm a scumbag remember?"

Giggling and slurring, I taunted him. "Hey, scumbag I know, but take off your shirt anyway, I really wanna feel your skin."

"You're drunk; you don't know what you're saying. Stay still so I can finish."

Squirming, I managed to get his shirt off and I started to maul him. I was surprised by the details of his tattoos and was totally fixated on their beauty. I kept circling them with my nails, and moved to gently pet his heart. I kept my right hand on it, trying to feel the beat, wondering if I wanted to possess it. I started to nuzzle at his neck, nipping at his ear, as I repeated my plea. I'm not sure if I was too drunk to do more, but I was starting to think I wanted to. *What? Did I want to do it here and now?*

He cleared his throat straining to maintain his composure. "Stop moving, let's rinse your hair. Try and stand so I can finish."

"Sure, I'll try." I replied, as he slipped his hand out from under me. I found myself sliding down the wall and caught myself by grabbing his neck. As I held on, I started to wrap my legs around him as he held me up against the wall with my head buried in his neck. I just wanted to rip all his clothes off because his skin felt so good against my inner thighs.

"Okay, that's enough water for you. Let's go, hold on tight to me," he whispered, as he walked out of the shower and placed my ass on the sink. Taking a towel from the shelf, he gently rubbed me dry. I thought I was going to fall apart; I was hanging on his neck like a rag doll, with my nose buried in his neck. *You're skin smells so good!* I started to lick his ear and nibble on his neck and slowly started to pull at his clothes. He was grabbing my hands while he was trying to dry me off. Poor guy was fumbling, soaking wet, but he didn't seem to care.

I murmured into his neck, "I think I'm dry, but you're drenched! I'm sorry!"

"You're a big pain in my ass!" Babe chuckled as he wrapped me in a towel and carried me to bed. "Now, stay there. I have to change."

I whispered, "Change here, and don't leave me alone."

"You're a pervert!" He said laughing. He walked over to his dresser and pulled out two pairs of boxers. Turning his back to me, he peeled off his pants and slipped on the shorts. Returning to the bed, he removed the towel and tried to put my feet into the boxers. I resisted and rolled around giggling. *So what if I'm playful, I feel like being naked.* Babe firmly grabbed my legs and somehow slipped the boxers on me as I was kicking and rolling around.

"Settle down; let's watch TV until you fall asleep," he said trying to divert my drunken playfulness.

"No! Lay down with me, I'm not staying here alone," I said not giving up.

"Move over, Fats!" he said, as he lied down next to me. "Hey, let me see your ears for a second."

"What, why?" I asked not sure if I could because my head was spinning.

"Just do it," he said as I slid closer and turned my head. He slipped earrings on me. "Hmm they look exactly how I wanted them to, beautiful!"

"What did you do? Hand me the mirror." He reached over and held it up so I could see the most beautiful pair of platinum diamond teardrop earrings dangling from my earlobes.

"Oh my God Babe! Thank you! I love them!" I said from the bottom of my heart. I wasn't one of those girls, I didn't need his swag or to have him put himself in harm's way to give me things. I just wanted the man, not the flash, but I was unable to express my feelings.

"Good, now settle back," he said, clueless; I was so emotionally torn over the gift.

"No, I want to look at them." I said as I continued to look at my reflection. "I can't believe you're giving me these. They are just perfect, I love them!" I said, as I grinned from ear to ear. They were simple and elegant, exactly something I would buy for myself. I had to accept them for what they were- a gift. I looked at him as he lay there smiling, all the while my heart fluttered.

I really hope you love me! Just looking into his eyes took my breath away; he was gorgeous and so easy on the eyes. "Didn't you forget something? I'm not wearing a shirt or did you do that on purpose?"

"Shush, I have to get something out of this night besides babysitting a bombed girl. Come on lay down and put your head on my chest. I need to relax, that shower took a lot out of me. So now I just want to see the diamonds and you," he said as he held his arms open for me to climb into.

I snuggled up on his chest, "Why didn't you try anything in the shower?"

"The first time won't be when you're smashed, I don't want you to regret it after. Why do I think I left you every time I took you home after drinking?"

"I had no idea." My tears spilled on his skin as I thought about all those nights he tucked me into bed.

"Now you do, so no more teasing, just relax, because it's getting harder and harder for me to be a gentleman if you know what I mean," he said as he flicked the channels until he settled on an old black and white movie.

I whispered, "Babe don't..."

He cut me off. "Listen I know what happened to you and because of that when I make love to you, you'll be sober."

I froze. "You know what?"

"Yes, I was told let's just say to tread light." Babe whispered as he was rubbing my back and kissing my head. "You okay?"

"Yes, that was a long time ago; I don't want to talk about it," I said as I crawled deeper in between his arm and body. Right on cue, he held me tighter. Whispering I asked, "What do you know?"

He whispered back, petting my hair. "You were a kid, your friend's dad tried to rape you. I want you to know I'm sorry it happened and it doesn't have anything to do with how I feel for you. Okay, Danielle?" Babe kissed the top of my head as he held me tightly, knowing I was stressed, drunk, and embarrassed. "I will make your nightmares go away, you never have to worry about him when you're with me. Never!"

I whispered thank you several times, as I kissed his skin. Babe was speaking to my soul, and I loved him more for it. I had to push the dark mood away quickly before I let it rob me of another milestone that I was entitled to.

His arm was over my shoulder, wrapped around me holding my hip, and his other hand was holding my leg that was draped over him. We lay there quiet for a while watching TV. Very easily, I could have just curled up and cried, but I forced myself to lock that memory very far back. He made me feel so safe and wanted; I knew he would never let anyone hurt me while I was with him. Babe had been gently stroking my leg, but now it was making me tingle. I started to giggle and squirm. Looking up at him, I reached up and kissed him gently and then more passionately. He was reluctant at first but then gave me a real kiss. I wanted this mood to pass; it was bringing my head down.

"Thanks!" I said as I nibbled on his lip. Babe slapped my ass and rolled on his side to kiss me more. Facing him, I wrapped my leg around him, trying to lose myself in the passion.

Babe held my hand laughing. "Settle down Peeper. I told you when and it's not now."

"When? Ha! You're pretty confident." I giggled.

"I told you, I get what I want, and I want you. And if I'm correct, you want me too. So it's not a matter of 'if,' it's a matter of 'when.' And when it happens you won't be drunk, because I want you to remember how good it was so you can be fucking sorry we didn't do this sooner," he said, laughing as he rolled back on his back and held me tight. "You're a nut!"

Soon enough, I was so comfortable I thought I was going to fall asleep, but I could feel him up against my leg. "Babe I can feel you against my leg," I said, but I didn't move away.

"Just noticed? I'm a good guy, honorable but not dead. You're lying on my chest without a shirt, I just washed every inch of you and you're sleeping with me in my bed, what did you expect?"

"Hmm, I like it. Hey why didn't you tell me you used to be married?"

"You never asked, and unless you stop your bullshit teasing, it's none of your business."

"Are you asking me out?" I said tensing up, but not moving, really hoping he was going to say yes.

"Nope," he said but gripped me tighter.

"Then I guess you're right, it's none of my business. But if that's the case, I should put some clothes on." I said, holding my ground as I snuggled closer.

"Suit yourself, but I promise you, you won't find anything to wear!"

"Really now? I'm sure I can find something of yours that will cover my assets!" I said as I snuggled closer.

"Not a fucking thing, so don't waste your time!"

"Babe?" I moaned.

"What is it, honey?"

I love you! "Ask me out already! Just give me what I need...I need you." My tears were spilling out on his skin, slipping down his side, and before I knew it I was sobbing uncontrollably.

Crushing me in his embrace, he quickly cut me off, "Peeper, I bet you'll be asking ME out soon. Shush, no more crying." He joked, as he kissed the top of my head. "You know I'm sorry about what happened at the bar. I would never want anything to happen to you. You know that, right?"

"I can't talk about that now either, I just want to lay here in your arms and forget all of it. Tonight, it's just us; nothing and no one else matters," I whispered, as I played with the hairs on his chest, trying to choke back my tears. His strong hands were holding me close, making me feel like the world could blow up and he would take care of me. *I just love you!*

I couldn't help but fixate on his tattoos; my mind became so preoccupied with all the marks on his chest. Some were beautiful and some were scary, but they were all his and I wanted to know them all. I wanted to know every part of his body intimately. My fingers traced the lines on his skin, making Babe breathe heavily "Did it hurt to get these?"

"No, not really." he said, as he started to tense up.

I climbed on top of him and laid low on his chest so my face was by his heart. I whispered, "What's prison like?"

"It sucks, what do you think?"

I pleaded, "I know, but what's it really like? Tell me something, anything."

"It doesn't matter. Stop," he said, strongly.

"I want to know about it so I can know you better," I pressed.

"I think I know you pretty well at this moment. Stop." he said, pushing back harder.

Whispering, I went for the kill, "No, I don't want to. Tell me how you could spend ten years without."

"Without what?" he said really tensing up now.

"Without a girl, without sex," I asked barely audible.

In a flash, he rolled over and was on top straddling me. He was fast and strong as hell. Babe pinned my arms above my head while he stared into my eyes, "You're unbelievable! You man up and not think about it. At this moment while you're in bed with me, this is what you're thinking about? Go to sleep!" Babe rolled off and turned on his side and shut off the TV. I felt terrible; I didn't mean to hurt him, I just wanted to know, because so far he had tremendous self-control, and had been so considerate of me.

I really broached that subject wrong and ruined the moment. Sometimes you have to let it be and not try to fix everything. I moved closer, spooning him. The poor guy must have been beat, because within minutes I could hear him breathe in a steady rhythm; I wrapped my arms around him tighter to snuggle. Not saying a word, he held my arm and kept me close all night long.

I don't know what he dreamed about, but it must have been bad. He tossed and turned, moving about all night like he was in a fight. Babe never made a sound, but he was all over the bed. No matter what he did he stayed close to me. I tried to wrap myself around him to drive away whatever demons were haunting him. His hard body was chiseled from stab wounds, gunshots, and tattoos. All the signs of his hard life- that would frighten most people- was just so beautiful to me. Wanting so much to protect Babe for once, I stroked his body while clinging to him. Breathing deeper each time, it seemed to make a difference. The sweat on his skin glistened in the dim light, making me wonder about his tormented dreams. *Would I ever know? Would I want to? Could I ever make Babe feel and understand what I wanted and needed?* I wanted to crawl deep within and find that one spot that made him who he was, a tough guy who did "things" and stroke it until he could let it go for me.

His life must have come back into full color to remind him every night, because I doubted it ever left him. *Could he ever fit me in somewhere to help keep those "things" at bay?* I know I decided I was going to try, if only just to let him see, he was so much more than a wise guy, but a good guy. As I buried myself in his arms, he held me in a vice grip throughout his restless nightmare, occasionally trying to choke the life out of me.

CHAPTER 17

My Gentle Man

I opened my eyes to a room so bright I felt like I needed sunglasses. Babe was sound asleep next to me, wrapped in the sheets. I stared, admiring what a truly beautiful body he had. I sat up on my elbow and started to trace the tattoos, each line and mark was so savagely carved into his skin. He started to stir. Rolling over, he pulled me closer to kiss me.

Looking incredibly sexy, he asked, "Hey good morning, how did you sleep?"

"Great, your bed's comfortable," I mumbled still in a haze.

"Good! I'm glad you were in it," he said as he kissed my hair.

"Hey, look I'm sorry I was such a mess last night. I think I had a melt down from all the stress of the bar, and then the call, I just drank way too much. I'm really sorry!" I said, knowing it was better to get over my embarrassment as quickly as possible.

"Sorry for what? You were great last night! Don't you remember?" he said as he touched my face, neck and then moved to my arms. He had a puzzled look while he stroked me.

Puzzled I asked. "Remember what? Nothing happened."

"Really you don't remember? You and me, you know," he said trying to keep a straight face.

"Know what? I remember everything and we didn't do a thing," I said gently laughing at him. "Why are you looking like that at me? Do I look so different in daylight?"

"Only kidding, you know you look beautiful, it's just I don't remember seeing all these bruises yesterday," Babe said as he focused on my arms. "Does this hurt?" He flinched as he touched one.

"Not really, you had a rough night sleep, tossing and turning. At one point you were choking me, but it doesn't matter. I'll be okay."

For once, he was turning red. "I'm sorry I did that, I've never hurt a girl ever."

"I know that, I'm fine. How bad do they look?" I asked grinning. "Hey, I'm gonna tell everyone you did this!"

"You better not! If you do, they'll think it's from having rough sex with me, because no one would ever believe that I raised my hand to a girl," he said in his sexy morning voice. "Now come closer for a little while longer."

I settled back down, and twirled the hairs on his chest. "I'm not sure how I can stay like this without you being my guy, because you're looking pretty sexy! This is too intense if you know what I mean."

"Really? I like intense!" He said as he held me tighter. "Why are you so hung up on me asking you out? I'm with you, isn't that all that matters?" He asked, grinning.

"No, a lot more matters than sex, because I don't just sleep around. You're either my guy or not. If you're not my guy, I'm not sleeping with you, plain and simple, but you'll become one of my best friends. By the way I can feel THAT!"

"Good, he's awake!" Babe turned over to kiss me. We were pressed up against each other and started making out like kids in a car. I was thinking way too much for someone who was in the position I was in. *Should I throw my convictions out the window because I was in his bed?*

Just as his hands were venturing in other areas, the phone rang. This time I didn't stop him from grabbing it, I've overheard enough voice messages to be gun shy. After he hung up, Babe turned to me and said, "We should get up soon. Some of the fellas are stopping by later to talk to you..." I interrupted his sentence as I started to kiss him hard and wrapped my legs around him. He moaned deeply when he felt my desire all over him. "Oh Jesus, Dannie!"

If I let you get up, this moment will pass and I just don't know if I'll ever be this position again. Once I get up, my pride will kick in and my morals won't allow me to be semi-naked staring at the most beautiful man in my world. The moment was here and I decided to stop thinking so much. My head was clear, and it was just the two of us in each other's arms. *Whatever happens happens.* We were about as close as two people could be wearing boxer shorts. Just as I shuttered in his arms, drenching his hands, his pager went off. I could see Babe's eyes look at the number with recognition and regret. "Hold up a sec, I have to return this beep."

This was the diversion that I guess I needed. Sucking on his bottom lip, I said, "Hey, are you hungry? I can make breakfast."

Babe held me for another minute and then kissed me on my head laughing, "I'm destined to live with this 'condition' being around you, I just know it! Okay, let's see if I have anything in the fridge. But I have one request, don't get dressed yet, they won't be here for a while."

My face turned purple. "You want me to cook without a shirt? Oh, good grief!" I got up and walked into the bathroom. When I returned, Babe was ending his call while he searched the fridge and pulled out milk, eggs, cheese, bread and vegetables. He turned around and his face said it all. "Well hello! Nice, that's exactly how I wanted to see you."

I was standing wearing nothing but his boxer shorts, which were rolled and shimmied down, hanging below my hipbone, and his diamonds dangling from my lobes. My long black hair was parted down the middle covering my breasts, but I was obviously topless. Without skipping a beat, I started to open the egg carton and asked, "Okay Boss, do you like them scrambled, in an omelet, or over EASY?" We both broke out laughing and started to cook forgetting everything, we just enjoyed each other. As I made the eggs, Babe came up behind me and flicked my right earring to get my attention, then started to nibble on my neck looking over my shoulder. I dropped my guard and let him kiss me. Gently, he put his right hand over mine, and put the wooden spoon down. His left hand wrapped around my waist and shut the stove off. Next thing I knew, my head was bent forward and he was groping me and biting my back while I held onto the counter.

He whispered in my ear, "I'm your guy and you're my girl. Got it?"

Shaking my head yes, I moaned as he touched me. The very thin material of our shorts did nothing to hide the fact that Babe was fully pressed up against me. He flipped me around and started to kiss me so perfectly I could have cried. Something in the way he moved and handled himself sexually made me feel like I couldn't live without him a moment longer. With one clean sweep of his arm he cleared off the island. In a split second, he picked me up placing me on top of the counter and started to peel off my shorts slowly and methodically all the while kissing me with his eyes open. He tossed them across the room and started to drop his. I was beyond ready, and started to grab at him, I couldn't get close enough, I didn't even want there to be air between us.

Babe pulled my hair back to face me eye-to-eye and said, "Tell me you want me, I won't go any further unless you do."

I dug my nails deeper as I moaned loudly. "Babe I want you with all my soul." With that, he kissed me like never before pushing me back as he moved to my neck. I held his head while he moved to my breasts, slowly licking my nipples. Gently biting my skin, he moved down towards my navel, and then licked his way back up to my breasts. Feeling his breath on my skin was making me crazy; Babe whispered my name as he stroked me. Arching my head back, moaning, he took me for the first time. He looked into my eyes, and that was it, my eyes rolled back as I lost it completely, screaming, barring down him. At that moment, a shadow passed the window. Babe pulled back, pushed me to the ground and whipped out a piece from the draw. Before I knew what was happening, two of his friends were opening the door and walked in dragging black garbage bags behind them. They stared in amazement just as I jumped up and froze in my spot as the alarm started to blare. There I stood, completely naked with purple choke marks around my neck and handprints on my arms! Stark naked, Babe jumped in front of me, but not in time to stop them from seeing everything!

Breaking my trance, he yelled, "What the fuck? You never used a doorbell before? Give me my key back!" I was mortified, as I ran to the bedroom slamming the door behind me. He shut off the alarm and followed me in a moment later, and pulled on a pair of sweats. "Listen, they came quicker that I thought."

I was so embarrassed with my arms wrapped around my legs covering my breasts. "You think?"

"Don't worry, they'll never mention it. I need you to come outside to talk to us about what happened, but put some clothes on first. They won't be able to focus if you're naked." Babe joked, trying to make me snap out of my pouting mood. "So get dressed and come out in a few minutes," he said as he leaned over kissing me again. "That was a pretty good second there."

I slapped his arm hard, "Stay here for another minute, and make them wait." Trying to pull him on top of me, I said, "It's still NOW!"

"NOW? You're more than a 'minute girl' so come on get dressed," he said amused at me.

Begrudgingly I started to get dressed in his sweats which hung on my hips, tied up with a knot in the back and had his shirt tied onto me with my hair up in a ponytail. Before I walked into the living room I looked in the mirror, and was shocked to see all the bruises! I look like I was tossed around and manhandled badly. Acting as if nothing was different, I walked in and kissed the guys hello, red-faced, but trying to act as if they just didn't see me naked on the center island engaged in rough sex.

"Hey, what's up guys?" I said casually.

Babe reached for me to sit next to him. "Listen, you have to tell us again what happened."

As I repeated the story, Sally interrupted asking me a million questions, like did I know them, see them before, what they looked and sounded like. I couldn't answer any of them, except that they looked familiar, maybe from Vibes, but that meant less than nothing, because everyone went there. Truly, I couldn't be sure, it all happened so fast and I was so scared. Babe could see I was getting more agitated, so he switched gears. He started to open one of the garbage bags and pulled out a beautiful black mink coat. "Stand up, I wanna see how this looks on you." Getting up on command, I tried on one coat after the other, until he went through both bags. Settling on the first one, he said, "Okay, I think this is the one. Thanks guys! Give me a few minutes, I'll meet you outside." They got up and kissed me goodbye, dragging the bags back out with them. "Okay, this coat is for you, I think you could use a little pick me up."

"Oh Babe, it's beautiful! I love it!" I said, as I showered him with kisses pushing him backwards onto the couch.

"Settle down, I have to go, BUT we'll pick this up later."

Panicking, I asked, "You're leaving me? Where are you going?" I stopped short of asking any more questions, because I knew he wouldn't answer them.

"You're going to be fine. Think of it as a mini-vacation, where you get to stay in bed and watch TV, just relaxing." He assured me, "Before you know it, I'll be back before I have to go to work. I'll grab dinner, what do you want?"

Feeling dejected, afraid, and slightly bitchy I blurted out, "Lobster and wine, we definitely need more wine. Don't forget dessert too!"

"Lobster? Hmm, you really are a nut! Okay, lobster it is. Who are you gonna eat it with this time?"

"I'm not sure, depends on who's coming."

"Hmm, now I don't have a shot in hell!" He said, laughing. "I have to go get cleaned up."

I followed him back, because I didn't really know what else to do, but then I realized he was going to take another shower. So I walked in the bathroom after him. He stopped and asked, "What are you doing?"

"I don't know. I just want to stay with you as long as you're here, come on let me in the shower."

"If you take a shower with me, I'll never leave, and I HAVE TO GO!" He said as he tried to get me back to bed. I pulled him with me as I flopped on the bed and tried to hold him, but no such luck. Finally, he got into the bathroom and stripped down. I saw him step into the shower, but he turned quickly so I couldn't see his face. Babe called out, "Hey Peeper, turn on the TV."

I playfully responded, "Jerk off!"

"Really? What you wanna watch that too? You're an animal!" he said laughing.

As I turn on the TV looking to be entertained by another show, he reached out and closed the bathroom door. Too bad, his show was better than TV.

CHAPTER 18

Red Rats

How much TV can one person watch? I stayed in bed almost all day. After my back started to hurt from lying down, I decided to get up and maybe clean his house. It was a two-bedroom, two-bathroom house with wood floors and high ceilings, decorated beautifully with neutral creams and whites, a real beach haven. I searched around, but couldn't find anything beyond Windex and paper towels. Just then I realized he really doesn't live here. He just visits; he must have a cleaning lady. There just weren't enough of his personal effects here for it to be his main place. *Where does he live? I took a shower with someone that I have no idea where they live? Oh brother! I better not drink so much tonight.*

Within a few hours, he returned with a group of guys carting a table, chairs, and bags. I stood in the window looking out as I saw them setup everything near the water and put a tablecloth over it. Turning, he waved when he saw me and then walked towards the door while his guys waved goodbye and left.

Babe walked in beaming like a kid in a candy store, and kissed me. "Hey, you hungry for lunch? I thought I'd surprise you, come out on the beach with me," he said as he took my hand leading me outside. It was cool, but beautiful. I held my hand over my eyes because the sun was so bright as we walked towards the water. The table was set with to-go containers from a Chinese restaurant, a bottle of wine, and a couple of glasses. Holding the chair out for me to sit, he saw I was shivering and excused himself for a minute. Babe returned and wrapped the mink coat around me, and handed me my sunglasses.

"This is such a nice surprise, I always wanted to eat like this! What's on the menu?" I asked as I grinned.

Leaning over the table he kissed me and then returned to his seat. "Hmm, Ming at the restaurant said you like Shrimp & Lobster Sauce, Peppered Steak, Roast Pork Fried Rice, and Cashew Chicken. So I bought it all, I hope you're hungry!" We opened the containers and shared everything while we talked and laughed for the next hour. What a sight we must have been, the two of us sitting by the water eating out of to-go containers with me wrapped in a mink coat all bruised up.

Babe leaned over to take a bite out of the container I was holding, and something about the way he moved made my stomach flutter. I leaned over too far, tipping on to him. He caught me making us both roll onto the sand. He lay on top of me holding the container up in the air so it wouldn't spill on my face. We went from playful to sexy in seconds. He put the container down and started to kiss me as I made him roll over. He put his hands behind his head, as I sat up straddling him. Opening my coat and unzipping my jogging suit jacket almost all the way, I exposed my breasts. Deliberately and slowly, I pushed my sunglasses to the tip of my nose, peering over the top, "So Babe what else would you like for lunch?"

"Anything you want to give me baby!" he said as he puckered his lips signaling he wanted me to kiss him. We were shrouded in secrecy with the big coat so no one could see me moving to Babe's neck biting and licking lower and lower until I started biting through his shirt. I held his wrists in place, preventing him from touching me.

The more aggressive I became the more I was making him moan. The more he moaned, the more turned on I became. I matched his moan and whispered, "Hmm do you like this? I can't hear you Babe. Umm I'm going to make you scream my name in a minute. And before I'm done the whole beach will hear you!"

I lifted his shirt with my teeth, exposing his waistband, and licked all the way around it. I nibbled his skin, enjoying the taste of him. When I tugged his pants lower, he pushed his wrists out of my grip, making me stop. I sang into his skin, "Nooo, no, no! Put your hands back where I want them, okay Boss?" I peered up at him with a look that said he meant business.

Babe grinned and whispered back, "Anything you want, you just tell me...anything!"

Tilting my head sideways, I purred, "Offering me anything is dangerous, Babe! I want your heart, all of it! Any part that might be used for another woman other than your family." I licked his stomach again. "I will make you scream for me every night and wish you were with me all day as long as you're mine completely, understand?"

"Oh baby, you got it, all of me!" He moaned so load, I grinned. Babe was moving in the groove with me as I rubbed myself all over him licking and biting him all wrapped up the mink.

"Say my name," I moaned, as I dug my nails into his chest biting his waist. "Say it, I want to hear you say my name."

The deepest growl came barreling out of his chest as he called out, "DANNIE!"

Yup, gotcha! You may cheat, but you will always remember this moment! "Again."

His hands quickly grabbed my head and pulled me up to his face. He couldn't stop kissing me hard, as he rolled over on top of me. He was breathing hard on my face as he moaned, "Oh Jesus Christ this is fucking great, but listen the guys are coming back any second, and as much as I want this, I don't want them seeing you like this."

I titled my head smiling. "Why?"

He was eye to eye with me. "Because I don't want them or anyone to see this side of you. This, all of this, all of you, is just for me!" He kissed me hard. "They respect you and I like that, and they know I care for you. You're not a dirty little secret you're my girl. Understand?"

Good, you passed the test! Scumbags wouldn't care as long they got what they wanted; it takes a real man to think about someone they care about first! I kissed him with a passion that almost made his honor waver, but soon he zipped my jacket and helped me up out of the sand. As I stood, he slapped my ass hard, knocking me forward. "You're an animal!"

I giggled, looking over my shoulder, and without a care in the world I hiked my coat up and mooned him. I took off, running at full speed towards the water, laughing wildly. Babe sprinted, grabbing me up in his arms swinging me around making me scream. I wrapped my arms around his neck burying my face because he starting tickling me. I screamed "Uncle! Uncle, please, Uncle!"

He slowed down, giving me a telling intense look before he kissed me. I think he would have continued, but we heard Vinnie clear his throat. Babe's forehead was pressed up against mine as he whispered, "I'm sorry!"

I whispered back, "I'm not! This is the best date I've ever had!" *I'm so in love with you!* We walked on the beach for a bit holding hands and kicking the sand while his guys packed everything up. The magical moment was ending; he had to walk me back to my gilded cage. I put my glasses on top of my head still wearing the mink, as I turned pink. "That was the best!" Standing on my toes I leaned up to kiss him, "Thank you so much for making today so special!"

Grinning at me with a twinkle in his eyes he said, "I like making you happy! This is only the beginning, just remember that!" He moved a few stray hairs away from my face and continued. "I have to run. Remember the rules, see you soon, be good." Kissing me one more time, he set the alarm and walked out.

Needing to do something, I set the table, started a fire and turned on the stereo and waited for him with the mink coat draped over me on the couch. I napped for a while until I heard the phone ring. No one left a message, but now I was awake and bored. Watching the waves from the window, as classic disco blared throughout the house, I danced. There I was dancing in boxer shorts and his button down shirt to Disco Inferno as the afternoon came to a close. Just as I turned around, I saw Babe staring at me with a huge grin and a hungry look in his eyes. He held two large bags of food; a garment bag with a shopping bag around it and something was following him in the room. That something was big and hairy; it was a German Shepard! He put the bags down while walking over to me, and peeked under the shirt to see if I was still wearing his shorts, "Nice!"

Frozen in utter fear, I stared at it and him and said, "What is that?"

Being a buster once again he said, "Um I thought you knew by now what that is!"

I slapped his arm and said, "No, I mean that," just as the dog growled at me.

"Dinner! Or do you mean my dog?" He grinned and let out a slight chuckle. "By the way, don't let me stop you from dancing."

"Oh stop, I was bored." I said grinning.

"Need a pole? I knew you were a stripper at heart!"

"Good grief! By the way what is that?" I said trying to deflect the attention.

Turning to the dog, Babe said in a commanding voice, more for the dog than me, "His name is Nero. Don't make any sudden moves until he gets used to you. He's trained as an attack dog. If I like you, he will too."

"Attack dog?" I said and sat down immediately. "Where was he last night?"

"At my house," he said trying to avoid my question.

Pressing further, "I thought this was your house."

Cutting me off, he said, "Listen, stop asking so many questions. Are you hungry?"

"Starved!" I said realizing I was famished.

"Let's eat! I want to rest before I go to work tonight; by the way, Nero is staying with you while I'm gone." He beamed.

I stood to unpack the bags but the dog growled at me, I sat back down in a flash. Then I tried it again and he did the same thing. Stuck not knowing how to proceed, I looked at Babe, but he was totally ignoring me. Finally he said, "Listen just be yourself, in control and don't let him smell your fear. Walk around and act normal." So I gave it a shot. I got up, he growled again, but I started to walk towards Babe anyway. The dog breached the space and stood between us snarling. Babe snapped his fingers and Nero retreated. "See you just have to learn how to communicate with him. Remember you're in command. Nero is an excellent dog; he'll take good care of you."

I asked, "I can't control him. Maybe he can stay in the living room and I can close the door to the bedroom until you get home?"

"No! You'll either get over your fear or stay terrified the choice is yours. Hey come over here and get on your knees in front of me."

"Excuse me?" I said nervously.

"Don't you trust me?" He said, clearly amused by me.

Without thinking I said, "Yes."

"Really?" he said with a smile. I think I surprised him with my quick answer. "Good! Come on get on your knees and close your eyes."

"Hey I went to camp; I'm not playing this game," I responded with a nervous laugh.

Laughing harder he said, "I thought you trusted me?"

"I do, but..." I said as my voice wavered, exposing my fear.

Cutting me off he said, "Suit yourself, but you'll be a prisoner if you don't."

I walked over to Babe and slowly lowered myself in front of him, and then I closed my eyes and waited. I felt Babe touch my face, head and stroked my hair while Nero started to sniff me. I was shaking like a leaf, while he mumbled something in German to the dog. Finally he told me to open my eyes, Nero was right next to me. Out of nowhere he gave me a tremendous lick on my face. Shocked, I laughed and put my arms around Babe's waist. Without thinking my face fell forward in relief and I landed right in his crotch! He grabbed my hair and playfully tugged it back away. "Hey, no dessert before dinner." Helping me up, we started to unpack the bags together and sat down for dinner.

Again, he served and I poured, but this time it was more relaxing. The lobster was amazing, just the way I liked it. It was fun cracking the shells and dipping everything in butter. Impulsively,

I leaned into him as he held the inside of the claw licking it and then gently removed the meat while sucking his finger. Babe's eyes changed from carefree to hungry, he was getting my message. He continued to remove the lobster from the shells and hand-fed me gently with the biggest grin. He was totally into foreplay with the food, and fighting the urge to pounce on me. The wine continued to flow and we moved onto dessert, and he started to feed me ice cream from his spoon. I pulled my hair back behind my head with my hands giving him a clear view as I swallowed, driving him completely crazy!

"You look fucking hot right now!" Babe said rimming my lips with the spoon.

I licked the spoon, then my lips, while I closed my eyes and moaned for effect. Once I opened them, I moved my head sideways and licked his fingers all the way down to his wrist just locking eyes with him. I raised my eyebrow and whispered, "I like the taste of your skin. How's this feel?"

Babe growled a deep laugh as he took the spoon and licked it himself. "I like it, but then again, I like it more that you like licking me." He picked up my wine glass and gave me a sip, watching my neck stretch to meet the rim. I licked my lips as I arched my back and I became distracted by Nero's eyes.

Nero was staring at us from the fireplace the whole time, but I no longer felt like he was going to rip my throat out. Turning my attention back to Babe, I kept thinking to myself that I wasn't rushing into anything and wanted to make our time together last as long as possible. Spying the other items Babe came home with, raising my eyebrow I asked, "Did you buy clothes? Do you want me to hang them for you?"

Casually, he responded, "Yeah, open the shopping bag, but leave the garment bag for later."

I walked over to the bag and brought it to the table. Taking the contents out, I found a black bra and a few pairs of panties. "Well, hello! What are these?"

"Do I have to teach you everything? Dense like a rock!" He said joking, "Try them on for me."

I looked at the bra and panties; they were from a little boutique I'd seen before. All black lace; they looked very delicate. I got up very slowly and deliberately, peeling off my boxers shaking my hips from side to side, as Babe's eyes darkened. I slipped on the bra and bent over from the waist, tossing my hair forward, and swayed as I slid the panties higher and higher, all to the beat of the music. Walking over to the couch with our wine glasses, he laid down in front of the fire to watch his own private peep show. "This is better than anything at the club baby! Keep it up and I'll break out the cash."

I held the sides of the G-string playing with them, turned my head sideways and grinned. "You can't afford what I'm actually capable of."

"Don't be so sure, I'll give you a bigger tip than you expected," he said, as I could clearly see he wasn't kidding. He couldn't take his eyes off me for a minute. "Hmm they're a perfect fit!" he said in a raspy voice.

I twirled around letting my long hair play peak a boo covering my body as I grabbed my breasts pushing them up moving to the beat. I know he likes to hear me moan so everything I said was in a moan-like, singsong whisper, "Mmm, Babe do you want me to strip for you?"

"We can start with that," He groaned deeply.

I seductively walked over to him and started to caress myself. "Hmm, if I do, you have to promise not to tell anyone, it's our secret." I picked up my foot and ran my toes over his chest. "I'll never admit to any of it!" I moved my toes all the way down to his waist. His face was dark and sexy as hell, as I traced his outline with my toes. "Babe, tell me what's your deepest darkest desire?"

He mumbled over the rim of his glass, "I want you to do everything for me." Like lightening he reached up grabbing me, but I waved no, as I chewed on my bottom lip. "I want every part of your body to be mine," he said with the deepest voice.

I swung my head back and moaned louder, "So you want what exactly?"

"What, you want me to tell you?"

Now, I lowered myself to straddle his chest as I bent to kiss it. As I licked up to his mouth, I moaned, "Oh, I want to hear everything, I want you to worship me, because I'm going to lick every part of you as you scream my name over and over again." Now I whispered in his ear, "Mmm, Babe, I need you so bad it hurts."

"Jesus Christ, you're killing me, purring dirty!" He moaned loudly.

Grinding him while he ran his hands all over me, I whispered, "Oh, I can stop and go back to being a good girl if you prefer, but I think you want me to be animal." As I moved up and down I asked, "Isn't that what you want? I'm going to be everything you want me to be." Just then, the foreplay got the best of me and I came screaming on top of him. He crushed me against him, burying his tongue in my mouth while I shuttered, with ecstasy. I whipped my hair back, and said; "Now you know what you'll have, IF I let you!"

Babe's eyes bugged as he repeated, "IF?"

Slowly, I sat up on his chest and reached for the ice cream. I took a spoonful and ate most of it, the rest I traced his tattoos. I bent down sucked the lines of cool ice cream. "Yes, IF, but first I have a few questions before I fuck you, Babe. And make no mistake, I'm going to fuck you until you scream devotions to me!" I raised my eyebrow, puckered my lips pronouncing each syllable, "Will you treat me like your queen, if I make you my king?"

"Mmm, you're my queen already baby, but what kind of questions are we talking about?"

I bent back down and bit his nipple. "Nothing like that, I won't ask THOSE questions, okay?"

His face returned to sexy and fierce as he mumbled. "Okay, okay," I cut him off by kissing him hard. I pulled back and continued to trace his skin.

Moaning, I said, "I did nothing but watch TV, set the table and start a fire. Oh, of course I wished that you would come home to me! I wanted to clean for you, but I couldn't find anything. I know you don't live here all the time, so where do you live?"

Taking a deep breath he asked, "Why?"

"There aren't any pictures or anything personal," I said as I traced the lines with my nails. "Babe, I know I'm going to fuck you like you've never been fucked before, so I think I'm entitled to know you better."

"Are you now? Questions, questions why, don't you trust me yet?" He groaned.

With a little ice cream in my mouth I sucked his skin gently. "This is the deal, McNeil. Sure, I DO trust you, but I don't really KNOW you, because you always keep me at arms length."

Grinning, he responded, "What do you need to know that you don't already?"

Leaning down over him, I nibbled on his lip again with a little ice cream as I moaned, "Everything!"

He growled, "This is your only shot, because you're on top of me, so be more specific."

Licking the spoon deliberately as sexy as possible and then running it down his chest towards my G-string I said, "I want to get to know you. Who you are, what you like, where you grew up, how old you are? Do you dance? Where do you live?" and very quietly, I asked, "I want to know most of all if you're involved with anyone, are you currently fucking someone else?"

He held my hips, moving his thumbs around the indent gently and very carefully said, "I live with my mother in Brooklyn, because I couldn't get released living alone." Then he traced the lines of the panties with his finger and continued, "I have a brother and a sister, both married." He continued higher to my stomach and then said, "This is one of my houses, but I have a few others." Grinning, he moved up to my bra and traced my breasts. "I like dogs, chickens, and pigeons. Oh, and I like these." Babe slipped one strap off my shoulder and said, "I'm eight years older than you." Cupping me, he continued, "I dance, a little." With the other hand he slipped the other strap off. "I have one daughter, and for the big one," he traced my lips with his finger as he said, "I'm not married anymore and I don't have a serious girlfriend. Are you satisfied?"

I bit and licked his finger as I pushed down grinding on him as said, "No, say it! Yes, you are fucking someone or no you're not."

He looked me dead in the eye, while he held my arms. "NO, I'm not fucking anyone!"

I moaned grinning, "Thank you! Do you want to know anything about me?"

He groaned, "What's your size?"

Giggling I said, "I'm a size two, why? That's what you want to know?"

"Yes, that's about it!" He said tickling my hips, breaking the hypnotic sexual energy.

Red-faced I asked, "You only want to know my size? You're a pervert!"

"Hey who's the pervert? Remember YOU were watching ME take a shower, I was just minding my own business. I'm completely innocent!"

Giggling at the absurdity that he was innocent of anything sexually, I continued by saying, "Okay, I'm a size 2, 7-1/2 shoe and a 34D bra as you know already." I said as I traced the line above his shorts with the cold spoon and stopped at the tip of where I couldn't return. I leaned down and kissed his neck.

He moaned, "Nice!"

"Pervert!" I giggled, but licked his ear.

"Come on, have some more wine, and lay down by the fire with me." Smiling, he was about to take control from me. Babe had to always have control in everything, but I actually liked it when the guy was the leader romantically.

As we started to snuggle, kissing on the couch watching the roaring fire he said, "Something doesn't feel right."

Alarmed, I bolted up. "What doesn't feel right?"

"Relax! I mean you have a bra on, and I think I'm used to you not if you know what I mean," his voice was sexy as he asked "take your bra off for me."

I leaned up on my knees and started to slowly unhook the bra, making a show of it I let it fall to the floor; slowly I covered my breasts, but he pulled my arms down, "You're so beautiful! You're my nervous, tipsy, sexy, fucking erotic girl, don't ever cover up with me." I just listened while the tears danced in my eyes as he opened up. "I love how you make me feel, how you love my body and all the crazy shit you've said. But you have something wrong, tonight you'll be screaming my name!" He pulled me down to kiss him.

Before we got too crazy, I made him slip his arms out of his shirt. Once his chest was bare too, I laid down on him, rubbing up against his warm body. My hands wandered all over his skin as I traced his marks and nipples. As soon as I touched his sides he gave off a little giggle. *Yes I found his weakness!* He was ticklish and I planned on taking full advantage of my newfound information. I quickly went from gently touching his skin to tickling him everywhere. Jolting up, he knocked us both off the couch onto the floor taking the mink with us.

He was on top straddling me while he restrained my arms, to prevent me from continuing. "Now, you will get it!" He proceeded to tickle me until I couldn't breathe. We were rolling all over the floor landing on top of the mink. Tickling became kissing and kissing led to caressing. I stopped struggling and bit my lip as I stared into his deep dark eyes completely surrounded by the luxurious fur.

I'm trying not to think about what is about to happen, because this was not part of my original plan, and I was terrified that when it was said and done, everything would change quickly. Wise guys have a short attention span. I didn't want it to be a one-and-done job. Babe was suspended over me leaning on his arms as he started to kiss me deeply. Making me pant as he playfully bit my lip, then moving to my neck and eventually licking every bit of me. Alarms were going off in my head, but so were the rockets and fireworks. His chest felt great against my skin, my legs were wrapped around his and we were totally exposed to each other in the soft fur. Babe's eyes bore into mine as I was breathing so hard because I knew there was no turning back from this erotic moment. He was naked on top of me and I was about to explode, I wanted him so badly. The crazier he got on me, the more my hips moved to match his. Gently Babe slid my legs open as he held my head staring straight into my eyes. I couldn't stop myself as I mouthed, "Babe, Babe"

Grunting he asked, "Yes?"

And just as he entered me, I said it loud and clear, "BABE, I LOVE YOU!"

For once his eyes rolled back as he cried out in my hair. The sweet, amazing, prefect moment came to a screeching halt when the phone rang. *No! No, no, no this can't be happening!* Babe tried to get up, but I kept pulling him back. "Are you kidding me, you can't get up NOW." I moaned as we struggled, not remembering my new rule of not overhearing anyone's messages.

"No, give me a sec, hang on," he said trying hard to get up.

"Hang on? Okay I'll hang on!" I said as I grabbed for him. Just then, the machine kicked on and a girl's voice was clearly audible saying, "Hey Babe, its Justine. Where are you? I thought I was going to see you again today? I miss you baby, call me back."

His whole body was rigid and stayed very still, but before he could say anything, I stopped the playful struggle and stared into his eyes and mouthed, "You just broke my fucking heart!" Furious and embarrassed for being naked, I started to cry hard. Covering my face with my hands, I rolled over burying my face in the mink. Sobbing, I wanted to curl up and disappear on the spot. I screamed over and over, "I LOVE YOU! WHY? WHY DID YOU DO THIS TO ME?"

Babe tried to turn me over while he talked to me. "Stop, let me explain! It's not what you think, stop!"

Finally getting me on my back, he pulled my arms down to see my face, but I yanked my hand up and slapped him hard across the face as I started to scream through the tears, "GET THE FUCK OFF ME! I HATE YOU!" I kicked him off and ran into the bedroom hysterically, slammed and locked the door behind me. *What was I doing? What an idiot I am...again! I knew better and shouldn't be in this position.*

Babe never came to the door; he never tried to talk to me. I grabbed his precious phone and started to beep every guy I knew to get me. What was there, some mob reunion? I couldn't get one fucking person to call me back. Two hours later, I walked back into the living room with my clothes on and bag ready to walk home even if I had to. But to my surprise, I was alone. He left for work presumably, leaving Nero behind.

The dog was guarding the door and I realized I wasn't going to get past him, and even if I did, I didn't know the alarm code to get out without setting it off. Maybe I could bribe him not to kill me since Babe was gone, so I turned to our left over lobster feast and put a little piece on a plate. Nero licked his chops and devoured it. "Nero you're as easy as me! Give you lobster and you're my friend." I cleaned up all remnants of our dinner, straightened up the house, and made his bed. Poor Nero, he must have had to pee but I couldn't open the door without the alarm going off. We were trapped!

"Okay Nero let's find something to read." I walked around the living room searching for a book, magazine anything. It was dark out, and I had all the lights on. I finally found a few magazines, and settled on the couch pulling the mink on me as a lap blanket and to my surprise, Nero joined me. I'm a total lap dog person, and extremely afraid of almost all animals. I was too afraid to try and get him off my lap so he settled in making me shake in fear. Into our third magazine, Nero's ears perked up and he gave a deep, low growl. A shadow passed the window. I fell off the couch and hid in front of it. Within a few minutes, the doorknob turned and Babe walked through the door. I peeked out over the couch and saw him; Nero bolted and sat at attention waiting for his approval. I wanted to run, but I just got up and sat on the couch waiting to hear whatever line of crap he was going to give me. He opened the door and let the dog out, turning to me he said, "Listen, before I leave to go to the city, I wanted to stop back and talk to you."

Drop dead! Dying inside, I cut him off as I said, "Don't bother, I need to go home."

"Listen, I'm sorry about before, that's just a girl I know from the neighborhood. We're friends, that's all," he said trying to minimize the situation.

Liar! I was like a tornado in a bottle, complete uncontrolled rage coursed through my veins, and I was about to snap. I tossed the coat at him along with the magazine, and my wine glass, responding, "Its none of my business! Go to work, or out or wherever you fucking go!"

Tossing the coat aside, he ducked the glass and slapped the magazine to the floor and said as he approached me, "Calm down! We have to talk about this, but I just can't until later. Listen, I think you should stay one more night, I don't have enough time to straighten this out with you, and I have to go, Phil's waiting for me. You can go back tomorrow."

Sobbing into my hands, because I truly wanted to rip his eyeballs out, I screamed, "I HATE YOU!"

"STOP! Please, stop! Let me explain."

"That's the best you can do? Really? Its twenty-four hours I need to get home and back to work. You're not the guy for me, I thought maybe you could have been but I was wrong! I can't even look at you; I never want to be with you again." Heaving, and almost throwing up, I said, "I think I hate you with all my soul Babe!"

"Geez, that's fucking cold," he said acting shocked and reaching for me, but he stopped short when I just looked at him with empty eyes.

Choking back the feelings of hatred, I hated every word that I said knowing there was no going back after saying it. "Thanks for taking care of me, I know you put yourself out and I appreciate it, but its time. Its time to go back to my life that has nothing to do with you, and never will because I'm better than this, all of this and frankly, too good for you! You're nothing but a fucking lying player!" I felt so manic, I wanted to be mature, but I just couldn't manage it. I buried my head in my hands, mumbling, "I'm so embarrassed, I took my clothes off for you, I let you in! I let you get to me1 I fell in love with you! You made me love you! And it was nothing but a joke to you!"

Ignoring my insults, Babe bent down and tried to move my hands, "Dannie you have to listen and believe me! I loved everything you did! That girl is nobody; she's nothing to me! You're the only girl I want!"

"Liar! Don't insult my intelligence with your gangster bullshit!"

"I don't have to lie, and I didn't have to come back to talk to you. You can't go anywhere, I won't let you!"

"I hate you so much, I can't do this...I really can't! You killed whatever I felt for you!"

"Don't say that, we can work this out!" Babe moved my hands away from my face and stared into my eyes.

"Babe, you're a liar! You intimidate people for a living, and now you're trying to get over on me too." The tears were streaming down my face as I just looked at him with total contempt. *Go ahead hate me it will make it easier! I want you to feel the hurt and betrayal I'm feeling and hate me just as much as I hate you!*

"You got that wrong, very wrong! I never lied to you, but I have to go. One more night? I'll take you back in the morning first thing," he said more as an order than a question. "We all square?"

If I hit you in the head with a shovel we might be square! "Sure why wouldn't we be?" I said in a monotone voice.

He moved a little closer and leaned in to kiss me. I put up my hand like I was going to hit him again if he got any closer. He got the message loud and clear, and slipped right into buddy mode because he had no idea how to handle the moment. "Good, see you later. By the way, did you get a chance to hang up the clothes for me?"

Are you out of your mind? "No, I thought maybe Justine would come over and do it for you PAL! And when she gets here give her the fucking coat too, I don't want it. Maybe she'll fuck you and strip for you too," I screamed, as I turned and walked away without looking at him. When I spotted a lamp I picked it up and tossed it along with everything else I could grab screaming, "I HATE YOU, I FUCKING HATE YOU!"

"You're gonna be like that huh?" Babe shouted as he ducked every missile aimed at his head.

"Like what, Babe?" I sneered, shouting a little louder with each word as I continued to walk closer and closer to him. I really wanted to fall apart and ask him how he could do this to me after everything he said, but my pride wouldn't let me. I bolted past him out the door, but he was faster than me and grabbed me, swinging me back in. I flipped, kicking and screaming roaring at him! "GET YOUR FUCKING DIRTY SCUMBAG HANDS OFF ME! I'M LEAVING BECAUSE YOU'RE A LYING BASTARD! I HATE YOU!"

Babe grabbed my arms, pulling me up short and yelled, "She's just a friend. Now STOP this!"

See, now I'm acting like an idiot, and showing you how much I actually cared! I'm a jerk off! I was like a caged animal seeing red rats. "Fucking friends? You must think I'm a complete jerk off!"

"No, I think you're pissed, but you have no reason to be, so stop all this now!" He put me on the couch holding my arms to keep me in place.

I seethed as I stared in his eyes, hoping I was going to rip his heart out with every word that passed my lips. "Pissed, nah! Why should I be? You don't mean anything more than a friend to me, so run off, do what you got to do, or should I say who you have to do, and see who you gotta see, because I will be right as rain as soon as I get out of here BABY. I'll never remember you as I take my clothes off for someone else! Mark my words; I have more guys waiting for the opportunity than you'll ever know! I could fuck a different guy everyday for a year before I'd have to go back for seconds!"

"Shut the fuck up!"

"As you climb on top of that broad, I'll be doing the same thing with someone else. And they'll fucking worship me!" I spit the words out such venom it took him by surprise.

Babe grabbed my shoulders shaking me so hard in an attempt to frighten the hell of me, but I just laughed at him. The look in eyes was lethal and all of the sudden it faded back to being hurt. "Yeah you, the girl who doesn't put out! Whatta you think I didn't ask around before I started up with you publicly? So shut up and stop acting like something you're not!" I was about to cut in but he firmly covered my mouth. "Shut up! Don't say another word, just don't!" I stopped resisting for a minute because I didn't want him to snap my neck. "Listen, stop this! I know you're just trying to get back at me. I didn't want you to stay here upset. I came back to sort things out, but I can see you're not in the mood to talk."

"In a mood? You have to be kidding me! What did you want to sort out?" I spit out seething with total disgust. "You going to sort out what exactly? Don't feed me a fucking gangster line of bullshit please."

"I don't deserve that," he said, trying to act hurt.

My tears exploded again because I was trying not to allow my raging anger to make me look like a lovesick moron. "I'm going to go ballistic! You don't deserve what? What about what I deserve, huh? I'm pretty sure I deserve to have a decent guy who doesn't have girls calling him saying she's missing them when he's in ME! I can't look at you, I don't ever what to see your fucking face again! Don't ever talk or come near me!" Standing, I demanded, "Give me the address so I can call a cab. I'm outta here! You got that?"

Towering over me, he became the gangster once again. "Yup, I got it LOUD and CLEAR, but here I'm the BOSS so you're going to have to wait until I say so! YOU got that?" He turned and let Nero back in and then walked back to the alarm panel, punched in the code and left without another word trapping me yet again.

I hate you! I hope you feel it deep down in your fucking black, rotten, cheating, lying heart! Fuming, I walked around. I wanted to kick something, but I thought the dog would rip my leg off. I found the garment bag and unzipped it and to my amazement, there was a beautiful dress inside. I took it out and laid it out on the bed to get a better look. It was black with a deep plunge in the back and looked like it was an off the shoulder number with a banded waist. I looked in the shopping bag and found stockings and a shoebox, all my size. The heels were high, black patent leather and gorgeous. A lot of thought went into this; I was impressed. It's pretty sexy to have a guy shop for you, but the reality was he probably did this a lot. I hung up the dress, along with the mink coat, and put the shoebox in the closet. I opened his top draw and was about to put the bra and panties in it when I started to cry again. *How did I get caught up like this? When did I become this girl?*

I tossed the panties in along with his t-shirts, briefs and boxers, and what looked like satin rolled up like belts. Red faced, I started to imagine what the satin strips were for and took them out and threw them in the garbage pail. *Fuck you Babe, they won't be here for Justine or any girl!* I grabbed Babe's phone and started calling my friends again, if I didn't talk to someone soon, I would lose my mind. I beeped everyone I could think of that could help me get out of this jam without feeing like a complete idiot, but no one called me back!

So angry, bored and tired from doing nothing, I finally crawled up in a ball on the couch and fell asleep to wait the night out. Early morning came and Babe slipped back in the house. I heard him, but kept my eyes closed, pretending I was sleeping so I didn't have to talk to him. I was peering through the slits of my eyes and I could see he was standing over me staring. He looked like a hot mess; I think I saw blood and smelled alcohol. He took a gun out of his waistband and put it on the mantel. I stayed still and waited for what seemed like an eternity for him to walk away. But Babe bent down and gently picked me up and carried me to his bed. He laid me down covering me. It was getting hard to pretend to be sleeping, but I kept going. I heard him go in the bathroom and turn on the shower, but I didn't hear him close the bathroom door so I had to stay still. When he finally walked out, I could see he was naked and carrying his clothes into the living room. In a minute I could smell the fireplace and something burning. Remembering Justine, I fought my instinct to go to him; I just stayed there listening.

After an hour, the house was still; I thought it was safe to get up quietly to check on him. Babe was sleeping on the couch naked in front of a dying fire. He looked exhausted and cold, so I covered him with a throw blanket. He must like the fire, since he started it when he came home, I put the log in and I noticed the gun was nowhere to be found. Something caught my eye in the ashes; it was a button his jeans. *Oh my God, Babe burned his clothes from last night.* I was afraid, not for myself, but for him. Torn up and confused, I just sat and stared at him. *He really is beautiful; honestly I could just look at him sleeping forever!* It was the waking up part that frightened the hell out of me. I could see scratches on his face. *They didn't come from me, yet! Hey, maybe he met up with Justine and she clawed him, but then why would he burn his clothes?*

I fell asleep in front of the fireplace, watching over him, completely conflicted. Bewildered, I woke up and looked around; I realized I was alone again covered by a blanket. He must have put the same one on me that I had put on him earlier. Babe was gone; he wasn't in the house at all. *Fuck, I can't be trapped here again!* I jumped up and searched everywhere. Finally, I saw him outside on the beach with Nero. They were playing catch with a stick. The dog was running in and out of the waves. Babe looked like a happy-go-lucky handsome man playing around, not a mobbed up wise guy. Gone were the remnants of last night's encounter. For a brief moment, he was just the guy I could really be with, except he was a fucking player.

My position was softening, because I was no one to judge him. I had my own admirers that called and pursued me. Shit, I was dating people when I met him and probably still would be if he didn't take up every free moment I had. I was determined that there wasn't going to be anymore fighting, so I made and decided to deliver coffee as a peace offering with a smile, because like it or not we swam in the same shark pool socially and I would have to run into to him.

"Good morning! Have some coffee before I leave?" I said as I handed him the cup giving him a hint.

"Thanks! You didn't have to do that," Babe said as he took his first sip.

"Sure I do, otherwise I wouldn't be a good guest. Listen, I want to thank you for everything, taking care of me, the food, wine, and everything."

"Stop, you don't have to..."

I broke in before he could finish. "I also want to apologize for being drunk, taking my clothes off, and all the other stuff."

Laughing he asked, "You're sorry you took your clothes off?"

Casting my eyes downward I started to cry. *I hate crying front of a guy, especially when it's about him.* "Yes, I truly am! The fireplace and wine got the best of me, but I don't want any of that to get in the way of us. I hope we're still kind of friends?" I didn't really want him to answer, so I just kept going. "I have to get home. Can you give me the number for a cab?"

"You sure you want to go?" He said sounding hurt and surprised I was still angry.

Sheepishly, I answered, avoiding his eyes, "I think I should, before things get out of hand again."

Moving closer to me he said, "Don't be like that. I actually felt really bad last night; I don't like to see girls cry."

Dismissing his advances, I said, "I really don't want to talk about it, you, her or anything."

Trying to be in total control he suggested, "Good so stay for the morning."

"Nah, please just give me a number for a cab and I'll get out of your hair."

"Cab? I'll take you. Let's have coffee and let Nero have a workout since he's been trapped indoors for a long time."

"I know how he feels!" I said glumly as I kicked the sand around.

"Ouch! I make you feel trapped? That's messed up." Babe looked at me with wide eyes.

Growing tired of the conversation, I let out a big breath as I squinted looking at him. "Oh come on, I've been indoors in someone else's house; it's not mine with all my stuff. I can't even use your phone."

"Who do you have to call that's so important?" He said laughing walking around the shoreline. "Your little friends?"

"Yes, kind of! I had some 'things' to take care of and need to make a few calls and stops." I said, trying to dish out enough sarcasm as I could.

Stopping in his tracks, he asked, "How do you know who to call?"

I tilted my head up and asked. "What do you mean?"

Sounding like the cat that ate the canary he said, "Your beeper was cleared of the history; there are no numbers in it."

Annoyed, but not shocked I asked, "You looked at my beeper?"

He continued to walk as he spoke, "You're kidding me right? Of course I did, what do you have to hide?"

Now I was pissed. "That's not the point; you have no right to do anything remotely like that or to clear the memory!"

"You're in my life, I have the right to know everything, and anything I need, and want to know about you and YOUR friends," he said as he touched the point of my nose with his fingertip.

Standing my ground, I countered, "First, I'm not in your life. Second, I know you're a street guy, but really? Does that rule apply for you as well?"

"Nope, you're on a need to know basis," he said, very matter of the factly, ignoring what I said.

I knew he was just breaking my chops, trying to provoke me. "All you need to know is that I'm tired, I want to go home, and I have plans before work and can't be late; AND I don't want to fight with you anymore, I just can't get caught up with you and get hurt."

Stopping in his tracks again, he looked me dead in the eyes and, as sincerely as possible, kissed my forehead. "I will never hurt you, ever." Babe took a cleansing breath and exhaled before asking, "Have a date?"

Smugly, I said, "Yes, I do."

"With who?" Babe said, blinking. Now he was hunting for information.

"Justine's father! Come on, Nero is done, take me home." I answered.

Walking around, he smirked at me. "Funny, you're a funny girl! Do you need me to call her for his number? Or is there anyone else you need me to call for you since you called the world last night from my phone?"

I shook my head, "I used your phone so what? What's the big fucking deal?"

"Well, I said don't make any calls and you did. What did you think you were going to accomplish calling Baby Paulie?"

"That's none of your business!" I snapped furious he would question my actions.

"Really? Everything is my business, I told you that before! And you should know after what happened, I programmed my phone to forward my incoming calls, so everyone you beeped called my mother's house. Oh and Paulie and me had a nice conversation, it was good to catch up with him."

I held my hand up to stop him in his tracks. "You're a complete pain my ass! Listen, whoever I beeped is none of your business. You truly are dead to me as boyfriend, let's try and remain friends. I'm just trying to end this nicely and quickly," I mumbled, talking more to myself than him. *Babe's world might be shaped in the way he wants in the street, but he doesn't have total control of his personal life! I'm not going to fall in line just to make it easy.* I cleared my throat, "Listen, please just lets get this overwith."

"Come on baby, forget all of this!" He grabbed me, swinging me around trying to make me smile; I only stared with total disgust, as I pushed against him.

He clearly had the upper hand, so I changed the conversation. "Hey, how was last night? Have fun?" I said trying to let him know I saw him come home.

"Not too much," he said trying to minimize the situation.

I knew what I saw and told him so. "You looked like you did. Have a little too much to drink?"

"I had a few, why?" he replied, dancing around my third degree questions.

"Because you came home reeking! Also you looked like you had a run in with a virgin or two, and you brought your work home with you." I continued with my teasing.

Now I had his full attention, "What are you trying to say?"

Eying him, I said flatly, "Nothing, except you smelled like scotch and had blood all over you. You don't normally look like that. Plus you put your tool on the mantel. I saw it, I know what they look like."

"You must have been dreaming," he said, trying to minimize what I was saying.

Very sure of what I saw, I countered. "Nope! I covered your naked ass up last night and it was gone."

"I know that, I covered yours too. But I took a shower when I came home, I didn't smell." He again ignored most of my comments.

"Oh yes you did! I know booze, I know you, and I know I saw you!"

"Peeper, were you pretending to be sleeping?" Babe said grinning at me.

"Yup! I didn't want to talk to you and from the looks of it, you appeared to need some privacy," I said, because I wanted him to know that I knew he had been involved with something.

"So you caught me, yup I was with a bunch of virgins last night. They were terrific!" Babe said, continuing with the joke.

Turning my head sideways I went for the kill. "So good, you had to burn your clothes after them?"

Now that comment brought him up short. Stepping in front of me, he held my shoulders square in front of him. "What did you say?"

Without skipping a beat, I repeated, "I asked you if they were so good, you had to burn your clothes afterwards?"

Turning his head sideways, he eyed me, "How do you know that?"

"Because when you carried me I saw the blood, then I smelled the fire as you torched your clothes. After I covered you, I put another log on to keep you warm, that's when I saw the gun and that the button that didn't burn," I said, as I took the small button out of my pocket and held it open in my hand for him to see.

He took the button and held it, "You're pretty perceptive. It's hard to hide anything from you. I'll have to remember that."

"Just noticed? It's none of my business; I just hope the virgins weren't too much for you. I'm speaking as a friend of course." I knew there weren't any virgins, but I also was sure I didn't want to know the true source of all the blood either.

"I think I handled them well, I didn't disgrace myself. Don't worry!"

Now I was the one who was serious, "Babe I don't want to know anything, but please be careful. I don't like this stuff; it's not good for business, friends, or families. I would go crazy if something happened to you!"

"You care, Peeper! I'm touched," he said as he held his heart.

"Don't call me that anymore! Stop! I hate you but in some sick way I was worried about you! Stop joking! I was so upset after I saw you. No matter what, somewhere deep inside I think of you as a friend and I would be sick if I thought anything happened to you."

"Thanks Dannie, I'm fine. When I woke up and saw you laying watch over me, I was happy. It felt good to have you close." He leaned in to kiss me, but instinctively, I pulled back. Overriding my physical apprehension, he hugged me tightly and in my hair he said, "I thought having the virgins would help me take my mind off you. They were great, but I really just wanted you!" I slapped his back trying to make him stop. All the joking around couldn't fix my broken heart; I just wanted to leave with a shred of dignity and dry eyes. "Okay, let's get you home."

"Great, do what you have to do. I'll be out here when you're ready," I said, trying to be casual. In a few minutes he returned with his keys and a leash for Nero. "Okay do you have everything before we go?"

"Yes, thanks I have my bag! Don't worry I didn't leave anything behind. Ready?"

"You're not taking your coat?"

Avoiding his eyes I said, "No, I don't think I should."

His expression turned tense. "I want you to have it, but you can leave it here if you want until you come back."

I turned to look at him taking a deep breath I whispered, "Come on now, you gotta know I'm not coming back here so I don't think I should take it." I stopped and started to take off the earrings, but he grabbed my wrist and held it. I stammered while I tried to be as sincere as possible. "You're not like the other guys to me; I care-cared-for you but you're no good for me Babe. I can't handle the girls and sneaking around. I'm not looking for a fuck buddy, so I'm not going to just take the coat and earrings. It would be a waste, because I would never wear them out with anyone else anyway. Do you understand what I mean?"

His face became stormy, and he looked like he could have slapped me. "Fuck buddy? Hmm. I guess you've had a few. Yup, I understand completely, my car is on the side of the house. Let me get the dog and lock up, follow me."

I ignored his comment, because I knew I hit him right between the eyes and my words fucking stung him! This was going to be the worst drive ever; I jumped in his car, dreading every moment ahead. Heading back, he said very little until we pulled up to my front door. As I was about to get out, I turned and said, "Thanks for the ride."

Babe leaned over and grabbed my arm strongly. "Nope, I'm walking you up, nothings changed! He got out and walked me in right inside; he stopped at the door and held me in place knowing I was trying to bolt. I know I'm not off to a good start with you, believe me, none of this is what I had in mind."

I stared at him, not sure I wanted to hear anything. "Babe just don't."

"Stop, just listen to me for a minute without talking. I want to take you on a date. Will you have a late dinner with me?"

This was a complete 180. I looked at him. He was clearly making an effort, so I held my breath for a second while making up my mind, "No I can't."

"I don't ask twice honey, so think long and hard." Babe was trying his best to be slick and play hardball with me.

"Good, don't, so we can remain friendly. I don't wanna to be enemies with you and we're going to end up there if this continues. I just need some distance for a while. I'll be able to be around you after it stops hurting." I grabbed his hand and looked at him dead in the eyes. "Whether you believe it or not, I don't fuck around. For me to take my clothes off and let you touch me it means I cared for you and I know I can't go there again." Babe tried to break in, but I hushed him and continued. "Listen, I'm fucked up when it comes to sex, you'll never understand. I know most of the girls out there, bang casually, but not me. I'm old school, sex is serious, personal, and I only have sex with someone I love. I'm falling for you and I have to stop this before I get fucked over." Again, he tried to interject, but I kept going. "I know you don't want to fuck me over, but the handwriting is on the wall, I'm going to get fucked over. Babe I'm going to quit the bar, I can't be around you every day, it's just too close for comfort right now." My eyes started to tear up as I choked on my words.

He let out a deep breath and took my fingertips and kissed them. When he looked up, my heart hurt, as he whispered. "We're all a little fucked up! I promise I will never fuck you over; I'll leave you first. But before that can happen I have to do this the right way. I'm not asking, I'm telling you I'm taking you out and you're going to go. Everything will fall into place, I promise. Trust me, don't quit!"

"No, and don't ask again." I shook my head no, as the tears spilled over cascading down my cheeks, making me burn with embarrassment.

"Come on, you hate me, but you owe me so you have to go out with me at least once. If you still hate me, then I'll leave you alone."

"NO!"

"YOU OWE ME!" Babe grinned at me with his best good-guy smile.

"Put it on my tab and leave me alone! I'm not going anywhere with you!"

"I told you, you owe me and I don't run tabs, so pay up! Tonight, you and me!"

I wanted to scream no, but against my better judgment I gave in, and shook my head yes. "Good grief, all right already! One meal, no touching, no nothing, and then we're square, all debts are paid in full!"

Beaming, he leaned in to kiss me, "Great! Tonight after work lets go out. I know the best late night joint in Chinatown, or maybe I'll take you to your favorite joint, Ponte's!"

Before we could get caught up into any heavy conversations, I opened the door and kissed his cheek. Then I was out and off; I never looked back to see if he was there watching or if he took off after I closed and locked the door. I jumped into my shower to wash off the embarrassment of the last forty-eight hours. Dressing quickly, I ran over to a little restaurant on Third Ave to meet Millie before work. We had such a good time catching up on all the gossip from the boys. I filled her in on what happened, Babe and this mystery girl named Justine. We decided we would have to do a little investigation on her to see what she was all about. When it was time to leave we asked for the check and the waiter told us it was taken care of already. Babe beeped me as we drank our coffee. I called him back from the pay phone and he said, "I hope you enjoyed your meal."

Confused, I asked, "I did, why wouldn't I?"

Laughing into the phone, he said, "Because it always tastes better when someone else pays. I approve of your lunch date by the way!"

"Are you kidding me? Thank you, but you didn't have to do that!" I said as I smiled, turning red. The boys always take care of their girls' checks. They have a network of people who tell them when their girls show up, what they do and who they're with. It's flattering and sexy in a possessive sort of way.

"You're welcome! Tell Millie I said hi and she's welcome too. Gotta run!" He said and then hung up on me.

I returned back to our table and said, "Guess who picked up the check?"

"You're kidding me? Babe?" Millie started to laugh at the situation.

Giggling I said, "Yup! Unbelievable! I told him I had a date today, so he must have tailed me."

I looked around at the staff and realized they were all looking at us differently than they usually do. As we left, I tipped the waiter and bartender as all the servers said goodbye, the manager even came over to inquire if our meal was satisfactory. No matter if you actually pay or someone picks up your check, you have to tip and tip BIG. It's a Brooklyn thing.

Tonight was going to be a mixed bag of nuts, very awkward and weird, because Babe's seen me naked and I said some dirty shit to him. He'll be there looking at me before our date...ugh! Going back to the bar, seeing Babe, worrying about who might come in, all of it is stressing me out! Not having Andrew and his big personality around was hard because he was one of the few guys I could talk to about all of this, even about being naked with his friend. The recent changes were painful, because I had such a connection to these guys. I truly loved them all, more so than any other crew or family I ever worked for, and that's saying a lot because I've worked for every family in New York.

I didn't know it, but Babe was going to be straightened out tonight. It was long overdue. The books had been closed for a very long time and there was a list of guys who were salivating at the chance to have their fingers pricked and burn a paper saint in their palms while they sold their soul. No new members had been allowed into this invitation-only society, the wait's been years long. It was a big night for him; Babe wanted this badge of honor more than anything or anyone.

Around nine, the bar was jumping and all of the sudden he came barreling through the swinging doors, walked behind the bar, and grabbed me to face him with a grip that could have ripped my arms off. His right hand was bandaged; I'm not stupid, I knew at that moment exactly what had happened. He looked different, he looked made. My heart sank, because I knew anyone who would ever love him, lost him at that moment. From now on, he would always belong to them. It wasn't "if" they would call, but "when" they would call and there was no mistaking that he would have to go, no matter what he was doing. If they said you couldn't be with this person or that person, he would have to listen. A million thoughts raced through my head as my heart pounded with regrets.

Babe gently untied my ponytail, fluffed up my hair, and kissed me hard in front of everyone. He deliberately held me against him during the kiss so that I could feel every ripple of his muscles. Every part of his body pressed up against me as he bent me backwards, burying his tongue in my mouth the whole time until he gently lowered me onto the floor mats. I remember the look in his eyes and the smell of his skin as if it were yesterday; at that moment, my heart stopped. I could feel his intense desire pressing up against my stomach.

My silent alarm sounded. *I'm cursed! Babe would never be the man I wanted him to be now, because he could never love me that little extra that I needed.* That little extra that makes men only think about one girl, and that doesn't fit into this life of ours. I remember there wasn't a sound in the bar except for the jukebox. There were so many jaws hitting the ground in complete and utter shock, because this was like throwing the gauntlet down. Babe reached for my hand and pulled me up from the mats and cupped my face in his hands after that oh-my-god type of kiss and smiled deeply at me.

This simple act sent a message loud and clear to his crew; no words were needed. Turning to the guys, he beamed with his arm around my neck shouting the drinks were on him. Everything was happening so fast, I didn't have time to think, let alone react, I flew up and down the bar pouring shots for everyone. The cocktails were flowing, the music was pumping and everyone had a great time. Every so often we made eye contact and he smiled wickedly at me. It seemed like he was the King at that moment. The boys were discretely cheering and toasting him. I was torn by my mixed emotions. On one hand I was happy to see him happy, but on the other I was devastated by his promotion of sorts.

Now he would go find some little Italian mafia daughter and marry her and I would be history. The bars and neighborhood were littered with girls like that. She would be a card-carrying member of the "Marias" club; every girl was named Maria, Marie or Mary for some reason. They were someone's daughter, cousin or sister and it would be a match made to keep the family ties strong. The silent smiles and attention would soon fade unless he intended to keep me as a side piece of ass. *Nope! Not happening. I would have to walk away, if I could.*

So I returned his smiles to avoid ruining his moment and tried as best as possible to look happy for him, all the while still seething from the night before. Watching all the guys rallying around him, I joined in on the toasts. Later, as I closed up, Babe wasn't with me for the first time in a long time, even though he was supposed to take me out on a date after work. He must have forgotten, because he didn't mention it as they all left to celebrate. I was sure the matchmaking deals were already in play, so as I washed the glasses consumed with sadness, I pictured him meeting one of the "Marias" in a club that was always willing, ready, and able to be promoted into the fat wives' club. I wasn't much in the mood to go out after work, so I just went home. For the first time, in a long time, I was home early.

Walking into my house alone was strange. I cleaned up and changed for bed. Wearing my fluffy robe, I looked at myself in the mirror, at the lines that were just starting to form at the corners of my eyes. The bruises were purple now; I looked battered. I thought about him out drinking and talking with all the girls around. Memories of Babe in bed with me as the daylight hit his face, his brilliant smile, and big hands on me, just made me die a little more as the time ticked away. My bed was too big and empty now. I kept thrashing around missing the smell and feel of his skin. After that night, I would never know him that intimately and innocently again. Our time had passed. Somehow, I missed the small window of opportunity I had to just be a girl getting to know a guy.

When my phone rang, I stared at it, unsure if I should answer. Wrestling with myself, I let the machine pickup. Within a second, I knew the caller wasn't going to leave a message, whoever it was hung up. This happened a few more times for the next two hours, forcing me to finally grab the receiver in frustration. I said hello a few times but after listening to my voice the person hung up. Someone wanted to know if I was home. It had to be one of the young guys who were trying to be a good scout. Probably to make sure I wasn't going to walk in on anything and create a scene. I was too tired and emotionally hurt, I didn't have any more fight left in me and took the phone of the hook. *No more calls for tonight.* Closing my eyes, I slept a dead sleep, filled with sadness, fear and remorse.

CHAPTER 19

Go Big

To my absolute shock his attention didn't fade, it only intensified. The next morning my front door buzzer rang around 8AM with a flower delivery. *Flowers? The doorman didn't ring me? How did the guy get up here?* Shaking my head, I put on my robe and opened the door, but I wasn't prepared to find Babe standing there with seven-dozen red long stem roses. Pleasantly surprised, "Oh Babe, they're beautiful! Come in."

He carried the vases in and put them on my dinning room table. "Before you say anything, I'm sorry about dinner last night. I didn't want to use the key and scare you. Let me make it up to you?"

"Oh you don't have to, its fine," I said trying to conceal my hurt. I was becoming accustomed to disappointment already.

Like the boss, he firmly said, "I don't have to, but I want to. So how about dinner tonight?"

Not about to be an idiot twice in twenty-four hours I declined. "I have to work tonight, I can't."

Looking so excited, he was pouring on the charm big time. "Take off, I'll make a call and have someone cover for you. I'll take care of it and whatever money you'll lose."

The boys will go to amazing lengths to get what they want. Jobs, responsibilities, and plans aren't barriers for them, only annoying obstacles. When they want to impress someone, their motto is go big or go home. Normal guys give a dozen roses; the boys fill rooms with them.

"No, I can't." I said holding my ground; no way was I going to give in to everything so easily.

Babe made me sit down as he took my hands in his. "Listen Dannie, you have a lot of guy friends like T, James, Vinnie and all the others buying you roses and bottles," I tried to break in, but he put his hand over my mouth. "STOP! Just listen to me! What you heard was just a friend, easily we could have been here and one of your friends could have called and said the same thing to you. I've heard you tell your friends you love them, it was the same thing! I'm telling you the truth, and if you stop being so mad for a minute you'll understand."

I'm focusing on your face listening to your excuses. Yes, they make perfect sense, but come on; its crap and you know it! That little place in my head that wasn't soaring in the clouds, was telling me nah-nah-nah- don't believe this bullshit.

Babe took a rose out of one of the vases and brushed it against my cheek as he kissed me gently. "Come on, say yes to me! I couldn't help last night, it was beyond my control."

I knew what he said was true, but I was so hurt from being ditched, I just couldn't give him 100 percent, so I settled to keep some dignity. "I'll work the day shift, if you can get the day guy to switch with me."

"Hang on, let me use your phone." Babe picked up my phone, made a quick call, turning smiling he said, "Done! You're off tonight."

Without another reason to say no, I gave in. "Oh, okay I guess I'm free then. So yes, sure I'll have dinner with you."

"Great! Take a shower, I'll wait." Babe said grinning from ear to ear!

Astonished, I asked, "Its eight in the morning, you want to go out now?"

"Yes, we're starting early. I have it all planned out, so let's get going." He beamed at me looking very excited. "Nothing is going to get in the way, even that robe of yours, so get your ass in gear."

Stupid me blushed, my heart was bursting, I was so flattered he was trying hard for me. Walking into the bathroom, I turned the shower on and called out to him, "Make yourself at home, I'm leaving the door open if you need me." Babe had a clear view of me from the couch right through my bedroom doorway. Turning on the TV, he sat on the couch but never took his eyes off me. I slipped off my robe, looking back at him as I slid the clear shower door open giving him an erotic view. Unlike when Babe took a shower, I had my back to the tiles as I made a show of shampooing my hair. Letting the suds rain down on me, I kept up steady eye contact toying with him the whole time. After I washed my body, he was standing in the doorway with a red rose in his hand smelling it. "Listen, you keep that up and we will have a very different date than I planned."

Giggling, I shut off the water and stepped out soaking wet holding out my hand for the towel behind the door. Placing the rose on the sink he put the towel around me and started to dry my skin off. Kissing my shoulders he picked my robe up and wrapped it around me, ending the show. "Go!"

Coyly I asked, "I'm going as fast as I can. What do you want me to wear for our date?"

On the verge of attacking me he said, "A pair of jeans should work."

"Anything else? Or am I topless again?"

"T-shirt. Go now!" He mumbled as he kissed me on the neck and backed away, letting me pass. Grabbing his index finger I pulled him with me as I walked into my bedroom.

Pointing to my bed, I said, "Sit and talk to me as I get dressed."

"You're killing me!" He moaned as he sat on the edge of my bed. Laughing at him, I climbed on top straddling him, pushing him back towards my pillows. Holding his arms above his head, I opened my robe exposing myself and kissed him hard.

Grinning at him I said, "Good, you deserve it! You stood me up last night!"

Boring his eyes into me, he tried to explain. "But..."

"Shush, don't talk I'm in control here. Got that, I'm the boss! You stood me up and that shouldn't happen ever! You've been a bad boy and now you will have to be punished!" He moaned as I continued to hold his arms as I leaned into kiss him. He pushed up slightly but I wouldn't let him up. *Now stay there and watch me, as I get dressed.* Raising my eyebrow, I smiled as I bit his lip, "Last night I took my clothes off, too bad you missed it, but today I'm putting them ALL on because you stood me up. Now you get to watch, but can't touch anything. It might be painful, but you deserve it." Pressing my whole upper body against him, I gave him one last kiss. Climbing off, Babe just lay there with his hands folded under his head intently staring at me.

I moved about, making a show out of everything, from putting on my bra and panties to turning my head upside down and drying my hair. Applying my makeup in only my underwear, I asked, "Did you have fun last night?"

"Yeah, it wasn't bad," he groaned.

Giving him a sideways look, "Hmm! Maybe I need to change my bra to punish you more." Bending down I grabbed my jeans out of the drawer and started to slide them up very slowly, knowing fully he was enjoying the show. "But if I do, we may never leave, so I won't." Pulling my tight t-shirt over my head, I was finally covered up. A pair of heels, sunglasses, jewelry and a blazer completed the look.

Turning to him I joked like a drill sergeant, "Show's over! Lets go." Babe stood up, adjusting his clothes as we walked out.

As soon as he opened the car door, I immediately smelled the sweet aroma of the roses from the car ride to my house. He put the top down and drove off, beaming from ear to ear. The first stop was the diner for breakfast. I was starved, and ate like a football player. Once satisfied, he drove me to a nail salon on Avenue U. He walked me into the store, paid and tipped the girl do my nails. Kissing the top of my head, he told me to walk next door when I was done. The manicurist was Korean and never made eye contact with me, but spoke to another girl in her native language the whole time. I presumed she was talking about me by the way they communicated and sneered in my direction. Once my nails were in perfect condition- long French claws- I went to find Babe. Just like he said, he was next door sitting at the end of the counter, with a few younger guys vying for his attention. Once he saw me, he motioned for me to walk over where he looked at my nails with great pleasure.

Running them across his jaw gently to tease him I said, "Thank you, that was so nice!" Leaning in, I kissed his cheek.

Beaming, he wrapped his arm around my waist and picked me up. "Ready for more? Let's go." We jumped in the car and drove to Coney Island Avenue. Babe and I went from store to store shopping. He picked out everything, from clothes to shoes and bought me a new wardrobe, and I knew I would only wear his clothes from now on, just to make him happy. There were so many bags he couldn't fit them all in his car and paid one of the guys to drive them to the club so he could grab them later for me. Everything was happening so fast before I knew it, it was early afternoon and I had to run to work. Babe reluctantly drove me, repeatedly asking me to just take off. Amazed at how excited he was, I kept grinning saying no.

I was only at work for an hour when he called to say he was returning because he wanted to talk. He was determined to wear me down and make me leave. Babe drove up to the bar and called out for me get in the car with the biggest grin across his beautiful face. I knew the more he grinned the more abuse I was in for.

"I can't, I'm working." I said from the front door as I walked out on the porch.

"Come on, get in for a minute."

"Noooo!" I repeated.

"Okay, you're going to make this hard on yourself!" he said as he got out of the car and walked up the front stairs. Before I understood what he was doing and could run away; he picked me up and slipped my shoes off my feet. He popped his trunk open and tossed them in and turned around and said, "Now let's do this again, get in the car."

"I can't, you took my shoes, you nut! Give them back!" I yelled.

Laughing he walked back to me and picked me up fireman style and carried me to the car. Depositing me in the passenger seat, he climbed in and drove off.

"Come on, take me back, I'm working!" I said joking around, because I couldn't believe he would really take me away from the bar, but happy I didn't end up in the trunk again, especially since this car's trunk was the size of a breadbox.

Totally ignoring all my pleas, he drove me to a house that turned out to be his mother's. Without any warning, he picked me up out of the car and carried me inside. Calling out in his booming voice "Ma! Ma! Where are you?"

His mother walked into the kitchen smiling and acted as if nothing was amiss. She had a warm and genuine smile, and I realized he got his smile and eyes from her. When Babe looked at someone he cared for, his eyes sparkled and his smile could light up the skyline. His mother was an understated, beautiful woman who was very easy to be around. The fact that she wasn't shocked meant she was used to her son being slightly crazy. To my amazement, Babe said, "Mom, this is the girl, Dannie that I told you about; she follows me everywhere because she loves me."

What are you doing? I turned green as I extended my hand listening to him spin his story to his mother. "Dannie is really a call girl, but I told her I can't date a prostitute. So if she quits, I might date her only if you like her. So here we are, I hope you think she's okay, because I would hate for her to go back on the streets." She reached over and hit him, laughing she told him to be nice.

I'm a hooker? I'm going to kill you, the moment your mother leaves the room! I couldn't help but go from green to beet red; mortified I stood there smiling and then leaned over to kiss her hello. She broke the ice and put me out of my misery by simply making coffee and putting out Stella Doro cookies. I could either continue to be embarrassed by what he said, giving him what he wanted, or I could turn the tables and just pretend this was normal. Proudly standing barefoot, I turned around and thanked her for the coffee and cookies, and sat down at her kitchen table. As we ate and talked, I could see the connection they had. Babe loved his mom so much; he was gentle with her and she doted on him.

They had their own secret language between them that no one else would ever understand, but everyone could clearly see. As we were leaving, she said, "Now Babe go buy this nice girl a pair of shoes!" Then she turned to me and with the kindest smile and said, "So nice to meet you. Please come by anytime. My son is a good man, I'm glad to finally meet you."

I smiled and said, "Thank you, I'm so pleased to meet you too. Please forgive me for walking into your home without shoes, but somehow they vanished off my feet."

Babe was grinning from ear to ear, "Okay ladies, time to go. Come on Dannie, I have to get you back to work before they think you ran away. So Ma, do I take her back to the corner or should I take her to dinner tonight?"

Slapping his shoulder, his mother said, "Oh stop teasing this poor girl. Take her to work, take her dinner, take her anywhere she wants to go, but give her her shoes back!"

We left smiling, walking out hand-in-hand until Babe picked me up when we hit the sidewalk and deposited me back in the car. Babe drove back whistling, and as we pulled up, he handed me my shoes. Putting them back on, I ran into find my regulars drinking and watching TV. They had poured their own cocktails, and wrote out how many they had, so I could charge them when I got back. Funny, each of them tipped me even though they served themselves. Only in Brooklyn!

I was getting so excited for our date. Babe said he was going to call Ponte's to make reservations at my absolute favorite date restaurant. He was going out of his way to make this night perfect. Around four, Phil came in with his guys, they all huddled talking together. Something must have happened, because he wasn't his normal outgoing self. My excitement turned into disappointment when I heard Phil say to Babe they had to go somewhere later on. He gave me a look, approached me to explain. I shrugged my shoulders and turned my back on him busying myself with a mindless task so he wouldn't see me looking upset.

"Hey, turn around. Listen, I'll make it up to you, okay?" He said knowing fully well I was pissed.

"No problem! I didn't say anything. Go, I get it." I was disappointed, but tried not to show it.

"If I get done early enough, we can still go. Either way, I'll see you later. Reaching over, he hugged me and kissed my cheek. I'll be back."

"Yup, sounds great!" was all I could manage under the circumstances.

The rest of the afternoon dragged on and before I knew it, I was working the night shift. The reservation came and went; time ticked on by and I was getting more and more annoyed. My coverage was sitting on the other side of the bar hanging out instead of working, because I was more comfortable behind the stick. Just as I thought about leaving, a delivery boy came in and gave me a beautiful blue Tiffany box with a big bow. I opened it and pulled out a cooked breaded pork chop on a rope. Like soap on a rope, but only a chop on a rope. There was a note inside the box that said, "Pork?" The bar erupted into roaring laughter. The open box sat on the bar all evening until Babe came in.

I said, laughing, "Hey Babe thanks for the chop, you nut! So, I'm confused, tell me do you want to pork me or eat me?"

"Eat you? I don't do that!" He said laughing and holding up his hand. "You ready to go?"

Giving him a sideways look I said, "Go where? The night's shot, the reservation was hours ago. I'm not hungry anymore plus I have my dinner now."

Ignoring the pork chop he said, "We can still get a table."

"Really? Should I choke the food down before you run off to work?"

"Come on, don't be like that, you know how it is."

"Yup, got it. It's the 'things' thing again," I said as I chewed on the pork chop. "So what's this pork chop supposed to mean? That you want to pork me, because tough guys don't dive?"

He blinked; his mood was getting dark because I gave him a verbal jab. "No, they don't, boy you are slow."

"Ha. Not as slow as you think! I can't believe I'm talking about this here and now, but let me get this straight, are you kidding me?" Pointing down below I said, "You expect someone to go down on you, but you won't reciprocate?"

"Nope! That's just the way it is. And I don't just want 'anyone,' I'm picky. Let's go already." The guys in the bar were watching us like a tennis match laughing and cheering each of us on.

"I'm not going anywhere but home. It doesn't matter to me, but I do think you're full of shit though. You probably searched a few times for the man in the boat!" Holding my hands in a v-shape pointing down again I continued to try to abuse him. "Come on admit it, it's not like I'm asking about dates with Mary Palm and her five sisters!" The room erupted into wild laughter.

"You have the wrong guy, that's not me." Babe sat back on the bar stool looking more pissed as the moments ticked away.

"Really, I think you'd go down in flames Babe! Who are you kidding Mr. Tough Guy? Admit it! You've been a pearl diver at least once, come on!" I roared at him. I just wanted to annoy the shit out of him, and I was succeeding.

"Don't make a scene! You got the wrong guy!" He said adamantly. "Listen are coming or not? Because I'm going to go if you're not! You're in a fucked up mood, maybe you need something, you sound frustrated."

Laughing at the absurdity of his comment, I went in for the kill, "Maybe YOU got the wrong girl! And NO, I'm not going anywhere with you, forget that; ain't happening! All my debts are paid in full out of default! And by the way, what kind of something would you be referring to?" Shaking my fingers at him I continued, "Ha, me frustrated? Hardly!" I took a step back laughing sarcastically and blurted out, "I don't think so! You're not the only one with friends, tough guy! They are always there if I need a hand, my list of admirers- oh, I'm sorry- my list of FRIENDS is just as long as yours, if not longer and I might call one tonight, but I promise I'll call out your name loud enough for you to hear! But then again, you may not recognize my voice as fast as..." But before I finished the statement, I knew I went too far, because he bolted out of his seat almost lunging at me.

"Shut the fuck up!" He didn't give me the time to answer; he flung his glass against the wall and stormed out. I ran out of the bar after him, calling his name as he jumped in the car and finally caught up to him at the corner red light.

Stepping in front of his car so he couldn't pull out of the spot, I could see the absolute rage in his eyes. "Babe stop! I'm mad as hell at you, fucking stay here and explain why you fucking stood me up again! If you drive away, I'm done!" He didn't say a word, he just glared at me with such hatred that I blinked. Not sure of what to do, I move to open the passenger door, but he screeched out of the spot leaving me standing there.

How come making you feel like shit doesn't feel better than this? I'm so angry that I forgave you and you left! This is another I fucking hate you, but want to fuck you moment! Feeling confused and totally stupid, I walked into the bar and sat down. There wasn't a sound; everyone stared silently watching TV. His friends were there, trying to figure out what to do next. I switched places with my cover and sat on the other side of the bar, sulking. Just as I started to move past the incident, a customer who was a banquet waiter walked in and gave me a to-go box of pork chops. That's when I found out he had ordered them from a local catering hall, having them made especially for me. The kitchen staff found it to be so funny, they decided to join in.

I started beeping him over and over again, but he wouldn't answer me. I left the bar, unsure of what to do, only to find pork chops hanging from my mirrors and door handles. I tossed them into the corner pail, shaking my head, if I wasn't so upset this would be pretty funny! I could either go out and forget this mess or go look for him. Without thinking twice, I drove past his mother's, but I didn't see his car. Continuing on my hunt, I drove past all his haunts and then, finally, to Breezy. I wondered what I was going to say when I found him. I guess I'll figure it out, but for now I had to just find him. Oh shit I realized I couldn't drive through the gate; I'd have to park and walk. As I came up along the side of his house, I saw his car.

Great! Okay, now to get him to talk to me, hopefully he'll open the door. I made the turn approaching the windows seeing the lights were dim and the fireplace was on. At that moment I should have figured it out sooner, but I didn't. I knocked and, without thinking, I turned the doorknob walking in to the alarm's beeping. Frozen in shock, I could see Babe was naked with a girl on the floor by the fireplace. I couldn't move. I couldn't think. I just stood there as the tears were flowing, and I couldn't stop them. *There he was, on top of a girl, my Babe on another girl!*

She finally noticed me and started to scream, just then he turned his face and saw me. None of us moved a muscle, suspended in mutual shock. Then there was too much noise all at once. The alarm started to blare and a girl's scream, his voice and noise, noise, noise!

I think he asked, "Dannie what are you doing here?" I saw him as he got up to wrap a blanket around himself. My eyes scanned the room, the dim lights, fireplace, wine and the naked girl with Babe. I was living through another nightmare. *What did I ever do so wrong to have this happen to me...again?* I couldn't hear him at all anymore; I knew he was saying something, but I just couldn't handle the humiliation, instead I turned around and ran out. I ran, walked and fell a few dozen times on the beach, blinded by my sobs, oblivious to where I was, I let the freezing water lick my feet until they hurt so much I could barely continue. Babe had told me I was at the end of the earth, but he was wrong. I found the Cabana Club at the end of his earth. I snuck into the club and threw myself down on a lounge chair and just cried myself sick.

I wanted to trust you even though I knew better. There is something about crying your heart out alone that makes it worse.

Misery loves company, and since I didn't have any, I did the next best thing; I fell asleep. I don't think I've ever been that cold. I woke up feeling sick as a dog, freezing, and completely miserable. *Oh good grief I had to walk back past his house to get to my car.* Snaking along the water I walked holding my head down so no one out for a morning walk could see my face. Finally, his house came into view and I ran past it quickly. With the main road in sight I tried to find my car, but I couldn't. I must have parked in a no standing zone, because it was gone or stolen. I never locked it; what was the sense locking a convertible? If someone wanted to rob it, all they had to do was slash my roof.

Stupid me, what would make me think my convertible BMW would last unlocked all night by the beach. I started to walk towards the bridge trying to think where exactly the trains were in the Rockaway's. I was going to have to hop the turnstile to boot, because I didn't have my bag. *Fuck me!!!* I pulled my hair into a ponytail and used the inside of my shirt to wipe the mess from my face. I stopped noticing the cars passing me on the road until one drove up in front of me. A guy rolled down the window. "Hey, you need a ride sweetheart?"

"No, fuck off!" I muttered.

"Okay, but its warmer in here." He said lingering before he pulled away.

This was going to be a long fucking walk! I had the bridge in sight when I saw his black Porsche coming across it. I kept my head down and tried to blend in, with whom I'm not sure but I was trying. I made it to the 'Welcome to Breezy Point' sign and there he was, pulled over with his engine running and window down staring at me. I knew I couldn't avoid him forever, so better not to start now. I stopped by the window and just waited.

"Get in the car, you can't walk home.""

Very quietly, I opened the door and slid in. Staring forward, not uttering a sound I waited. Somehow I felt I've spent most of my life waiting. Waiting to grow up, waiting to move out, waiting to meet a good guy, waiting for this or that, waiting, waiting, and waiting. He pulled the car forward and drove toward his house. We pulled up and he got out of the car, but I didn't move. Babe walked around and opened my door, and extended his hand to help me. Ignoring his gesture, I got out on my own and followed him into his house and immediately sat by his kitchen island with my head down.

Sounding sarcastic, he started the conversation. "Hello? Do you have anything to say to me?"

Completely heartbroken and trying to hide the fact I was shattered, my voice cracked as I whispered. "My car was robbed. I have to call the police."

"That's it, your car was robbed? Nothing else? Like what the fuck you were doing here last night?"

Trying to control my temper and disguise the hurt in my voice I said, "I made a mistake, Babe. Fuck my car, I don't care anymore." I would rather lick my way home than look at him one moment longer. I jumped up and bolted out of his house. *Fuck him, fuck my job, fuck my car, fuck it all!*

Babe was after me like a rocket and caught me on the sand. As he grabbed my waist, I just screamed, completely crazed, kicking and screaming. He held me fireman style bringing me back in the house. I finally stopped when he pinned me in a chair, because I didn't want his hands on me for even a split second.

As he stood in front of me, he roared, "STOP IT NOW!" Babe moved my hair away and wiped my face with a towel. Once I was still, he let me go and said, "Danielle you almost gave me a fucking heart attack walking in here. You're lucky I didn't blow your head off! Besides you fucking intruded on me and then disappeared on the beach."

"I made a mistake." I mumbled completely devastated.

"You sure fucking did!" His anger was starting to chip away at his control.

"I've made a lot of mistakes. Don't worry I will never DO that again!" I said on the verge of ripping his eyes out. *Please just disappear from my life!*

"Say what you have to say without the drama, stop talking in riddles." He taunted me.

Spitting the words at him, I continued, "I have to go home." I starting to choke on them, I was barely able to say anything intelligently. "I have to get away from you and I'm never coming back here; this was all a horrible mistake! That's what I'm trying to say."

"Really? So that's it then? You made that pretty clear last night, so why did you come here?" He asked as if he could slap me.

Blind rage was pushing past the hurt and I wanted to kill him right there and then. If I carried a gun I would have shot him on the spot. "YOU must be out of your mind. I walked in here and you were with some pig girl, so yes, that's it, I'm done. I'm not going to be with someone that I have to worry every time we fight he's with another girl! You piece of shit, you couldn't stay home for a few hours alone?"

He ignored my insults. "I'm not the one who started all this, you did! Then you walked into my house uninvited, unannounced and then disappeared all night, you're fucking kidding me right?"

"First of all you have keys to my house, so walking into your house shouldn't be an issue since you do it all the time to me! For your information, I walked to the Cabana Club and slept there. Listen; if my car wasn't stolen you wouldn't have even known I was still here. I would've been long gone." I said running my hands through my hair on the verge of ripping it out.

"Your car wasn't stolen, it was towed." He said as he walked around the island to the coffee maker and turned it on like a cold-hearted prick.

This was no surprise to me; I thought it was a possibility. "I must have parked in a no parking zone. Where can I pick it up?"

"You can't. I had it towed, it's at my shop." Babe said with an air of a King who could do anything he damn well pleased.

I'M GOING TO LOSE MY MIND! Outraged, I shouted, "YOU STOLE MY CAR? AGAIN? Why would you do that to me?"

Completely composed, he toyed with me, "Why would you come here and walk into my house?" The wilder I got, the calmer he was, just to annoy the hell out of me.

"That's notthesamething, onehasnothingtodowiththeother. WHY WOULD YOU TOW MY CAR AGAIN?" I continued to shout getting to the point of red rage homicidal maniac status.

"Again, why would you walk in here? What were you looking for, what did you want?" He asked continuing to torture me with his stupid questions.

Spitting the words out at him, "I wanted to find you because I'm a dick!"

"Why?" he asked maintaining his calm tone.

"Why? Because you took off like a bat out of hell and I was concerned that I hurt your feelings more than I meant to! You stood me up Babe you fucking stood me up! So like a moron I came looking for you and look what I found. You having sex with some girl! I don't want to talk about this! Just please give me my fucking car back!" Now I was banging my fists on the counter instead of his face, because honestly if I truly went off on him, I'd never stop.

"Later, you can get it later." He turned his back to me and started to pour a cup coffee.

"Later? Are you fucking kidding me? No, I'm tired of the waiting game, I want my car now!" I demanded, shooting up like a rocket out of my chair. I grabbed his arm shouting like an animal. "Look at me; I can't stand talking to your back all the time! LOOK AT ME!" As soon as I turned him around, he grabbed me by the back of my hair and kissed me hard. Before I realized it, I slapped him hard across the face! I started hitting his him on the side of his face, kicking and shoving him, but he had me in a vice grip. He was staring me down with a deadly look. He caught my arms in mid swing as I continued to go after him and pinned them behind my back and lowered me on the floor. Thrashing like an animal, I tried to get out, but I was completely overpowered with his full weight on top of me. I just couldn't get out of his grip.

Babe finally came up for air growling, "So you saw me fucking some broad is that what you needed to see? You need a reminder that you have a little competition to act right?"

"Get off me! I hate you!" I spit at him screaming.

He ignored the spit and hissed, "You hate me? Liar! Admit it, you love me!"

"I hate you, I'm never going to sleep with you, ever!" I screamed with as much venom as I could muster.

"Really?" He said as he started to grind me. "Something tells me differently!"

Thrashing under his grip I screamed, "You gonna force me?"

"I never forced anyone in my life, I don't have to! You wanted to go with me the other night. TELL ME!"

"YOU'RE A PIECE OF SHIT! I hate you..." My voice trailed off because I was choking on my tears.

Completely serious, he growled up against my lips. "Honey, I want you more than anyone else, but I'll never ask or try again, this is it for us! That girl meant nothing, I just want you!"

How quickly we went from wine and roses to tears and fears! You're everything I knew you would be! He was like a vice grip squeezing my heart. I couldn't find my voice. *What, he wasn't trying again? I must be crazy that I would even want him to?* He saw the look on my face and returned to kissing me so hard I thought my teeth were going to break, but now I wasn't struggling anymore. In fact we both were holding each other. Getting lost in him, we ripped each other's clothes apart. *The men in the white coats need to come and lock me up, because I'm a loon!*

"Tell me, I can't go any further until you do. Tell me you love me. I want to hear you say it, because I love you," He panted over me.

Now I was crying harder, if that was even possible. I whispered, "Yes, I love you!" and in an angry, frantic, chaotic way we made love for the first time on his cold kitchen floor never breaking eye contact the whole time. He watched me intently, trying to make me feel every movement of his body. Babe was a pure animal holding my face in his hands until I started to roll my eyes and scream in submission. We moved together so fluidly, it was if we were made for each other. Babe fed off my ragged breathing, my moans and how I arched my back, but what he really wanted was to stare into my eyes.

Every time I closed them, he growled, "Open your eyes, look at me"

I tried, but I'm not good at following directions, I just wanted to do what comes naturally. I slid his thumbs from my jaw so I could bite and suck them as I moaned his name, "Oh Babe, Babe, oh my God Babe." The more I said his name the wilder he became. We were speeding together and as I screamed his name loudly, he came with me, in me. *What did you just do?*

Babe remained on top of me, sweaty and breathing hard and asked "You okay?"

Shaking my head, I moaned, "Ah, ah, oh my god, I think so. How about you?" As much as I didn't want to, I held onto him for dear life.

"Whew, I feel fucking great!" he moaned and started to kiss me again. Biting my lip he whispered, "Danielle, I love you, do you hear me? I love you." I shook my head mumbling my devotion to him incoherently.

"I heard, but is it real or just the sex talking?" *I am the biggest idiot and I deserve all the misery that's coming my way! You will be the death of me!*

Babe kissed every part of my face passionately, as he moaned; "I've loved you from the first day I met you, that's why I gave you so long to come around. By the end of the day, I'll look into your eyes as you come for me."

In a matter of minutes we were doing it again, this time with less force and more passion. It was pure and simple, completely sublime because he was on top focusing completely on what worked for me. Slowly bringing me closer and closer to where he wanted me. With his face in my neck, breathing into my hair, his raw sounds were the biggest turn on. I couldn't control myself; I began digging my nails into his back, as I cried hearing him say my name over and over again. I pushed Babe over the edge, making him follow me. Moments later, he was kissing my neck, while I gently cried. These were tears of passion, but he felt them and whispered, "Did I hurt you?"

"No!" I said burying my head in his neck.

"You okay then?" Babe asked so tenderly.

"Yeah, I think so." I answered unsure I could form a sentence because I was emotional.

Grinning at me nose to nose he said, "Me too!"

I wrapped my legs around him sobbing while I kissed him whispering. "You're mine, all mine! Do you understand? Babe if anything ever happens again, I'll never forgive you!"

"They'll never be a next time. I promise you, never." Babe whispered in my ear. After a few silent minutes he started to stir, "Let's go take a shower." He said as he helped me up to my feet. I was so amazed at how gentle he was, kissing and caressing me. My big tough guy was now a strong caring man in total control of the situation. Bending slightly, he picked me up and started to carry me into his bedroom.

Where was Babe hiding my whole life, this was the most amazing sex I'd ever had! Maybe you have to be on the verge of murdering someone to feel that extreme sexual attraction and satisfaction? I must be more fucked up then I ever thought possible! My head was buried in his neck and I asked him to wait because I wasn't sure if there were any remnants of last night's guest.

Confused he asked, "What's wrong?"

Whispering my fears to him, I asked, "Did you bring her in here last night?"

Babe cleared his throat. "No, you are the only one in my bed. She's a casual friend, nothing more. Don't make it more than what it was." I was about to say something but he sat down on the bed still holding me in his arms and continued, "I was so angry at you last night! What the fuck were you thinking talking to me about being with other guys? That was way out of line. Don't say anything, just listen, you can't do shit like that. Don't play with me, remember what I am, I'll walk away from you if you do that again no matter what. Teasing is one thing but that was out and out disrespectful. I'd kill someone else for that, you do know that right?" He paused to make sure I understood him clearly. "After I left, I ran into her and the rest is history. When you walked in, I sent her home. I found your car when she left; I didn't want to miss you, so I had Vinnie tow your car so you had to come back. We walked the beach looking for you until I went to work. I left the fucking door unlocked for you even with all the crazy shit going on, I didn't want you to be stuck locked out."

Stroking my hair, he was so gentle with me. "I wish you would have found me, in a strange way I dreamed you would." Tears were spilling down my cheek as I whispered, "You broke my heart Babe, you don't understand what this means to me. Cheating is the ultimate betrayal, I wouldn't have done that to you no matter how mad I was."

"I never thought you would stay out all night, let alone try to walk home." He said sounding completely sincere. "I wasn't cheating, you made it clear you didn't want to be with me, and she did. I guess we misunderstood each other, but now you gotta know if you ever go with anyone else after me, I'll never look at you again. You'll be dead to me. Get it? I never go back, never."

I sat silently, listening to his story, and in a crazy way, I understood. I couldn't even count the amount of guys I knew that would jump in a heartbeat to help me forget him if I ran into them upset. There were just two things I wanted to really know at this moment, who she was and if it was going to continue.

"Aren't you going to say anything?" He asked as he smoothed my hair away from my face and wiped the tears away.

I choked the words out. "Are you going to continue to see her and who is she?"

"No, I'm not going to continue to see her! You don't need to know her name. Come on we're not going there." He said as he held me tight.

Unable to forget and forgive so quickly I pressed the issue, "Yes we are."

"No, we're not." Babe said trying to close the chapter on the sordid details.

"How can you expect me to forget it? I want to know who she is."

"Listen from now on, it's different." Babe said talking page out of the wise guy deflect-at-all-cost playbook.

"Why?"

Finally, giving me what he thought I needed to hear, he said, "Why? Because I love you. Isn't that enough?"

"No, it's not." I said truthfully.

"It's going to have to be. We're not going to talk about that anymore, that's the past. Okay?" he said trying to move past the moment. He turned my palms upside down and kissed them. "Tell me what you want, I want to give you something you really want. What do you dream of?" *You don't get it; you can't buy your way out of this! I'm not that kind of girl!*

I stood up, about to walk away, but I just didn't want to fight anymore. "Babe what I want you can't buy, just do right by me. That's what I want, treat me good and love me."

His eyes focused strangely as if my simple statement was too foreign for him to process. No other girl would turn down all he was offering. "You're a nut, I love you more than you'll ever know."

Why should I give him up so someone else could have him? Random girls, middle of the night calls and crazy behavior was what I signed up for, so I had to man up and deal with it all, because regular guys are fucking cheaters too. Yes, I'll sell my soul to the devil to be with you! Falling back into his embrace, I allowed him to take control completely. Babe was kissing the top of my head and held my chin up when he whispered the rules that I already knew. This was not my first rodeo. "Okay? All right no more other people for both of us. No more dating at all, you're taken from now on. I'll treat you like a princess just do the right thing. I will do things for you, you can't even imagine! Anything you want, you'll get it! Believe me I really mean anything! Just don't fucking act up and disrespect me especially in front of people. Listen to me real good on this one because you'll never be the same, I promise you! If I ever find out you're with someone else, I will kill him in front of you! No questions asked, no excuses, and no favors. I will kill him!" The look in his eyes said more than his threats.

What, you think I don't know this already? I could write the fucking gangster girlfriend handbook! I gave him the respect and paused before I spoke. "How about what happens when I find you with someone?"

"No problem, because that will never happen." He beamed his big boy wise guy smile. "Oh, and ask me before you make plans. I'm first, got that? I want to know where you are and who you're with, just run everything by me first. Tell me everything, got it?" I shook my head in agreement, because I was going to break most of them anyway, except for cheating because I simply wasn't that way and I knew what he was capable of, so I pacified him while he continued. "I want you to take a shower with me." Pulling away, he slapped my ass and walked into the bathroom. Without another thought I followed him in and proceeded to have the best shower of my life. Babe's hands were so strong, and tender as he explored my body. He kissed my neck gently as he whispered, "Are you on anything?"

I hate this conversation! "You tell me first how you feel before I answer."

Babe held me up against him tightly wrapping his arms around me as he pulled my face up to meet his. "I just wanna know, but it doesn't matter. I won't be sorry if you get pregnant, I'll take care of you and the baby." He didn't flinch he was too perfect.

The tears flowed fast and furious as I kissed him hard. When I pulled back, I whispered, "I'm on the pill. Babe that was the exact present I needed but wouldn't ask for!" I couldn't have said anything more sincere and personal to him, and he knew it and I was rewarded with his soul; the real guy, the one I loved. We washed each other and made love repeatedly until we were prunes; followed by the most amazing mid-morning nap ever. Eventually, I jumped up like a bat out of hell when I heard him groan. I had forgotten where I was.

Sitting up, he asked puzzled, "Hey what's wrong?"

"I...I forgot where I was. You scared the shit out of me. That sound, it freaked me out," I said as I wrapped the blanket around myself, all of the sudden I was self-conscious, being naked.

"Come here, lay down. You can't be scared with me; I'll take care of you. I'm going to make those nightmares go away." He gently coaxed me back into his arms and held me protectively until I felt safe again. Sleeping with Babe was life altering; at least for me. It was much more than physical, it was as if I'd just given him my soul, what I felt for Babe could easily push me over the brink of insanity. Add in all the craziness, forget about it. I've been shot at, held up, tortured by people, forced to jump into moving garbage trucks, almost run over, and couldn't leave my house without an escort, all because of his "things," and then there were frigging hoe bag girls everywhere. To make matters worse, I had my own hang-ups, and now I was madly in love with the exact person I swore I would never date again! All of it and the situations plagued and tortured me in my waking and sleeping hours!

I was just a nice girl who worked and partied hard, was I ready for all this? I wondered how he could live this nightmare daily being hunted like an animal by former friends, not knowing who may have switched sides during the night. Crew jumping became the reality, along with guys becoming rats for the Feds, joining team America. I was used to the life but not the war; this was a whole new animal for me. One thing was for sure, I would always, and I mean always love certain guys as brothers no matter what side they were on, because taking sides was part of what they did in the life. It had nothing to do with me, and I was going to make sure it stayed that way.

Babe stirred, holding me even closer than before, as if right on cue to push all the fears to the back of mind. His scent, warm body and mighty grip held me in check until I was able to drift back to sleep.

CHAPTER 20

....

Come-Fuck-Me Look

It was early afternoon when I awoke to Babe kissing my back. Giggling, I said, "Hmm, that's feels so good, but I'm not sure if I can do it again. It's only been four times today already."

"Are you sure? Just lay there and we'll see." He said smoothly as he gently rubbed my back and shoulders moving over them and down until, he reached his goal. He instinctively knew I wanted him to explore all of me, and explore he did. Babe moaned, caressed, and straddled me, resting his nakedness against me, and before I knew it, it was happening again. I couldn't do anything but lie still, which, as it turns out was all he wanted me to do anyway. Gently nibbling my neck, he started to pull my hair and his desire was growing more every minute. Babe licked and kissed my neck, whispering and moaning as he buried himself in me. I was chewing the pillow as I arched my back, until we both fell apart and came with each other. He was holding my hips so tight and had his legs intertwined with mine to the point we were both lost and I whispered, "I love you!" over and over again until it ended.

Babe was the perfect lover, he made me feel alive and every way he moved was more amazing than I could have ever imagined. A few minutes later, he kneaded my arms and shoulders asking, "Hungry yet? Come on we have to get up."

"Actually, I'm starved! What do you have?"

"Go check, I'll be there in a minute, I have to make a quick call."

I got up and walked into the kitchen on a mission, searching for something delicious. As soon as I saw the to-go containers in the fridge, I knew they weren't there the day before. They were from her. No way was I going to eat their left overs, I tossed everything in the garbage. *Goodbye whoever you are and your Chinese food.*

Moments later, Babe walked in spying the containers in the pail, and quickly switching gears he said, "Get dressed, let's go out and eat before we have to go to work."

"I don't have any clothes. I need to go home."

"No, put on my sweats and a shirt, you look sexy in my clothes. Plus you have a set of panties and bra here, we'll get all the bags later."

"Good grief! Let me see what I can do." I said as I disappeared in the bedroom and started to pull myself together. Within twenty minutes I came out wearing his sweats rolled and a white t-shirt tied up in a knot and button down shirt completely opened. My hair was wild and my freshly applied makeup all added to my look of happiness and the just-fucked look.

Grinning like he could toss me again instead of eating, he said, "Nice! You look like you just got laid!"

Scarlet red, I asked, "Do you want me to change?"

"No way, I like it! As long as you're with me you can sport the just-fucked look, because I'm the one who did it."

"I couldn't wash my hair, you only have shitty shampoo and no conditioner."

"What do I know about that stuff? I've been washing my hair with crap for years in jail. Buy whatever you want." He slipped on his leather jacket, grinning at me. "Let's go, I know a little place by the water."

Grabbing my new mink, I put on a big pair of black glasses and we jumped in his car and took off. What a sight we were, pulling into eat at a little restaurant by the water. He ordered one of everything and we dove in like we had been rescued from a deserted island. Unlike most girls, I never pretended to be a lightweight, and Babe loved watching me eat like I was going to the electric chair.

"Oh Fats, you ready to go to work tonight or do you need off?" He asked as we ate.

"No, I'm fine I can go. Hey, where is Nero? I didn't see him."

"He's at my mom's. I 'm not here all the time and it would be unfair to leave him alone so long." He said as he tried each dish. "I have a couple of stops to make unless you want to take the ride?"

"I'll go with you but I have to get dressed, I can't go to work like this, can I?" I asked unsure of what the rules were about looking like I had been fucked all morning by this picky wise guy.

"Sure, you look cute." He said obviously approving of my appearance.

"I do?"

"Yes, you do and you know I like the way you look."

"Really?" I started to toy with him as I slipped my foot out of my shoes burying my toes in his lap.

"Nice! Watch out down there."

Now I had both feet buried in his lap and I wiggled my toes as I watched his face turn colors. He was trying to concentrate on our meal, but he became increasingly distracted. Every so often someone would come over to say hello or to see if we needed anything. Babe remained seated and never got up when he spoke because he was holding my feet firmly in place, and then he turned grinning as he growled. "Stop teasing me or we are going home again."

"Is that a threat or a promise?" I teased as I leaned in and kissed his soft lips, licking them lightly before I sat back grinning.

His eyes darkened and he said in a low voice, "I never threaten, I make good on every promise. If we go home, you're not going anywhere! I'll keep you all night long and you won't be able to walk tomorrow."

"Geez Louise, take me to work!" I said, sounding afraid of more sex, joking with him.

With that, we settled up and left. Driving back to the neighborhood was fun and relaxing. We hit the avenue and made a few stops along the way. I said hello to everyone and just enjoyed the afternoon sun. Finally, we arrived at the bar and I leaned over to kiss him goodbye, but he wouldn't have it and walked me in. I was self conscious, walking in dressed in his clothes, but as long as I looked cute, it was okay. What I wasn't prepared for was the crowd; the bar was packed with the guys. Each one took noticed the outfit and either laughed or shot Babe a questioning look. I said my hellos as I walked behind the bar. Within a few minutes, Babe came over to the opening and put his hand on my lower back and kissed me goodbye. "You're going to close when I get off from work, I'll pick you up."

Smiling, I said, "Have my car delivered and I'll meet you if you can't get here."

"We'll see," He said leaning in again, kissing me hard.

"Later Babes!" And with that, he left, and just as quickly, the barrage of questions started. The first face I saw was James and he was smirking like the cat that ate the canary and looked like he was up for a wiseass, ball-breaking, but good-natured time.

"So? Anything new with you?" James teased.

Trying to be aloof I said, "No, why?"

"You're wearing guy's clothes, that's why! You look...well you look like you had some night Pal." He said roaring as he slapped the bar with his bear paw hand.

"You don't know the half of it, but it's nothing compared to you in my elevator, so yes, to answer your question, something happened and I'm very happy!"

"I told you to just give him a shot, he's a good guy. Hey, by the way, nice mink! You must have been pretty good, Pal, to get that!" He said as I hit his arm laughing over the comment and recent events. I smiled thinking about my earrings.

The night started to roll and I quickly put the day's events on the back burner. Before I knew it, it was late. *Where's Babe?* It wasn't like him to be late, so I beeped him. He called back quickly telling me he was still around the corner at the club playing cards, and needed a little more time. I started to check over the liquor inventory, when I realized an hour had passed and he still wasn't there. I decided to take matters into my own hands. I went into the bathroom carrying my mink and an extra pair of heels from my fetish stash that I kept under the bar for those that rather drink out of my shoes than a glass. Reapplying my makeup, I took off all my clothes, slipped on the heels and the mink. I looked smoking hot as I locked up the bar and snuck around the corner. His car was there along with all the others. I stopped to say hello to the smokers outside and made my way inside to find him sitting at table playing cards just like he said.

Bending down I kissed him and ran my hands through his hair, "You on a roll?"

"Nah, just having fun, sorry I got caught up." He said not really paying attention to me.

"Oh that's okay, you sure you're not playing anything too serious?" I asked as I playfully tugged his ear.

"No, why?" He said as he looked up at me and noticed I was all dolled up. He started to smile when I stood in front of him, cornered so only he could see the front of me and I opened the coat to reveal I had not one stitch of clothes on.

He grabbed the front of the coat and quickly closed it as he asked, "Are you fucking crazy?"

This guy had no idea what he got himself into; I was really ballsy and crazy! Holding the collar closed, I grinned as I leaned down to kiss him. "Still want to play with the boys or would you rather play with me?"

He turned, laughing, and said. "I fold, gotta go!" Pushing the cards forward to reveal he had a full house, all the guys looked at him like he was nuts. Babe kissed and hugged them quickly as I walked towards the door holding the coat closed grinning from ear to ear.

When he got to Phil, Babe leaned in. Phil held him for a second talking quietly. Standing sideways, I smiled with my right ankle up and eyebrow up as I chimed in, just in case Phil was going to try and change his mind. "If it's okay Phil, I really NEED Babe!" Then I moved my coat a little, threatening Babe that I might open it completely. His face flamed red for a moment and he looked at me silently saying, don't you dare! I loved seeing him squirm, so I adjusted the collar just a bit challenging him.

Fumbling with his words, he said, "Phil, I'm making it an early night."

Phil was a man about town and got the hint. "Sure you guys have fun!"

Babe made it over to me in a flash and held my elbow escorting me out the door and into his parked car. As soon as he closed the door, he turned to me and started to laugh. "Are you crazy? Where are your clothes?"

"I lost them in a card game!" I said laughing.

"Funny, better not." He said giving me a look, but with the biggest grin as if I was his first real meal after being released.

"Hey, you kept me waiting, I had to take matters into my own hands. I wouldn't really flash the guys anyway, just you. You taking me home?" I asked knowing I didn't really want to go there, but would play it by ear.

"No, after that show you and the mink are coming home with me!" He said as he ran his hand over the fur covering my leg.

"Okay, sounds great, but I need some clothes and stuff. Can we swing by my house first?" I asked.

"Sure thing, but make it fast before I rip that coat to shreds!" He joked as he made a U-turn and drove towards my apartment.

Before we got out the car, I thought I'd give Babe a present. "Babe, do me a favor?"

He turned his head, as he was about to open his car door. "Sure what's up?"

I bit my lip. "Put your seat back."

He turned his head twice, and started to grin. "Its back as far it goes."

Leaning over I started to unzip his pants, and before he could react, I was on top of him. Babe held my waist as I wrapped the mink around us. As quickly as I started is as quick as I finished, leaving him looking raped. Before I climbed off, he kissed me hard.

"So you still think playing cards is more fun than playing with me?" I giggled as I licked his earlobe.

He grunted as he shook his head and tried to smooth my hair. "Come on you animal, let's grab your shit and go home!" *Home, that sounds perfect!*

We bounced into the building laughing like school kids. It seemed like I was gone for so long. We walked in and were startled to see the condition; everything was trashed. Someone must have broken into my apartment. Babe put his arm in front of me and pulled out a piece; he started to walk room to room to see if anyone was still there. But of course, no one was and there wasn't any real damage just everything tossed about. It looked worse than it was. All my jewelry, furs, designer handbags and electronics were all still there.

"Why would someone do this to me? They didn't take anything." I said more as a statement then a question.

"Come on grab what you want, let's go." Babe was red hot and wanted to leave, presumably to do whatever guys like him do during these situations.

"What should I take? I have a headache, what the hell is happening?" I sunk to my knees in the pile of furs and cried my eyes out. Everywhere I looked I saw my beautiful things thrown all over. My coat was off, and I felt Babe try to slip a jogging suit jacket on my naked body. Slowly, he tried to lift me up, but I panicked and scrambled around looking for my box. "Wait. I want my jewelry, I keep it in a travel case." Within 20 minutes I had my Pullman luggage packed to the brim and in the process straighten up. Babe was standing by my answering machine that was blinking like crazy.

"I think you should check your messages."

Without thinking about who would have called I said, "Okay hit the button." There were several messages from my girlfriends, then ten hang-ups back to back and finally two messages from guys, One was asking me out, and the other to meet up as friends, only Babe didn't know that.

Thank God he didn't call me Lucky! How did Carl get my number? Trying to pretend he didn't just hear the message I focused on the hang-ups. "That's weird, I never get hang-ups."

"You're kidding me right, who the fuck was that? Two guys?" He asked shooting me a beady-eyed look.

Grinning because I had an innocent opportunity to stick it to him, I answered like a ball buster. "You have your fans, I have mine Babe. Don't worry, one I never went out with, yet! If you're a good guy I won't either! And the other is just a friend!" Raising his eyebrow, he was about to get crazy until I started to laugh and wrapped my arms around his neck giggling. "Stop, he's been asking me out for a while, way before you. He's a big tipper!" Sometimes a little lie can help smooth things over. I just remembered his friendly female call and added, "He's an old neighborhood friend, you know, just like yours!"

"Ha-ha, you're a riot! What kind of tips are we talking about?" He saw I was laughing, that this was just stupid teasing and eased up. "You talk to this guy, you do that tomorrow. Come on let's get out of here." He grabbed my bags and we left. We flew back to Breezy. As we got out of the car, Babe was quiet and on edge looking everywhere. Once we were in the house, he finally relaxed a bit. "Okay, listen unpack some stuff, take a drawer, whatever you need, but leave some clothes in your bag. We're leaving tomorrow."

"Oooh, you're giving me a drawer? Where we going?" I asked teasingly, trying to break the tension.

"I'm not sure yet, but you're not going back to work for a few days. We're leaving your car out back, okay?"

"I'm scared." I said as I stood over my bag contemplating what I was going to unpack.

"Good, it's okay to be scared, then you'll be aware of your surroundings." He said, trying to make a point without alarming me too much.

"Before we go tomorrow I want to go to a bank and get a safety deposit box, I can't imagine someone stealing my jewelry."

Babe patted the bed for me to come close as he asked, "Hey bring your jewelry over here."

"Umm, why?" *Oh come on, this is my private memory box.*

"Peeper, I'm on parole I need to know what you have there, I can't get jammed up over this stuff."

Nervously, I tucked my hair behind my ear and shimmied up next to him pulling the case with me. I positioned myself with it on my lap and slowly turned the dials until they all clicked and the latches opened. The top level was filled with rings, the next with bracelets, with two pull out sections for earrings. The necklaces were all placed in the bottom drawer, but there was a whole area filled with my rainy day money. Like a little girl playing with princess jewelry, I stacked the rings on my fingers, one on top of the other filling up every available space.

Babe's eyes were wide as he was momentarily speechless. I moved my hand in front of his face, as he was motionless sitting back against the pillows propped up in bed. He looked at my hands and back to me over and over a few times before he spoke. "Dannie, what the fuck is this?"

"Well, it's my jewelry and rainy day stash." After, I took out my rubber band stacks and neatly piled them up, and nonchalantly said, "Every time I make an extra grand I cash it into hundred's and add it to the box. Whatever I declare, I deposit in the bank and the rest I split between a safety deposit box in LA and pay my rent early with it." Proud of my hard work, I added, "My rent is paid up for a year. I also have about a thousand in reserve with each utility company too. I tried to give them more, but they started mailing me refund checks!" I had to giggle at the situation as I watched Babe pick up my monster bracelet and examined it with the eye of a jeweler and thief. When he didn't say anything, I continued. "I need about another ten thousand to feel comfortable. I should also mention I own both of my cars outright. Lately I've been thinking about buying my apartment."

Babe twirled the bracelet around. "And what about this stuff?"

I started to squirm, because I just knew he wasn't going to like hearing about the jewelry. "Well, that piece is from my ex-boyfriend, why?"

"You have some nice costume pieces here."

My eyes widen as I blurted out, "That's not fake!"

I could tell he knew, but was just picking at the scab. "You sure about that, Peeper? Seriously, you know you can't keep this stuff here, I can't get jammed up for it."

Turning white, I blurted out, "Well it's mine, I just can't leave it in my apartment to get robbed next time! Like I said before, I need to get a box at a bank ASAP!"

Babe ran his hands through his hair, not liking what I said. "I told you, I'll take care of that. You won't be getting robbed again!"

"The reality is that my apartment, in a doorman building that has tons of locks and an alarm system was tossed, not robbed. Let's not even mention that my alarm never went off, someone knew the code. Whatever they were looking for, wasn't there, and that was either you or me, and since it's my place it was probably me!" I blew out some air, fingering the jewelry, before continuing, "Listen, can you take me to the bank tomorrow?"

"First thing! Now that's settled, I gotta know is this all from guys?"

I turned beet red, as I mumbled, "No, I bought some of it." I played with the rings on my gypsy fingers. I put my hand up to inspect them, and without thinking I asked, "What do you think this hand is worth?"

"Well if they're real."

"Everything in this box is all real!" I cut him right off, raising my eyebrow and grabbing his hand for support as I leaned over the bed to grab my handbag on the floor. My diamond tester was at the bottom and I fished for it so I could prove to Babe my prized possessions were all real. I pulled the top off, exposing the needle and turned on the battery; I started to push it up against each stone. I'd checked everything many times, so I knew it was real, but I wanted Babe to know. I handed him the tester and put a pile on his lap to pick from. Again each one came up as genuine. Babe became fixated on the engagement rings, looking closely at each one. "One, two, three, four, five, six...you have six engagement rings here. Is there anything you want to tell me?"

"Nope, not a thing, but if you have a question, ask me, don't beat around the bush."

"Why would guys give you jewelry like this unless you're in a relationship with them? I gotta ask. How many guys have you been with?"

"Date or have a relationship with?"

"Is there a difference in numbers?"

Tilting my head, I asked, "Well, how many people have you been with?"

"No one, I'm a virgin!" Babe laughed more at himself than me.

"Umm yeah okay, I believe that one!" I elbowed him giggling. "Anyway, how about how many people have you fucked, but didn't date?"

"I have amnesia, so move on."

"Yup, I suffer from the same affliction so lets not talk about this." I started to slip the rings off my fingers, but turned and looked him right in the eyes. "Babe, listen. I don't fuck around, that's all you need to know. I've never been a blowjob and no one can say a bad word, sexually about me that's real. I know guys have lied about being with me, but everyone knows they were blowing smoke out of their asses! I know it bothers you, but I'm not a virgin." Babe tried to break in, but I stopped him. "Also, I've never dated assholes except one guy named Joe AND I'm sure you heard all about me robbing his car and the stupid shit that went on. The whole neighborhood jokes about it. He was a huge cheater, and I'm sure I only knew a quarter of how bad he actually was, but he embarrassed me publicly by fucking everyone! We were a 'match and gasoline' couple from the get go! Like I said, I'm sure you know everything I'm telling you and everyone I went out with, but just hear this from me; I'm a good girl, and my ex's only have nice things to say about me. Some jewelry is from customers, even one of the engagement rings, so don't get hung up on stuff like that. The others are from relationships that didn't work out." I winked, trying to break the tense mood. "I told you I was a keeper, well this proves it!" I giggled nervously. *If you can't handle the truth, then let's not waste time.*

"I'm not saying a word, not because I don't have more questions, but because I believe you. We should have had a serious conversation before getting to this point, there's a lot we don't know about each other. Just know I don't want to hear about your ex's anymore after tonight and I never want you to wear their stuff either. You're going to need a new box for me to fill."

I took a deep breath; this is a tough conversation for any guy to have let alone a street guy. "I don't need a thing! Don't go crazy getting me anything."

He cut me off, "Oh and another thing just learn to say thank you and take what I give you!"

I shook my head rolling my eyes at him. "Fine, thank you! But listen I know we didn't talk about it before we had sex, but we should have. I really didn't expect to get caught up in the moment and not use protection. I kind of think of that as the guy's job!" I shoved his arm playfully as I continued, "When you came in me, I was too caught up to ask why you did that, and I was even more oblivious to you not using condom, which I swear by. So let me ask you something, am I going to catch anything from you?"

He put my hand to my heart and said, "Hand to God I'm all good!" He winked asking, "Are you?"

I mimicked him, and said, "I'm all good too. Just like the paperwork said! But it was nice to know that if I wasn't on the pill, you would be okay with it."

Now it was his turn to be embarrassed, as he avoided the conversation, by asking, "So you're the marrying kind of girl, and you're in your twenties, so you must have started to date when you were born for this collection, hmm?"

My face turned stormy looking down at the box. "No, I got my first one when I turned eighteen. For my birthday in fact, but it didn't work out." I picked up a huge seven-karat ring and twirled it on my fingertip. "This is the first one. Its beautiful, I still love it! But I won't ever sell it even though I know it's the best piece I have. You know some are cocktail rings and some are engagement rings...right?"

"For a guy not to ask for that kind of ring back, he had to be a street guy!" He bent over and took a loop out of his night table, looking at it closer. "You got that right, this is some stone!"

I beamed with pride as I said, "I fucking know it! I know jewelry. Jewelry, property, and oil are the only things worth holding on to as an investment. I have the paperwork for that one, with the serial number engraved in the stone."

Babe didn't say much for a few minutes while he rolled the ring around in his hand. I started to pack up my treasure. Babe handed me the ring and leaned over to put his loop away. When I was about to close the combination locks, he stopped me. "Listen put this in the box. It's five-G's, so your half way to your goal."

I just stared at his open palm and then back to his face. "No! I don't want your money!"

"When are you going to learn not to tell me what to do with my fucking money? Take it and do what I told you to do!"

I just held the money as I narrowed my eyes. *He's buying my forgiveness! This is a payoff to forget all about the girl! Does he really think this will work? Please, a fucking car couldn't make me forget! I will get over it, because of the baby comment, and he knows that, but I'm not letting him know he's off the hook so fast!*

I genuinely smiled and was grateful as I kissed his cheek softly. "Thank you!"

He broke the silence, "Pack a bag for a few days, you're not going to work. I'm taking you far away, until I can sort this out."

"Ooo, where are we going? I'd love to go away and spend some time with alone with you!"

He put his arm around me trying to comfort me, as I looked disappointed. "Listen honey, I'm taking you, but I can't stay. I have to go to the half way house this weekend. But pay attention, I just gave you some cash, put it away, before you loose it."

"Oh good grief, when you talk to me like I'm stupid, I really get scared." I said as I grabbed his hand tightly as if I were a child looking for that it's-going-to-be-all-right smile.

Babe kissed my head gently and pulled me to stand up. "Come on let's get settled in and go to bed." I followed his advice and unpacked some clothes, and started to undress. "Nice! Come on come over here I want to really look at you, especially after the big show with the coat." Babe said with a big grin as he stood by the bed. "I guess you liked it?"

Smiling from ear to ear, I said, "I love it! It's absolutely perfect!"

"Good, it looks good on you too." He put his hands in his pocket and pulled out something shiny. "Come here."

I walked slowly towards him; there wasn't any part of me that was hidden. When I reached him, I reached out and touched his face. Babe kissed my hand and gently slipped a beautiful diamond watch on my wrist. He looked at it for a moment and then started to kiss my arm moving up slowly until he reached my neck. I glanced down to look at the diamonds and saw it was a Patek Philippe. He whispered in my ear, "Do you like it?"

Turning my head sideways to give him a better angle to kiss my neck, I purred my thanks. "Oh Babe of course, I love everything you give me! Thank you!" *You're making me dizzy with the gifts! I hope you're not trying to compete with the ghosts of my ex's!*

Ever so slowly, he moved towards the other side of my neck as he held my shoulders. "It's beautiful, like you, and it's only the beginning. I'm going to enjoy spoiling you!" I could feel he was removing his shirt as he moaned slightly unzipping his pants. As they dropped his beeper went off and the phone rang at the same time. Groaning, he reached for the phone catching it before the machine picked up with one hand and grabbed the beeper with the other. His whole facial expression changed as he walked out of the room talking on the phone.

I curled up on the bed and turned on the TV as I looked at the watch. It was gorgeous and very expensive; Babe was showering me with amazing gifts, but I never asked for this. *All I want is you!* As I drifted into twilight, he returned and started to get dressed. "Babe, I'm waiting." I said dreamily, as I patted the bed.

"Got to run, be back later." I could plainly see he was not my boyfriend at the moment; he was now one of them.

That moment came quicker than I thought it would. The phone calls that will make him drop everyone and everything. He chose them, not me. "Really? Now, come on stay with me a little longer. Tell them you got stuck in traffic!" I said, as I tried to pull him down to me.

Grabbing my arms, he pushed me off roughly. "Hey stop! Wake up and grow up, I gotta go!" He said, so easily it shocked me.

Completely taken aback, I stared at him in total disbelief that he could just slip a thirty grand watch on my wrist and, like the flip of a switch, become a cold-hearted prick. Without saying a word, I got up and slipped on a pair of sweats without looking at him and stalked into the kitchen. In matter of a minute he was walking out the door mumbling some sort of lame goodbye. I stood in the kitchen, stunned, alone, feeling like a complete fool thinking about what just happened. Crawling up on the couch, I started rethinking every move I had made in the last six months.

CHAPTER 21

Grow Up

Instead of waking intertwined and facing each other, I woke up cold and alone on the couch. Rubbing the morning out of my eyes, I wandered into the bedroom to find it as empty as it was last night; he never came home. I took a shower, made breakfast and waited, and waited, and waited for two days. Babe left me alone to worry, with not even a phone call. In fact, the phone never rang at all. Chain-smoking, I watched TV non-stop, hoping I wouldn't see a news flash, while the hours dragged on like months. I stopped beeping him after the first day, knowing he wasn't going to answer me. *Did he get locked up? Did someone shoot him? Was he hurt or God forbid dead?* Every possible scenario was running through my head.

Around 3AM on the third morning, I felt completely abandoned, trapped and desperate. Thinking Babe might slip in and out without me knowing, I put my pillow up against the front door and slept there wrapped in the mink just in case he came home. In my dreams, I heard the same footsteps approaching the door, but it had only been wishful thinking so far. Then, there was the tap on the glass that was different enough to make me open my eyes; I turned to find Babe with Sally and Vinnie waiting for me to move so they could open the door. The expression on his face said it all; he was pissed finding me like that.

Maybe he forgot I was even there, who knows, but he definitely didn't expect to see me sleeping on the floor by the door. He walked in like he had gone out for milk. Giving me a quick peck on my cheek, he breezed past into his office with the guys trailing behind as they all said their hellos, closing the door, leaving me alone again. Obviously, I wasn't going to get an explanation; he was in full gangster mode. Without saying a word, I grabbed a piece of paper from the island and scribbled a quick note to him, "I grew up!" Tossing it on the bed, I grabbed my bag with my jewelry case, the mink and walked out. Jumping in my car, I drove like the wind crying all the way back to the world that I left in complete shambles, all because I fell in love with a card carrying member of the mafia.

My beeper started to vibrate non-stop, but I didn't bother to look at it. I didn't care anymore, nothing mattered except that I had to figure out what I was doing with my life, because no good would come if I stayed on this emotional rollercoaster wearing a love sick blindfold. It was time to take off the rose colored glasses and either stop caring so much that it hurt, or give back the presents and walk away. If I wasn't locked up, none of this would matter, my own life would occupy my time and I probably wouldn't even notice his disappearing acts as much. Pulling up in front of my building, I double-parked and ran inside for a minute. As I returned, a car peeled around the corner and stop short in front of me. Two guys I knew, Gene and Nick jumped out and approached my car door, but I had enough, I threw the car in reverse and took off leaving their toes barely intact. Panicked, I grabbed at my bag and felt for my jewelry case. *Whew it's here.*

Unsure of what to do or where to go, I drove to Sunset Park to a pay phone that I used to use when I didn't want anyone from my world to see or hear me. Checking my beeper, I saw all the numbers were his. Disgusted with myself, I cleared the memory and ripped the battery out disabling it. I sat outside of the phone booth thinking and crying. *Nope, I'm not calling him or anyone! Fuck him! Let's see how Babe feels being abandoned without an explanation!*

My mind was made up; I wasn't making anything easy for him. *No calls, no messages, no nothing! You want to know where I am, fucking find me!* Throwing the car in gear, I drove with the music blasting. Two hours later, I pulled into Caesar's Palace in Atlantic City, feeling exhausted from everything. Checking into the hotel, I paid for everything in cash so I would be untraceable. I had to leave a five hundred room deposit, but who cares; I was flush with cash thanks to his five-G's. It was my time now. I took a long bubble bath and when I felt like a prune, I stepped out and wrapped myself in the robe. Feeling mentally shot, I lay down and slept the kind of dead sleep that only comes when you are exhausted to your core.

It was about 9PM when I woke up, feeling refreshed and starved. I pulled on my sweats, put some makeup on and headed to the casino floor. I couldn't care less what I looked like, especially compared to the stretched pants and over sized t-shirt crowd. Slipping my big black glasses on, I walked around scouting the tables until I found one that gave me the winning feeling. Pulling up a seat, I dropped a grand and the dealer smiled big at me.

I looked over to find my old friend, Pat the Bookmaker sitting there. *Jesus Christ!*

He smiled and gave me a big hug. "Hey sweetheart! What are you doing here so far away from home?"

He must have thought I was joking, but I was dead serious. "I ran away! Let's play cards and see if I learned anything hanging around you guys!"

"Bring it on! Hey, you talk to Johnny lately?" Johnny was my dear old friend from childhood, except it was my childhood, not his. Johnny was sixty-five when I was eighteen and proposed to me after whisking me away to LA to be with him. He was a big wise guy and had adored me since I was a child, roaming the streets of Little Italy. All my monster jewelry came from my mobster ex-boyfriend. It would have been so easy to marry him since his wife had died, so he was really single, just not gangster single. We would have had an amazing life, but it's not the right thing to take someone's love and adoration when it's not reciprocated. I was never a gold digger and just couldn't marry him. So I kept Johnny as a close friend, my backup big guns so to speak.

"No, but I might call him tonight. Who knows! Don't get mad at me, I love you, but I'm just in a bad mood." I said.

"Does it have anything to do with all those bruises on you?" He stood up and looked at me closer moving my hair away from my neck. "God! What's going on with you?"

Annoyed, I pulled my hair back over my shoulder. "Nothing's wrong!"

"You looked like you've been choked! Who the fuck would do this?" He said with a look of disgust and concern.

"Pat, stop it's not what you think." I tried to brush it off and minimize the purple finger marks all over my neck.

"Then what is it? You either got choked, because someone grabbed you or you were fooling around. Either way honey, this ain't good. Which one is it?" He said shaking his head nervously moving the toothpick from one side of his mouth to the other.

Completely scarlet red I snapped, "No one grabbed me!"

Retreating to his seat, he mumbled, "These young guys like all this kinky shit! You know better than to ever let anyone leave marks on you. Who's your guy? What's his name? What the fuck were you thinking?" Doing an about face, he grabbed my arm and pulled up my sleeve, not seeing any track marks he sat back down again. "Drugs and this crap go together. If I find out you're doing drugs I'll kick the shit out you myself! Got that?"

I could either be pissed or flattered, so I chose flattery. "Pat, I'm NOT into drugs! I'm too cheap for that, plus I can't even sing Karaoke because I can't embarrass myself in public let alone be a junky! But I love you for watching out for me. I'll introduce you to Babe soon, if I keep him." I said winking at him. No way could I explain Babe's sleeping habits to Pat. He would have thought the guy was nuts, so it was easier to have him think he was into rough sex.

"Soon! Got it! And stop this kinky shit! I'm just saying John is a gentleman and would never leave marks on you. You should have stayed with him! Just saying!"

"You're a good friend to John, I love you for that and for being a good friend to me too! You'll like him, he's a standup guy, but now lets play cards so I can take all your fucking money!" Without realizing it, everyone at the table had stopped playing during our conversation and now was ready to resume the game.

A half-naked waitress dressed like a roman goddess took my order, quickly returning with a bottle of champagne. I must have cut a real sight with choke marks wearing a Patek Philippe watch, huge diamond earrings, drinking pink champagne and dressed in a tracksuit. I drank, playing better than I thought I would, because I was up a few grand as I let the hours slip away. Before I knew it, it was 4AM and I hadn't eaten anything and was getting smashed. Now I had way too much expensive jewelry on to be wandering around, and too much cash on me for my own good. Time to go before I get stupid, but first I needed to find the cage to wire the money into my account so I didn't lose it.

As I filled out the slip, I noticed a few guys were looking at me. Finishing up, I slipped on my black glasses and walked towards the hotel elevators. One guy called out to me by name "Hey Dannie, stop I want to talk to you!" I never looked back or acknowledged any of them; I flashed my room card to the guard to gain access to the elevator bank and walked briskly into an open car. As I turned to hit the button to close the door, the guys made it past the guard calling out as they advanced towards me. "Stop, Dannie! Stop!" I smiled as the door closed, cutting them off. *FUCK THEM, FUCK THEM ALL!*

Once the door opened on my floor, I high-tailed it into my room and called the front desk, requesting another room on a different floor immediately. They said I could come get the key at once. Slipping the do not disturb sign on the knob, turning up the TV volume, I grabbed the mink and left. It was like playing beat the clock taking the elevator to the hotel lobby to pickup the key just as the guys from the casino found my original room. As soon as I opened the door, the phone was already ringing, and I answered to find a panic-stricken desk clerk. "Excuse me, but there are three VERY large men who are looking for you outside your other room."

"I have no idea what you're talking about. I don't know anyone like that." I said as I chuckled.

"They are demanding to get into your room. What would you like me to do?" He said with a high pitched voice.

"Nothing! I don't know anyone like you're describing." I answered, trying to sound intimidating.

"Excuse me, but are you sure?" He asked, sounding frighten to his core. They must have been right next to him, because they heard our conversation and I could hear him get smacked and cry out for them to stop.

I didn't flinch, even though I should have felt sorry for the poor guy, but I just didn't give in. "Of course I'm sure! Good night!" I said as I hung up.

Jumping on the bed, I turned on the TV and pulled the mink over me. My phone continued to ring and never stopped; the calls were constant. I ignored it all until the knocking starting at 6AM. First it was a light wrap, but then someone was pounding on my door. Totally annoyed, I put the chain on the door, flipped on the light and opened it, expecting to see the guys from the casino. They were there all right along with ten other guys and

Babe, who was standing in front of the door looking like he was going to kill me.

I tried to slam the door closed, but he put his foot in and pushed the door forward ripping the bracelet the chain was attached to right out of the door. So much for a fucking security chain and security door for that matter! That was it, he was in and I was trapped. Looking past him before he slammed the door closed, I could see the guest across the hall opened his door to see what was going on, only to be rudely told to mind his own fucking business. Calmly, I sat on the bed and lit a cigarette waiting for him to say what ever was so important he had to break my door for. The calmer I was the more crazy he was getting, pacing the floor screaming at me.

"What the fuck do you think you're doing?"

I said nothing, just took deep drags.

"I asked you a question, answer me!"

Again nothing.

"You fucking kidding me right? You're going to answer me!"

Nothing.

"Don't ignore me, I'm asking you to explain yourself!"

Nothing.

"You answer me NOW! I'm not asking, I'm telling YOU!"

Nothing.

He grabbed the cigarette out of my hand snapped and tossed it, but I only lit another that he smacked out of my mouth without touching me. Immediately, he knew that was too close for comfort and momentarily snapped out of his mood. "Oh come on now, stop this nonsense."

As far as I was concerned, it was like smacking me. I very quietly got up and picked up my bag and walked to the door. He stood staring incredulously at me as I opened it and walked past all the guys towards the elevator bank. *My mind is made up, I'm done!*

Babe stormed into the hallway and called to me again. "I said stop! Where the fuck do you think you're going? You better listen to me NOW!"

Everyone stared unsure if they should do something as I ignored him, until he the magic word- "now." I turned and pointed my finger at him. "No, you did not just say NOW to me! I don't know who you think YOU'RE talking to, but FUCK YOU!"

One young guy, Peter grabbed my left arm stopping me in my tracks. I turned and tried unsuccessfully to pry my arm away, but couldn't so I smacked him hard across the face. "Get your fucking hands off me! Don't you ever touch me!"

I hit him again because he wouldn't let go. I tried to pull back, but he was practically breaking my arm. Just as I swung at him again now with a solid fist instead of an open hand, I connected breaking his nose as he backhanded me really hard knocking me to the ground. The sound of his nose breaking was unmistakable. I've been in quite a few fistfights, and been hit before, fighting my way out of situations, but this was the hardest crack of my life. He was 6 foot 4 and 350 pounds of solid, juiced-up steroid muscle, but at least I know his nose broke and we all heard it! That was it;

all hell broke loose. Babe ripped the kid off me and beat him to a pulp as I held my face crying.

Once Peter fell to the floor, Babe was kicking the guy's head in while he growled. "Don't you ever touch my girl! You got that? NEVER TOUCH HER AGAIN!"

I seized the moment and started to get up to run, but he grabbed me dragging me back kicking all the way into the room and flung me on the bed. I don't think Babe realized how hard he tossed me, because I bounced off the bed hitting the wall and back onto the bed. As I struggled to get away, he grabbed my foot dragging me back towards him, when James and Vinnie jumped in between pulling him off me. Vinnie grabbed his shoulders shouting, "Stop, you're gonna kill her! STOP!" I knew when I saw the look on his face he was lost in complete rage. Vinnie's words started to snap him out of it.

James was all over me, checking to see if I was hurt as he whispered, "I'm so sorry!"

Babe grabbed James' shoulder yanking him, "Get your hands off her!"

But James wouldn't back down; he stood in front of me shoving Babe. "NO! DON'T YOU FUCKING HIT HER AND I DON'T CARE IF YOU AND ME HAVE A PROBLEM OVER THIS!"

I blinked a million times, because this was turning into a really bad situation! Vinnie moved next to James, blocking me. "Hey Babe, enough! You can't do this, we're all tight, but THIS can't happen!"

His eyes changed and his whole face became completely remorseful. He put his hands up, backing off. "I love her, I'm not going to hit her!"

James leaned in threatening, as he pointed to me. "You better never hit that girl Babe!" He turned and walked out. Vinnie held Babe's shoulder looking at him with a mixture of friendship, fear and warning. He turned and tapped my leg, smiling before he walked out too.

I was a fucking mess, bleeding all over the place, as Babe sat down on the foot of the bed with his head in his hands. "I never meant for any of this to happen. I know you don't want to hear this, but we have to get out of here. They called the cops, and I'll violate my parole for being in a casino and a different state!" When he looked up at me, his face went white. Babe jumped up for a wet towel, but I snatched it from his hands before he could touch me. My eyebrow was split, the steady stream of blood just poured down my face.

I could still hear the other hotel guests scream from their rooms, and knew he was right. "Fine, let's go" I said as I stared at him with complete hatred. Babe picked me up and carried me out of the room.

The guest right across the hall was screaming, "Oh my God I think they killed her, she's being carried out bleeding! She's dead!"

Babe kicked their door so hard it rocking it on the hinges. "Shut the fuck up!" We made it into one elevator as another was opening, filled with police. We could hear their radios. I avoided looking at him, instead focused on James holding my bag and mink. James was a threatening-looking guy all on his own, with the power to back up his look. I've seen him do severe damage to quite a few people. *I'm glad he's on my side!*

The elevator door opened to a beautiful suite, with a living room, and a few bedrooms. Everyone from the melee were there looking sheepishly at me. I just held Babe's neck, as he carried me into the master bedroom. After he placed me on the bed, he tried to look at me closer. "Look up, let me see your face." He said as he moved my hands away. "You're in bad shape you need stitches."

I slapped his hand away and stormed out for my bag. James had it under his arm, guarding the contents. He knew exactly what was in there; we've sat up in wee hours of the morning looking at my jewelry contemplating the value of each new piece. He was my boy, and I trusted him completely. "James, I don't want to bleed all over you, but can I have my bag?"

Standing he towered over me, his fierce face melted as he looked at me. "Sure thing Pal! You okay?"

"Yeah, I'll be okay. Thank you for what you did back there. I never want to get in between you guys, I'm sorry about all of this!" I couldn't hug or kiss him; otherwise I would be gushing blood all over him. I knew this was all superficial, my eyebrow split because it's thin skin. My lip took the hardest hit, but it would heal. All the real damage was done from Pete, not when Babe tossed me on the bed, because I hit the wall rolling, but my shoulder felt like I just played hockey. Babe's adrenaline was pumping when he threw me, and grabbed my ankles. I would bet my last dollar that he would never hit me on purpose, but I wouldn't let him know that.

I walked back inside with my bag and dumped the contents on the bed as he called the front desk. "Hey I need you to send me the house doctor. Yeah, up to my suite."

Seething I grabbed the phone and barked at some poor person that I didn't need any medical assistance before hanging up on them. I found my butterfly stitches and ripped open the wrapper with my teeth as I held an alcohol wipe on each cut. *Jesus Christ!* I never said a word, or made a face, even though it burned like a motherfucker. Babe stood right next to me looking at me through the mirror as I closed up my brow and lip. When I was done, I muttered. "No fucking doctor is coming near my face with a needle! If it heals badly, I'll have a plastic surgeon take care of it back in NY, not here in Jersey and you're paying the fucking bill!"

I lit a cigarette and sat down so I could put my head back to help the clotting. I didn't say a word, I just silently cursed him while he pulled up a chair and sat in front of me. He took my hands out of my lap and held them. "Listen say something, you're making me fucking nuts."

I whispered, "It's bad enough that guy hit me, but you smacked the cigarette out of my mouth, threw me against a wall and dragged me by my ankles! What kind of man are you, that you would do that to me?"

"First I didn't hit you, I hit the cigarette." He said, looking ashamed.

Looking at him for the first time in the eye. "It was an eye lash away from my face."

Babe gently touched my cheek. "If I wanted to crack you, I would have. I don't fucking miss, but I would never hit you. All the other stuff, I'm a hundred percent wrong!"

"Ya think!" I said, sarcastically.

"Listen, you were making me nuts! It just went down hill when I was trying to talk to you and all you would do was smoke."

"You weren't talking, you were screaming," I said slowly for effect.

Pulling back surprised, he said, "You walked out without a word, what did you expect me to do? Do you understand I could violate my parole just being here? Get it through your thick head, I'll go back to jail!"

Disappointed with his behavior, I shouted, "You didn't come home for days. You left me to worry all alone with nothing, and locked up! Fucking locked up Babe, like a fucking prisoner AND FUCK YOUR PAROLE!"

"Stop! Hey, come on I would have called if I could. You have to understand." Babe said spewing the same line of shit, they all thought was an automatic pass for being MIA.

Interrupting him, I hissed, "No I don't understand, why you couldn't call once in three days or have someone call me? No, I don't! One minute you're amazing, the next a girl calls you, then you're amazing again, then you're fucking some girl, then you love me, then you tell me to grow up, leave and don't come back! When you finally waltzed in, you didn't even try and explain."

"Come on." He said, trying to convince me with a gangster con job!

I wasn't having it and I snapped. "Let me finish! You didn't call, you left me to think you were dead somewhere. I didn't sign up for that! Someone, anyone, could have called. I was sick, worrying and then you come in and breezed past me like its all some fucking joke. Do you know I slept by the door so you couldn't sneak in and out again?"

"Honey I'm so sorry I scared you, but you're not new to this, so why are you so upset?"

Pulling my hands out of his, I wiped the one renegade tear that escaped with the back of my hand. "I thought you were DEAD! DO YOU KNOW THAT? DEAD! I guess I AM new to this part, because I never expected you to up and leave me after giving me the watch. You were off the fucking wall!"

"STOP, I'M FINE, I'm fine really! Just don't talk like that." He tried to soften his tone, smiling with a sympathetic look. "Okay, I'll try to keep that in mind, but you have to stop trying to run away, every time I turn around you're busting my balls! Really, do I deserve this aggravation? Come on!" For the first time, I could see he felt terrible.

"I went to the club naked to get your attention and then you abandoned me. I think I had good reason to walk out!" I cringed in pain, not from the assault, but because I was truly hurt.

"You didn't even answer my beeps, it was one more thing for me to worry about." He broke in, clearly exasperated.

"You figured it out quick enough to send Gene and Nick to my house to get me."

"What are you talking about? I didn't send them." He said looking like I hit him from left field.

I told him what had happened as he sat stone faced, not giving up a crumb of what was really going on. "I pulled up and ran into my apartment for a second and when I came out they pulled in front of me and jumped out to talk to me. I thought you sent them, so I took off."

"I didn't send them, but forget about all of that." He tried pulling me into his lap, but I pushed him off.

"Listen to me very clearly all you do is make me cry! If you make me cry anymore, I'm gonna make you fucking cry big time! I had it with this bullshit. You got it? This crazy crap ends now, no more! I swear to God you don't know me very well and I'm not putting up with you, this fucking war crap and getting knocked around by you or anyone." He tried to cut in but I put my hand up. "No, let me finish, you owe me that much respect for all my pain and suffering! I'm a good person, I'm already in love you and will role with the life but if you ever pick up your hands to me I will kick your ass to the curb. And before you say anything I know you didn't mean to bounce me off a fucking wall, but you shouldn't have thrown me to begin with. You dragged me! You fucking dragged me like a dog! I'm a fucking woman, not one of your jerk off hoods! And if this doesn't work out between us don't get any big ideas of thinking you'll intimidate anyone who looks at me after I leave you, because remember I don't deserve it and I'm VERY well liked. I won't stand for your terror tactics!" I gave him a look to kill when I finished. I started to smoke to control my temper, because my hands were shaking badly.

Babe's face was unreadable as he was measuring me up. After a few minutes of silence, he finally admitted, "You're right, all of it. I won't make an excuse, I'm wrong. All I can say I never wanted any of this to happen."

"I never said you did any of it on purpose, I'm just letting you know it can never happen again…ever!"

I know this bothered him, he was taking long drags and looked very tired all of the sudden. "I gotcha." He put his cigarette out and got up but stopped and looked at me seriously. "I never meant to throw you against the wall! You do know that right?"

"Yes."

Trying to be funny, he joked, "You need some meat on your bones, you're too fucking light!"

"Fuck off!" I knew he didn't mean it; he was just caught up in the moment. I tucked my hair behind my ears as I looked up at him. "Babe, you better not have a problem with James and Vinnie over this. Don't go pulling rank and all that street shit! I couldn't ask for two better friends."

"You know I love them both, they're my best friends! I would have done the same thing. Fucking guys did the right thing, I admit it, they did."

Tapping my leg Babe said, "Give me a second." When he returned from the living room, I was already curled up about to fall asleep. "Hey don't fall asleep. If you hit your head, you could have a concussion." He started to feel my scalp, but I swatted his hand away.

"I hit my shoulder, not my head. I'm fine, but if I do die, I hope it eats you alive!" I said smirking, playing with him.

I slept for what seemed like an eternity, and finally woke up because I felt like I was suffocating. Babe was asleep on top of me, almost smothering me. Gently, I tried to move his arm, but he jumped up, spooked, holding me down, looking totally deadly, before he realized it was actually me. Babe released his grip and started to hug me hard and wouldn't let go. "You make me crazy, even in my sleep! I can't fucking believe what happened, I can't get over your face." I tried to break in, but he covered my mouth. "You're the most beautiful girl I've ever seen, but now you look like a prize fighter. It's my fault, I'm sorry, but you're not making it easy!"

"Babe, I love you too, calm down." I said as I tried to look at him, but couldn't get him off me. "Shush, I may get mad at you and need space, because of your bullshit, but I'm not leaving you." *What was I saying out loud? Oh no! Shut up you idiot, don't promise anything you know you can't commit to!* My internal voice was screaming to get the hell out of this relationship, but my heart was talking instead.

"No, I have too many things going on to worry about this and you. Stop running or walk, the choice is yours." He said laying his cards on the table.

"Shush, okay, okay I'll try." I said as he pulled back and rolled over. Trying to soothe his wild and hurt feelings I started tracing his stubble, while I wondered how I'd fallen so in love with this man. He fell back sleeping as I lay there, watching him, thinking about how bad it must be for him to go through all the craziness right now. The things I was seeing and hearing lately weren't good.

As I played with his hair, I wondered what would have happened between us if we had met during a different time.

Babe whispered, "I like that, it feels good having you with me."

"Shush go to sleep."

"I'm sorry Danielle, really you gotta know that!"

"I know it, really I do." I mumbled choking back my emotions.

Babe pulled me onto this chest and held me until he whispered. "I want to see your face."

You must be a sadist to want to see my black and blue and bandaged face! "Forget it, it will only make you feel worse."

"Awe, I love you honey! I promise this will never happen again, I'm never going to look at your face all fucked up again... quit working...ahhh...go the spa...I'll give you everything." I felt his heart break with sadness and regret. Pulling me up, he kissed me over and over again. Together we drifted off to sleep holding each other.

Soon, I felt gentle kisses on my shoulder as he whispered, "Hey Peeper, how you feeling?"

"Banged up, everything hurts." I meant every word I said, every inch of me was throbbing with pain.

He deeply kissed my hair whispering, "I'm sorry!" I groaned from being held tightly. He released his grip on me mumbling more apologies. Babe stood up running his hands through his hair yawning and when he looked down at me, his whole expression changed.

Now I know you really feel bad, I can see it in your eyes. "Hey Mr. Cranky, getting banged up brings out your soft side. I'll make a mental note to remember that." I tried to break the tension by joking around.

"Keep that under your hat, I don't have a soft side out there." Kissing me, he said, "Get serious for a minute. In a little while I'm going to take you to another house, but I can't stay."

Alarmed but annoyed, I blurted out. "Again? Oh come on just let me go home already, I'll be fine!"

"I have to check into the half way house, and just can't be around." Babe said, looking embarrassed.

"Can't you check in and leave? Better yet, pay someone off and not go!" I knew he had to go, but I just hated all of it.

Laughing at me, he said, "I like the way you think but no I can't! You'll be fine, don't start to worry now."

"You can't leave me alone somewhere strange again after all this shit. I'm tired, I just want to go home."

Babe said, trying to ease my fears, "Rockland County, it's a little over an hour away from home."

On the verge of wanting to run away, I asked, "Why can't I stay here? I'll be fine"

"No, there are so many of us and them here, you just don't realize it. Half the casino was beeping me when you sat down to play cards. Besides your friend, who thinks I'm beating the shit out you, who do you think was playing cards with you?"

"No!" My face was pink, because I thought I was so independent and did everything on my own, now I know he heard our whole conversation.

"Yes!" He said, smiling at me.

I asked, "Did I win fair and square? I can't believe you! I thought they were all bad card players!"

Pulling me close, he grinned. "What do you care, as long you won? If you have fun, that's all that matters! Who do you think paid for your champagne?"

"I did!" I said, sure that I paid and tipped big.

"No, you didn't. Check your account, the money was put in there." He said laughing at me.

Going from pink to red, I realized that here in the East Coast's Sin City, of course the boys would know every move I made. I suggested, "Bring me to Breezy and get Nero."

Babe shook his head no. "Nero has to stay with my mom."

"Can I stay there without the dog?" I said trying to pretend I was okay being alone.

"I think it's better you go somewhere quiet." He said as he kissed me. "I can't leave the half way house if something happens. Unless you have a better idea, its upstate for you!"

"Florida? Anywhere besides Rockland County or upstate, it's all so boring. No Pine Bush! I hate the country." I said as I started to nibble on his ear.

He giggled, "You have no idea how long this weekend is going to be for me. After chasing you, I'm going to need to rest."

"Old man, do you need to rest already?" I teased.

"I think I can hold my own, you don't have any complaints do you?" Babe smirked.

"None that I can think of yet! Do you?" I held up my hand and said, "Don't answer because I don't want to know. Pretend you like it for me okay?" Giggling, I crawled out of bed like I was being held down by a ton of steel. "I'm starving, let's eat!"

With that he rolled over an ordered room service, which was delivered with lightning speed. Once our appetites were appeased, we jumped in the shower. Soon we were washing each other and enjoying every inch of the exploration. I couldn't take my eyes off him. Babe was like a drug that I needed to survive.

"Turn around, let me wash your back, I wanna take care of you." Babe was so gentle as he spoke in his sexy voice.

"No fair! I can't look at you," I said, but turned anyway.

"You've done nothing but stare at me, now it's my turn." He said as he proceeded to wash my back as he gently spread my arms on the shower wall.

I was on the tile wall soaking in every sensation of his wandering hands, while the warm water soothed my aching body. Coming closer, I felt his gentle kisses on my neck, then tracing my spine all the way down to my ass as he whispered he loved me. He was on his knees, caressing and kissing my ass as he moved lower and continued on to my thighs and calves and, eventually onto the arches of my feet. He washed and kissed me from head to toe except for the one place I wanted him to go to.

"Babe?"

"Hmm?" He moaned.

"You missed a spot." I said playfully.

"What spot?" Acting as if he didn't have a clue.

"Hmmm, THE spot!"

"I told you, I don't do that."

"Really? You have to be kidding me! Come on its just you and me here." *Was this guy for real? Come on now; are you the last of the old fashion wise guys that don't dive? Good grief! Even the old men were carpet munchers, but of course, my luck not him!*

"Nope! But if you're in need of some assistance let me help you out." He moved back up to my neck and kissed me from behind. Lost in his embrace, he made love to me very gently in the shower.

"I want to hear you." He whispered in my ear.

The more he moved, the louder I got, until I was screaming hitting the shower tiles. This time, the experience was explosive.

"Dannie, I love you." He whispered in my hair.

"I love you too." I moaned as I clung to the wall. "You'll never last all weekend without me."

"Don't worry; I'm going to sleep it away. Come on let's get dressed." He moaned.

We dried off and went inside to change. I pulled on my sweats and put on a ton of foundation and makeup. The makeup could only hide so much, I still looked like I was abused or was in a bad brawl. We walked outside and there were guys everywhere. Some were sleeping, others were watching TV, but there were just so many of them including my card playing buddies. I spotted my mink lying over James on a chair while he slept. Just looking at him made me smile, I loved James. Turning around, I spotted Frankie standing up, stretching, not realizing I was there, he started to scratch himself through his loose boxer shorts. I wouldn't have noticed, except that he was standing over a guy who was sleeping on the floor. Babe and I both saw the same thing at the same time and doubled over laughing. Frankie was sprinkling his pubic hair all over the guy's unconscious face.

We couldn't stop laughing as we said our goodbyes. As we left AC, I asked Babe to run me over to the bank as soon as we got home. Just as I requested, our first stop in Brooklyn was a bank, and before I ran in, Babe handed me another $5000 emergency money. I kissed him, not for the money, but for the sentiment behind it. I wasn't about to say no, after getting tossed around. The boys always stash money anywhere they can for rainy days. Five-G's at a clip was nothing to sneeze at and now he'd given me ten; he obviously was investing in me. I ran in and purchased a safety deposit box. In went my jewelry along with my 7-karat diamond ring from my friend Johnny, bankbooks, passport, car title, and all the cash. Now I felt better, no matter what happened, no one would get his or her hands on my shit. Babe waited the whole time outside by the car. When I returned, he was talking on the corner pay phone with a tough-as-nails expression until he spotted me and hung up. We pulled out, and his beeper started going off like crazy.

"Maybe you should pull over and call the number back," I said, concerned, but he totally ignored me, like the beeper. Babe kept driving, looking at the screen after each beep, while we both pretended it wasn't going off. It was either a girl or the boys, and either way, I didn't want to know. I didn't ask any more questions and sat there, waiting to figure out where we were going. Finally, he got off at an exit and drove to a pay phone. Babe got out and made his calls. He spoke in a hushed voice, but he was clearly in gangster mode by the look of his face and body language. While we were sitting there, a hick cop car pulled up. Babe never got off the phone but just looked at them.

Rolling down the window, eyeing the Porsche, one of the hillbilly cops, Officer Barney Fife, asked, "You folks okay? Do you need assistance Ma'am?"

I answered sweetly, "No officer, but thank you for stopping." Waving I said, "Have a good day! Thanks again!"

"Okay Ma'am you have a good day too." Officer Fife said as he eyed us, surely noticing my black and blue face before he slowly rolled away.

Babe hung up and jumped back in the car. Slapping my thigh, he said, "You okay?"

"Sure, are you?"

"Never better honey, never better." With that, we were back on the road to God's country laughing all the way to hell.

CHAPTER 22

Nuts & Buttons

He drove forever; we passed Rockland County and were heading west on Route 17, when I complained, "Oh come on, Pine Bush? I know where we are."

"Nope, a little past there. Sit back and enjoy the ride."

Enjoy the ride? We're flying past a green landscape and nothing more. We passed anything of interest, like the Outlets, a long time ago. I'm not a country person. The road was tree-lined and very desolate, if you were lost, there wasn't a soul to ask for help, so I guess that was the point of having this house. The whole ride, my beeper was going off, first Millie, then Bri, but no one beeped 911, so I wasn't overly concerned. I was having too much fun with Babe and put them on the back burner.

Babe drove into a long dirt road, the driveway to his beautiful arts-and-crafts style house. There wasn't another building close by. Babe pulled the car into the garage and closed the door. This house was amazing, just like the beach house. The windows at the back of the house were floor to ceiling overlooking a beautiful lake.

Grinning proudly, he said, "You like it, I can tell."

"Who wouldn't, it's beautiful! But how can I stay here alone? A bear could eat me."

He laughed at me. "Eaten? There you go again all you want to do is get eaten! Seriously you don't have enough meat on your bones to get eaten."

"No, come on, anything and everything can hurt me here." I said truthfully.

"You will be fine. Listen, be serious, do you know how to use a gun?" Babe asked trying to gage my real knowledge of firearms.

"Yes, I'm a decent shot pointing at cans and paper targets, but people and animals are completely different. I don't want to shoot and kill anyone." I said, looking at him seriously.

"I'm not asking you to shoot anyone. I just want to know that you can handle yourself." He moved over to a built in cabinet and unlocked it. Inside was assortment of riffles, shotguns, and handguns. I couldn't tell the difference, not being a gun person. "Okay, come over here. This cabinet that has to be locked all the time, open it only if you have to use one. Here take this." And he handed me a shotgun as I blanched at the cold metal in my hands. He proceeded to show me how it worked and everything I had to do to protect myself. I was so grateful when he locked the cabinet again and gave me the key. "Keep this with you until I come back. Now let me show you the house." I followed as he took me on a tour; it had a massive basement, with multiple rooms and a fireplace, and it led directly out to the lake. The first floor had a master bedroom, living room with another fireplace, kitchen and laundry room that led to the garage and then upstairs, which had five bedrooms. There was a wraparound porch and floor to ceiling windows. Looking outside, I could see the dock and a boat. Babe started a roaring fire and said, "Keep this going all weekend. Toss a log every two to three hours and it will keep you busy."

"Babe this is amazing! Where are we? What lake is this?" I asked looking at the panoramic view.

"Isn't it? I love coming here. We're near Roscoe; this is Indian Lake. Most of the homes here are only used in the summer or during hunting season. Just try and stay in, believe me, the weekend will fly."

I stood with my arms around his waist staring out at the lake as we held each other for a while. "This is going to be a long weekend for me. As pretty as it is, and it really is, it's scary to be alone here."

Babe turned to kiss me, holding me in his vice grip for a while, before he brought me to the fireplace and said, "You have no idea what being alone really is, this is nothing compared to what I've seen. Just enjoy yourself and the house. I'll be back soon, but before I go I want to give you something." He tossed my mink onto the floor, lowering me onto it. Babe stood above me, methodically removing each piece of clothing until he was completely naked, they were in a pile next to us, with his gun on top as a cold reminder of the life. He noticed a rubber-banded stack was sticking out of his pocket, and pulled it out. "Listen Peep, take this just in case." As he tossed it towards me, the band broke and the cash flew all around us.

Then he started to take off each piece of my clothing slowly, tenderly, focusing on me. Babe lingered, playing with me in each area that so needed his attention, as I stared at the barrel and the money, while I sunk deeper into the mink. I was panting by the time he was on top of me, and more so as he swatted the loose hundred dollar bills all over that stuck to our skin. The whole experience was sexy as hell! He held my hands above my head and kissed me deeply as we made love. I was getting used to him staring at me while on top, he must have liked to watch, because he never lost his control or turned away. Whew, as much as I wanted it to last forever, I knew he couldn't stay, and sadly, our afternoon ended sooner than it should have.

He stayed on me for a while; kissing and bringing me back to reality slowly and then said, "Okay, its time for me to leave. Stay inside and keep busy, I'll drive straight here from the Bronx. If something should happen I'll send Vinnie for you."

With that, I became startled, "What?"

"I'm just saying, just in case crazy shit happens."

"I kind of thought the bar incident and maybe all the craziness was getting resolved when you came home and burnt your clothes." I asked, probably sounding naive.

"Stop!" He said as he was trying to get off me, but I was holding him down on me.

Ignoring his uptight answer, I held him looking into his eyes. "I love you Babe! Hurry back, I'll miss you!"

"Ditto! Hey hang on; I want to give you something." He took out a chain from his jeans and slipped it around my waist. It had something dangling from it.

I took a closer look and it was the button from the fire with a diamond in the middle. "You're a nut. Is that the button? I'm not sure I want any more gifts, because every time you give me one, something crazy happens."

"That's all behind us, don't sweat anything." He said smiling. "Yeah, it's the button on a gold chain. Looks cute hanging on your hip; that's my favorite part of your body. Did you know that?"

"My hip? Really?"

"Yup! It's sexy." Babe said with a deviant smile as he started getting dressed. "And you thought I was only a B&B guy!" In a matter of minutes he was heading towards the garage. I followed him naked, wearing only the chain and tried in vain one last time to get him to stay just a little longer.

"Nice! That's what I want to see when I come to get you!" He kissed me and jumped in his car. I watched him to drive away feeling both fear and love. *Time to get dressed, I can't just sit around naked.* Before we left Breezy, I packed his sweats, just in case I felt I needed to feel him near me for security.

The first thing I did was check all the locks on the windows and doors. The alarm was on and he gave me the code, so I started to relax. I unpacked all the food we picked up before we drove here. With all the domestic issues resolved, I jumped on the couch with a book I wanted to read. Day light stared to fade and I put another log on the fire, hoping to keep the chill out. Funny all the sounds you hear when your alone in the country. Every little thing made me jumpy. In Brooklyn, I could sleep through screeching cars, garbage trucks, and screaming children playing in the street, here I could hear the squirrels fuck. I guess I dozed off, because when I woke up, the fire was almost out and it was two in the morning. I threw another log on and searched for the TV remote. He had TV's in each bedroom along with a lot of videos. I curled up on the gigantic bed and popped one in that turned out to be porn. *Next! Porn again?*

I looked at the labels and realized the stack was filled with porno movies. *Really, why am I surprised, of course porn was perfect to watch when he's on the lamb, occupying his time in the mountains.* I moved to the next pile and they were old black and white movies. Awesome, I started with the Maltese Falcon, and then moved to Casablanca before I fell asleep. I passed the night away dozing in front of the TV. I woke up Saturday morning tired from doing nothing the day before.

After making coffee and some eggs, I walked from room to room, trying to feel his presence somewhere in the house, but no such luck. He was there only because he was in me, I carried him around in my mind and my heart. I switched gears and went into his closet looking for his clothes. I had no idea, what his style was, or favorite color, or even size. Maybe I could get some answers to the mystery since I was trapped. The closet was ordinary, filled with the kind of clothes all the boys wore. I felt like such a snooper, but hey what else was there to do? I tried on some of his jackets just to feel him; it was just then, when I was looking in the mirror staring at my bruised body in his clothes, that I noticed a bottle of Drakar Noir cologne and picked it up. It smelled just like him. I sprayed it on me, and then I walked over to the bed and sprayed the pillows. If I couldn't have him, I could at least smell him.

Curling up on his big bed, I popped another video in. I wasn't really paying attention, because I was looking at the lake through the window, but the music caught my attention. There was a bride and groom dancing, laughing and spinning in a circle in the middle of a dance floor. I stared at the happy couple trying to figure out what movie it was, until the groom's voice boomed over the music. Then I heard him; now I looked at the TV sharply. *Oh my god it's my Babe! This was his wedding video. He did say he was divorced but he kept his wedding video.* I watched him dance with a beautiful girl, then they cut a tall tower cake and the video messages started. I never moved a muscle. Watching Phil and all his friends that I knew wishing him well made me so sad. Poor Babe, he looked so young and in love. They look like they should have had the perfect life, how awful it didn't last. Even though I was in love with him, I loved him enough to feel his pain over this. I hit rewind several times, putting it on a loop and watched it as I fell asleep.

I woke up, not because of the fuzzy sound of the video ending and about to restart, but because I heard the doorknobs turn. I opened my eyes, but didn't move. Looking out at the windows I could clearly see two large shadows moving across the patio. I slid off the bed and crawled into the living room towards the gun cabinet. Fumbling with the key, I managed to unlock it and grabbed one. Scurrying into the laundry room, I jumped into the closet. My heart was pounding; I could hear them moving from door to door and window to window. The sound went away, but I knew no one would drive all the way up here and just leave without getting in to make sure no one was here. They had to be outside somewhere. I didn't move for what seemed like hours. All of the sudden, I heard the sound of the garage door opening,

I started to panic. My heart was racing; I got ready and held up the shotgun to the laundry door and waited. *Oh my god, I knew I shouldn't have let him take me here! Fucking Babe couldn't stash me in the Goddamn Bronx! I'm all good in the hood and would have gone shopping, instead of hiding in a frigging closet!*

Finally I could feel a presence outside the door, my mouth went dry and my hands were sweaty knowing I only get one shot, so I better make it a good one. The door flung open and I saw James and his Cousin Richard standing there. They went white as a ghost and jumped out of the way as I pulled the trigger, but nothing happened. Frighten beyond belief I dropped it and ran out after them.

"HOLY SHIT WHAT ARE YOU FUCKING DOING?" Roared James.

"Protecting myself! What are you doing here?"

"Babe wanted us to check on you!" James demanded as he rubbed his head in shock. "Where is it? I wanna see it!"

"Over there on the floor, I'm not touching it again. I pulled the trigger but nothing happened."

James bent down and picked it up checking it out. "Hey brainiac I think you forgot to do something!"

"What?" I said, completely drained and frightened.

"Load it!"

I broke down crying. "He didn't tell me to load them, I thought they already were!"

"Who do you think loads them, the fairy? You have to do it yourself! You're fucking unbelievable, but I give you credit for pulling the trigger."

"How did you get in? I locked everything!"

"You did, but I used my garage door opener to find his frequency and popped it myself. You should have unplugged it, not just closed the door."

We all went into the kitchen and I put on a pot of coffee. Poor guys were totally freaked out and we all needed to calm down. "Are you staying the rest of the night? There are lots of bedrooms, pick one," I said, trying to sound cheerful.

Richie chimed in, "There is no way I'm driving home now in the pitch black after that experience!"

"Great! Are you guys hungry?"

"No." He stopped speaking when he heard a noise from another room. We all followed the sound until we were standing in front of the TV with Babe's wedding video running on a loop. James and Rich stopped short, looking dumbfounded. "What are you watching?"

"Oh come on, I found it by accident and couldn't help myself. You were there, I saw you in the video. You looked so young!" I said, trying not to sound like a stalker.

"Yea, I was a kid. He was married a long time ago." He said, sounding as sad as I felt.

Richie broke in. "Listen I'm tired, I'm going to bed. Call me if you need me."

"Thanks! I'm sorry about before. Good night," I said, turning from Richie. That left James and I alone, but I didn't really want to talk about the video or anything serious.

James asked, "Listen, before I go to sleep too, anything happening?"

"Na, I've been alone since he left, doing nothing but watching TV."

"Yeah, I can see that. Anyway, I'm going to sleep. Love you! Good night!" He bent down and kissed my head and walked off to what I guessed was his bedroom when he visited. Now I jumped into bed and popped in another video, making sure it wasn't his wedding or a porno, both of which would make me nuts as I slept. I woke up while they continued to sleep. I was so stir crazy I decided to slip out; disarming the alarm, I opened the back door leading out from the bedroom and stood staring at the lake and pulled out a cigarette. There was a dock, a boat, and some jet ski's all waiting for someone to use them. I walked down and sat dangling my feet in the water thinking about what would have happened had I shot James by accident. *How did these guys live like this? Never knowing how and if they were going to die. Terrible!*

I just couldn't imagine losing Babe. The touch of his hand on my cheek, the feel of his lips kissing my thigh, or the look in his eyes when he stared at me, was enough to make me crazy. How could I ever live without it again? Shaking my head, I could almost hear him say, "Don't you worry!" as I walked slowly back up to my beautiful prison, ready to wait out the rest of my time.

CHAPTER 23

....

Bullet Fairy

The beautiful windows overlooking the lake let in so much sun, I was up early. I had the coffee on and a big breakfast, waiting for the guys to get up.

Rich said, "Morning Dannie, hmm that smells good!"

"Hi Rich, hungry? I made a feast, so dig in!" I said laughing. It would haven been so good having them around if I could forget about the recent turn of events.

Rich grabbed a plate as he smacked his stomach, grinning. "I'm on a protein diet so eggs and coffee sounds good."

"Hey, what's that smell?" James said as he came bounding down the stairs. "What did you make, Fats? Smells great!"

"I love you guys! Come on eat up." I said smiling. "What's there to do up here? I've seen the lake, the trees and all that stuff. It's as much fun as watching paint dry."

"You can't go anywhere. Babe will be here tomorrow, but until then you're staying put. Get it, got it, good! Plus you can't go out looking like you were kidnapped with those bruises!"

"Oh come on, its not that bad, plus I'm with you guys. Who in their right mind would bother with me?" I said trying to be as convincing as possible.

James seemed disturbed looking at me. "What did you run out of makeup? You didn't look like that before."

"No! I just washed my face, so I don't have any on." I blushed with embarrassment.

"Hmm, you need some Fats, before you scare the fucking bears! You know I'm kidding! By the way you, would be surprised how many people would want to get to me, so the answer is still no, before you ask again! Any who, next!" James said, as he grabbed a big plate and started to devour it as he plopped on the couch. "This is my spot for today. You know you should have brought Rotten with you. We could've had tons of fun!"

"I can tell you like Millie, James!"

"Absolutely! You would have to be bent not to like her."

"Okay, when we get home lets all go out one night and see where it goes."

"I know where it goes, don't you worry about that." He roared laughing.

"Good grief! You're such a pig!"

"Yup Fats, yes I am. And proud of it! You only live once." He continued to tease.

"I can't sit around here doing nothing, as you think of ways to fuck my girlfriend ALL DAY LONG!" I said, laughing at him.

James playfully pointed his fork at me. "Babe said no, so no it is. Rich, let's see if we can catch a game on the satellite."

With that I walked into the bedroom, trying to find something to do. Showering alone seemed so boring now. After a very long, hot shower I settled on top of the feather bed and started calling each girlfriend while I flicked the remote. Starting with Bri, I knew she'd abuse me for being MIA.

"Where the fuck you been, stranger?" She teased.

"Oh please, you have no idea what's going on. Way too much to explain over the phone." I knew I just couldn't adequately describe any of it; we would need lots of alcohol and be face to face for this story.

"You need to tell this guy, you have to come home once in a while. Enough with this shit!" She teased.

"Easier said than done. What are you doing?"

"Listen I'm having a house party this Sunday. Can you come?"

"I would love to, but let me ask him and I'll call you back." I knew I said something stupid as it came out of my mouth.

"Oh my god! Ask him? Ask him what? If you can go out?" She roared into the phone.

Laughing with her at the absurdity of my situation I said, "I know, but it is what it is. I won't see him until tomorrow, so I'll call you then."

"You do that!" Still laughing at me, she teased, "Can you remember where I live?"

"Ha-ha, you're funny! Shut up, see you Sunday!" Hanging up, I started to miss my freedom big time.

Next up was Millie, who said that it was a tense weekend. Seems a lot of the boys weren't around and the local hangouts were empty. The war drums were definitely loud and clear. Before I knew it, it was well into the afternoon. Sporadically, I would hear James and Rich cheer for a pass or interception; at least they were having fun. The day was dragging on and I dozed from time to time until finally it was evening. After checking in on them, I poured a full glass of wine and sat with them watching a game.

"How can you watch this shit! Stop and go stop and go! Oh my God, this is so boring!"

"Oh Fats, you don't know what you're talking about! I got a lot of money on this game!"

I squinted at the TV. "On who, the fat ones or the hot ones?"

He jumped up cheering and high giving Rich as the score changed. "I don't wanna fuck em, I just want them to win!"

I slipped in casually, "Whatever! I like boxing and hockey this stuff sucks! Hey James, by the way Bri's making dinner tomorrow before she goes to work. You guys want to come?"

Turning his head to look at me, he asked. "Sure, did you ask Babe?"

"What are you talking about? If you could go?" I asked slightly confused.

They both started to laugh and gave each other a look like I was stupid. James said, "No, did you ask him if you could go? We know we can, but do you?"

"I go where I want, when I want."

"Not anymore! You gotta ask from now on." He said, trying to get me to understand.

My face flashed red, he confirmed what I already knew but didn't want to admit. I stood up and poured another glass of wine. "I'm not talking to you!"

"Don't get pissed Pal! It is the way it is," James yelled as he focused on the game.

"Look where your advice got me PAL!" I said as I walked over to gun cabinet and unlocked it. I took one out and a box of ammo and walked out the back door. Knowing Babe well, I knew there had to be a homemade gun range setup close by on the property. Last night I saw bails of hay and figured it must be where he went for target practice. I found it in the dusk and put my wine glass down to load the gun. There were a bunch of spent shells in a can and everything was easy to figure out. I started to shoot, hitting every target. The sound must have made the boys jump, because they ran out were quickly trying to coax me back inside.

"Hey! What the fuck you doing Fats?" James asked from a safe distance.

"What does it look like? Shooting something, instead of someone!" I said as I hit every mark dead on.

"Come back inside, you're making too much noise!" James shouted as he approached me from behind.

"What, am I going to wakeup the bears or bodies? Come on, I'm having some fun. Plus, I'm just checking to see if I'm still a good shot. I might need this skill sooner rather then later at this rate!" I said smirking at him over my shoulder.

James walked over and took the piece out of my hand and unloaded it. "Nope! You're drinking and you're mad, that's a bad combination."

"You're no fun!" I said as I begrudgingly went back inside to the bedroom like a spoiled child. *Maybe if I just go to pass out this nightmare might end sooner.* So I slept on and off, watched stupid sports and reading until my prince charming finally came to free me from my prison. The sun was setting on the lake and I woke up to see it, feeling something breathing on me. I focused my eyes in the dim lights and I saw Babe lying down next to me, sleeping. It was nice feeling his body next to mine. I snuggled closer, while he slipped his arm over me. I stayed half asleep for about an hour, until he started to move.

Rolling over I whispered, "Hey!"

"Hey to you too."

I moaned, "Missed you!"

"Me too." He said snuggling in my hair.

"How much?" I giggled.

"Give me your hand, I'll show you how much." He growled as he put my hand on him.

"Animal!" I said giggling more.

"Don't start the engine, if you're not going to drive the car." He growled in my hair.

"Don't you think of anything else?" I said giggling as I grabbed his hair and moved his face closer to my neck.

"Not when it comes to you! You have no idea how much I missed you baby!"

"Yeah, then next time take me to the Bronx so I can be closer! I'm dying here, its horrible!"

Babe laughed into my hair. "I can only imagine you in the Bronx! But tell me how much you missed me!"

I giggled as I whispered. "Lots!"

"Ditto, sleeping with a bunch of skells isn't as good as sleeping with you."

I moaned, "Thanks! Jerk off!"

"I haven't done that in a while, now that I have you." He said as he pulled me closer kissing me again. "Did you have a good weekend?"

Biting my lip I asked, "Hmm, did James tell you what happened?"

"Ah yeah, that's fucked up."

"I didn't think, I just grabbed it, but he would have died if it was loaded. I love James and Rich, I couldn't imagine hurting them."

"I hear ya, they know too. Relax we'll figure it out soon." He said trying to calm my fears.

"Figure it out faster!" I said without thinking.

"Stop!" Babe tensed up immediately.

"I don't want to know anything, except when will life go back to normal! When is this gonna end already?" I pressed.

Now he was in gangster mode again. "You don't have any rights with this. If you keep asking, or talking, we won't be."

That was like a smack in the face. "If I ask or say anything, you won't talk to me? What kind of shit is that?" I said as I pulled away. "Plus I want to go back to the way things were! I hate this, all of it!"

"Listen Dannie, no questions, no conversations about this, that's it. There are things I can't explain you need to just trust me. This...this between you and me has nothing to do with that. You have no place in it, so just don't go there." I felt the dread creep up leaving bile in my throat. I started to cover myself and silently got out of bed and went into the bathroom as he called to me. "Hey don't go away like that. Come back here, come on."

I closed the door without responding and locked it. Everything I always knew and hated was coming back to say I told you so. I took a fast shower and got dressed. When I left the bathroom, he wasn't in bed, so I packed everything. When I was done, I walked in the living room, bag in hand. They were talking together in the kitchen and quieted down when they heard me. I said blandly, "Babe I'm ready, let me know when I can get in there and clean up before we leave."

He called out to me. "Come on in honey, the guys are about to go."

I walked in the kitchen and saw they were all standing by the island pretending to make small talk. James broke the ice by speaking first, "Hey what's up Dannie? Listen Babe is here, so we're going to take off. Thanks for not blowing my head off Pal."

"Jesus, I'm never going to live that down. I'm so sorry, I love you!" I said as I hugged him hard. "Rich, I'm sorry too! Love you!" I kissed Rich over James' arm as I thanked them both. We all walked to the door and I stopped as they started to get their cars calling out, "Wait a minute! Guys, I'm going to Bri's house tonight. She's making dinner, if you want to come it starts at 9:30." They looked at each other and then back to me.

Babe moved closer putting his arm around me, "I was going to take you to dinner, but if you want to go, we'll talk later."

"No, I don't think you understand. I'm going, if you want to come that would be great. So we don't have to talk later, just swing by and meet me there." I said holding my ground.

"Hold on, I'll drive, why have two cars afterwards?"

"No, I was thinking of going out afterwards with the girls so I might need my car. I'll figure it out when I get home and let you know later." Not waiting for a response I waved goodbye and walked back. As they said their goodbyes, I started to clean up. James and Rich stared at me before saying their goodbyes and walked out the door with Babe, hanging their heads, not wanting to get in the middle of a brewing argument. When I was satisfied the house looked fine, I sat on the couch and waited. *Waiting, waiting, waiting...I'm always waiting.*

Eventually he walked in the living room and sat next to me. "Listen let's not go home like this, there are some things we need to settle and some things that you need to know are off fucking limit."

Looking him square in the eye I said angrily, "I'm under the impression, you expect me to ask permission if I wanna go out and that's not happening! I've never asked anyone permission to do anything in my adult life. Plus, nothing should be off limits."

"You know how it is, so not permission, but what's so wrong with running your plans past me first?" Babe said looking annoyed at me.

"That sounds like asking permission and nope it's not happening. THIS, this is the part that I never wanted, I just wanna go home."

"Home? You mean my house right?" His eyes narrowed, I knew he was on the verge of getting nasty.

"No, I need to go check on my apartment, I haven't been there in a while."

Babe wrapped his arms around my waist kissing me as he whispered, "Forget going to Brianna's, just come back to Breezy and stay with me baby."

I pushed back on his chest. "Noooo, I'm GOING to her house. I can't stay MIA much longer, plus I want to go back to my life. Come on let's close up the house."

Now he was angry. "Your life?"

Getting flustered and angry I started to shake my head. "I'm saying this, all this stuff is your life, not mine. It's too much, too soon!"

"I don't want to fight either. Too soon? Forget it let's get outta here!" He stormed off mumbling curses while he closed up. Finally, he got in the car and we took off. There was very little small talk and we made it home much sooner than it took for us to get upstate the first time. As soon as he pulled up, I was about to get out, when he said, "Wait up, I'll walk you in."

"You don't have to do that," I said quickly.

"I'm not planning on staying, so don't fucking flatter yourself. I just want to make sure you get in, don't cop a fucking attitude." Babe barked trying to maintain control.

"Hey why are you being like that? Flatter myself? Fuck you! I can get in just fine." I said as I stormed out of his car.

I heard him follow me in all the way up to my door, which I slammed without a word to him. Needing to get away from all of this mayhem, I decided to call Millie. "Hey you going to Bri's tonight? I think I wanna go to Vibes after too. I need to go out, can you pick me up?"

Millie shouted, "I miss you Mama! Of course but isn't Babe's taking you?"

"I'm not sure what's he's doing. If he wants to come, he can drive there. Come get me, see you soon," I said, sounding clearly annoyed. I set about to straighten out my turbulent apartment, and got dressed. Millie picked me up and we drove down the block as I told her everything.

"Oh no, Dannie! Look at you, those marks, and your face! What did you get yourself into?" Millie was crestfallen, hugging me in the car. "You need more concealer in bright light!"

I looked in the vanity mirror, and gave up. "I'll do it before we go out, for now, its good enough. As for Babe, I have no idea, I'm so confused," I said shaking my head. I didn't want to get into anything at the moment. "Let's just go out and not think about it."

We went to Bri's and acted nonchalantly as we said our hellos. They were hanging out, munching on the amazing dishes Madelyn and Bri whipped up. There isn't a person who doesn't love Madelyn's macaroni and gravy and Bri's lamb chops. What a feast we were having. Everyone looked shocked when they saw my bruises, I knew I looked like I went ten rounds with a boxer, but they avoided the subject. They all asked about Babe, and I felt uncomfortable that he was a no show. Her dog started to sniff around me like crazy, and when I reached my slobber limit I asked her to get it off me. Brianna tugged at his collar as she asked if I was a near a dog, forcing me to admit to spending the night with Nero.

Madelyn asked, "Where's Babe? I thought he was coming."

"Don't think he can, I guess, I don't really know." I stopped to sip my wine as I mumbled over my glass, "Babe's mad at me anyway."

Madelyn asked, "What the fuck did you do? I gotta ask what the fuck did he do to you? You're all beat up!"

Holding my hands up, I tried to save his reputation. "He didn't hit me, someone else did, but that's all squared away now. But getting back to why he's not here, I didn't do a thing! I just wanted to go out and I think I didn't follow the rules or something. All this crazy bullshit is stupid." Now I had the guys' attention as well.

Leaning in, Pete said, "You should beep him and square it up."

"Ah, no! I didn't do anything wrong to square up."

Bri broke in, screaming, "Are you married to this fucking guy? No! You don't have to ask him anything! Plus don't think we didn't notice your face, neck, and arms the moment we saw you. My fucking God, just look at you! Don't get me wrong, I like Babe, but this is just too much!"

Ignoring the bruise comment, I laughed. "See! I can come and go as I please. He's not my dad, he's my special friend, all right he's my boyfriend. There I said it finally."

Fat Jerry said laughing, "Friend? I don't have a friend like you."

"Who are you kidding Jerry! You got tons of them!"

"Shut up, Jerry! She's her own person! Case closed!" Bri said, taking control of the situation. "Eat up mother fuckers, I gotta go to work soon!" With that the conversation went back to normal and I was no longer in the hot seat. Sooner than we wanted we had to leave so Brianna could go to work.

Millie and I jumped in the car. Our first stop was Turks, but our crowd wasn't there yet, so we moved on. We went to Vibes, which was always a rocking party. Bri had just settled in behind the bar when we made our way up to her. "I didn't think you were going to come out after dinner, I thought maybe your ankle bracelet wouldn't let you out this far. I thought you were gonna fall off the face of the earth again," Bri said, teasing me.

Waving my hands, I said, "You still have no idea! Can't talk here."

"Gotcha! What are you having?" Bri said as she winked at me.

"A bottle please." In a matter of seconds she was back with my glass, bucket, and bottle followed by five empty shot glasses.

"Here you go, you have five more coming to you from Tough T, Anthony, Tommy, Rock, and Dodgy." Bri laughed walking away. In a second she returned. "You have another bottle from Carl."

"Nice to be home! Cheers! Wait a minute, who's the last bottle from? Carl?" She shook her head yes and pointed. There he was, smiling and talking to a group of guys I knew. His pointed collar was extreme, meaning he was high up the gangster food chain. I smiled and nodded my thank you, as he tipped his head sideways. No way was I going over to him; I just went on as usual being me, not Babe's girl, just me. Just when I was relaxing, talking, and dancing, among my friends I spotted James. He saw Millie and shouted "Hey, Rotten!"

"Shut up, James!" Millie screamed as she kissed him hello.

"What are you doing Dannie? Long time no see or hear! Yes, I went there!" He said laughing and giving me bear hug. "Ohhh, yes, ahhh-ha...oh that's so good!" He said mimicking us. "Jesus Christ really?"

"Elevator man you're an ass! I don't want to talk about it or him." I said clinging to him as I hugged him for dear life.

Looking down at me, he made my heart melt always, because I just loved him. "Are you still mad at me?"

"I could never stay mad at you!" Slapping his arm, I reached up on my tippy toes and kissed him.

Leaning in, he whispered, "You know he's gonna find out you're here, right?"

"I've been here, way before he was in my life. The world does not revolve around Babe. I'm going to dance." I said storming off.

"Oh boy, what are we drinking ladies?" James asked.

Millie whispered. "James, she's drinking a bottle and she has five backed up. Save your money."

He lowered his head whispering in Millie's ear. "Rotten, listen I have a dilemma, I know he's been beeped already by other guys, but I have to let Babe know she's here myself; he's going to tell me to make her go home."

"So he can tell you, but if she says no, you can't drag her out," Millie said trying to defuse the tension.

"We'll see. Come on let's have a drink and you can tell me how much you love me," he said as Millie hit his arm laughing.

Before I returned to the bar, I stopped by each bartender to catch up and say hello to all the customers. I started to see Babe's guys scattered around and then I spotted him talking to Brianna. *Oh my god!*

As I approached, he took command of the situation, kissing me putting his arm around my waist leading me to the bar. "Hey having fun?"

Looking smug and annoyed I shot back, "Absolutely! I always have fun!"

"Great! What are you drinking?" He asked trying to settle in.

Smirking I said, "Champagne, like I always drink, what do you wanna drink?"

"Black with a splash of water."

Giving him the no-no look I said, "Absolutely not! You're not drinking that with me, have a martini!" Scotch brought out his demons badly.

"I can't even order what I want? You order whatever, I don't care." He said sounding annoyed. "Nice to see you out and catching up on lost time and your life." He put each arm around me on the bar and locked me into a facing position.

"Ha! I guess it's not much to catch up on. You do know this is my second home, whether we're an item or not."

"I know, but now you know, I KNOW EVERYTHING." He said as he bent down and kissed my ear whispering, "Don't make a scene."

Leaning in I bit his ear. He pulled back and cursed as he rubbed it. Out of the corner I heard someone calling out. "Babe, is that you?"

"Hey Babe someone's calling you," I said.

Blocking my view was the first sign something was wrong! Then Babe locked me in place so I couldn't move and that made my stomach twist as he casually said, "Ignore them."

My Brooklyn radar was up, as I pressed further. "It's a girl's voice. So don't give me any shit!"

"Ignore her."

Oh you must recognize the voice! "Oh no, I don't think so. Move, I want to see who it is," I said as I heard her repeat his name. Now James and Millie heard it to; they looked around trying to assess the situation.

Babe glared at me trying to be intimidating as he ordered, "Ignore HER, she'll go away."

You must be kidding me! Again Babe didn't know me as well as he should. "All right, okay, calm down. Geez, what's wrong why can't I meet your friends?" Now the voice was closer right behind him. She put her hand on his shoulder, not knowing I was standing in front of him, because I'm shorter than Babe and she came up on his side.

"Oh, now I know why you didn't answer me." She said with an attitude.

Not moving his arms from around me, Babe mumbled, "Hey, how are you? I'm a little busy at the moment."

I stared at her and then it hit me, she was the Breezy girl! I was not going to let this opportunity pass, I interrupted her as she was trying to speak to him and said, "Hey, haven't we met before?"

"No, I don't think so." She said trying to blow me off. "Babe what are you doing?"

Trying to get her to go away, he said coldly, "I'm busy honey, talk to you later."

"Honey! Whose honey? Excuse you, who you gonna talk to later?" I said being as antagonistic as I could.

Embarrassed, she glared at me. "You're kidding me, right Babe? Who's this?"

I shouted "Hey honey, who are you?"

Babe interjected quickly, "This is my girlfriend, Dannie."

"Girlfriend? You said you didn't have a girlfriend." She shouted as she put her hand on his arm trying to pull him to face her.

"Get your fucking hand off his shoulder honey! Hey, I know where we saw each other. You're the girl Babe was fucking on the floor! You're the Breezy blowjob!" I said knowing I was firing the first verbal shot, but I did it on purpose so she would swing first and I could beat the crap out of her defending myself. It didn't take more than a second before we were swinging at each other and Babe was stuck in the middle.

He shouted, "STOP!!" Growling in my hair he continued but in a whispered voice, "I'll violate for a stupid girl's fight!!"

"You should have thought about that before you BANGED THIS PIG!" I screamed as I was still swinging at her, finally connecting. When he locked me in place, I stepped on his leg hoisting myself over his shoulder. James held the girl by her waist, trying to separate us, but I had her by her scalp with one hand and was punching her in the face with the other over Babe's shoulder. I found leverage when my foot hit the bar and used it to propel myself right over Babe's shoulder. I landed right on top of Justine and knocked her to the ground. Now I was smashing her face in with my right hand while I held her neck down with my left. Vinnie grabbed my wrists as Babe grabbed my waist and peeled me off of her.

One guy yelled out "Babe no shortage of girls, huh?" Another called, "Need me to take one of them off your hands?" Still another, "I'll take Dannie for the knock out! Any takers?" I could see their amused faces laughing, and then I spotted Carl staring at me smirking over his glass as Babe carried me out, over his shoulder out the side door, but not before I screamed out "Justine!" I saw her turn her head responding to the name. Her face was completely unrecognizable and covered in blood. Now I knew; I matched the face to the mystery name! Soon, James and Millie followed us out. After he put me down next to his car, he held me there and tossed money at James to go back in and settle up. He turned to me pissed as he snarled, "DANNIE END IT NOW!"

"ARE YOU FUCKING KIDDING ME?" I struggled against his grip trying to get my arms free.

"We're going home NOW! Don't say another fucking word, I swear to God, not one more fucking word!"

Fuming, I wasn't going to be ordered home because of her. "You go home and leave me alone!"

"No, we're all going home!" Babe said trying his best to be forceful.

"First you're not my fucking boss! Second she hit me first; third I'm not going anywhere, forth I don't want to, and fifth I don't have to! But most of all, you never told her you were in a relationship after we got together. I asked you if it was going to continue and you told me NO!" I stopped to take a breath. "And sixth, GO FUCK YOURSELF, with this broad that you said was just a friend!"

"Stop! This is a private issue keep it between us! Don't you scream at me in the street, EVER! Hey James, I'll see you later. Millie, can he catch a ride with you?" He said as he opened the car and tried to put me inside.

"NO! YOU NEVER TOLD ME THE GIRL ON THE PHONE WAS THE SAME ONE I SAW YOU FUCKING AND I DON'T CARE WHO HEARS ME!"

He leaned in talking into my ear. "Lower your fucking voice now! Do you hear me?" Immediately I stopped struggling, and just glared at him. Again he leaned in, "I'm going to let go of you and if you think you're going to smack me here, you're making a big fucking mistake! Understand?" I didn't respond I just kept staring at him as he let go and leaned in again. "Now get in the car!"

I shook my head no. "Babe, you have two choices I'm going to the diner, you want to come fine, or you can go inside and hangout with Justine, but you're not gonna punish me by sending me home! You're just not!" Holding my ground, I was not about to be ordered home by anyone.

Millie trying to break the tension said, "Oh I'm hungry too. Let's all go to the Florida Diner! James I have my car, want to come with me?"

James beamed his hungry horny boy look as he hugged her. "Everyday of my life! But I guess breakfast will do, onwards, Rotten!" James said laughing as they walked away.

Now slightly calmer, because I said what I needed to say, I settled into his car but was still seething as we headed up 86th street. Turning to him, I said, "So that's Justine?"

"S-t-o-p! By the way, nice shot over my head; I always wanted to be between two hot girls but not like that."

I wanted to smack and fuck him at the same time. "Jerk! She's a dirty mutt! You must be kidding me, thinking I'm going to let this twat get away with swinging at me! She had a lot of fucking nerve to come over when you were with me!"

Laughing at me, he asked, "You would never do that RIGHT?"

"Shut up! She's not me! I talk to everyone because I CAN, and I never, ever get in between a guy and girl unless he's my guy! So the big question is, are you her guy?"

"No! You know that. Listen..." Babe said, trying to dismiss the whole situation.

On the verge of flipping out, I interrupted and screamed. "No, YOU listen if you're NOT her guy; she has no right to do what she did. Settled! You need to have a conversation with this broad, or I will. Come to think of it, I'm going to pay her a visit and bash her teeth in tomorrow. Make no mistake, this bitch is dead."

He grabbed my arm and locked eyes with me. "Don't go looking for trouble. I said I'd take care if it and I will."

Calming down, I pleaded, "Yeah, I don't believe you! Please don't make an idiot out of me. This is why I didn't want to start up with you, because I just didn't want to go down this road. Disappearing for days, fucking girls coming out of the woodwork and things! Next, a string of kids will pop up!"

Trying to make a joke out of the situation, he started busting my chops. "I can't help it if my fan club gets out of control once in a while."

I turned and punched his shoulder hard. "You're not fucking funny! I'm fuming!"

Flinching, I hit his arm harder then he thought I could. "Minch'! Stop!" Pulling up to the diner, Babe leaned over and tried to make me laugh, "You can't keep beating up my fans! Come on Feisty, after we eat come home with me."

"No!" I fired back.

"Should I call Justine?"

"Jerk! I'll eat your fucking heart for breakfast, and your eyeballs will be my mints!" I smirked as I left the car. We entered the diner and met up with Millie and James. We quickly ordered and moved past the incident, because I always knew this would happen dating a guy like him. *You proved me right pretty early on!*

Afterwards, we returned to Breezy just before the sun was coming up. Stopping to look at the amazing shades of purple and blue stretching across the sky, I grabbed his hand and walked toward the water instead of inside the house. I whispered to Babe, "I'm amazed each morning, it's so beautiful here." The sand was cool and felt so good slipping into my shoes. I bent down to remove them and dug my toes in as we walked. It was still dark out, not enough light to see how close we were getting to the water. I jumped into his arms at the first kiss of the cold water on my toes. After the chill passed, we ventured as close as possible waiting to watch the beauty unfold. I had my head on his shoulder holding his hand as the spray gently hit our faces. Babe turned and kissed me as the water licked at our feet. It was a gentle, romantic, kiss. Turning my head sideways, I opened my eyes to see him staring at me. As he sucked my lip I had to ask, "Why do you always kiss me with your eyes open?"

Kissing me more deliberately, he whispered, "I like to see who I'm kissing, I want to see your face." Batting my lashes at him, I thought that when it's just the two of us, I'm crazy in love, but when his world collided, I become insecure. Pushing up on my tippy toes, I wrapped my arms around his neck and allowed him to lower me to the sand. Within a moment, he was kissing me softly and intensely, making me wish I could make the moment last forever. He held my neck, adding fresh bruises to my assortment by keeping my face in position, as he kissed me, watching me intently as my eyes started to roll back. Whispering he loved me, we both were lost in the moment like the waves rolling around us.

"Babe, I love you too much for my own good!" I said, biting his lip.

"I love you too! You o-" Babe froze mid sentence, because we heard hushed voices in the distance. Mouthing to me he said, "Shush."

I stayed stock-still and looked into his eyes as I could see he was alarmed that someone was creeping around his house. I was able to differentiate between the waves, and the intrusive voices saying, "His car is here, but it doesn't look like he's here."

"Maybe he's in another car?"

"Nah, I bet ya he's here, somewhere. We just have to find him."

Leaving my shoes behind, we crept along the water farther down the beach, while the two guys walked around the perimeter of the house. Holding my hand tightly, he pulled me towards the cabana club, but they must have seen us moving in the shadows, because all of the sudden we heard shots firing past our head. Ducking low, we ran past the side of a house. Once near the parked cars, he shoved me under one and told me to stay there. Terrified, because they were still shooting in this direction, I stayed stock-still waiting for it to end. Babe looked back to check on me just as one of them took aim. I screamed so loud he jumped, as the gun went off, but it was dark, and I really couldn't see what happened to him. Now I was beside myself, flipping out, thinking he might have been shot. *God, please don't take him from me. I don't think I can handle this. Please God!*

Car alarms were blaring, neighbors were screaming along with the distant sound of sirens, but my mind was very quite for the moment. I peeked out from hiding my face by the tires when I saw him run towards them gun drawn. A few more shots went off and people started to turn on their lights. Surveillance and floodlights illuminated the area. I could see the two guys take off running toward a car, probably afraid of being caught on the cameras now that the whole neighborhood was awake. Once they turned around, I saw their faces. Frozen in horror, anger, and terror, I realized they were from the other side of this nowhere land of nonsense war. They knew Babe and came to kill him in the middle of the night.

As soon as the car took off, I crawled out and ran toward the house. All the lights were on, I ran from room to room, but couldn't find him anywhere. Alarmed, I ran outside shrieking, searching franticly calling for him. I called his real name out for the first time, since we met. I was hysterical standing on the beach just screaming his name over and over again as I fell to my knees sobbing. Finally, picking my head up, I focused my eyes and saw Babe running towards my direction. He sprinted like a marathoner scooping me up, holding me tightly and carried me into the house.

Closing all the lights, we went into the bedroom and stayed there all night. He crushed me against him, telling me over and over again how grateful he was that I was okay. Holding him as close as humanly possible, I didn't say anything, except that I loved him more than anyone. Babe knew how I felt; it was enough that he was alive. I knew he had bigger problems to deal with than me. What could I ask him that he would be able to answer? Nothing. I'd only make him crazy with the conversation, plus, I knew who they were already and why. In that moment, I gave up, and grew up a little bit more.

CHAPTER 24

Go Die In A Corner

Waking up in Breezy with Babe became normal. Technically, we didn't live together, but I slept there every night. I returned home only to check on my apartment, pay my rent, and pick up my mail. He gave me more than a drawer; I had keys, part of the closet, and counter space in the bathroom. Things were naturally smooth with us, but not in the outside world. As much as he wanted me to be home, he knew I was unhappy and felt trapped. Eventually we just learned to do go about our business without compromising too much.

One night the bar died down early enough to go out after work, and since Babe wasn't coming for me, I went out. I headed into the city, not knowing exactly where I wanted to go, but ended up at the Japan Club to meet up with Pino. He was in rare form with two red heads on his arms, but when he saw me, he left them at the table and gave me the biggest bear hug. "What are you doing baby?"

"Nothing, the bar was dead, so I closed up and came out."

"Sorry kid, do you need any money?" Pino took out his wad of cash and started to peel off some bills.

I stopped his hand, kissing his cheek. "Nah, I'm all good, but thanks!"

He gave me a sideways look laughing. "You sure? Come on take it, I'll only piss it away on these broads!"

Shaking my head giggling I had to ask the million-dollar question. "How the hell did you find two red heads? That's pretty rare!"

"Fucking tourists, but they're sisters, so it should be interesting!"

I laughed hard as I hit his arm. "You're so fucked up, but that's what I love about you! Hey just make sure they're over twenty-one!"

As I hugged him, he called out to Alex the bartender who knew me well from working there. "Hey, give us a bottle over here."

Just as he was toasting with me, I felt a hand on my arm and I turned to find Carl behind me. "Lucky, how are you?"

"Oh Carl, hey how are you?" I said as we kissed cheeks to say hello.

"I asked first." He laughed slightly, trying to be funny, and then turned to Pino. "Good to see you Pino." They hugged gangster style and turned back to me.

"So, Lucky, tell me, how are you? The last time I saw you, you were beating some girl up!" Carl grinned wildly, enjoying having me on the ropes.

Pino cut in, "Dannie who did you beat up now?"

"Oh, I thought it was a one time event, but it sounds like you do this often." He looked at me sideways.

As I tried to answer, Pino cut in. "Rocky over here is a strange combination of a brawler, fucking awesome bartender and a class act lady! Carl, she works for me on Grand Street, you should stop by one night."

He smiled as he sipped his drink. "I didn't know that, but I'll be sure to stop in!"

"It will be good to see you there. So, how do you know each other?" Pino asked.

I stood watching the two of them discuss me as if I wasn't there. Carl told Pino about the money, getting pulled over and Vibes. They laughed and traded a few stories and when they realized I was still there, they broke out laughing apologizing.

"Listen guys I hate to break up this party, but Pino, your red heads look bored." I motioned with my head towards the table, because they were chatting it up a few younger guys.

Pino leaned in kissing me, "Listen baby, come over and sit with me, I'll dump the broads..."

I cut him off, "No! I'll stop by before I go, but don't chase them for me."

"Okay, if you need anything I'm right over there." Pino called out to the bartender again, "Alex, anything she wants is on my tab! Understand?"

Alex called out joking around, "We still have strict orders not to charge her, so I'll charge you double!"

I had to laugh, because Alex and I still worked with each other and we never charged each other anyway. I thanked Pino before he went back to claim his prized red heads. Carl looked at me smiling, sipping his drink. "So its nice to finally talk to you. Do you come here a lot?"

Blushing, I giggled tucking my hair behind my ear. "Kind of, I work here and used to go out with one of the owners."

"You're turning red, that's a nice look on you!" He took another sip. "I've never seen you working here, I stop by weekly."

I put my hands to feel my cheeks, knowing fully well I was crimson. "Well, I used to be here a lot more, but I moved over to the Slime, so I only work every other Monday now, plus like Pino said, I work for him on Grand, and I also work in Brooklyn."

He looked surprised. "You certainly work a lot!"

I shook my head laughing. "Yeah, I like it that way."

Carl cut me off, "So, who did you go out with, I know all the guys."

"Here? Oh, John, we're still very close friends."

"John? I know him well, we meet up in Vegas every couple of months."

I had to laugh, because if he was in Vegas with John, he must have been a big gambler. "Do you now? Well, I remember those trips well! They were always tons of fun! Listen I'm glad I ran into you." His face brightened, probably thinking I meant something completely different from what I was about to say. I looked around to see who was standing within earshot, before I continued. "Listen Carl, I appreciate the interest; I'm flattered, but I'm in a relationship and don't want you chasing a run away horse. You understand?"

"I respect that, thank you. After watching you fight, I figured it out. I have to say you're very well liked; everyone I spoke to only had good things to say. Plus you have some right hook!"

My smile widened and tried not to laugh, because as much as I knew I had a solid reputation and a good swing, but it was nice to hear it. "Thank you, I invest in my relationships and am a hard worker."

Carl took out his wallet and handed me a business card. "If you're ever free, I'd still like to take you out and get to know you." I shook my head no, as I waved off the card, but he was determined and pressed into my palm. "I know you have a boyfriend, but that doesn't mean we can't be friends, so keep it and think about what I said."

I blinked a few times, before I answered. "Carl don't get the wrong impression; I'm not looking to date, fool around or anything like that. But it was nice to get to know you a little more. I'm sure we'll see each other again and become friends."

"I understand. You never know, we may never run into each other again, but I'm gonna to remember what you did for my friends so if you ever need anything don't think twice, call me." He replied, but his expression told me he would be visiting me soon nevertheless.

My stomach shifted, making me feel as if I was doing something wrong, talking to Carl, holding his card, and being in city alone without Babe knowing. *I'm always out, what's the big deal? Something about this whole thing isn't right, time to go!* "So I'm going to go, but thanks for understanding and it was very nice to actually meet you this time!" I leaned in and kissed his cheek, and quickly walked to Pino to say goodbye. "Hey Pino, I have to bolt. Have the waitress bring the bottle over, I can't stay, but thank you."

Pino's sly smile let me know he was watching my whole conversation. "We'll talk; come to work early so we can eat together. You be safe honey!"

I kissed him, as the redheads looked on stupidly. "Sure thing, love ya!"

I made my way to the door, just as James and some of the guys walked in. *Oh Jesus Christ!* We hugged and kissed, and when I explained I was leaving, he picked me up and carried me to the bar over his shoulder! He started calling out to Alex to set us up, slapping the bar in excitement. All the boys were trashed, but in great moods. I giggled slapping his shoulder to put me down, and he did, right on the bar. They all kissed and hugged me, as Alex popped a bottle for us.

"So Fats, I'm glad to see you!"

I cupped his face and kissed his cheek. "I love you wild man, but I have to leave!"

"Where you going? We just got here?"

"Brooklyn, I'm going to see Brianna."

"Fuck Brooklyn! Stay in the city, hang with us!" He said as he hugged me hard downing his glass.

I kissed him as I slid off the bar. "I know, but I have to get up in the morning. Plus there are tons of girls waiting for me to leave so they can have you guys all to themselves!"

I didn't wait for him to try and change my mind; I said my goodbyes and weaved through the crowd to get out fast. I was back in Brooklyn quickly and walked into Vibes to meet up with my girls. I think the phone calls were made before I even touched the bar. I could feel the eyes watching me, but it really didn't bother me. If I was there to hookup I would have hated being under a microscope, but I wasn't like that, so it was all good.

Talking to Brianna at the bar, I spotted my ex, Joe, out of the corner of my eye. He was standing on the side sipping a drink talking to another guy. *Ugh, this night completely sucks! Babe must have put a hex on me as punishment for going out!* He spotted me and walked over, stepping in front of me, "Hey what's up?"

"Fine, Joe, leave me alone," I said sidestepping him.

"I just wanted to say hello. You don't have to be so nasty." He said to my back as I passed.

"I want to. Later." I knew it wasn't going to end that easy. *I hoped he would just go off with his own friends and die somewhere, but I knew I had no such luck.* After a few minutes, Bri came over with an upside down shot glass, "You have a drink with the cunt, Joe, when you're ready."

Giggling at her description of him, I blurted out, "Fuck no! I would rather not; I don't want his drink. Plus I'll never drink what I have backed up."

"Joe, she doesn't want your drink, but I'm charging you anyway for annoying her and me!" She shouted loud enough for the whole bar to hear and everyone broke out laughing.

Now he thought he was a big shot because Brianna had acknowledged him, "Okay, very funny Dannie! Just about as funny as you stealing my car!"

"Oh here we go again! Please go die in some corner and leave me alone." I could hear the guys mumble that I was pretty funny and then one of the guys called out, "Did you really steal his car?"

"Joe, leave me A-l-o-n-e!"

"Looks like your new boyfriend is a handy guy! Nice face!" He voice trailed off.

"What did you say?"

"You heard me bitch!"

"Bitch? Stop talking about your mother! Did I start talking to you? No! I don't want to talk to you, be nice to you, or even stand next to you! Go away!" I fired off in rapid succession without stopping to hear his lame attempt at any comebacks.

Brianna chimed him, "Joe, you're acting like a little cunt, cut it out!"

"Really, just noticed? Go away!" I turned my back on him laughing at the Brianna's comment again, but I saw his face just as he was trying to swing at me. "Really Joe? You're such an asshole!" I said, completely exasperated with his constant stupidity! .

I really didn't have to finish the sentence, because all the guys were on their feet around me and not because of Babe, but because they liked me. They knew Joe too, but he crossed the line by yelling at and harassing me in public. Joe was taken off to the side and eventually he left on his own accord. I stayed drinking with my friends until the club closed. As we walked out to pickup our cars, I found Babe standing by mine with his friends in another car next to me. "Have a good time?" He asked.

"Of course, why wouldn't I?" I said, unsure of how much he knew already.

"Anything interesting happen?" Babe asked.

Trying to change the subject, I asked, "Why? Hey, aren't you supposed to be working?"

"I get out at 4AM, so I'm here. Where are you planning on going now?" He said as he wrapped his arms around me starting to kiss me.

"NO! I'm done for tonight!" I said, thoroughly enjoying his attention. Before we could say another word, Joe approached us, shouting incoherently obviously drunk. Babe stood in front of me and put his hand out to stop Joe from getting closer. Joe tried to slap his hand out of the way and Babe punched him, knocking him backwards. All his guys jumped out, but Babe didn't need their help. Babe was on him; he was punching him so hard I heard something break. He hit him so many times, so quickly; I thought he'd kill him. Babe's hands were like sledgehammers. Once Joe was down, Babe stomped on him, kicking his head in.

This was the beating of Joe's life! He kicked his ass from the car to the curb, leaving Joe in a bloody heap, while his guys watched for the sign to finish him off.

"Is there something you forgot to tell me?" He said as he turned to face me. Babe grabbed my arm, opened the car door and shoved me in just as Joe was up at us again. It was an unfair fight; Babe was just tougher. After Joe fell on the floor again, he didn't move much. Babe said something very close to his face and I saw Joe turn white. The look in his eyes said he was deathly afraid, I doubted he would ever approach me again if he were to live through the night. Babe jumped in the car and took off. I told him the whole story as he drove.

"Babe, I'm so sorry! I feel terrible about all of this; you're not hurt are you? Did you hurt Joe badly?"

"I'm fine, and what do you care if he's fucking hurt? I should've killed him! He was looking for trouble, and you're fucking lucky I was there," he said as he drove toward the highway with his guys in tow, shadowing us until we were home. We made small talk the whole ride; I decided not to mention anything about my night. *Nope don't say a word!* As soon as we walked in the house, I put the whole night on the back burner, I was just happy to be with Babe. It was a huge turn on to see him defend me; he was no slouch and could handle himself well.

"Hey, so why was your ex-boyfriend around? I want to hear this again." He said as we jumped into bed.

"I have no idea. Like I said, I was dancing and I looked up and saw him watching me. It's not my fault he was there."

"Really? Do you want me to believe that?" He said as he rolled over on top of me. He started to kiss me and roam within a second he was making love to me. Not normally rough, he was aggressive as he stayed on top holding my arms above my head nibbling on my lips asking, "Why are you worried if Joe's hurt?"

"Joe who?" I said trying to be cute.

"Do you still have a thing for him?" He said very deliberately.

"Joe Schmo!" I played.

"Answer me!" He shouted as he bit me.

"What's the question?" I said smirking not letting him know he was bothering me.

"Don't be cute! DO YOU HAVE A THING FOR HIM?" He demanded a lot rougher.

"I am cute, I can't help it!"

"Tell me!" He said more intensely.

"No! I have a thing for." I moaned.

Pressing he asked, "For who?"

"Hmmm!"

"For who?" He asked over and over again.

"For you!" I said screamed. "For you!"

We jumped over the edge together. He whispered in my hair "I love you," as I panted "Ditto!" The next morning I woke and made us breakfast in bed. For the first time, I could see a little grey hair in the morning sunlight as we ate. He looked so sexy naked, eating with me. As I settled back into his arms eating toast, I asked, "How did you know where we were and where the car was last night? I gave it to the valet, so how exactly did you know?"

"Never mind, I just knew!" He said laughing holding me tighter.

Feeding him toast I playfully asked, "Why didn't you come in to see me?"

"I wanted to see you walk out," He said biting my hand as he went for the bread.

"See what?"

"See you and whomever," He said smugly.

"Hmm, I like the thought of you being on your toes, and not too comfortable, but really you know I'm not like that."

"You think? Come closer and show me."

"Hmm how did you ever live without me?" I giggled as I turned to get up to put our breakfast tray on the floor, but stepped on a box. I jumped back, "Ouch! What's this?" I bent down and found a little box with a bow. He leaned over the side of the bed smiling. I looked at him and back to the box. "What's this?"

"I don't know why don't you open it and see?" Babe grinned leaning over the bed.

I slipped the bow off and found a beautiful diamond tennis bracelet. He slipped it on my wrist and pulled me on top of him. *What a way to start the day.*

CHAPTER 25

....

Shooting Gallery

Time was moving in quickly on us, only we didn't know yet. Every moment was edgy, filled with danger and desire. It was so distracting to be around him, because I couldn't think clearly. When I wasn't with him, my heart ached; Babe had become the big love of my life. My mind was in the clouds and I had to fight to keep myself grounded. We spent most nights together in Breezy and days back in the neighborhood. The few times I went home, it was uncomfortable. During dinner one night in downtown Brooklyn, Babe broached the subject.

Taking me by surprise, he asked, "How's your apartment doing?"

"Fine, I was there two days ago. Thank God I'm not into plants, because they would all be dead," I said trying to figure out where the conversation was going.

Looking at me, he asked, "How much do you pay in rent?"

Uncomfortably, I answered, "$1250, it's a score, I used to pay $1500 down the block."

Smiling he asked, "Do you like it, your apartment? The building?"

I answered, unsure of where this was going. "It's nice when I'm not getting held up. The neighbors hate me, mostly because of James fooling around in the elevator. It's a clean building and the owner is a nice guy. Why? Why do you ask?"

"I was just wondering," he said playing with his food. "You spend a lot of time in Breezy..."

He didn't finish his statement. My stomach started to sink. I pushed my dish away and looked at him. "Does that bother you, having me in Breezy? You're the one who keeps bringing me there. You know if you don't want me there, just tell me." My eyes were getting teary. "Excuse me." Not waiting for a response I left the table and walked to the rest room. Once inside, I went into the stall and started to cry. The bubble was about to pop, and I knew he was trying to figure out how to let me down. Trying to compose myself, I retouched my makeup and walked back to the table. When I approached, he stood up and held my chair out for me.

"You okay? Is the food bothering you?" He said with concern in his voice.

Trying to sound normal and not let my voice crack I said, "The food's fine, I'm good. Where were we? You were asking me about my apartment."

"I was just thinking that maybe you would like to be with me in Breezy. You shouldn't give up your apartment, but maybe sublet it." He said smiling at me.

He took me completely by surprise. Elated, I jumped on his lap right in the middle of the restaurant showering him with kisses. I'm sure people thought he proposed to me; I didn't care. "You want me to move in with you?"

"Apparently, yes." He said with his arms wrapped around me laughing. "You're a nut! So what's your answer?"

"I have to think about it!" I said playfully as I kissed him.

Tapping my lower back, he chuckled. "Unless you want to have me do you on the table and give the waiters a show, you better sit in your own seat. But I also want you to start thinking about a business you would want to have. I have some money on the side, and I want you to open something that you'll enjoy doing to make your own money." He fixed my shirt a little smiling at me, before he continued. "I really don't want you behind the bar anymore. Find something that makes you happy and I'll finance it, but it's gonna be all yours."

Settling back, my heart was racing and I couldn't hide my tremendous grin. "I'm not sure, I have to think about it."

Grinning he said, "Really now? You look pretty excited for someone who has to think about it."

Trying to look serious, I expressed my sincere gratitude; "First, you don't have to do that, but thank you! I really want you to know I'm not with you for anything more than being with you! Truly thank you for everything you have done and want to do for me, but please don't anything that'll send you back!"

"Don't tell me what to do with my money already! I'll buy the building, and you can have the storefront. Fuck it you can have the building too!" He buried his face in my neck making me giggle.

"Oh Babe, thank you, thank you, thank you!" I smothered him with kisses.

He pulled my shoulders back. "Now, what about moving in?"

"Well, you have to tell me more, like what are the arrangements?"

"What arrangements? I'm asking you to live with me." He started to laugh and make fun of me. "Are you really a blonde? I think you might be with all these silly questions! Dense!"

"Oh, so you are actually asking me officially to live with you, because I know you think I'm always a mind reader. I want to make sure there's no misunderstandings."

"You are such a ball buster!" He laughed.

"Thank you very much!"

"Okay, okay Danielle, come here baby. I love having you with me you know that. So why don't you move in?"

I grinned from ear to ear moving my food around on my plate as I sat there staring at him and finally said, "Do I get to use the phone? Can I answer it?"

Trying to sound nonchalant he said, "I'm installing another phone for us, but my first one will only be in the spare room."

Pressing further, "The locked room, I've never been in?"

"Yes, it's my office." He said as he sipped his wine giving me the eye.

"What about your daughter, are you ever going to introduce me?" I asked nervously, as I drained my glass.

Touching my face, he assured me, "Of course, lets plan it at my mother's."

"So let me get this straight, Breezy will become your main place, right? You will be coming home to sleep every night? This isn't going to be a place for all the guys?"

Babe took my hand and held it as he said, "I know you love the beach and the house, so I think it would be perfect for us. Plus it's really not a secret anymore since I've been with you."

I was on the verge of crying, my eyes danced like jewels. "So you will be sleeping there every night right?"

Reverting back to being a ball buster, "Unless you don't want me to, I'm joking. I have to check into the half way house, but there are conditions to living with me that you have to know."

I put my fork down and gave him my full attention. "Go ahead, what are they?"

He took my hand and turned serious. "You know I'm out on parole, if I violate the conditions in any way I will have to serve the rest of my sentence. That's five more years, so you can't do anything or bring anything or anyone into the house that would compromise my parole."

"Well, that's pretty easy, I don't do drugs. I only smoke cigarettes and drink; both are legal." If you're old school like me, drugs are a no-no and now I knew I would never indulge again. That part of my wild life was over for good, it just wasn't worth the stress, plus I just didn't enjoy it as much as I enjoyed him.

Continuing, he said, "Dannie there are people I can't be around, anyone else who's out on parole. Understand? So talk to me first before you invite anyone new over."

Beaming, I said, "I can do that, no problem. I thought it was something more serious."

"Well, I'm not done yet. I'm going to ask permission to officially move in here, so you and the whole arrangement will have to be approved by my parole officer."

"Oh, okay, I've never been in trouble, or arrested so I should be fine. I'm as good as a girl scout! Now I have a question for you."

Laughing at me he said, "Shoot."

"Very apropos, is there anything in the house, or should I say will there be anything in the house that would get me in trouble if it was ever searched?" I said delicately.

Narrowing his eyes he looked at me like I hit a nerve. "Very perceptive again Peeper, I'll take care of everything, don't worry."

I went a step further. "Bills too."

He laughed at me asking, "Are you making a statement or asking a question?"

"Definitely making a statement!" I said cracking up.

"I don't want your money, I don't even want you to work! Your new job is supposed to be looking good, keeping a clean house, and being there for me. You're a nut! Come on eat before everything gets cold," He said as he leaned over to kiss me.

"I have a lot of stuff; this is going to be interesting. I've lived on my own since I was 18 and my closets show it. I don't want to give up my apartment, because it's a good deal," I said totally overwhelmed, but in a good way.

"Listen, those are all good problems. Don't stress! I just don't want to waste any more time, I have a lot to catch up on. You figure out what you want and I'll make it happen." Babe leaned over and kissed me.

"I love you!" *You have no idea how much I really love you!*

"Ditto, now let's eat!" he said as we started to dig into our meal. I was famished and ate everything in front of me.

The next day, I went home and started to pack up my belongings. Wasting no time, I was ready within the week. I left all my furniture and everything as if I were going away for a weekend.

"So this is the last box. I guess you're officially in. How many pair of shoes do you fucking own?" Babe said, as he placed the box on the floor in our bedroom.

"I know, I have more shit I didn't even look at yet, but I'm here! First we have to change the answering machine outgoing message and then let's go shopping."

"Shopping for what?" Babe asked confused.

"Sheets, towels; stuff like that."

"I have all of that, you use them every day." He said as he sat on the end of the bed.

"That's different, I was a guest. Now I'm not and I don't want to sleep in the same sheets that anyone else did," I said as I climbed on and straddled him. "I'm marking my territory Babes!" Playfully kissing him, I ran my fingers through his hair.

"If you keep doing that I'll be saving lots of money today!" He said as he laid back and drew me into him. After we rolled around making out, I slid down and reminded Babe of what he was in for. Moaning he wrapped my hair around his hands, until he couldn't hold out anymore. He pulled me back up, kissing me deeply. "Ouffa Peeper, what was that for?"

As I touched his face, I whispered, "I thought it would make shopping easier to deal with."

"Fuck shopping! Let's stay in bed!"

I titled my head, narrowing my eyes. "Nope! I will burn these fucking sheets tonight with you in them if I don't get new ones!"

He held his laughter, but couldn't help grinning at me. "Okay Peeper, lets roll so we can make dinner with Vinnie after we're done."

Giggling, I whispered in his ear, "Perfect!" I jumped out of bed and freshened up, while he got dressed. My poor baby, he looked so tired, his lifestyle was taking a heavy toll on him.

We drove to Century 21 on 86th street and went on a shopping spree. Babe let me pick everything; as it turned out, we had very similar tastes. Bags in tow, we walked through the women's department stopping in the handbag section. He was looking at a display counter, while I rummaged through the racks; shortly, he came up behind me and kissed my cheek. Smiling, I turned around and he was holding another shopping bag. "Ooh, what's that?"

"Just a little something from Fendi for you! I hope you like it." He said holding it above my head. Kissing me again, he grinned as he spoke, "I like seeing you happy."

"You make me very happy, I love you!" I said kissing him back. Babe put his arm over my shoulder and we walked out of the store. It was one of the happiest moments of my life; just the two of us enjoying being with each other. The boys love to shower their girls with presents; usually it's to buy their blindness; you're less inclined to get mad that they stayed out late when they come home with a designer bag.

Soon after we stopped for dinner, I guess he picked the restaurant so he could mix business with pleasure. I sat at the bar sipping my wine while he moved from one small group of guys to another. Some made small talk with me, the waiters were polite but I could feel the tension in the air. Taking it all in, I watched the dance of this life unfold in front of me. Eventually, we moved to a table and were joined by another couple, close friends of Babe. Vinnie and Gabriella; I liked them very much. Vinnie and Babe were inseparable, and I began to feel like we had been friends forever, even though Vinnie had been my boy for years.

Soon we were toasting and Vinnie joked around, "Who knew this is where we would end up, after I towed your car! Chin, chin!" We clinked glasses and laughed as our meal was being served.

Since he opened the door to the conversation, I walked in. "So Vinnie, you towed my car huh? I don't remember calling you. I hope you flat bedded it away, instead of hitting every pot hole in town."

"Flat bed? Nope! Babe asked me to only use one chain and make it swing while I dragged it all over town. I put the top down and drove through the car wash too! Hey I was your friend before you met Babe, of course I flat bedded it, that's a sweet little convertible."

We all laughed and talked making the meal pass quickly. During coffee and dessert, the guys took their cups doing the walk and talk thing, even stepping outside to smoke, leaving us girls at the table. Gabriella and I didn't mind; we were having our own fun. There was a noise coming from somewhere, and after looking around, we realized it was coming from outside. My instincts kicked in and I started to get up to find Babe, when Gabriella grabbed my wrist. "Sit, don't get involved. You have to learn to let them be, and ignore everything even if you want to rip their hearts out. You're not the bartender here, you're the girlfriend and there's a world of difference." I've said the same exact thing hundreds of times before, but it's very different when you're in the drivers seat.

"Believe me, I know, but..." I said as I sat again.

"Whatever he's in, you can't help. Believe me, Babe would be so pissed if you went outside now. You guys are just starting out, do it on the right foot," Gabriella said, as she sipped her coffee taking a bite of her cake. Of course I knew all of this already, but it was hard for me to sit inactive, though I tried not to show it. After a loud shouting match, Babe stormed in with Vinnie trailing closely behind. He was patting my hair with his big bear paw hand as he stood over me, talking to the restaurant manager.

Finally, Babe sat down as our after drinks arrived. He tried to act as if nothing had happened, but I could tell by the stormy look in his eyes he was pretending. He fell into a conversation with Vin as I sat sipping my Tia Maria. I wanted to keep the night positive, so I tried to make light conversation with Gabriella.

"One night we should go out to the city for dinner and dancing when the guys are busy. I don't think I've seen you at any of my haunts. Where do you go?"

"I really don't, unless I'm with Vin." She said, as she smiled at him.

Trying to be friendly, I offered, "Oh, okay then we should all go together it'll be fun! Pick the date and I'll get us a table at Regina's, The Slime Light, The Japan Club or anywhere you want to go. I've worked in all the hot clubs and one of the perks is I get in everywhere and always have a great table."

"Oh that's sounds like fun; it must be exciting to work in those places. Do you like it?" Gabriella asked sounding interested.

"I do! The night flies by so quickly. I create a fantasy world, where you come in and forget that your life stinks, or that you're not that special. For the price of a drink, you get the whole show; I pay as much attention and make as much small talk as I can. By the end of the night, the guys think they're rock stars and the girls feel beautiful. I get paid to have fun, what could be better than that?" I meant every word and I could see Babe's eyes boring into mine. *Did I say something wrong? Am I not supposed to like working?* I couldn't figure it out so I toned it down, "What do you do?"

"I stay home. Nothing as exciting as you, but I like it," She said without sarcasm. Switching gears Gabriella asked, "Do you like kids?"

Turing pink I said, "Yes, but not now I'm still having fun." Now, I was turning purple, hoping I said the right thing, because I knew better. The last thing any guy wants to hear is that a girl wants children when they are newly dating. The topic of children and marriage makes guys run in the opposite direction. I could tell I was failing miserably at small talk, so I turned my attention to Babe and put my hand on his leg. He didn't notice, so I slid it higher, still nothing, he kept talking until my hand was in his lap. Babe put his hand over mine and just held it there and put his other arm over my shoulder pulling my chair closer. He leaned in and kissed my forehead while he continued to talk to Vin. *Whew! I guess I didn't say anything too awful.*

The night was coming to a close and we all got up to leave. I thanked the restaurant owner and waiters profusely and walked out holding Babe's arm; I was so happy to be on it, and I let him know with the way I held it. I knew he liked it because his free hand was holding my fingers that were wrapped around his arm. As soon as we walked outside we lit cigarettes and stood on the sidewalk smoking and bullshitting. The mood was light, and some other patrons were outside milling about. I was looking down the block at the sunset, when I saw a car make a hairpin turn. I grabbed Babe's arm as I pulled him down hard throwing myself on him just as it passed. I saw the car; it had smoked windows and was slowing down as popping sounds came from it just as we hit the concrete, and then there was screeching sound of tires pealing out. Glass went flying everywhere; windows were shattering all around us! I felt something warm and sticky dripping down my neck and face, the sharp pain was intense.

Babe looked at me wide eyed and said, "You're bleeding!"

Amazingly, I was level headed and calm for just being almost shot, because I was more worried for Babe then myself. "I don't know, I think so, are you?"

I looked around and there was broken glass and blood everywhere. He didn't answer he was on his feet staring at me horrified as he pulled me up. We had parked in the front; thank God the car was there. Babe dragged me through the driver's side. Everything was happening so fast, he started the car and pealed out of the parking spot without saying a word. I was amazed that he seemed very calm and was in total control, even though the world around us was in complete chaos. As he drove, I could hear those jungle drums of war again beating louder than ever. I didn't say a thing; this was just too serious for idle chatter.

Babe pulled up in front an apartment building I had never seen before and got out. He carried me up the stairs double time. I couldn't figure out why, I thought I could have walked. The door was open and he ran right into a bedroom. As he lowered me on the bed, the look on his face started to make me nervous and I asked trying not to cry, "Babe what's wrong? I wasn't shot right?"

"Shush, stay still." Babe quickly but very gently inspected me. My skin was on fire, and I started to cry hard from the pain as he touched me. "Shush, it's okay, don't cry come on it's okay." He inspected every inch of me, including my scalp. Very gently he parted my hair and searched my head, "Oh boy, you're lucky. You have a lot of cuts but I think it's from the shattered glass." He shook out my clothes and glass came tumbling out on the floor. "You had your back to the restaurant windows when they blew out. You're really fucking lucky!"

Grabbing his hand, I kissed it thinking about how close I was to losing him. "You too! You're not hurt?"

Trying to make me calmer, he tried to minimize the situation, "Rocky didn't you say you would protect me? Remember? Well, you did good, real good!" His eyes spoke right to my soul, more so than anything he was saying. "James is coming to take you home, he should be downstairs." Quickly, we figured out my clothes were not going back on. I had way too many cuts; I just couldn't manage it.

Shaking my head at the thought of slipping anything on over my shredded skin I said, "Listen give me a sheet, I'll wrap it around myself and go. I just can't get dressed. You're not coming right?"

"Honey I can't, James will take care of you until I get back," He said as he gathered everything and helped me get ready. Within minutes James was there and Babe helped me into the car. Before he closed the car door, he leaned in and said, "Listen to James, and you know...you just know don't you?"

"I do, and I love you too! Be careful!" with that he closed the door and James took off.

He followed the letter of the law, and stayed within the speed limit the whole way, because if he were to be pulled over, how would he explain a naked, cut and bleeding girl wrapped in a sheet sitting in his car. I sat quietly, because my mind was racing. I watched the water fly by on the belt Parkway, and before I realized it, we were in Breezy. James pulled up and opened my door to help me out. There was a guy walking his dog nearby who stopped to look at us.

"That was some toga party!" I joked loud enough for the dog walker to hear as I limped towards the house. Once we were in, he went into the bathroom and turned on the tub as I followed.

"Come on you, get in the tub. I'll hold the sheet and you get in unless you need me to help you lay down?" James saw I was crying so he tried to break the tension by joking around. "It's not like I've never seen a girl before, you don't have anything different from your girlfriends."

I was just dying from the pain of a thousand cuts. "I fucking couldn't care less what you see; I'm in so much pain right now."

"Okay get in and I'll get you a drink, plus I have to get salt."

"Salt for what?" I looked at him like he was crazy.

"The water, it'll help with the cuts." He tried to calm my nerves, "What do you want to drink?"

"Don't tell me anymore, please, just help me in." I said as James reached over and helped me take my sheet off and then held my arms as I sunk into the bathtub. The warm water was like an electric current going through my body. I cried out at first, but after a few minutes it felt heavenly. "Hey James, do you have my bag? I need a cigarette."

"Let me run to the car and get it, be right back. I'm going to get us a drink and the salt too." He turned and walked out leaving me to soak. He quickly returned with the salt, a bottle of wine, two glasses and a pack of cigarettes. He poured salt into the water and told me to swirl it around. I could feel the sting immediately. He handed me a glass of wine and lit a cigarette for me.

Trying to make the best of this situation, I joked, "You know this isn't exactly how I thought I would be if I took a bath with someone."

He shot up, "WE ARE NOT TAKING A BATH TOGETHER. I'm helping you, that's totally different. Babe would kill me if he ever thought differently."

I looked at him like he had three heads, "Oh stop, you know what I mean. He knows we're friends. In fact we've been friends long before he entered the picture."

"There are no friends when it comes to this sort of shit. Make no mistake; he would go ballistic if he thought otherwise." He sat down on the toilet and took a big swig from his glass of wine. It seemed to do the trick because he started to relax a bit. "So, you took my advice and gave him a shot. Now you guys live together."

Smiling at him, I joked, "Oh my God yes, but look where your advice got me, almost shot! I'm kidding, yeah its strange how this all worked out. I think I need to have my cuts looked at, I hope I don't have glass in any of them."

"I can do that, but from the looks of you, the glass went through your clothes. I have them inside they're frigging shredded." Turning serious he asked, "Did you ever have a tetanus shot before?"

Thinking back, I said, "I had one last year, because of the rusty pipe I stepped on. I think I'm done with the bath; I need to take a shower I want to wash my hair. Can you help me?"

"You wanna get me killed!" James said as he came over and helped me up in the tub. I flipped the drain switch and stood up with his help. "You didn't hit your head right?"

"I don't know, I don't think so. Why?" I said as I turned on the shower. "My scalp is killing me!"

"Because I want to make sure you don't have a concussion. Come on wash your hair so we can get out of here." James leaned against the wall next to the shower and kept his hand against the wall for me to hold on to. I could see the sparkly pieces of glass hit the tub while I rinsed. I finished quickly and shut off the water.

"Okay James, I'm done. I'm not sure I can put my clothes on though."

He gently placed a big robe around me and walked me to the couch in the living room. He started a fire and went into the bedroom, and came out with his arms full. "Okay let's try this first, lay back and show me your legs." He inspected them and put peroxide on all the cuts. He thought I looked okay, no glass in my cuts so I decided to put on sweats. Then he moved towards my chest, back and neck; all looked good so I put on the hoodie. It was big and soft and the zipper made it easy. James moved to the arm of the couch as I sat facing him with my head down. He started to comb through my hair parting it looking for glass. "You have glass in your scalp, stay still and I'll take it out. I took your tweezers from the bathroom."

I wanted to scratch my head, but couldn't because it hurt so much. "That's why my head is on fire. Thanks, I really appreciate it."

"You owe me, big time!" He joked, as he started to pull the little shards of glass out. "So, you did good, Pal!"

"I don't know what made me look in that direction, but I kind of knew something was wrong when the car made the turn." Thinking about the car and those eyes made me want to throw up.

James held my shoulder for a second as he said sincerely; "Well you probably saved his life, when you pulled Babe down."

I sat there, thinking about what had happened tonight, as he filled an ashtray with the glass. There was something about the eyes I saw through the window that was bothering me; they were so familiar. *Could they belong to a close friend, or an old friend that jumped crews?* A million questions ran through my head, I couldn't rest, thinking about those eyes. I was amazed when James was done. There were just so many cuts; he poured a bottle of peroxide on my head. It burned like hell, bubbling and foaming up. Afterwards, he brushed my hair and braided it like a champ.

"Whew James, you know a lot about hair for a guy who buzzes his own. Where did you learn how to braid?" I said, smiling at him.

Being a wise ass, he joked. "Your girlfriends! Okay, how do you feel, better?"

"So much better, thanks! But I'm tired; how about we go watch TV inside."

"Are you crazy? I can't go watch TV in Babe's bed! You go, I'll bring a chair to the door." He helped me inside and sat in the doorway talking to me until I fell asleep. I had such nightmares; I kept reliving the shooting over and over again. The sound of the gun and the glass shattering made me wake up screaming. Babe and James ran into the bedroom to see if I was okay.

"Shush, rest." Babe said as bent down next to me touching my cheek.

"What's happening? Are you all right?" I asked totally foggy.

"I'm fine, go back to sleep," he said, as he kissed me again and walked back into the living room. They talked quietly; I couldn't hear them, but they looked intense. I was drifting in and out of a restless sleep, smelling cigar smoke. On the verge of throwing up, I finally got out of bed and walked inside. There were guys everywhere. Babe was in his office, but walked out talking as soon as I entered the room. "No one called the cops. How are you feeling honey? You need something?"

"Fresh air! The cigars are killing me!" I said smiling as I walked over to the refrigerator to get a glass of water. "Anyone hungry?" All the guys started to crowd around the island and before I knew it, I was making potatoes and eggs. Everyone loved it, especially James who kept dipping his Italian bread into the pan, sopping up the olive oil.

"Hmm, that was delicious! I'm so glad you woke up Pal, I was fucking starving!" James mumbled as he munched on the bread.

"James thanks for before, really I can always count on you. Love ya!" I walked over and gave him the biggest hug. Nothing beats a great friend.

Babe came over, puffing on his cigar and gently slapped my ass. "Look at this love fest! James you did good my friend, thanks."

Laughing, he playfully slapped him on his back and went back inside his office, which quickly became the war room.

The boys face this kind of situation more than the average person knows. Very few incidents get reported, forget the neighbors, they'll never call the cops. Almost always, it's between them and it's like housekeeping for the mob; occasionally a civilian gets in the cross fire and then it's bad. Every neighborhood had the old Italian ladies who dressed in black for a hundred years, tossed salt over their shoulders, went to church every Sunday, wouldn't step on a crack, and wore red ribbons safety pinned onto their bras to keep the evil eye away; they would rather die than call the cops. They just closed the blinds and pretended it never happened. Usually, their sons were mobbed up too, so they too were in this life.

CHAPTER 26

Living In The Fast Lane

Like the shot heard around the country that set off the American Revolution, the drive by started a chain of events I could never have imagined. From that moment on, I had to look both ways, more so than ever, when I was walking in and out of anywhere. Babe was keeping crazy hours; I was alone more and more at the beach house. Our hours were very different from other couples, because we both worked nights. Early one morning before we fell asleep, we were in bed watching TV, Babe pulled me close to talk, "I think you should take a vacation from working in the city and the bar for a while."

"Oh come on, I make terrific money, you really want me to give up a minimum of three-G's a night? That's on a regular night, not counting the special nights when big shots come out." I said resting on his chest. "How many girls do you know who can make that kind of money legitimately and with their clothes on?"

"Funny! You're hilarious! You better keep your clothes on out there, but not in here. If I could, I would throw them all out so you'd have to be naked all the time here."

"Suppose I don't. What are you going to do about it?" I teased, playfully.

"I told you about making guys blind again. I'm spending too much money on sticks!" He said as he gently tickled my side. "All kidding aside, behave yourself."

"I know that! Hey, I'm no slouch either; so you better ride on the right side of the road too! Remember I know E-VE-E-R-Y-O-N-E and they all gossip. But really, you want me to take a break from work? If I stop the momentum, it will never be the same. The cash will dry up and someone else will take my place. As it is, just being labeled your girl affects my wallet. Guys who would normally flirt and tip big are giving me ordinary money and keeping their distance now. Before you 'noticed' me, you have no idea what I'd been tipped! I had a guy tip me with a car trying to get into Fort Knox, another made me a hand-carved bed and brought it right to the front door of the restaurant in Little Italy to give it to me, and let's not forget the guy who gave me a mink coat as a tip!"

"I don't wanna hear about any of that shit! First, I don't want you working so much, second, I can't be everywhere all the time, and third, I want you home more." Stopping to kiss my head he continued, "I have a lot of time to catch up on."

Titling my head I smiled at him. "What does that mean? How are you going to catch up?"

Babe rolled over to face me. He started to touch my cheek while I lay on his arm, looking at his beautiful eyes when he asked, "How do you feel about kids?"

"Kids? I just moved in." I said biting my lip, breaking into a sweat.

"Come on, it took long enough to get here. We love each other; think about it."

"How many kids do you want?"

"A lot!" he said as he rolled over on top of me. Holding my face in his hands, he started to make love to me.

"A lot? Hmm." I moaned, "That sounds like ten."

"Okay, ten!" He whispered

"Not ten! Ahh!" I said, licking his ear.

"Eight!" he said, as he moved with me.

"What are we orthodox? Fuck no!" I said as I dug my nails in his back.

"Six!" He pressed.

"Six? I'm not a Mormon!"

"Four!" He said as he moved in me.

I pushed him back a second to see if he was playing me. "Are you serious?"

Looking at me like never before, he said, "I couldn't be more serious, I'll even buy you a bigger house. Whatever you want, you just tell me!"

"I just moved into this one," I said stunned.

"Four!" He kept the pressure up.

"I didn't even unpack fully," I countered.

"Two!" He pushed.

"I didn't even go food shopping yet." Trying to focus, as he was distracting me by biting my neck.

He was gripping my face and burying me with deep kisses; when he surrendered and shouted, "Start with one!"

I surprised myself as I moaned, "Okay!"

Now he was really mauling me, whispering, "I love you!" Somehow I had fallen in love with someone I didn't want to date, moved into his house in the middle of nowhere when I always wanted to live in the center of all the action, and am now talking about children, all within a few short months. My head was spinning. I could hear him say in my mind, all good problems, so I relaxed and enjoyed the moment.

The boys rush through life much faster than most people, because everything changes on a dime for them. At any minute they could be pinched, and spend half their life or more behind bars. Living in the fast lane, it's easy to get swept up in their whirlwind excitement. They love lots of children; big everything including homes, meals, cars, boobs, butts, parties, and families.

When we got up, it was with a whole new feeling. Babe started pressuring me to ease up at work right away. "I really don't want you working anymore, but I know I won't win that battle yet! Really, you don't have to work at all let alone that much, I just want you around more. You think about a business yet?"

"We've been through this and yes I've been thinking, but I don't know what I want to do." I said, tiring of the conversation, because deep down, I was afraid to give up too much control of my life. *Suppose things didn't work out and I quit my jobs, I would be left without anything.*

"Think faster! And no, you've been through it. I'm not giving in; you have to make a decision here," he said, taking a stand.

"Okay, maybe I'll give up one night in Brooklyn, but I'm keeping Little Italy and everything in the city. There is just too much money at stake," I said, as I started to get dressed. Picking out a really cute little black outfit for the night in the city, I turned to him for the stamp of jealousy or approval. If he wanted me to change, it was because I looked too hot, and then I knew I was making money tonight! "I'm taking my car; I need to fill up my tank before heading into the city. You need anything before I come back?"

"Why are you taking your car?" Babe asked getting more annoyed by the moment.

As nonchalantly as I could, I said, "Most likely I'm going to The Zone Club after work, with some of the girls and Pino."

Now he was pissed. "Really, when were you going to tell me?"

"What? I don't know, I guess later when I firmed up my plans. What's it matter, you're working anyway?" I looked at him, confused at his attitude. When we were single, he loved I was out all the time, but quickly, he was changing. *Why do guys try to make girls home bound after they meet them out?*

"Are you kidding me? You can't just go anywhere; you need to use your head. Things aren't good, come on," he said exasperated. "Your safety is important."

I sat down on the edge of the bed and looked at him. "Babe, listen, this thing of yours has nothing to do with me, no matter what. You said it yourself; I grew up with everybody, worked with and love them all, which will never change. All this crazy shit that's happening, is about you and your friends not me. Plus I go out, a lot! You know it, that's not going to change any time soon. I have a life with my friends, and it includes girls and guys." I grabbed his hand and put it on my heart. "I love you, I really do! So much more than I thought I would, but I'm a girl, and again, you said I have no place in this. I'm getting nervous at how I've been a target lately and how fast things are changing. I don't want to give up working, going out and my life just yet."

"What the fuck are you talking about? You're my girl! You live with me! I just asked you, not the girl next door to have kids with me! EVERYTHING FUCKING CHANGED, you can't expect it to be the same. I think you need a fucking reality check." Taking a breath, he continued, "What the fuck! You grew up in this, and I'm not the first guy you dated so you need to stop and think about what's going on here."

Raising my eyebrow, I smirked at him, "You asked me while we were having sex. Are you serious, really?"

Looking offended, he said, "Of course I am! I meant every word."

I sat down and gave him my total attention, "Listen, do you really want to have a baby? You can't change your mind, and leave me holding the bag literally."

Gripping my hands, he was more serious than I'd ever seen him before. "Do you think that little of me? Why would I do that? Do you really think I would leave my kid?"

"You know, I don't think badly of you at all! Well, no, I meant do you really want them, or were you just caught up in the moment?"

"No, I really meant it! I want to have kids now." He said as kind and sweet as any man could be during this kind of conversation.

Now I was thrown for a loop. "I, I, I, listen do you want to talk about this all now? I would love kids! I want a big family; I want you to chase me around the kitchen when I cook. I want our friends to come over with their families, but most of all I want to grow old with you." I was about to cry. *Then ask me to marry you, don't ask me to get knocked up!*

I couldn't say what I was thinking, so I bit my lip instead. "I gotta go to work. We can talk about my reality check later. But for now, I'm your girl who works, has friends and goes out. You need to be okay with that. I won't cheat on you, but come on, you're not my father, and you're my guy. As for growing up in this, you're right, but then again that's one of the reasons you pursued me, so lets not pretend. Just remember what you like about me, is also what you're trying to change quickly!" I choked out, trying to be as sincere as possible, although clearly frustrated.

"Hey, why are you crying?" Babe grabbed my arm as I put my earrings on. He turned me around and straightened my dress. "This is way too short!"

"It's not new, you always like it before." I wiped the tears away and leaned in hugging him.

He repeated. "Hmm, why are you crying?"

"You are offering me everything I've ever wanted, you've been so generous and I'm loving you more than I could ever have imagined, it's just I'm afraid the other shoe is going to drop. That's why I want to say yes, but I can't exactly stop on a dime. Supposed it doesn't work out the way you want it? If it doesn't work, I'm not sure I can handle it." I tried to shake off my fears as we moved trapped in a very awkward situation. I could tell Babe didn't like to hear about anything negative. My fears and his unpredictability always made me feel like I was walking on eggshells. My life so far had been very chaotic, and it didn't seem to be slowing down any time soon. When it was time to leave, I kissed him very gently, knowing how agitated he was. It didn't help that I was dressed in a skintight little black spandex dress; the look on his face let me know he disapproved.

"Shush, I get it, come on baby we'll talk later. Beep me, spend the money and park in a lot, don't street park." He said trying to salvage the conversation.

"Yup, will do. Love you!" I whispered as I walked towards the door.

I stopped, as he called out, "Don't fucking bend over in that napkin of a dress."

Shooting him a playful look, I left and jumped in my car. I couldn't wait to get to the city and away from the Brooklyn ways. The city vibe was perfect and suited me just fine. I couldn't help but think as I drove that I didn't want to change that much so fast. *Give up my job? Crazy talk; I would never take a night off let alone quit, thousands in cash a night was just too much money to say no too.*

I had to figure out something else. I decided to compromise and park in a lot and walk down the block to the restaurant. The neighborhood was buzzing with tourists, street hawkers, and the boys doing the talk and walk. You know when you look hot and can see the heads turn as you walk on by, it definitely gives you pep in your step. Just as I crossed the street, a cabbie whistled at me, but didn't watch where he was going and hit the cab in front of him. *Nice, I caused another car accident! Do I really want all of this to change?*

The night flew by. My regulars all poured in and the money flowed like the Nile. Pepe, who owned a pizzeria, started the night off by inviting a group of tourists in for drinks. Good grief, I knew those girls would never understand what was happening, but it was my job to make sure everyone had a great time. I turned up the music and flashed my big smile. Jerry joined the girls and started to spin his web of stories. One girl asked what they did for a living, which was always a fun question to hear. Jerry laughed sadly, "I'm retired, not because I want to be, but because I had an accident at work."

"Oh how sad! What happened to you?" One girl asked. I stopped and looked at him as he continued. "I was a pearl diver. Pretty famous too, maybe you've heard of me?"

"No, I don't think so." The girl said.

"Well, in America I'm pretty famous. I've been a diver for a long time. Black pearls, white pearls, fresh or salt water don't matter."

He said with such enthusiasm, I almost died laughing. "But one tough dive, I encountered the little man in the boat. We had a terrible fight it was a real battle! Thankfully, I made it out alive, and now I'm unable to dive." He said muttering as if he lost a limb in battle.

I couldn't keep a straight face; I was crying laughing, doubling over. The girls looked confused and upset for him, they tried to console him. He whipped out a Benjamin and tossed it to me, winking, as he said, "Ladies lets go somewhere else where I can tell you more about finding pearls." *What a bunch of gullible girls! They had no idea he was referring to oral sex! Jerry was certainly famous for being a pearl diver, but not the kind you could string together. Ha!* When it was time to close up at 1AM, I cleaned up the bar while Millie hung out waiting with the owner, Pino, Cousin, JP, and Craig.

Hurrying we ran out and headed over to the Zone on the West Side Highway, an outdoor tiki-style club. Some of the girls were there already and we met up and the fun began. Before we knew it, it was 4AM and the club was about to close. A small scuffle broke out with some guy who was rough with a waitress. Within moments, the girl was screaming and our guys walked over to investigate. Pino told the pedestrian to keep his hands to himself and not touch the waitress.

This pedestrian mouthed off so Cousin and Pino grabbed his throat and tossed him into the Hudson River. He screamed like a girl when he hit the water! The waitress was so grateful that someone stuck up for her; she bought us a few rounds. By the time we finally left I was shocked how late it was. Pino wanted us to go to Williamsburg to his after hour joint, but the ride seemed too far so I decided against it and opted to go home instead. Just then, I realized I never called or beeped Babe. I never even thought about him or checked my pager. Saying goodnight, I rushed to my car and found the valets totally bewildered.

"What's up guys?" I asked feeling a little uneasy because they were all around my car. Once I walked past them, I saw my car was filled to the brim with newspapers. Oh my god, Babe must have tossed them in because I had my top down. They didn't know what to say. You kind of know if someone does something so off the wall, they must be connected, and not to fuck with them.

Valet kids make outrageous money and would never jeopardize that for anything, so no one was talking. It's not like I needed their input anyway, really I knew all along who it was. Where to dump the papers was my biggest problem; it's not like you can get rid of a carload of papers in NYC without being noticed. Millie walked over and started to laugh, "Oh my god! He's a psycho, how fucking funny!"

"I know, but what I am going to do?" I said as I popped the trunk open. "Sweet, my trunk is empty. Help me grab some papers and stuff them in my trunk."

We shoved piles and piles into my trunk; my rear end was hanging a little low. *Prick, if I blow my shocks and struts I'll kill you!* Finally, I cleared the two seats and we jumped in and jetted out of the city with the radio blasting TLC. *So, now I have to think, do I let this go on without retaliating; no I don't think so!* Once back in Brooklyn, I drove to my friend's carting company and dumped all of the papers except for one.

We went to the Chinese deli that stays open all night and bought flowers and then headed to Breezy. Once there, we found a vase and rolled the flowers in the newspaper and left them on the center island for Babe to find. It was getting late, so we curled up on the bed to watch TV.

We must have fallen asleep, because when I woke up Millie was next to me and Babe was on the couch. Oh poor guy, he was hanging off looking so uncomfortable. Millie and I snuck in and stood over him and started to gently call his name out while we played with his hair. "Ooh Babe, Babe, hmm where are you?" We sang in a whisper by his ear. "Ooh Babe, wake up. Baby we need you."

Moaning like he was half dead, "Funny! You girls are a fucking riot!" Rolling over he grabbed my wrist and dragged me down on him. "I thought it was Christmas when I walked in and found both of you in my bed! You're both lucky I'm such a nice guy, otherwise I wouldn't be on the couch."

Giggling, kissing his face I teased him. "You would never survive! Please!" Holding his face in my hands I said, "You have to know we're a package deal. Whoever is with me, has Millie in their life too, but not the way you would like."

Millie broke in, "Do you know how many guys have propositioned us throughout the years? Please, you're all a bunch of dogs! Wake up; we're hungry! Hey, I need a drawer too, and I'm leaving my toothbrush and pj's for sleepovers."

"Make whatever you want, the fridge is full!" He said trying to shake the cobwebs out of his head.

"No, I want you to get up and look for me." I said trying to be cute.

"Nut, I saw the flowers and paper already." He said laughing. "Nice, I like fresh flowers, thanks, but you didn't have to deliver the paper too."

"Huh you either! My leather seats have newsprint marks on them." I said as Millie roamed the fridge.

Laughing at me, he played right back, "Really, I thought you needed a reminder of the time. Did you have fun?"

"Next time, buy me another watch instead. My shocks were low; my car is used to my tiny hinny, not a truck load of papers." I said nibbling on his lips. "As you know I always have fun!"

"Next time, answer your beeper. You're lucky you're easy to find, but if I didn't FIND you, I wouldn't be so nice today."

"Please, next time, I'm going to after hours in Williamsburg, good luck finding me then." I playfully snapped defiantly as I got up.

He pulled my arm and brought me back down to him. "Oh no way! No Williamsburg, and absolutely no after hours. They're filled with drugs and that's a no-no! Got it!"

"Hey, I have my own juice in the jungle, I don't need you in Williamsburg! And drugs? We're not into that! I'd rather buy a mink coat than snort one. Please! Why no Williamsburg?"

"Out of my realm, that's why. Plus I told you, I want you home more," Babe said as he released his grip on my arm.

"Please, Babe who would I hang out with then? You can't take my partner in crime away. You can't imagine what our nights are like." Millie said as she started to scramble the eggs.

"Oh I think I know what your nights are like. I have ears, I've heard things." He said in a coy tone, "Hey Millie, what's the deal? I know you and Joe are long over, but when are you going to say yes to another guy so you two wild ones can settle down." Babe said as he poured the coffee.

"Oh please with Joe! All Joe's suck! Her ex and my ex are both named Joe and they both stink! I didn't want to go out with him to begin with; his ex-wife talked me into it. Please he's still in love with her." Millie said waving her hands at Babe.

Leaning on the island, sipping his coffee, he asked the million-dollar question, "I gotta ask, did you girls really rob him? I mean I heard the story, Joe told us the night it happened, but it takes big balls to do what he said."

"Listen Babe, he took my beeper and wouldn't return it. Fuck him, why should I have to buy another one. Plus everything we 'stole' I bought with his money, but still I bought it."

I was laughing sitting at the island watching the two most important people in my life talk, joke, and get to know each other better. This was a precious moment; I savored every minute. "Babe, listen, Joe took her beeper and locked it in his car. So we went to the guy he bought the car from and asked him for the code to open the driver's push pad on the door. He didn't want to give it to us, but we were dressed in hot shorts, little tiny halter-tops and killer heels. Poor bastard! We told him, we locked the car keys in the car and Joe would kill Millie if he had to break the lock. He felt sorry for us, and gave us the code."

"I will never buy a car with the door push pad!" Babe declared.

Millie laughed as she continued, "Then, we drove in my grandmother's car so he wouldn't recognize us to New Springville and waited outside the building's garage he lived in. Correction; where we both lived together. Once a car opened the community garage door, we drove in behind them and found Joe's car in the parking spot. It took two-seconds to get in using the code, so I got the beeper. Then we sat and waited."

"You cased his house?" Babe asked, getting a kick out of the story.

"Yup! As soon as he drove out of the garage, we went up in the elevator to the apartment. In a matter of ten minutes the whole apartment was in garbage bags. We took everything except the furniture and his guns. We laid those out on his mattress."

"I heard you took the food out of the freezer and fridge; even the ice cubes! We all laughed so hard when we found out you took the toilet paper and soap."

"Don't fuck with us and you can wipe your ass! Cheat on us, and screw us and you have to shake and dry!" Millie said. "We've all had our Joes! But all and all Dannie and me actually like him as a person, not as a boyfriend! He's a good hearted and funny guy."

I shook my head in agreement and told Babe the rest of the story of how we robbed a wise guy. "As soon as we packed the bags that belonged to Millie, the rest we threw in the buildings dumpster and left. We were in my apartment for less than an hour when Joe called me, looking for Millie. I told him she was out with her mother and asked him why he sounded so upset.

It took less than a second, and he spilled his guts telling me that he went home for something and went into the bathroom. 'Dannie, listen I went to take a piss excuse my French and I look down and I'm standing on the tile floor, not my rug! I flush, and see the toilet paper is empty. I look around the bathroom and it's completely empty. My fucking soap was gone; I couldn't wash my goddamn hands! I went into the kitchen to use the sink and the same shit. The whole fucking apartment looked like I was robbed to the bone. Nothing's left, nothing! Not a dish, glass, towel, soap, shirt, shoe, nothing! The fridge is clean as a whistle.' Of course I tried to sound sympathetic, but he was reading me like I was reading him. Millie was right next to me listening on the other house phone."

"Poor bastard! I feel sorry for him," Babe said as he sipped his coffee.

"Fuck him! Who feels sorry for me? Nobody, that's who. He dumped me and held my beeper hostage, so he got what he deserved!"

"Listen Babe, take no prisoners. It costs too much to feed them! All kidding aside, what can he really do to us? Nothing! He had to man up, we had him in this one."

"So how did it end?" Babe asked.

"I asked him why he wanted to speak with Millie and he said 'I was thinking I was robbed so I ran to my car and that's when I saw her beeper was missing. So tell your girlfriend to call me.' I laughed and said sure."

"I ain't fucking calling him! Ever! Joe and I say hello and goodbye, we're friendly in public but that's it!"

"So now that Joe's gone, who do you like? I can't have the two of you rooming loose on the rough streets of the city. You guys may hurt somebody." He said laughing, but I knew he was trying to say he didn't want us out gallivanting around so much.

"Please, I keep finding frogs instead of princes! I'm taking a break for a while. So let me ask you something Babe! Why is my girlfriend locked up all the time here?"

"She's not locked up...yet! Maybe I'll try that later!" He grinned at her.

"Nah, nope, no locking me up, no handcuffs, no bondage what's so ever! I'm all about a good time, I don't like the dark stuff!" I laughed at him waving my hands no.

"We'll talk later about that!" He laughed grabbing my ass. "What do you girls have on tap for today?"

"Not sure, why?" I asked, as I started to do the dishes.

"How about you two hangout here at the beach today? Looks like it's going to be beautiful. You'll have the run of the place; I've got to run soon."

"Babe, why don't you bring home a friend later and we'll all eat together, before you go to work?" I suggested playfully.

"Sounds like a plan. Okay, I'm going to take a shower, if you girls are done with the bedroom." Babe said as he slapped my ass and walked inside.

Millie looked at me and we broke out laughing. "Oh my god, Dannie, he's gorgeous! He's so nice; I can see how happy you are. Tell me all about him." We grabbed our coffee and moved to the couch and I started to tell her our story. There wasn't anyone I would rather share this experience with, because Millie and I were no strangers to adventures.

CHAPTER 27

Promises

Millie and I took off and hit all the markets to make dinner. I bought everything Babe loved and we spent the afternoon cooking. By the time Babe returned, he had James in tow grinning with boxes from Arthur Avenue, filled with every pastry we could ever want. Babe walked over to the island and started to open all the lids taking in the aromas. He slapped my ass and kissed my cheek. "Oh Fats, this smells great!"

I titled my head and kissed the tip of his nose, "Thanks but don't get too excited until you taste it, you might hate it! Remember I'm not that domesticated!" .

He stayed close nuzzling my neck, "Don't you worry about that! I'll teach you what ever you don't know, and I'm sure I've had worse, so it's all good." *His smile could light up a city! I love seeing him being just a regular guy!* He picked here and there and finally couldn't fight the urge to dunk the butt of the Italian bread into the gravy. His groan of approval made me feel like I won the first round, and when he dunked another piece and gave it to James, I knew I was home free.

"Ohhh, Dannie this is great!" James said devouring the bread.

Babe broke in, "Enough with the 'Ohhh, Dannie' shit! I hate that name!"

I had to laugh, "Out of all the names you call me, that's the most normal one! Fats, Peeper, and Rocky...hmm?"

James laughed, "I can handle Fats, but I don't even want to know what Peeper's all about! Rocky, I definitely understand!" He turned to Millie grinning, "Now Rotten, you have the best name! You know that right?"

She smirked and tossed the towel at him, "Ugh, I hate it! Please, Babe, tell James here calling me Rotten is horrible! Tell him!"

James burst out laughing as Babe slapped his back, "What's wrong with you? How the hell did you come up with that one?"

He cleared his throat; "Well we were all out in Long Island at a club and some guys were hitting on these two loons so I spoke to them. They weren't bad guys; they backed off and just hung out with our group. Well, you know how they are, the dancing and crazy shit hanging all over each other and me and the guys. They asked if I was going with one or both of them, so I said I wouldn't dare because Dannie's my sister and Millie's a virgin!"

The tears were running down his face as he told the story. "Fucking guys said no way, that she was too hot, and couldn't be a virgin. So I called Millie over and said tell them, go ahead tell them you're a virgin! I thought she was going to kill me, but she turned and said that she was. I turned to the guys and said see she's a virgin and too bad because by the time anyone gets anywhere with her 'it's' going to be so underused, it will be rotten! And that's where Rotten comes from, and I love to freak people out saying it still!"

Babe's jaw was hanging open as he looked between Millie and me. "Millie are you a virgin?"

She burst out laughing, "Umm I was back then! That was two years ago!"

I was dying laughing as I sipped my wine, "Babe, I swear to God, she's telling you the truth! Do you know how many guys tried to get at her because of it? Oh my God there are no words!"

She bumped her hip into mine as I laughed into my glass, "Yeah Babe how about your girlfriend over here trying to auction off my virginity at the club! You have no idea what's she's done to me. None! I've had old, and young from all walks of life beg me, then even one guy who was mental! A fucking mental case tried to give me money in the VIP lounge. Like my snatch was for sale all because this one over here was whacked and taking action on me! She fucking took bets on when I would lose it too!"

James spit his wine out. "Holy shit I forgot about that! I was in on that! All of us were!"

As the tears ran down our faces from laughing, Babe just held his glass staring grinning, "This is one of the first times, and I feel bad I was away for so long! I can't even imagine what you guys are really like, I've heard, but I think the stories are all watered down for my benefit."

We all moved to the table and started to eat, while James told embarrassing story upon story about us. "Oh Babe did your girl ever tell you how I had to fly to Paradise Island while she was away with the girls?"

I cut him off making the don't-say-a-word gesture as I tossed my napkin at him. "Shut up! What happens on vacation stays on vacation!"

"Oh no, not when I have to hop a fight and come down with a ton of cash, because you gambled yours all away!" He turned his head towards Babe but pointed at me, "This one right here, and don't take her gambling! She's crazy! Yup, this one right here, your girl! They all went to Paradise Island, and she started to gamble, well the first night she hung out like a normal person, but by the second night no one could find her! She took off and was playing cards with a bunch of guys from Taiwan! Yes, Taiwan!"

I started to pelt him with bread, "Blabber mouth!"

Babe grabbed my hand pulling me closer under his arm, "Oh I want to hear this, go ahead!"

James grinned and continued, "Yeah, so where was I, oh this one left everybody and went to another hotel and played cards for two days!" I get a call, that she disappeared but she called to say someone had to bring her more cash! So like the good friend that I am, I jump on a flight, no bags, and no nothing just eight g's in cash in my pocket. So I buy a ticket at the airport counter, I have nothing no luggage, so I was checked so many times I thought the agent should have bought me a fucking drink after it all! I land, take a cab to the resort, find the rest of the motley crew all drunk on the beach, they tell me what she said.

I take another cab to some skank joint and find her in room playing cards with guys who don't speak fucking ENGLISH! I don't mean like a few words, I mean NOT ONE FUCKING WORD! She sees me and riffles through my pockets, takes all my cash while I have to sit on some fucking folding chair in the corner like a dick! I don't know what she's doing with these sweaty guys, because no one is FUCKING TALKING! They just keep drinking, tossing chips and wiping fucking gross sweat from their greasy heads. I must have fallen asleep, because I feel someone sticking their hands in my pants. I wake up and this one over here is shoving money into my pocket! It turns out she fucking won!"

There wasn't a dry eye at the table: we were crippled with laughter. I turned to Babe, snorting I was laughing so hard, "Wait let me finish the story! So I'm playing and I'm down, but I knew I would eventually win so, I called for more cash. When James walked through the door, I almost fell off my chair; I had no idea the girls called him. I didn't give James a chance to say I word, I dug my hands into his pockets and fleeced him. But he seemed to bring luck with him, because I started to win again and when I won all my money and his with a profit, I left the game."

Babe blinked, his eyes laughing, "When was this?"

I cried laughing, "Last year! But that's not the end of the story! Oh no, James, you know my brother from another mother, your friend over here! Well, he comes back to hotel with me and we keep him with us for the rest of the vacation! You know people go there on their honeymoon. Well, this one, your friend JAMES, meets a couple staying at the resort with us and can you guess what he did? Can you?"

James kicked back laughing, "I don't care Fats, go ahead!"

"Well, this one over here turns around and hooks up with the bride! Yup, he's banging this broad on the beach, in the ocean, in our rooms while her J-O of a husband thinks she's sick with sun poisoning! The fucking flight home, he gets up and she follows him into the bathroom, and the two of they are going at it fast and furious in the mile high club. The doors banging, she's panting on the door, I could hear him coaxing her 'Yeah baby, just like that, yeah!' Everyone on the plane can hear him, except of course the idiot husband!"

Babe wiped the tears from his face with his napkin, "I can only imagine! You're fucking crazy James! Dannie what's this you think you can play cards? You may have to teach me what you know, I'm not that good at it!"

James grinned, "Oh Babe are you fucking kidding me? Dannie don't believe one word coming out of his mouth! You know most people come out of prison fucking skinny, looking like shit! Not this one! Oh no, this one eats like a fucking king in the joint! He can beat anyone at cards, anyone! Fucking forget dominos! Well, he beats everyone and gets fucking food! We were in the same cell for a year, when I was transferred I left fat! And Babe, I'm just saying, be careful don't bet with jewelry with this one, because she has a nice collection of watches she's won from guys! I bought two from her already!"

Millie was doubled over laughing so hard; she had to drink some water to recuperate. "Babe, did you hear how we were thrown off the island of Jamaica?"

I cut in, "We were escorted to the airport, and we didn't get thrown off the island!"

Babe's head spun around, "Sweetheart, being escorted is just as good as getting tossed off the island. So let me hear this now!"

Millie choked back her laughter as she wiped her eyes. "Well, can you guess why? If you can't let me enlighten you, it was for fighting! Yup, fighting! We were in a club and this one." She jabbed James' stomach as she mimicked him, "This one, you know your girlfriend over here. Well, we were all dancing and these local guys come over and we're hanging and drinking. Well, one guy's wife comes over and freaks out. Dannie tells her to take her broken down husband and get the fuck away from us.

Well the wife didn't come alone she came with back up! Fucking girls jumped us, and this one, cracks the girl with a table and rips the leg off and beats the bitch with the table leg! Fucking table leg! The cops came as we were leaving. We all get locked up; she makes a call and gets us bailed out! But not bailed out to go back to the resort, no, bailed out and escorted right to the airport! We had to fly right out! Yup this one over here did that!"

I shrugged my shoulders giggling, "So it was one time! Big deal! I'm really very quiet and calm!"

James and Millie looked at each other doubling over laughing. James shouts, "One time? Calm? Yeah how about that idiot, Frankie, hmm?"

I put my finger on my temple grinning, "I don't remember anyone!"

"Well, let me remind you of him! Babe, Dannie's went on a date with this guy, we all told her not to, you know the type, a real Shem!"

Babe broke out laughing, "Really, you with a Shem? You should be ashamed of yourself!"

I poked him "Stop that!"

"Anyway, Dannie gets sick while she's out, wait I forgot, first he takes her to a local place so everyone can see he landed a date with her." James slaps the table crying, "Jerk off! Okay, so she's with this short Shem with the world staring at her. Well, she gets sick, and asks the guy to take her home, but he grew a set of balls for a half a second and said no! He said he would take her when he was done. So this one over here gets pissed, but in the mean time the bartenders start removing all the shit off the bar because they all know she's going to beat this dick up, only thing is he didn't know it! Well, Dannie gets up, walks outside, goes to the valet and gets his car delivered to the front of the joint."

I dropped my head right on the table and covered my head with my napkin. "Go ahead!"

"Well, the whole place is at the window watching while she goes and rips his radio out tossing it in the street, then she pulled his seats out and tossed them out too! Right on fucking Third Avenue! He drove a jeep, so now she takes his fucking doors off and tosses them! In ten minutes his whole car looks like a fucking erector set! Fucking guy was shaking in fucking fear! But the best is she's at Shorts, the restaurant is three blocks from her house! She could have walked or asked me for a ride because I was right there!"

Millie wiped her tears. "No, I have better stories then that!"

I stood up waving my arms, "Millie shut up! I know what you're going to say!"

"Oh come on its funny! I don't care; you owe me after my virginity! Babe this guy Sam was so in love with her! Oh my God since she was really young like fourteen or something like that. Anyway he used to show up fucking everywhere she was. Well, as the years passed he would still stalk her, and she was going with this other guy, Ricky. Well, Sam goes over to her boyfriend and tells him that he's in love with her and, man to man, wants Ricky to dump her.

Well, Sam got beaten up, but Ricky yells at Dannie over it! Dannie waits for Sam to walk out of his house while she stakes him out from across the street with a shit load of roman candles. She fucking lights them and shoots them off at him and his car. Poof, poof, poof is all you could hear. When it was over the guy was passed out and his whole car had burn holes all over it!"

Holding the napkin in front of my face as the tears ran down, I mumbled. "I got that from some movie, it seemed like a good idea at the time!"

James, starts counting on his hand again, "One, how about Cancun when you got held up and chased the guy down the street with the shank they tried to rob you with? Two..."

"That's it, no more! Nope!" I stood up cutting him off and started to load the dishwasher laughing. I wasn't angry, because hey, I did everything they said and worse, I just didn't want Babe to hear about my ex's all night.

Babe grabbed my ass, "Get over here! The dishes can wait! So you act like a goodie two shoes, but..."

I broke in, "I'm feisty! Can I hear about your antics? Hmmm?"

"Nope! Lets open another bottle."

We laughed and continued on for hours until we ate so much I thought I gained ten pounds. After coffee and dessert, we went back to wine and I could see Millie getting tired. She had her toes curled up in James's lap snuggling low on the couch, while the fire crackled. Babe tapped my shoulder holding a bottle and two glasses, "Hey guys we're going to take a walk on the beach for a little while. You wanna come?"

James waved his hand, "You crazy kids have fun, and I'll stay here and let Rotten tell me how much she really wants me!"

We laughed as we stumbled out the door. The air was crisp, but not too bad. We walked a bit, until we found the spot by the water that we liked. I sat in front of Babe, leaning against his chest, while he held me. We could sit and talk about nothing or just sit with each other for hours, not saying anything, because we truly enjoyed each other's company. While the wind whipped my hair around, Babe grabbed a piece in the air and tried to tuck it into behind my ear as he whispered to me, "Are you really happy with all of this?"

I kissed his hand that was wrapped around me, "Yes, very! Are you happy with me?"

He kissed my hair, "Yes, that's why this is going to be hard to say." I tried to move, but he held me in place facing the water instead of him. "Shush, sit still and listen. I may have to go away for a little while. Do you understand what I'm saying?"

What? No, this can't be happening. "I think so. Can I ask how long you'll be gone?"

"Well, I'm not sure if I'm even going, but if I do it will be sudden. I promise I'll find a way to let you know. I hope it won't be for long, but I want you to listen to me real good. You have to keep a low profile. I hate to say this, but stay away from my friends we don't see anymore, if you know what I mean. James, Vinnie and the other guys are okay. If they're actually not away with me, you can stay close, but don't ask them anything! Nothing, not a word!"

"Okay, but should I go home to stay at my apartment?"

"No! This is your home now! I'm going to start giving you money to keep on the side, besides your allowance. Pay whatever bills and put the rest away for the lawyers. And don't tell anybody about it, I don't tell nobody about how much I got."

What did I really want to ask? The answer was nothing! In my heart I wanted to know everything, but then in my head if I truly knew anything it would be too much! I was going to ask a million questions, but I stopped short wishing I could hold onto this moment for as long as I could. Taking deep breaths, I realized I wanted to know something very important. I asked, "How would I know if something happens to you? Will someone tell me?"

"Nothing's going to happen, but bad news travels fast, you would know." He said in a very low voice.

"I love you so much I would need to know!" Shaking, I desperately asked, "Can we move?"

"Move where?" Babe asked very gently, knowing this was tough for me.

Trying to convince him I suggested, "Florida, California, Vegas, even Maine if I had too; anywhere!"

Always in control, Babe answered in a strong voice, "I would be who I am anywhere we go, that wouldn't change. So why go somewhere else?"

I whispered asking, "I know, but who exactly are you?"

"Who do you want me to be?" Kissing my hair gently he had patience with me. Keeping the pace going.

I pressed further. "Do you always answer a question with another one?"

"I'm the man who loves you. Isn't that enough for you?"

"It's never enough; I'm always going to want more. I want the fairy tale, I want Prince Charming, I want the family; I want it all!"

"And I will give it all to you! I will!"

I kissed his hand again, "About the lawyer, should I just give them money, or wait for you to tell me how much? One more thing, when you go, can Millie stay with me?"

"Sure if that's what you need, but keep a low profile with her. As for the lawyer, I'll let you know. The money can really disappear fast." He kissed my head and gave me squeeze. "You good?"

"Yes, I think so. If the money disappears, I'll sell the stuff you gave me, it's only things." I said, meaning every word. *It wasn't what you bought me, but why you gave it to me that made me fall deeper and deeper in love. I'm pretty sure I am the first and only one who doesn't want you for your money!*

"No! You keep everything I gave you! Its yours!"

I tried to turn again, but he kept me locked in place. It was cold; he was rubbing my hands and bringing them up to his lips to kiss. I felt something slid onto my left hand and saw a beautiful platinum pear shaped ring on my finger when he lowered it. I sucked in my breath. "Oh Babe its beautiful! Oh my god!" *Are you proposing to me?*

He sat silently kissing the top of my hair, "It's all going to be okay, and I just need to know your going to listen to me."

The tears streamed down my face as I watched the water roll up close to us. "Babe, I got your back! I'll be here if you leave, when you come back, and in between I'll do the right thing! We'll get through this."

He buried his face in my hair kissing me, breathing deep. After a few more minutes of quiet time, he started to get up and helped me to stand. He hugged me rocking back and forth whispering he loved me as I sunk into his arms taking it all in. When I finally pulled away, I had my game face on, "Okay, 'if' isn't a sure bet, so until 'if' happens lets just go on, and 'if' happens we will get through it. But we can't let that hang over our heads and change how we live. We'll deal with it all as it happens, but I don't want to dwell on it."

Babe bent his head holding my face as he stared into my eyes before he kissed me hard. When he pulled back, his eyes sent a thousand silent messages he knew I needed to hear. He cleared his throat as he stepped back to admire my hand, "It's as beautiful as you! I like seeing you wear everything from me."

Was this guy proposing to me? He didn't ask, so I didn't know what to say. "I don't know what to say, this the most beautiful gift I've ever been given."

"More than the Audi? The frigging bed? Or the mink coat? How about all those trips you never told me about?"

"Please, what, did you run a background check on me? First, you need to know something, I never slept with any of them, not even a date! The trips, well that's another story, my ex-boyfriend took me away a lot so that's not a tip." I looked at him and said, "Hey, I only said it was a car. How did you know?"

"I know you didn't, but you kept most of the gifts though! I told you, I know everything, and the car, bed and coat were all white!" Babe said laughing as he wrapped his arm around my neck. "How did you exactly get the bed as a gift?"

"It was all white lacquer with hand carved doves facing each other. It was pretty ornate, but not my style. You know Jules from the furniture store in Chinatown; well he brought the headboard part of the bed to the restaurant window. I was staring at him like he had two heads, but I didn't want to hurt his feelings so I went outside to look at it. There he was standing next to this huge king size head board."

We both sat on the sand and dug our toes in laughing as I continued the story. "Well, what does one say to something like that? I smiled and said thank you, but that it was just too special a gift to give me. I remember his face turned red, and in his Italian accent starting getting upset saying I didn't like it. If I said no, I didn't want it, he would be embarrassed and become spiteful, but if I accepted it he would think I wanted him in the bed."

"Hey Shem! Like he wasn't giving you the hint already by giving you the bed."

I avoided his eyes, because this was the other side of being a girl in the know that no one ever talks about. "I know that! But being a girl, you have to play it right, or I could've been fired."

"So where's the bed now?" He asked tensely.

Taking a deep breath, I continued, "I told Jules, the bed was beautiful, but I couldn't keep it because my dad gave me my bedroom set and would want to know where the new one came from."

Smiling, he asked, "Your dad? You're kidding me?"

"Nope! He respected the 'dad' line."

"Where is your dad? You never talk about him," he said as he reached for my hair to pet me.

"Dead. I have no family." I said without inviting any further questions.

Pulling me closer, he said, "Come here, don't worry about it, we can make our own family!"

Clearing my throat, I continued, "I mean, don't get me wrong, it's very flattering in an odd way to have someone make that bold statement and give you a bed, but pretty difficult to get around the fact he's telling me he wanted to fuck me in a very public way. The car and coat were a lot easier to accept."

Busting my balls, he said, "An Audi was a pretty nice gift!"

"The Audi was a gift from a customer, but my ex-boyfriend gave me a car too, a Vet. So laugh all you want, not too many people can say they were tipped like me."

"Where's the Audi?"

"I lost it in the city outside of Bloomingdales. It was picked up by the police in a raid and towed to the Whitestone pound to be held for evidence. By the time they were done with it, I didn't want it anymore. It was trashed!"

Looking at me sideways, he asked, "Raid?"

Laughing, thinking of my car I told him my crazy story. "Yup, the police were staking out the block and moved in after I parked the car. My car was collateral damage. The fucked up thing was I lost all my photos from vacation of us topless on the beach that I just had developed, along with a trunk full of clothes and shoes and some spare cash. I'm sure the cops stole everything!"

Babe put his head in his hands shaking it laughing, "So there are photos of you out there?"

"Oh please, there are photos of all of us girls, group shots and we were only topless!"

"Great!"

"Oh stop! Let's get back to the car..."

He cut me off, "We have to look into getting you something, because that little convertible is getting old. You need something newer."

Smirking with a raised eyebrow, "I'm never selling the BMW; it will have to be garaged. I've had too many good memories in that car."

"Buster, I think I'm buying you a minivan! You'll look great in it!" Babe said covering his arm laughing at me.

"Ewww! NOT HOT! I want a fast little convertible, because I'm still young! When I get old it can be a hardtop! My car has great memories!" I giggled.

"I don't want to hear about those 'memories,' unless I'm included in them. Let's go back." He reached over and kissed me, before we walked back to the house, to find James and Millie sitting by the fire.

James waved his hand at us "Shush, she fell asleep!"

Babe and I leaned over the couch and Millie was curled up on the couch arm with her feet on James, "You're the man buddy! She fell asleep!" Babe said chuckling.

"Listen, she shoots me down all the time, but you can't blame a guy for trying! She thinks of me like a brother, isn't that fun!" James said staring at Millie.

"James, you look tired too. Close your eyes, take a nap," I said running my hands on his head. Bending down, I kissed him on top of his head. "We love you like the brother we never wanted, but are glad we have."

"You girls are the sisters I never wanted and still don't! I always wanted to be around two hot girls that I can't touch, and one almost shoots me. Fun right? Love you too!"

Babe gently tugged his arm and started to lead me to the bedroom. "James, we're gonna rest up before I have to go to work."

"Oh yeah, I remember how you guys rest. Don't make too much noise resting, I wouldn't want your resting to wake up Sleeping Beauty!"

He didn't fully close the door when he was ripping my clothes off. We didn't make it to the bed, but instead made love on the back of the door standing up. There was absolutely no way James didn't hear it, but at that moment we could have cared less. Giggling and moaning, I clawed the door while Babe was on me. "Shush!"

"Shush, yourself!"

Practically eating my hair, he growled in my neck, "They can hear you."

"And your point is? Are you embarrassed?" I decided to give him something to be embarrassed for so I started to moan louder and pound the door. "Oooh, Babe! Yes, Babe! Ah, ah, ah! Yes, yes! Oh you're so...so...I love you!"

"You're fucked up, shush!" He said trying to cover my mouth as I bit his fingers.

"I'll show you fucked up!" I threatened. Then I screamed, "Oh YES now!"

That put him over the edge; he was pulling my hair with one hand, while he bit my neck and slammed me into the door. And then there was nothing but silence and our breathing. After a few minutes, Babe picked me up and carried me to the bed. I kept thinking about our conversation, and I couldn't help but hold him tighter than I ever did before. I slipped into a twilight sleep and when I felt him move away, I opened my eyes.

"Don't go," I whispered in a sexy voice.

"I have to get ready for work."

Caressing him, I begged. "Five more minutes!"

Babe touched the tip of my nose. "No! I'm jumping in the shower," he said looking like the most handsome man on the face of the earth.

"Leave the door open, I want to watch you," I said as I wrapped my legs around him.

"Hey Peeper, you want to come in?" Babe asked playfully.

"I'm not sure, maybe I just want to watch. Make it a show for me," I said teasing him.

"Who would have thought you're such an animal Peeper? You surprise me everyday." He smiled with his eyes and his Brooklyn swagger.

Laying there naked staring at him I asked, "Am I really so different from you thought I would be?"

Leaning on the door he laughed, "Yeah, I didn't think you would be so much of a handful all the time."

I said as I leaned on my elbow, "Yes, you're as crazy as I thought you would be, but you have another tender side that pulls at my heart."

"You think? Even tough guys have a heart, but don't spread that around," he said as he winked at me.

"I can't fully describe how you make me feel when you're looking at me, except that I know you love me by the way you watch me sleep, make love, move around; it's an intense look."

Returning to the bed, he pounced on me, "Is that a bad thing?"

"No! Its kind of that look you have when you're around someone you really care about. You look at your mom in a way I can see you love her so much, there isn't room for anything or anyone else in the room when you're around her."

"You and my mom are both important to me. I've spent enough time staring at the inside of a cell; I want to look at the things that make me happy now. Give any thought to our conversation?" He said still on top of me staring into my eyes.

"About going away? I can't stop thinking about it."

"No, about our other conversation?" he said as he ran his fingers up my thigh, stopping on my hip.

"You mean the tribe?" I said, trying to be cute.

Babe eyed me trying to read my reaction, "Yes, What you think?"

"Oh I don't know. That's a lot to think about. I don't know enough about what could happen to me, if something happens to you."

Babe propped me up and held my face in his hand, "If I was a sanitation worker and we had a family suppose I died. What do you think would happen to you?"

Flipping the coin in my head, trying to think of every side, I asked, "I don't know, I never thought about it like that. But what if we have a family?"

"Well, it's the same thing. You don't know, and you never will. If you love me, enjoy the moment; I can't promise you anything more than anyone else."

Thinking with my head and not my heart I asked, "Regular people have insurance."

"Listen, you're supposed to be okay, but very few guys follow the rules. I don't plan on dying or getting locked up, just so you know, but if I do get pinched, if someone comes by with an envelope. You take it- no questions asked- and use it."

"And if they don't?" I asked, already knowing, wanting to hear him say it.

"Then they don't, and you have to work. If we have kids, your number one job is them. You raise the kids first and everything else comes second."

I asked, "Who would I call if you get pinched?"

"My lawyer and Phil, they know what to do. Man you got a lot of questions! I have one for you now."

Smiling I said, "Wait I'm not done yet. If we have kids, are you going to keep me locked up all the time?"

His eyes narrowed as he carefully thought about what he wanted to say. "Danielle, do you really think you're going to be out roaming around like you are now?"

"You know Madelyn's water broke on the dance floor right? She still goes out." I smirked, because I knew he would think I was immature, but the reality was I liked my life and didn't want to stop being me, just to make him happy. *Why can't we compromise?*

"It's funny when its someone else's girl, I love her, we've been friends for years, but I want you home."

I shook my head no, as I looked at him. "I'm never going to be like Vinnie's girl, and if you try and make me a homebody, I'd grow to hate you."

He exhaled, realizing our lifestyles and priorities were miles apart. "We'll take one day at a time, I understand what you're saying, but you have see my side of it to."

"I do, I wouldn't be out all the time, but I would still go out, and I don't want you to be bent out of shape. So if you love me for the person you met, you'll love me for the person I will remain."

Babe looked deeply into my eyes so intensely, I was frightened for a split second, until he broke the silence. "I love all of you, okay?" I kissed his beautiful lips with my eyes open as a few tears slipped down my cheeks. He gently wiped them, as he caressed my face. "Baby, I just need you to start slowing down with this going out every night. I need you around more, especially until we have kids, but we'll work out something so you can still have 'your' life. Okay?" Babe raised his eyebrow as he poked my side. "By the way how do you know you're not pregnant now? It's not like you take your pills all the time!"

"Good grief, you know way too much! Let's take a shower."

"Peeper, you joining me?" He gently kissed the tip of my nose, stood up and walked into the bathroom. Once in the shower, I was washing my stomach when he put his hand on mine and said, "I think you would look cute pregnant!"

"Yeah? I'm nervous…"

Babe said with confidence, "I'll be right there, beside you as much as I can."

"Okay, but we don't have enough room here for my shoes, let alone a baby," I said playing around with him.

"I told you, I'd buy another house." Babe always had an answer for every problem.

"I love this house!" I said beaming.

"Then we keep it and build up?" He said smiling like a King.

"Can you do that?" I asked getting caught up in the excitement.

"I can do anything! Would you like that?"

I thought for a long moment, looking at him with the water spraying all over his skin, his hand on my stomach and simply said, "Yes, yes I would. Yes, to everything!"

I've never seen Babe so tender than at that moment. He bent his head and buried it in my neck, and held me tight while we both cried at our happiness.

"Hey, I want you to know I think you're going to be an amazing dad," I said as I held his hand on my stomach. Babe picked his face up and kissed me more tenderly then ever before.

CHAPTER 28

Fuck Me, Feed Me &
Paying My Bills

ow life moved even faster, within a month Babe had an architect come to the house. We sat at the island and he asked me what I wanted. *What I wanted? No one ever asked me that before. People always tell me what they think I need, or what they want to give me.* I didn't know what I wanted; my head was spinning. I sat there while Babe explained he wanted to add another floor with three bedrooms and two baths.

I finally chimed in that I would love a large walk in closet and storage. "I'm sure I'm going to need more storage for Christmas decorations and stuff like that. Oh how about another fireplace in our bedroom? And I would like a deck outside of our bedroom to have breakfast with you in the morning. Can we do all that?"

Leaning into me, Babe kissed my head and whispered, "We can do anything!" Sounding upbeat, he said, "Christmas is my favorite holiday! I want the house done by then and plan on having a great party here. So how fast can we get started on the renovation?"

"We need to file for permits, but I think we can start within thirty days and rush through it." Getting up and shaking our hands, the architect walked toward the door and said goodbye.

"This is a reason to celebrate! We're going to dinner at my favorite place, Karl's. Get dressed, invite Millie to come with us and meet me there tonight," he said as he gave me a bear hug.

All day I moved with a purpose, I was so excited. Everything I wanted, the guy, the family, and the house were all happening faster than I ever expected. That evening, I dressed deliberately in a seductive dress; decked out with the earrings, bracelet, watch and ring Babe gave me. I picked Millie up and we headed to Williamsburg to meet Babe. Pulling up, we parked and went inside. I didn't have to give Babe's name; the maître knew him well and escorted us to the best table right away.

Millie took my hand smiling at the ring and asked if he proposed yet. We were both puzzled and talked about it often, but so far Babe had been a complete mystery in every way. I couldn't pry a thing out of him, no matter what I did. We noticed "the eyes" were on us as we spoke, but after forty-five minutes we were still sitting alone.

The waiter had already brought us a bottle of wine and appetizers- their famous jumbo shrimp and slab bacon. We picked lightly, waiting, but when I finally looked at my watch, my stomach sank. I just knew something wasn't right; Babe was never late. I excused myself and beeped him with my code. After a few minutes, he called back to give me a new seat on his roller coaster. I walked back to the table stunned, but in control.

Millie asked, "What time did he say he was coming?"

"He's not coming; he's on the lamb," I said trying to be upbeat so as not to draw attention.

"What? Why?" Millie looked grief stricken.

"I have no idea, I really don't know. It's this crazy thing I guess between all the guys. He said we should eat and go home after. Can you stay with me? I don't want to be alone in Breezy."

Grabbing my hand, squeezing it she said, "Of course. Do you want to stay with me?"

"Maybe, but tonight lets go back to Breezy. I want to do exactly what he asked me to do," I said as our waiter, Otto, came to the table carting the largest steak I'd ever seen and every side dish on the menu. "Excuse me Otto, but I didn't order yet."

"I know, but Babe called the order in when he made the reservation, he always does."

"Oh I'm sorry he won't be joining us after all, it will be just us." I said trying to be in control.

"I know, he called back and told me to pack all the left overs for you take home when you leave. Enjoy, if there is anything I can get you ladies please let me know. By the way the check has been taken care of too."

"Babe took care of the check?" I asked confused.

"No, his friends at the bar," Otto said pointing to a group of guys I didn't notice when we walked in. I took a better look and realized I hadn't seen them in a while. *What did Babe say to me?* He mentioned something, I couldn't remember exactly.

Millie said, "Hey I haven't seen those guys in a long time. Isn't that Frankie, Bobby and Jo, they haven't been around? I guess they hang out in Williamsburg now."

I turned and they raised their glasses and toasted us, and it was then that I remembered. "I can't let them buy dinner, Babe would be furious! He told me to stay away from old friends. We should go." I called the waiter over "Otto thank you, but we can't stay after all. But most of all I can't have them pick up our check. Please give me the check and I'll take care of it. You can charge them our after dinner drinks if you feel like you need to appease them. Can we have two Frangelico's straight up please?"

Otto returned quickly with the bill, and I paid cash, of course, left him a two hundred dollar tip, and asked him to have the valet load the wrapped food into my trunk. We grabbed our glasses and walked over to the bar, "Hi guys, thank you for offering to buy us dinner. It's way too generous of you, we can't accept, but we did order drinks. Chin-chin!" I said as I raised my glass and clinked Bobby's glass.

"Oh don't be silly! Dinners on us!" he said as he tried to flag down the waiter.

"No really, I already paid, thank you! You're always so generous, thank you!" Trying to sound sweet and friendly I said, "We're gonna run guys. Have a good night." As I turned to walk away, Jo grabbed my arm and said, "Hey what's the rush? Where's Babe tonight? Hey is that an engagement ring?"

I looked down and glared at his hand, he knew it but kept it there anyway. Smiling, I looked up, ignoring his ring remark and said, "He's great, why he wouldn't be?"

"So where is he?" He asked still holding my arm.

Smiling but eyeing him I said, "Jo, you're his friend so you know better than me, Babe doesn't tell me anything, but I'll be sure to tell him that you asked though." I thought he would have kept it light and released my arm, but he didn't. I looked at him in the eye and moved my arm out of his grip. Then I leaned in and kissed him on the cheek before moving on to the rest. "Thanks for offering to buy dinner and looking out for us. You're all too sweet! Have a good night guys!" Without waiting for a reply we walked out. Glasses in hand they followed us and watched from the door. I gave the valet kid a twenty-dollar bill as we jumped in my car and took off.

"What was that about?" Millie asked looking in the side view mirror.

"I don't think they were the welcoming party. Weird, that they were there and Babe wasn't," I said.

"I know, maybe you should sleep at my house tonight", Millie replied

"No, he told me go home tonight, I think I need to be in Breezy just in case he's looking for me." I jumped on the highway and headed back. Upset, thinking about what tonight was supposed to be; I put the pedal to the metal. Pulling up, we looked around before we got out of the car and quickly went inside the house. I went into the bedroom and looked around, but everything looked the same. We decided to stay home and watch a movie.

I asked, "You want a pair of sweats to change into?"

"Sure, but I think I want to get cleaned up. Can I take a shower?"

"Yes, let me get you fresh towels. There's shampoo and body wash in there." I said, as I went to the closet and pulled out two towels. I handed them to her and she opened them to drape across the sink, when something rolled out on the floor.

Millie bent down and picked up a wad of cash, "Hey Dannie, I think I found something."

"Like what?" I said as I walked in the bathroom. She handed me a rolled up wad of cash in a rubber band. I unrolled it and found a thousand dollars. "Geez, I will never get used to this. This fell out of the towels?" She laughed and showed me the towels. "Let me give you another one and I'll put this back on the shelf." I went to the closet and pulled out another set of towels and the same thing happened.

"Get the fuck out of here, are you kidding me?" I said as I bent down to pick up the money. I took a closer look at the towels and found every one had a roll of money stuffed in it. There was ten grand in cash in there! "I guess its rainy day money. Just use the towels anyway."

"He's crazy!" She said as she walked into the bathroom. After a few minutes of the water running, Millie called me, "Dannie come here."

I walked in and she popped her head out and showed me a covered travel soap dish. "That's not mine, I only use liquid." I said as I took it out of her hand and opened it. Inside were another bunch of hundred dollar bills neatly folded where the soap should've been. "I guess he is trying to tell me something, like he's going to be gone a long time, because this is a lot of money."

I sat on the floor getting really nervous. It was definitely meant for me to find, so I decided to collect it all and put most of it in the safety deposit box for safekeeping. *Where else did he stash money?* If I wasn't careful I could throw it out by accident. The floodgates opened and there was no stopping. I cried until I was cried out. When I was drained, we sat in bed and watched TV, and polished off a whole chocolate cake.

Around 3AM the phone rang and we jumped. I grabbed the phone on the first ring and I heard his voice, "Hey having fun without me?"

"Oh my god, I miss you!" I said without realizing I was crying into the phone already.

"Shush, don't do that or I won't call you." He said clearing his throat. "Did you enjoy dinner? I heard you looked hot!"

"Who told you that?" I said giggling.

"Never mind, I just know. So did you get the surf and turf?"

"I had it all wrapped up and took it to go. It's your favorite restaurant; it's not fun being there without you. I paid and tipped well."

"Good, tip the valet?" Babe asked.

"Who do you think you're talking to? Please! Some of the guys tried to pick up the check, but I politely declined and paid. I allowed them to buy us an after dinner drink so I wouldn't offend them. They asked for you."

"Yeah? I'm sure." He said sounded agitated.

"They were creepy, and walked outside as we drove off."

"Don't worry about it, you won't be going back there for a while," he said, more as a demand than a suggestion.

Cutting in, I asked, "Hey, I have to ask."

"Don't ask me."

"No, silly. I meant do I have to pay any bills? You know cable, gas, electric, and phone?"

Sounding a little more relaxed he said, "Not yet, everything is good for two months."

Laughing to myself, I realized I didn't know the first thing about my basic, domestic life here in Breezy. Babe told me where the bills were, and that there wasn't a mortgage, or car payments. He lived a lot like I did; he paid in advance for everything in cash. Before he hung up, he told me to "use" whatever I would find, which meant look for the cash and use it if I needed it. I tried to be upbeat as I told him I loved him and hung up. I didn't even have time to take a deep breath when the phone rang again. Babe's voice was sexy, but sad, almost lonely as he told me he missed me.

"I miss you too!" I said holding back my tears.

Laughing at me, "Yeah me too more, especially when I jumped in the shower. That's all I wanted to say."

Now I didn't want him to go, as I said, "Wait!"

"Anything else, Peeper?"

Giggling, I added. "No. Wait I love you! And I tossed my pills."

"Yeah? Now that's the best thing I've heard so far. I love you too!" I waited to hear him hang up, then curled up and fell asleep.

The next morning came quickly, and my beeper was jumping. Millie and I were up, meandering through the morning, when I started to return the beeps. The first one was from the restaurant, so I called back. It was Pino asking if I could come earlier to work to count for the bank deposit. I agreed, because it was a quick $100.

I loved him I would have done it for free, but I never told him that. The next beep was from the bar. When I called back, the bartender asked if I could cover tonight for someone. Unfortunately, I couldn't be in two places at once, so I had to decline. Finally, the last one was from the super of the building from my apartment. As soon as I called him back, he asked if I was okay, because he didn't see me from a while.

Calls returned, and dressed, we went off to Little Italy. We stopped for coffee and walked to the side entrance to the building above the restaurant. We walked passed Bruno, who was sitting in a yard chair, smoking a cigar, reading his paper, wearing a guinea t-shirt, guarding the door. We smiled and kissed him on his bald head and handed him a cup of espresso.

He said, "Thanks baby! How are ya, girls?"

"Wonderful Bruno! How you doing?" I said.

"H-I B r u n o!" Millie said as she sauntered passed him and headed up the stairs. There, we ran into Lenny sitting, guarding that door, reading the racing form. We repeated the process of handing him a cup of espresso and I kissed him on his balding head.

"Lenny, you're never gonna get laid if you keep smoking those gross Tiparillo's!" Millie said holding her nose.

"I'll only quit for you baby!"

"You're too cute, Lenny!" She said, as she kissed him hello. Once inside, there were more hellos and we finished passing out all the coffee we'd bought at Figgalo's. Pino gave us huge bear hugs and pulled me over to the corner to ask, "You okay?"

"Yeah, I'm okay. So you heard?"

"Hey, let's go outside for a minute," he said as he walked me passed Lenny and Bruno again. We walked down Mulberry Street doing the talk and walk, passing all the old timers, enjoying the good weather, tourists, and unmarked panel vans of undercover cops. I snaked my arm through his and leaned in while he talked in my ear, "How you holding up?"

"Good, I guess! Your guy's going through some crazy shit." I said shaking my head at what I could only imagine they went through daily.

"Yeah, well it's the way it is. Just be careful, hey you need any money to hold you over?" Pino said with a heavy heart.

"Thanks, but no, I'm good!" I smiled.

Pino sincerely asked, "Babe, is he good to you?"

"Very!" I said without skipping a beat.

"Good! Don't get caught up in nothing! Do you hear me?" Pino said, warning me.

"I don't get involved in anything, I don't know anything, and I'm too legit to quit!" I said, trying to inject a little humor.

"Stay out of it and stay out of Williamsburg," he said very seriously.

"What do you mean?" I said looking up at him.

Starting to cough in his hand he said, "Don't go there for now, NO Karl's either! I heard some guys were there, trying their luck at the bar."

"You heard about that?"

"That's my world over there. Fugeddaboudit! If you're ever stuck or scared over there just go to my club. You know where it is right?"

"I do, Millie and I went there last year. Thanks!" I said cracking up, "Pino, don't you remember when Millie worked in the Dominican Club?"

"Oh that fucking crazy joint! Listen, if I'm not there, tell my guys you work for me. You'll recognize a lot of them from here. I gotcha back baby! You're always gonna be my little pal," he said as he kissed the top of my head.

"I love ya, thanks! Oh, I don't know if you know, I moved in with Babe, and look what he gave me."

"Are you engaged?" He said, eyeing my ring.

"I have no idea, he hasn't asked yet."

"Okay sweetheart, everything will work out!" He said as he stopped and hugged me. "Okay let's go back to work." We walked back and off I went to count, count, and count! While I counted Pino, Millie, and I laughed our asses off retelling the Dominican Disco days.

Millie was asked to work in a club, to help boost profits. It was a Spanish club in Williamsburg. One night I went to pick her up, but for some reason I took one of my bartenders, Ava with me. Ava was also blonde and blue eyed, but very innocent. Well, we pulled up to a massive street crowd. There wasn't a parking spot to be had, so I pulled up on the sidewalk in front of a bodega. As I weaved through the crowd, I realized Ava wasn't behind me; she had been separated and now surrounded by the drunken customers. I pushed my way back and grabbed her hand dragging her out of the middle.

When we walked in the club, I thought it was strange that everyone was walking around looking at the floor. I asked Millie if she was ready, and she said to give her a few minutes, as she needed to look for something. Always being a good friend, I offered to help, thinking maybe it was jewelry or a beeper. We walked around through the crowd looking, when I finally asked what exactly the missing object was, Millie said an ear. There had been a fight and guy had his ear chopped off, and he needed it to have it reattached.

Ava stood stunned, asked if it was a real ear, and almost threw up when she found out it was. Of course, she would be the one to find it, almost stepping on it. Millie picked it up, threw it in a plastic cup of milk and the three of us made our way to the front door. Once we pushed our way through the crowd outside, we decided to take it to the hospital for the guy. Only in Brooklyn will your bartender deliver your ear foryou.

The customer was so grateful, he offered us cash for the ear, but we didn't take it; after all, if I lost an ear, I would hope someone would do the same thing. When we were leaving, the club DJ, Mo, asked us for a ride home, because he had gone in the ambulance and was now stuck at the hospital. I agreed, because what the hell was another pit stop in our adventure! He lived in a burnt out building on a derelict block with groups of guys standing around open fires in the metal garbage cans, drinking. Mo was a squatter, and had to climb up the fire escape to get in.

I had made so many detours; I became distracted and never looked at my gas gage. After we said goodbye to Mo, I tried to start the car, but nothing happened, because I ran out of gas. Ava was on the verge of crying as Millie and I laughed at the fucking timing. With no other choice, we got out and started to walk, but Ava was afraid of the street guys.

I explained she could stay in the car, but would probably become one of the guy's, from the open fire pit crowd, new girlfriend. She turned white and quickly joined us instead of being passes around by the crack heads. Poor Ava cried as she walked with us, asking over and over again how I knew where to go.

We walked about two blocks to a blackened storefront that I could tell it was a card club. I knocked on the door and was greeted by a few knock around guys. I told them who I was, and whom I worked for, and they invited us in. It was like entering Ali Baba's den; this place was packed with swag everything! The guys were great, treated us like daughters. Someone went and syphoned some gas into a can and filled my tank. Ava was freaking out that I had handed my car keys over to a prefect stranger to gas it up, and deliver it to the club. *What a pedestrian!*

What she never understood was that we may be strangers technically, but we all connected and that made us family. All three of us were gifted leather jackets, fed, and escorted to my awaiting car outside. I'm still friends with those guys today, because they were Pino's crew. He laughed thinking about what he heard the next day from the boys. I could count and talk as long no one mentioned dollar amounts. Within two hours, I had all the money bundled into piles of a thousand each. Paid and tipped with a free dinner of our choice, we went out to pick the restaurant.

This was no easy task. There really wasn't a bad restaurant on the strip, each known for one delicacy or another. One only had to figure out what they wanted first, and then find the place that specialized in it. I grew up coming to Little Italy twice a week from first to eighth grade. Most of my school girlfriend's parents were either in the restaurant or funeral business. I remember always thinking I'd never starve in either business, because everybody eats and everybody dies.

I chose Flora's Restaurant and we decided to sit outside. Millie and I settled in to eat and enjoy sightseeing; we kept on our oversized sunglasses so we didn't have to make eye contact with anyone if we didn't want to. Sipping wine and twirling our pasta, we huddled in deep conversation discussing my stressful life, in code, without actually mentioning anyone.

"I don't think you should keep a regular schedule anymore. Switch up your routine. Sleep at my house, we'll sleep at Breezy and even go back to your apartment too." Millie pleaded.

Thinking more, I said, "Yeah maybe, sounds like a plan."

"You know he would understand, in fact he would probably suggest it if he could. Maybe he thinks you'll realize it on your own." She said, holding my hand.

"You're right, I'll start tonight." I thought about how I would get word to Babe so he wouldn't worry.

"Want to go out later?" She knew I was upset and tried to cheer me up.

"I can't, he wants me to stay home this week in particular, but we're working so it doesn't count, if we stay here in the neighborhood," I said giggling.

Our plans were set; if it turned out to be slow, and we closed early, we would bounce on Mulberry Street. Finishing up, we strolled a while stopping at the local card game to see the boys. This is where I would pickup Old Man George whenever I worked. He was the nastiest, crustiest curmudgeon around, who I knew since my little girl catholic princess days.

I'm not sure how it started, but it was my job to pick George up and walk him to the restaurant, holding a black umbrella over his old bald head. He would complain the whole way as he shuffled, never saying thank you. Once inside, I would have to cook his meal, no one else was allowed, and I was the only person who could serve him.

As he ate, he would toss a bill on the floor, sometimes it was a $10, $20 or $50. George would tape a piece of clear fishing wire to it and if you were stupid enough to bend to pick it up, he would pull it out of reach and laugh at you. This happened to me once and I never fell for it again. Every time I saw it, I would walk over it and say, "George I won't bend down for anything under $100, and if it's not there, you have to give me double." I ruined his fun every day. When he was ready, I would have to walk him back. Even if the joint was packed, I would have to leave to take him.

Depositing him back at the game, I would give him a little peck on his cheek and he would give me a $50 bill. I would always say, "Thanks George, I'll say a prayer for you, not that you deserve it."

The night started the same as most nights, with the same cast of characters. Old Man George playing his money jokes, Ray singing Frank Sinatra very loud, torturing all of us, with Jules the furniture maker, and all the rest in their assigned spots. We had a great bar crowd and every table was filled. My girlfriends stopped by regularly and really cranked up the party. How they can drink so much is beyond me. They could hold their liquor more than a man. They were trying, in vain, to get us to join them after work, but I promised I wouldn't go out so I passed.

"Millie, if you want to go, you can. You don't have to stay here with me," I offered, not wanting to hold her back from having fun.

"No way, are you kidding me." She said giving me a hug behind the bar.

Around 1:30AM, a truck pulled up to the front and out popped a guy. I didn't take much notice because trucks were there all the time. It took me a few minutes before I realized Babe was standing in front of the window grinning at me. I jumped over the bar and ran outside and jumped on him. My legs were wrapped around his waist while my arms were wrapped around his neck kissing him. He held the bottom of my cheeks to support me. Every person in the restaurant was ogling us at the window. After a minute he gently put me down.

"Oh Babe, I can't believe it's you!" I cried!

"Who did you think it was? I hope you don't kiss every guy in a truck like this?" He said, joking and grinning.

"Of course I do, it's the truck stop special!"

With that, he slapped my ass hard, "I know I heard about that from the guys on the route, so I came to see for myself."

"Ouch! Jerk!"

He grabbed me to pull me close. Whispering he asked, "You okay?"

"Yeah, but I miss you!" I said wanting to cry, but I held my tears in check.

Being serious, he whispered, "Me too, listen I gotta run, but I'll try to stop by every night you work here. Keep a low profile and stay out of trouble."

"I will, you too! Do you want anything to eat or drink before you go?"

"No, gotta run, I have a schedule to keep. Love ya!" he said as he buried me with a major kiss.

I stood there on the sidewalk as he jumped in the truck and drove away. When I walked back in, all the guys went crazy, shouting, "How come you don't say hello to me like that? Hey, I drive a truck too!" Shaking my head, I went behind the bar completely flushed with embarrassment.

As everyone started to leave to hit the clubs, we cleaned up and readied the place to close. Pino didn't come in and we were left holding the bag; literally, we had the night's take. That definitely meant we had to stay in the neighborhood, because we had way too much of someone else's money to lose. There are no friends when it comes to money.

Millie and I walked around the corner to one of the restaurants that stayed open later than the others and sat outside sipping some wine, recounting our night's adventures, people watching. The owner bought us our first round, and some of our patrons stopped by and started to back us up. We had six drinks in reserve, more than we would ever drink because we would be too hammered to drive if we drank that much. We started talking table to table and soon the whole place was having a group conversation.

The owner's son, Frank, joined in and quickly he became the main focus. He was extremely charismatic. I could see Millie smiling at him and he was moving closer and closer to her. They had a history already, having dated over a year ago; they just drifted apart without any bad blood between them. It appeared the old flame was relit.

Before we knew it, it was 4AM and our night was coming to a close. I could see Frank was trying to hang with Millie, but she didn't give me the signal she wanted to stay alone, so I busied myself and went behind the bar and made coffee for everyone. No matter where we were, I wound up behind the bar. The morning haze reminded us we were still out from the night before.

Frank asked, "You girls okay to drive home?"

"Sure, we didn't drink that much. I had three glasses of wine in ten hours, I think I'm good and I'm the driver. Millie's the passenger tonight," I said, sipping my coffee.

"Good! I think Sugar here had a little more than you. She's staying with you?"

"That was the plan, unless it changed." I said teasing him.

"Sugar, hey you going home with Peeper here?"

Jumping up in total shock I asked, "Oh my god! Where did you hear that name?"

"Where do you think? I got off the phone with Babe by the time you were on your second drink."

Shaking my head, totally red faced I said, "You're too funny! I can't believe he told you that."

Frank winked, "He knew you would know I really spoke to him if I called you that. I can see it worked. So tell me if you girls want to drive home tonight or stay in my apartment upstairs since it's late."

"Frank! You have a one bedroom upstairs, where would we sleep?" Millie said, clearly interested in him again.

"I'll take the couch and you girls can have my bed," Frank said as he put his hand over his heart. "I'm always a gentlemen you know that."

"Dannie, we have clothes in the trunk, and always have our toothbrush and makeup with us. What do you think? You said Babe wanted you to stay home."

"Really Peeper? Then why are you out?" Frank asked.

"I'm not out really, we just got out of work and this is our neighborhood. What did Babe say on the phone?"

"He just wanted me to keep an eye out for you girls, make sure you're both okay," he said winking at Millie.

"Is that the only reason you're talking to us Frank? Because Babe asked you to?" Millie said teasing him.

"I think you know that answer. Hey, can you tell me why we stopped dating Sugar?"

"I don't know, maybe it was because you're so busy," Millie said as she got up and excused herself to go to the bathroom. Turning around she gave me the eye and I jumped up to follow her. Once inside the bathroom, we broke out laughing.

"So what do you think? Do you still like him?" I busted out barely able to contain myself.

"I always have. We have so much fun together, but I don't want him to think that just because we're staying, I'm gonna go with him."

"He knows you well enough and knows you're not like that. It's your call; he's your ex, not mine," I said as I brushed my hair in the mirror. "But I can tell he's clearly taken with you."

Millie pleaded, "Let's stay, I'm tired, but don't leave me alone with him!"

"Gotcha! Let's go." I said as we returned to the dining room. Frank straightened up and was ready to close.

"Okay Frank, we're going to stay with you, but before you do a tap dance remember you're not getting anything," She teased him with her hand on her hip and the other pointing at him.

"I promise to be a perfect gentleman! Follow me ladies," he said as he walked towards the kitchen. There, in the back, was a door going upstairs to his apartment above the restaurant. He was another neat freak! Millie walked around not skipping a beat, because she was familiar with his place. Frank went into his bedroom and came out carrying two pairs of t-shirts and sweatpants. "Okay, the room is all yours. There's a bathroom in there and another in here. Help yourselves to anything."

"Thanks so much I'm going to change," I said as I kissed him on his cheek and walked into his bedroom, leaving them completely alone.

I could hear her clear her throat trying to get my attention, but I didn't look back because I wanted to give them a minute to be alone. Frank didn't skip a beat; he offered her a glass of water for her throat. I could hear Millie mumbling yes, and thank you, probably cursing me as I walked away. Once inside, I changed and cleaned up turning on the TV, I put my bag on the bed as I jumped in. Not much later Millie walked in with Frank and they started to laugh at me. "You don't have to sleep with your bag; I'm not going to rob you!" Frank said laughing at me.

"Good grief, if it was just my money I'd give it to, but I have the restaurant money, so I can't lose sixteen-G's." Tapping the bag I said, "Just call me Estelle Getty tonight! I'm sleeping with my bag!"

"Well, let me find something to sleep in and I'll get out of your way. I can't sleep naked with Sugar and Peeper in my house."

Frank changed and said good night leaving Millie and I alone, giggling about the situation. We were extremely tired, and fell asleep quickly.

How could we not wakeup with a smile on our faces? Frank had a beautiful breakfast set up for us when we woke up. He sent a busboy to the parking lot to pick up our bags from the trunk of my car, and was waiting for us to stir, sipping coffee and reading the paper.

"Oh Frank, this is beautiful! Thank you!" Millie said as we walked in. He turned and looked at her with that look; the look Babe gives me. *Hmm, I think we may have started something here. I'm sure it couldn't hurt that we were in white t-shirts and not wearing bra's either.*

"Anything for you girls! Come on sit. Coffee?" He said as he poured two cups for us. There was everything you could think of to eat; it looked like a brunch buffet in a restaurant. We were famished and dug in. "I hope you like everything. If you want something else, I'll call downstairs."

"No, no, everything is just perfect! Thank you, you didn't have to any of this." I said, extremely grateful for his hospitality. "I hope we didn't inconvenience you too much!" Millie's cheeks turned a light pink as she turned to him, "I hope your girlfriend won't get mad that we're here."

"Sugar, I don't have a serious girlfriend, just dating around," he said laughing, knowing fully where we were going with this. "I'm not going to ask you the same, because I know you don't have one either."

"How do you know that? I might but I don't at the moment," she said with a teasing tone. "I don't need one either."

"Oh really, that's too bad. I like to be needed," he said, boldly taking her hand in his.

"I feel like I'm watching a good movie, this is fun! Millie, he got up earlier than us, so he already knows every detail about you. I know from firsthand knowledge. Frank, I think I'm going to read the paper over there, way over there." Without waiting for a response I took my coffee and his paper into the bedroom and jumped on the bed to read what was going on in the world.

About an hour later, Millie walked in followed by Frank carrying our bags. "Oh thanks, Frank!" I said grinning at them both.

"Take your time girls, but I have to jump in the shower first. You guys can stay as long as you like, I have to get downstairs." He leaned in and kissed Millie on her cheek. "Later, Sugar."

As soon as he was out of the room, we started to giggle, not saying anything we didn't want him to hear; we made chit chat until he was in the shower. "Millie, oh my God is all I'm saying."

"Shhh, I'm sure he can hear everything! Let's get out of here and go home to shower." We made the bed, cleaned the dishes, put away the food and got dressed so fast we amazed ourselves. Frank was out of the shower and getting dressed in the bedroom. When he came out, we were sitting waiting to say goodbye.

"Wow you don't have to leave, just because I have to. If you want to take showers you girls can stay."

"No, we don't want to put you out. Plus, you have things to do." Millie laughed as we gather our bags. Thanking him and kissing goodbye, we walked out the back of the restaurant, through the courtyard to the street around the corner, so we didn't have to walk past the boys. Not that they didn't know we were there the moment we walked in. Nothing went on in Little Italy that they didn't know about.

CHAPTER 29

Hump & Smile

"Here, your beeper is going off," I moaned as I handed Millie her beeper from the night table.

"I'm so tired, who's looking for me already?" She said, as she fumbled trying to read the number. "Oh, its Frank!"

"Here's the phone, call him back while you still have the sexy morning voice." I handed Millie the phone and she gave me a look to kill before dialing him.

"Hey Frank, you beeped me?" She moaned in her best come-fuck-me morning voice. "Ha-ha I just woke up, thanks for everything. Hmm, I'm not sure if I'm free, what do you have in mind? Oh a late dinner tomorrow night? No, I think I'm busy." She said winking at me. "How about the night after? Sounds good, I'll meet you after work, swing by the restaurant to pick me up. Okay, thanks! Bye." She hung up and was totally red faced.

"So you're having dinner with Frank? I knew he was going to ask you out!"

"He wants to grab a bite after work. Do you think he has a girlfriend?"

"I don't know but let's find out tonight." I said starting to hatch a plan. "You up for a little Mannix?"

Millie grinned, "I was just thinking the same thing. I need to know, I can't have this nonsense happen again. He's a player, but I'll give him the benefit of the doubt. Let's get up and get dressed."

"Let's call around and see what the girls have to say. I'll start with a waitress I know." I dialed and asked. "Hey Gia, got a quick question. Frank from the restaurant, the one Millie used to go out with, what do you hear about him? He asked Millie. She does, they dated last year. Oh great, thanks!" I hung up and turned to Millie, "Gia said he's a nice guy and that she's never seen him with any particular girl, he's always with the boys."

"We'll see tonight!" With that we were up to start our day. We decided to go shopping before work, and headed to 86th street. We picked off store after store, filling up the trunk. Each outfit I chose was with Babe in mind. I wanted to look good for him; as a matter of fact, I wanted to do everything to make him happy.

"Babe's a lucky guy, he's not going to recognize you after all the new clothes."

"I know, but where am I going to put them all? I maxed out his closet already with all the stuff he just bought me!" I said, giggling.

"What about that other door I've seen? Can you make that room a closet?"

"Are you kidding me? I'm not even allowed in it, let alone to put up a California closet system." Smiling, I grabbed her hand and decided to tell her about the kid's conversation. "I didn't tell you yet, but he wanted to blow the house out and add another floor and he asked me about kids again!"

Her jaw dropped, "Oh my god, really already?" Quickly giving me a huge hug and starting to cry, she said, "Oh Mama I'm so happy for you! I can't believe how much everything is changing so quickly."

Surprising myself, I started to cry too. "I know it's been a real whirlwind lately. I'm kind of scared! Kids? That's a huge commitment!" We walked outside the store to smoke a cigarette.

"Did he talk about getting married?" Millie asked gently.

"Nope, not a word! I thought he was old fashioned, so I didn't expect the baby conversation before the wedding. But it's the boys thing I guess."

She asked the million-dollar question. "Would you marry him?"

Without skipping a beat I blurted out, "In a heartbeat! I don't want to be with anyone else."

Raising an eyebrow, she looked at me. "Is this sex talking or is this about him?"

"I've never had anyone look at me like I was the only person in the world. Babe just does everything I want and stuff I didn't know I wanted him to do." Giggling I said, "The sex doesn't hurt either, he's an animal!"

"I guess there's no need to be on a diet! But we better hit the gym more to keep our asses! Come on let's look at shoes!"

We went about our shopping excursion, laughing and talking about everything as we moved store to store. On the corner was a baby furniture boutique. We passed by and stopped. Looking in through the window, I put my head on her shoulder and just stared at the window display. As we stood there, a face came into focus inside it was Babe's sister, she was looking at us, smiling and waving at me. Jo-Anne walked outside and I introduced her to Millie.

"Come inside!" She said, "We just changed the window display."

Swallowing hard, not sure what I should say, "It looks great! I didn't know you work here."

"I own the store, my brother bought it for me! If there's anything you guys need, let me know," She said in her usual friendly way. "Who's having a baby?"

My face flashed completely red and she saw it, "Oh my God are you pregnant?" Giving me a big hug before I could explain, she pulled back and saw my ring and started to cry.

I stuttered quickly, "No, no! I'm not." Trying to figure out what to say I turned even redder. "I was just looking." *Shut up! Who just looks at baby furniture unless they're having a baby, shopping for a baby or wants a baby?*

Looking distressed she backpedaled, "Oh I didn't mean anything, but are you guys engaged?"

I was starting to fumble with my words, "Umm, well its like this, he just gave me the ring as a gift."

"Silly me you don't know me very well," Jo-Anne said, now more nervous than me. "I love my brother so much; I just got excited for a second."

Now I felt worse because she was so uncomfortable. "Oh please don't feel bad. I'm fine, we have to run." Trying to get out of the conversation we moved towards the door. "You have such a beautiful store, I'll tell all my friends to come here." Kissing her goodbye, we made a mad dash out the door. That was it, no more shopping. Stuffing every bag in the trunk, we jumped in the car and took off. We flew back to Breezy and changed for work. Just as we were leaving, the phone rang.

"Hey Peeper, what's up?" Babe asked, sounding like the King.

"Hey Baby! I miss you!" I moaned.

"Ditto! What are you doing?" He asked sounding glad to hear my voice.

I was missing him terribly, "Getting ready for work. I guess you talked to your sister."

He pressed, "Yeah I did, she feels bad and I figured maybe there was something you needed to tell me."

Feeling stupid and embarrassed over the whole scenario, "No, I was just looking. I had no idea she owned the place, I just stopped to look at the window after leaving the store next door."

Babe sounded less excited as I spoke, "Okay, just checking. Be careful tonight, park in the lot please."

"I'm in Brooklyn tonight." Taking a deep breath I continued, "I'm so embarrassed! I just threw out my pills but I think I would need to be near you for anything to happen."

His mood bounced up again as he turned on his sexy voice. "Ooooh, okay I'll solve that soon, but you never took them anyway so we'll see! Love you!"

"I love you too." I listened to Babe hang up, and sighed.

I was getting used to our brief calls, but not the separation- it was unnerving. Millie was right by my side, supporting me through the turmoil. She worked in another bar close to mine for the same family, just a different crew. We tried to stay in the same borough at the same time. That night, she was going to drive me to work and pick me up, just to switch up our routine a bit. Brooklyn wasn't as much fun now that all the boys weren't around. I didn't expect a long or prosperous night ahead.

Walking into an empty bar was depressing, and for some reason I was edgy, so I spent a lot of time on the porch smoking until I closed up. Picking up Millie, we headed to the city to have a little look around. We headed right to Mulberry Street and jumped around the restaurants. From what we heard, we were one step behind Frank; we just missed running into him at each place. Sitting in the car around the corner, I started to tell Millie about a white van that was probably filled with Feds that I saw across the street from the bar all night.

As we sat there smoking and talking we had an idea, thanks to the Feds. We left the car and walked up behind the restaurant and looked at the back of the building. Knowing his apartment was on the second floor and his bedroom was at the back we looked for any movement or shadows against the existing lights. After a few minutes, we decided to take a better look and jumped over the fence.

We banked on the fact we were such common faces in the area, that no one would take notice of us. Sizing up the building, we moved some crates and garbage pails around until we made a pedestal of sorts. How no one heard us whispering and giggling I have no idea. I jumped up first and then Millie followed me; climbing on me, holding onto the bricks, she stood on my shoulders and peeked into his bedroom window. Having her weight on me gave me such an uncontrollable case of giggles that I almost peed myself. She held onto his window ledge and caught his friend on top of a girl fucking her.

With every hump he picked his head up slightly and smiled at us through the window. He liked being caught and put on one hell of a show. After a few minutes, the weight was too much for the crates and we tumbled down onto the floor. The lights started to go on and a few people opened their windows only to find us collapsed on the floor with our skirts up laughing. Apologizing for making noise, we took off, running. Frank never came to the back door of his restaurant, so he had no idea we were trying to spy on him. Millie and I cried laughing all the way back home.

The next day, I worked in Brooklyn again, and was hoping Babe would call me, but he didn't. Not that I would tell him on the phone, but I just wanted to hear his voice. I drove myself and parked right in front and there was the van again. It was becoming so obvious, I'm sure they didn't try to hide it anymore. They just wanted to be intimidating. Most of the customers who were regular guys even commented, referring to them as the fuzz,

Hawaii 5-O and Kojack. The very next day the feds came busting in; the place was swarming with so many agents it was like a fucking convention.

The men were professional and stand-offish, but there was one Spanish girl who broke my chops. She actually went through my handbag and looked at my checkbook. She kept asking me if I knew this one or that one, and when I said I didn't, she ripped a check out of my book and stuffed in her pocket. I protested, but it fell on deaf ears. No big deal, it was a blank check I could void it out. I'm sure they knew I had a bank account already, so it didn't really matter. When I left after my shift, I waved goodbye to the van like a true ball buster.

Millie finally went out with Frank, so I went home alone after a long day at work. I opened the door, busied myself heating up some dinner I'd brought home and walked in the bedroom to eat in front of the TV. I switched on the set and went into the bathroom to change into one of Babe's button down shirts. Wearing his shirt always made me feel close to him. As I was just about to jump on the bed, I heard a noise from the other room. I froze, because I'd never heard anything coming from that room before. *There it was again!* I backed into the bathroom closing and locking the door. I sat in the shower in the dark for what seemed like an eternity. Then I heard his voice calling me, "Hey where are you?"

I didn't answer right away, just in case it wasn't him. He repeatedly called me, but until he used the word Peeper, I didn't move a muscle. All at once, I jumped up flung the door open and pounced on him knocking him to the ground. He was flat on his back, with me on top of him kissing him. Never saying a word, I ripped his clothes off and took total control for the first time. He never had a choice, nor did he fight it; I barely let him come up for air. I missed him and was showing him exactly how much.

I stayed on top crushing myself against him, while I bit his neck roughly until I couldn't hold back. I brought him right over the edge with me as I screamed his name over and over again.

After a few minutes of sweaty panting, I giggled "Are you alive? Did I hurt you?"

"I think I may need stitches but you can kill me like this everyday!" He beamed rubbing his neck. "You're wearing my shirt Rider! Nice!" I started to peel myself off him and help him up off the floor. He fell back on the bed stretching out, "Now what was that for?"

"I missed you so much! Are you back?" I asked standing over him, with my finger touching his nose, chewing on my lip.

He grabbed me by the waist and tossed me next to him. "No, just needed to grab some stuff and I wanted to see you quick before I go to work." Grinning he said, "You did say I needed to be closer to you."

Flaming red, I knew exactly what he was referring to. Trying to change the subject, I reached over and grabbed some papers off the end table. "Listen Babe, I was invited to a baby shower this Saturday, and we also have a wedding for friends of yours. There's Phil's fundraiser Sunday night too. What should I do?"

Running his hand through his hair, he exhaled, "Well, I guess we have a busy weekend. Didn't you take off already?"

"Yes, two months ago when we responded to the invites, but I'm not going if you're not going. By the way, you've been gone a long fucking time!" I said, teasing him.

Looking guilty, he said, "I know, but we're definitely going. Add dinner at my sister's this Sunday too."

"Really?" I was nervous all of the sudden. "I never asked but does she know that we live together?"

Babe started to laugh at my immaturity and nervous chatter. "I'm not 20 years old, of course she knows."

"I'm so excited, we have the weekend together! I can't wait I hope it drags! I'm going shopping in the morning."

"Pick up cards, for the envelope gifts," he said, as he got up and started to pick out his clothes. "Buy a generous baby gift; go see my sister."

"I'm not cheap, don't worry on that mark. Plus, I'm spending your money, I'll be extra generous!" Smirking at him, I made the inch gesture with one hand and I need money gesture with the other.

"Gotcha, you only want an inch, I thought you liked it by the foot? I have to go soon; I need to take a shower." He said slyly as he walked into the bathroom laughing and turned on the water. "Peeper, come in here and work off the cash!"

"For an inch you get a hand shake, for a foot of cash you'll get a happy ending!" I followed him as we both cracked up and I proceeded to remind him of what he'd been neglecting.

Kissing me gently after he tucked me in for the night, he whispered in my ear, "I want to take your car tonight. Where are your keys?"

Moaning, I surrendered my car over to him. "On the island, the papers are in the glove. Do I get to drive your car?"

Moving my hair away he kissed me gently as he said, "You like the speedy little Porsche's don't ya? I'm leaving I love you! I'll leave the other keys on the island with a foot."

Tugging on his neck, I kissed him hard, hoping to make him stay I said, "Hmm, sounds like a plan Boss! Love you too!"

I heard him hit the alarm pad and leave. I drifted off to sleep with a huge smile on my face, even though I had the little birdie whispering a warning in my ear, After all, Babe was a mobbed up guy, who did "things." I knew it even though it was never actually said to me and he never alluded to it, but I had a brain.

I had just given the keys to my car over to a person that's main livelihood was doing dark things; my car could be used in a hit and traced back to me. On the other hand, this dangerous trigger-happy guy was my man and I loved every inch of him. I often wondered how he separated work from everything else and still kept his sanity.

I never really knew what Babe did that earned him all the money he had. The expression "things" is pretty broad and could cover a lot of different mob related ventures. I'm not sure I could sleep with someone who chopped heads off regularly, but beating, shooting or shaking them down didn't bother me as much. He was kind of like an exterminator taking care of removing all unwanted pests.

My dreams that night were a weird mixture of murder, and sex. Somehow, I still smiled all night long.

·

CHAPTER 30

President Of The Fan Club

The next day, I woke up like I owned the world. I got ready and decided to call Millie. She was up already getting ready for the gym. I told her I would swing by to pick her up and we could grab coffee, go to the gym and head off for a day of shopping, but most of all she could fill me in on her date. Grabbing my beeper, bag, sunglasses and the strange car keys, I saw a fat envelope with a note on the outside. "Buy yourself all the pretty outfits you need for the weekend, besides the baby gifts because you earned it! Check out the furniture for the nursery! XO Babe"

I stuffed the envelope in my bag and ran out the door with a huge smile on my face. I walked to where I parked and I saw a strange car there. It wasn't Babe's, but a Jaguar XJS, black on black turbo convertible. I looked at the keys in my hand and hit the alarm button. The lights flashed and the car unlocked. *Wow, this is a beautiful car.* I opened the door and looked inside; the car was pristine. I popped open the trunk to toss my gym bag in, and found a note and gold box of Godiva chocolate. My hands were shaking as I opened the note and saw Babe's handwriting. "To the

President of my fan club, enjoy the ride!" I ran in the house and beeped him right away.

Babe called me back laughing, clearly waiting for my beep, "It's about time you woke up! What, were you tired, Peeper?"

I blurted out, "I just went outside and found a car."

In his ballbuster tone he played with me. "Really you found a car? Who do you think it belongs too?"

"I don't know, maybe you should tell me? The note said the car was for your fan club President," I teased.

"Oh well, leave that it there and walk, she'll be over as soon you leave!" He started to laugh, "You fucking nut, the car's for you! Do you like it?"

"Are you kidding me? I love it!" Giggling I said, "It matches my black hair!"

"Beats an Audi and Vet, huh?" He asked, busting my chops.

Giggling, I teased him back; "I can't even remember those cars anymore! Thank you so much I love, love, love it! Baby wait to you get home and I'll show how much I love it and you! Maybe, just maybe I'll thank you on the car!"

"You're on big shot, I'm loving how you've thanked me already and I'm gonna enjoy your gratitude more than you know! All kidding aside you needed something newer and I almost got you a Porsche, but they are all two-seaters, and you're gonna need a back seat soon!" He said, laughing at me on the phone, but clearly he liked that I made a fuss over all his presents. It made him as happy to give me elaborate gifts, as I was to receive them.

"Really, I thought you had me signed up for a baseball team! Please don't get rid of my old car! Store it in your shop, but keep it for me. It has a lot of good memories," I begged.

Babe hated hearing about other guys; he had a major jealous streak. "I told you already I'm not interested in the old memories that I'm not part of. When the team comes I'll get you a mini van!"

"Silly! No, I bought that car with my OWN hard earned money, that's what I mean! I never did anyone for presents; I'm not that kind of girl! Just so there's no misunderstanding, I WILL NEVER DRIVE A MINI VAN! How hot would I be sporting a mini van? Really come on now, that's an anti hard on vehicle!"

Laughing he said, "Okay, okay I get it now! Don't worry your old car will be in the shop. Enjoy the Jag! Gotta run, love you!"

"Thanks again I love you more! Beep me later," I said and hung up. The boys never gave Toyotas or Saturns; they wouldn't even steel one unless it was on the list for parts needed, let alone sleep with a girl who drove one. When they give a girl a car, it's flashy! Showering girls with expensive gifts is a sign of success and power, only a broken down valise would drive or give a crap car.

I flew in style to Millie's. What a dream the car was to drive, Millie loved it. We ran to Starbucks for lattes and then hit the gym. Starting off on the treadmill, I figured it was a good place to talk for 30 minutes solid about her date. She gave me the 411 on their small talk and how he was smooth and didn't try anything.

"So how was your date?" I asked with a grin.

"We had a lot of fun! He's crazy, he took me to Ray's for dinner and then we went to Regina's dancing."

"That's the condensed version, so what else?" I asked, prying.

"He held my hand a lot and kept petting my hair. Every guy pets my frigging hair! Ugh! He kept his arm around me the whole night, but he was good. Frank asked if I was interested in anyone and if I would go out with him again. So, I said I'd think about it. I don't know I have to take it slow, and see where it goes. He wants me to go to Rockland County for a party this weekend."

I asked, "He wants you to stay over?"

Smirking she said, "Yes, because it's his mother's birthday party and I love her!"

Shaking my finger I said, "Well after the party, you'll be stuck with him you know!"

"I'm fine, he's not that kind of guy with me," She said laughing. "Frank's this big tough serious guy with everyone, but with me he's a lot of fun. If I don't want to do anything, he'll be good."

Smiling, I said, "I know he's a sweetheart! I love when he's on the news looking all serious, but with us he's just so different! When do you leave?"

Milliesmiled,"Frank's pickingmeupat 7PM, in BROOKLYN!"

Shocked, I said, "That's big, he never comes out here!"

"I know, he's strictly a city guy," Millie smiled knowing that the simple act of going to Brooklyn was huge for Frank. "Forget the machines, let's finish up and go shopping! I want to buy a new outfit for the party." We had too much to do to get ready for our parties, so we hit the stores. First stop, Babe's sister's store to buy a baby shower present. We pulled up and found a spot in the front; the car was certainly eye candy, because heads turned as we got out sporting our cute jogging suits and oversized sunglasses. Jo-Anne met us at the door, welcoming us in.

"Hey, come in, come in!" She said giving us a big kiss hello. "What can I do for you guys?"

"I was invited to Benny's wife's baby shower. I really don't know them, what do you suggest? I think she's having a boy," I said walking around looking at her beautiful store.

Millie called out, "Dannie, you have to see this, come here!" She was in front of the most beautiful display of baby clothes. "Oh, my god look at how cute this is! It makes you want to have a baby just to buy this!"

His sister giggled and started to pull different outfits out. Before we knew it the whole counter was filled with clothes. Talking and laughing, we were having so much fun. I was fingering a little tiny pink onesie, with a matching hat and pink satin ribbons and receiving blanket.

I said, "I'm going to take them all! Ring it up, and could you wrap this pink set separate please?"

"Oh that's great! I'll give you the total, my bother can come in and pay later."

"No, I'm paying cash." I said and whipped out the envelope from Babe without realizing his handwriting was clearly visible.

She read it at the same time I did, and I turned flaming red, but didn't say a word. Four hundred dollars later, with boxes upon boxes stacked and wrapped in jumbo baby blue and brown polka dot ribbons and bows, we took them outside to load into the car. As soon as I popped the trunk open the box of Godiva and Babe's note were sitting there for everyone to read. Millie and I started to load the boxes in and quickly Jo-Anne moved the note card and chocolate out of the way. She held them and couldn't help but read his message to me.

Smiling she said, "Congratulations on the new car! Its beautiful!"

Grinning from ear to ear I said, "Thank you! I love it, but not as much as your brother!" I said, just because I thought she should know I cared for him and wasn't just after the expensive gifts. Girls in this life of ours are either standup girls or gold diggers. Plenty of gangster cock chasers only wanted the flash, and cash, but made the mad dash when their guy had the first sign of trouble. Very few visited them in prison more than once; not me, I felt like I was a member of a frequent flyer program.

I wanted Jo-Anne to know I was in it for the long haul, a keeper, and the type who visited even though I hoped never to have to. As we were arranging the packages, a Cadillac pulled up next to me and with a few guys in it. The windows were open, and I could see their faces, they were the same group from Karl's.

Not skipping a beat, I smiled and said, "What's up fellas?"

"Nothing honey, nice car looks new." Grinning as they were checking out the car. "Hey Millie! You girls look pretty today!"

"Thanks guys," Millie said with her very best fake smile.

"Thanks, I like it," I said slyly.

With vicious smiles, they turned their attention towards me, "How's Babe? We haven't seen him in a while, where's our pal been?"

Even though Millie and I were extremely feminine; very girly girl, we had a sharp side to us. Now I turned my attention directly to the passenger and with my hand on my hip and cigarette in the other I snapped impatiently, "Now what's this about? You know me long enough not to ask me anything because I don't know ANYTHING, I'm not part of this and I resent you fucking asking me. Stop already!"

"Ooo, don't be like that. I'm just asking a fucking question!" He shot back.

"Well, don't! How about I start asking your wife fucking questions about you?" I said with my eyebrow raised. "Or did you forget I served you for years and would have a lot to talk to her about. I'm sure you would be pissed, so remember the rules and leave me the fuck out of this."

"Take it easy, take it easy! We were just stopping to say hello, that's all. Say hi to Babe for us." And with that they peeled out and left. These idiots were bothering me, breaking a big rule that the boys follow; families are off limits. Babe's sister was more used to this, she stayed right next to me instead of going inside. Trying to get us to go back inside, Jo-Anne offered to order lunch, but we declined. Saying our goodbyes, neither of us mentioned the situation. We had some power shopping ahead and little time to get all dolled up. We left the car, and walked to all our favorite shops, planning on hitting Kings Highway next if we couldn't find something dazzling.

All the stores had ears, we couldn't talk without everything being repeated, plus half of them were bugged anyway. Millie and I never brought the subject up. I couldn't find the perfect dress I was looking for, but Millie found the most amazing jumpsuit and dressy shorts sets. She had long legs and wore killer heels.

We moved from store to store, each owner was friendlier than they used to be. Funny, all of a sudden the owners wanted to show me the dresses from the back room that weren't out yet. I always thought I had great service, but now it was definitely different.

Running out of stores, we jumped in the car and drove to Kings Highway to the Russians. The Russian boutiques were incredible; they stocked one-of-a-kind dresses but you needed to be rail thin to wear anything they sold. The idea was if you look good enough to charge a couple of grand like a Russian hooker, then you've achieved the right look. I've always thought if someone thought I looked good enough to charge for it, then I must be looking pretty fucking hot. I don't mean a $20 blowjob from the boardwalk, I mean a $5000 a night girl from the swanky city hotels.

I found two dresses, all beaded, low cut and slinky. One was champagne gold and the other was pale silver. In the next store, I found a few shorts sets, a dressy black, cropped blazer, a navy with a military style jacket, and a pure white one. All would be cute with a pair of high heels. Next, I needed something for dinner at his sister's house. This was harder; I didn't want something too casual, but not dressy, not short, but not frumpy either.

Getting frustrated, we walked into a high-end lingerie store, and it turned out to be the one Babe bought my bra and panties in. With Babe in mind, we moved from rack to rack, pulling different sets out to try on. Oh my God Millie and I loved lingerie. I found a few nighties that were all screaming sexy when I tried them on. When you date one of the boys, you know you need to keep their interest with lots of provocative clothing.

"Dannie, you have to try this one on! Look, it's perfect!" She said handing me a little black satin number with a cream lace trim that hugged my hips and just barely covered my breasts. It was really beautiful. I purchased it along with a full black sheer body stocking, five lace bras all different colors, with matching lace panties, three different nighties and two robes; one short and one long.

"Millie, you have to buy this! Look at this color against your skin." I handed her a mocha lace number and a cream bra set. She fell in love with them.

"Who am I buying this for? Please!"

"Hey, you never know." I said laughing, but I knew she wasn't going to be wearing these for anyone but herself right now. Frank was in for the chase of his life; better men had tried and failed. I was sure we would be calling him Frankie Blue Balls by the time she made up her mind.

"I know, but I'm buying it anyway. If I don't wear it you can have it for Babe!" She said laughing. We walked to the counter and the cashier started to ring us up, and I noticed the girl looked familiar. Millie did too, and gave me the eye. "Do we know you?"

Giving us a strained look while she stared at my ring, she mumbled as if she couldn't wait for us to leave her alone. "No, we never met."

"Oh you look so familiar, maybe it's from the clubs or a restaurant," Millie said as I pulled out Babe's envelope and put it on the counter. Her expression changed from contempt to out and out hatred, as she read his writing. Another chunk of change dropped. We were done and went to the car parked in the front to load our treasures into the trunk. There was a little café across from the lingerie shop so we stopped in for a quick lunch.

As we ordered, Millie noticed the cashier walk out and go into the shoe shop next door. She was talking to the girl behind the counter and waving her arms around, and then she started to point at my car. The two girls were looking out the window when I saw her- Justine. I slammed my fist on the table, zeroing in on her, I watched her every move. *THAT CUNT!* I was in predator mode and this girl was definitely going to be my prey. Justine walked outside to smoke a cigarette and stood right next to the car talking and nonchalantly looking at it.

I called the waitress over, "We're not done, but might step outside for a minute. How much is the check?"

She pulled the dupe pad out and tallied up the bill, "It's $24.25."

I tossed her a $50 bill and told her to keep the change and our food on the table. Grabbing my bag, I got up from the table. While Millie tried to get me to take a wait-and-see approach because she's always been more levelheaded than me, I ignored her and walked out. Lighting a cigarette, I hit the remote to make the lights and alarm chirp. Justine looked at the car and then around to see where it was coming from. That's when she saw me standing in front of the restaurant, staring at her while I took long drags from my cigarette, contemplating if I was going to just going to beat the piss out of her in broad daylight. After a minute, she flicked her butt and went back inside. I did the same. Millie had my back, watching what might unfold with guarded amusement. I was no longer interested in eating, so we talked for a minute and then decided to leave.

We walked over to the car with that Brooklyn bitchy swagger staring right at the window. There was another store next to the shoe store I wanted to go into; quite frankly, I wanted to go shoe shopping too, but I thought I'd look for another place. We went into the other store and I found the perfect outfit to wear Sunday. I was almost back to my normal self when I walked out to find James sitting next to my car.

"What's up James?" Millie asked as she kissed him hello.

"What are you girls up to?" James asked grabbing me and swinging me around to face him, instead of the store- he knew, Justine must have beeped him.

"Nothing, shopping. Why?" I asked annoyed.

"Oh nothing, I just thought I'd wait to say hello." He said as he started to look at my car. "Nice! This is fucking beautiful!" He grabbed his stash from his pocket and tossed in a bunch of bills for good luck. "Good luck with the car!"

"Thanks sweetheart! So why are you here?" I asked looking right into the window of the shoe store.

"I told you, I wanted to say hello," he said, with that don't-start-any-shit look.

"Great! I'm almost done; I think I need a new pair of shoes before we leave. Come with us. I guarantee it will be a great show!"

"Oh no, no, no! Shoes? Let's go to 18th Avenue, there's some good stores there." James grabbed for my hand trying to divert my attention, but I sidestepped him.

"Are you kidding me? Nope I want shoes from this fucking shop..." I didn't finish my sentence when I bolted right in and started to look around. Justine just stared at me with such hatred; if she had the wherewithal, she would have stabbed me on the spot. James and Millie looked panicked, as I stalked the shelves trying to figure out if I was going to shove a shoe down her throat or not. Millie and I picked several pairs and asked for assistance to get our sizes.

Justine didn't say a word, she just walked in the back and returned with the boxes and threw them in front of us. Putting aside the bitch face sales girl, the store really had the most beautiful shoes; I wanted them all. And so, I decided to buy them all.

Millie wanted one pair of killer heels. "James, what do you think of these?" She said as she modeled them in front of him.

"Hot! They defiantly are sending a message," he said sitting back grinning on the couch.

"Oh Millie I love them! They will look cute with the short set."

"Sold, I'm getting them!" She said beaming.

We took our boxes over to the counter and waited to be rung up. She rang Millie first and then turned to me. My total was $950. I pulled Babe's fat cashed out envelope out again and proudly placed it on the counter so she could see his handwriting and my big ass ring. Justine's eyes watered, she look like she was going to bust out crying. I paid, put my envelope away and grabbed my bags. Right before I walked out the door, I turned and said, "Hey Justine, don't think calling for backup will save you next time. Oh and by the way, keep your hands and mouth off my guy and his dick!" Staring at her with a huge grin I walked out.

Trying to fit more bags into the packed trunk gave me the opportunity to regain my composure, so I could frighten Justine down to her core. Anyone can slap or punch someone without scaring the life out of them, but when you are towering over a person in total control of their very breath, you scare the living shit out of them. I knew Justine was watching me, seething; I could feel her hatred sink into my flesh like I was an ear of corn. Crunch! Closing the trunk, I turned and she was losing control fast. I tossed my handbag in the car, pulled off my hoops, turned my rings around and boldly walked right up to her face. My actions and physical aggressive stance definitely let her know I was ready to wreck her. "Do you have something to say to me? What do you want?"

The tears were gushing out as she shook with rage, "I already called Babe and told him you were here. He's never staying with you, he told me you mean nothing to him! Nothing!"

She picked up her hand to slap me, but it was game on; I grabbed Justine by the face and kicked her knees out from under her at the same time. As she fell forward I gripped her neck and moved my hand to her mouth. I started to rip her tongue out. She clawed and bit me, but it was no use because my fist was already stressing her jaw to lock open, and I was standing while she was on her knees, too bent forward to do any damage. Justine was panicking; then she started to gag and threw up just before she passed out. It happened so fast, I was calm and methodical, never breaking eye contact with her, and I even frightened the crowd that gathered around. James tried to get in between us, but as fast as it started was as fast as it ended.

What they didn't know was I hit her pressure point causing her to lose consciousness. While she was on the floor, I bent down and wiped the vomit from my hands on her clothes. I really wanted to kick her face in, but too many people came out of the stores. A few boys, who were in the restaurant, were staring at me, grinning in approval. I just couldn't help myself; I had to say something to James, "James, I love you but do NOT get involved in girl shit!"

James said, trying to control the situation, "Stop are you fucking crazy? Listen its broad daylight, relax." He bent down and started shaking her until she came to.

As soon as she opened her eyes she started in right away coughing and screaming, "I was with Babe before her, James! You gonna let her do this to me?" She turned her head towards me, "You're fucking dead! Babe will never look at you again!"

I took a step towards her, but she backed up right behind James. I jumped on him and dove over his shoulder and grabbed her hair trying to lift her off her feet almost tumbling head first over his shoulder on the concrete. "Oh I guess you're not afraid to approach a guy with a girl, but you're hiding now?" I growled at her and I wasn't letting go for shit.

James was taking a pounding being stuck between us. I held her hair and just kept punching her over and over again. Two guys across the street came running over and separated us. She was wild, crying and screaming while I stood composed, plotting the moment I had the opportunity to jump her and finish the job.

I lit a cigarette because I was starting to truly feel like I was going to kill this girl. "You look different with clothes on, cunt!" As soon as I said the magic word, all the guys turned towards her. I sidestepped James and got right up to her and grabbed her throat pulling her face up against mine. I think she thought I was going a little Silence of Lambs on her and bite her face, but all I wanted to do was tell her something. I had my nose jammed up against hers as I whispered all while the guys tried to pry my fingers off her neck, "You dirty hoe bag, this isn't about Babe anymore, and this is about you and me. If you ever look at me, talk to me, or about me I'll come to your house and slit your fucking throat from ear to ear; then I'll go to your parent's house and do the same for having you. Mark my words, you will fucking die, slow and painful. Don't fuck with me; I make Babe look like a priest!

Her eyes bulged out of head. Justine froze in shock, and in fact, so did James and the boys. I released her and stepped back. I looked back at James; poor guy took a pummeling from both of us, and looked it. I calmly got in my car as Millie jumped in. Justine was holding her face crying, "Did you hear her, and she threatened to kill me! But he was mine first! You had no right!"

I looked at her and I shouted, "Are you kidding me, I live with him! James won't always be here to save your sorry ass, remember that! Don't forget what I said, this is about you and me!" Then I peeled out of the spot. We said very little as I drove, Millie knew I was serious. I dropped her off, wished her a great weekend and headed back to Breezy.

I was finally able to breathe by the time I got in the house. It took several trips to unload the car, but once I did, I jumped on the bed to unwind. Flicking through the channels, I decided to beep Babe, because I wanted to have this conversation once and for all about this broad. He didn't call back, so I beeped him again. *Hmm, where is he that he can't get to a fucking phone!* Getting more annoyed, I beeped him a third time, vowing if he didn't call back I wasn't beeping him again, but go out instead. Well, by 8PM, he didn't call so I made up my mind. First a nap, then a shower, I was ready by 10PM and headed out. It was weird not working on a Friday night; I called Madelyn and swung by to pick her up.

Her boyfriend was working and we knew eventually we would wind up at Vibes by the end our night. We drove around Dyker Heights, hit 11th and 13th Avenues and moved up to 18th Avenue, and beyond, hitting all our types of places; The 30th Hole, Hettie's, and when we got to Club K, we decided to stay for a while to hang out with Dodgy. He always treated us like queens and their club was packed. Dancing was such a big part of our lives, as New Yorkers, we took pride in being better dancers than any other area.

There were so many local guys there; it was like old home day. I started to dance with a few of them, but it quickly turned to an extreme club music moment, when the crowd surrounds a group and the dancing resembled having sex, but only standing up. I guess I was looking to bust chops and push the envelope a bit, because I started to go off with a kid named Lenny, when a hand grabbed my shoulder. Turning around I came face to face with my friend Matt, "What the fuck are you doing?"

"Hey Matt! I'm dancing, come on dance with me!" I said as I tried to coax him to break loose, but he wasn't having it. I even undid his tie and slipped it around my neck using it as a prop as I danced.

"Time to go! Come on you can't do this here," He said as he grabbed my hand.

"Please you guys act like a J-O all the time, it's my turn tonight! Leave me alone, I'm not wearing stockings so don't go grabbing anything!" I said as I stormed off the floor wearing his tie.

Really what double standards, guys can do anything, but girls have to be perfect all the time? Please, fucking spare me! No one is master of me, for some reason I had to remind myself of that.

CHAPTER 31

I'm Not Married

"A re you sure you want to go to another place," Madelyn asked, as we jumped in the car.

"Why not? I'm not married! Plus, I want to hit Bundles before Vibes," I said, taking the tie off and putting it in the glove box.

"Okay, you know best!" She knew I was having fun, and just went with the flow, even though I was still pissed. I wanted to pass by his mother's house to see if his car was in the driveway before going to Bay Ridge. We were at the red light on 86th street facing Dyker Heights when a car driving erratically started blowing the lights with its high beams on- it was heading our way.

I threw the car in reverse and hit the gas. I was driving in reverse down 86th street with my foot pressed to the metal. Madelyn turned white and held on for dear life. The car was on us, coming perilously close to hitting the nose of the Jag. I made a right hand turn in reverse onto 5th Avenue and then a left onto 90th Street; pulling up right in front of Vibes all the while I had my forearm on the horn. Everyone jumped off the street and sidewalk as I pulled up and jumped out. We ran into the vestibule of the club, way too pumped up with adrenaline to cry, we ran right to Bri.

The whole place was in an uproar over my arrival, bouncers were pressing in on the crowd to see if anyone was about to start something. When I turned down the street, the car that was chasing us, whipped a U-turn on the corner and they took off; they would have to be fools to go any further.

"What the fuck happened to you?" Bri asked, seeing I was visually shaken.

I screamed, "Somebody was trying to kill me! A car blew a bunch of lights and tried to hit me head on."

"You outdrove them?" She asked, as she poured a Jack Daniels straight up for me.

"You bet your ass I did, the alternative wasn't an option." I said as I downed the shot. Jack was a burning pleasure I only indulged in when I was extremely nervous or looking for trouble. "I think Madelyn aged ten years!" She was just catching up to me after talking to her boyfriend. I turned to her laughing. "I'm impressed you didn't puke on me!"

Madelyn said as she shook her head. "Puke? I thought I was going to be ejected; for sure, I thought we were going to flip the car."

"I think Babe would kill me, if I demolished it the first day I had it!" I said with my head in my hands.

T walked over a put his hand on my back. "Hey I just heard, you okay? I'm taking you and Millie out to dinner, next Wednesday after work. I want to know what the fuck is going on here."

"That's if I make it to Wednesday!" I said, hugging him.

"Don't you worry about that, you call me any time and I'll be there. Need a place to stay?" He offered.

"No, thanks so much!" I said as I poured myself another drink from the bottle Bri put up on the bar. I had to calm down so I could go home, I had way too much to do, than sit here and get drunk, "Okay I have to go, am I driving you?"

Madelyn put her hand up shaking it, "No offense, but I'm not getting in your car right now. Love you!"

"Suit yourself, but you lived. Anyone else would have crashed," I said as I made my way to the door saying goodbye to everyone along the way. As soon as I got near the door, I was stopped by the bouncers, "You can't go now, someone has to come and get you."

Trying to be as convincing as possible, "Stop, I'm good. See you."

"Hey, she's fine, I'm here." Babe said, looking annoyed. He put his arm around me, kissing my head. The boys all kissed and hugged goodbye, and he led me to my car. Opening my door, I slid in, knowing I was in for an ear full, but my blood was boiling; all the day's rage was returning.

"Where's your car?" I said, as he jumped on the highway.

"That doesn't matter, I gota ride, when I heard what happened." He said sounding more like a parent then a boyfriend.

"What part are you referring to?" I said wanting to bust his balls big time just to keep myself in check. "Shopping, your friends, Justine or the ride?"

"All of it, I heard you handled yourself just fine with the guys." Taking a break to light a cigarette, he continued with a hint of humor in his voice, "What about the shoes?"

If looks could kill, he would have died in that driver's seat. "I went shoe shopping, why? How did I know your Breezy cunt friend would be there?"

Laughing outright, he moved on. "Anyway, where do you learn how to drive like that? What did you drive a get away car in another life?"

"No! I drove on the Autobahn in Germany. There are no speed limits, prick! You're awfully calm, I thought you would be a lunatic!" Feeling proud of my driving skills, I smirked as I contemplated how far I wanted to press the issue. I had a sinking feeling we were about to have an argument over Justine.

"Listen, after everything that's been happening, I'm happy to find out you're not helpless and can take care of yourself." He said, holding my leg as he drove.

I couldn't hold it in anymore I went for the kill. "So you're not going to mention Justine? Seriously? I almost tore the girl's tongue out of her head and choked the life out of her and you have nothing to say?"

His face went hard and dark, but he kept his composure. "Couldn't have been too bad, I didn't hear a thing. So stop patting yourself on your back, you couldn't have hurt her that much."

I lost my mind at that moment. We were at the red light before we merged onto the highway. I turned and started slapping him everywhere I could before I jumped out of the car screaming. "Fuck you! You want me to trust you to have kids with?" I ran holding my bag into the pitch-black park crying hysterical as he called out after me. *How could you minimize all of this? They were all pieces of crazy shit, all of them, and if I was the only sane one, then we're all doomed!* I sat on the swings seething, too angry to continue to cry when I saw the headlights.

Babe drove into the park to look for me, and as I sat still on the swings, he got out and walked over to me. "Get in the car."

I didn't answer right away, nor did I move. If I got in the car, I was allowing him to abuse me, and if I didn't well then it was over. *Decisions, decisions, decisions!*

He repeated himself, "Get in the car."

I looked up and just glared silently at him waiting for some word or sign to swing the pendulum either way. He sat on the swing next to me and looked down at his folded hands hanging between his legs. We sat for what seemed like an hour, but was probably 20 minutes as I waited for lightening to strike him dead. *Tick-tock, waiting, waiting, waiting.*

Like a teenager, he leaned in and kissed my cheek softly whispering, "I don't give a fuck what you do to her, let's go home."

Tick-tock, what to do? "Are you fucking her?"

"No, I told you I don't give a fuck about her."

Tick, tick, tick should I give up his dick? Something said ride this out, because she could be just a troublemaker. There are tons of girls like that, and I seem to meet them all. "K, I'm ready."

We made small talk until we went home. My adrenaline was slowly coming down and I was feeling the crashing sensation. It felt good to walk in and shed every ounce of clothing, along with my problems. I jumped into bed and was about to pass out, when Babe joined me and with a bag. "Hey you left something at my sister's." He handed me a beautiful bag; I knew what it was when I saw it.

"I'll put it away tomorrow," I said with my face buried in the pillows.

He pressed. "Hey you have another shower to go to?"

"No…" I mumbled feeling more exhausted than usual.

He moved closer and whispering in my ear, "So who's this for?"

"Shush!" I whispered, drifting.

Touching my hip he pressed further. "Shush yourself. Who's it for?"

I rolled over and looked at him. "Don't make me feel stupid. It was so pretty I couldn't help myself!" My eyes were closing as I whispered, "I can't keep my eyes open, I'm so tired and I feel sick."

"What's wrong?" He asked sounding concerned.

"My head is spinning and I've been exhausted for days, way before the fight. I feel like I'm getting sick." I grabbed his arm and squinted at him. "That girl said I stole you from her. Were you dating her or just banging her?"

"Stop!" He said trying to move away from me.

"No, you stop! She said it and you told me it was a one-night stand. So which one is it?" I demanded wanting to know the truth.

"She's just jealous. Go to sleep." He kissed me again and held me close, as I drifted off.

Waking up behind the eight ball sucks! I was in a rush because I knew I had so much to do and had to look good doing it, I jumped up to take a shower, but felt sick to my stomach. I barely made it into the bathroom before I threw up, only feeling slightly better after I was done. *Maybe I ate something that didn't agree with me last night.* Trying to shake it off, I jumped in the shower. While I washed my hair, I heard him moving around.

He looked in and asked, "Hey, what are you doing?"

My eyes were closed, because I had a face full of suds as I felt him touch me before I could even answer. He was rinsing my long hair in the water and wiped my eyes to kiss me. "Stop I have to get dressed soon," I pleaded.

"It's 10AM, you don't have to be there until 1PM, we have time," he said as he smothered me with kisses. It was pretty easy to forget time and contemplate being a no-show completely, when he kissed me like that. Holding me under the waterfall he asked, "Did I hear you get sick? You okay?"

"I did, but I feel better now." I said, trying to avoid the conversation.

"So you went shopping and I didn't get a floor show. Aren't you gonna show me something for all the money?" Babe asked playfully.

"Don't worry I have change, I didn't spend it all." Kissing him back, I said, "But I was thinking of going shoe shopping again and spending the rest."

It was a like flipping a switch. "Find a new frigging store, will ya!" He said as he started to wash himself.

Hey now, I hit a nerve. Last night you were all I don't care and now you're edgy? Something's rotten in Brooklyn! I dug deeper. "What are the odds I would go to that store? You know I had no idea she worked there until I saw her. Plus, now I know where you bought my bra and panties, at her girlfriend's store. Jerk!"

"I've been called worse! Don't make this a game, just go to another store and keep the fucking change." Babe said, sounding like I was the enemy.

"Touchy Mr. Grumpy? You've lost your funny bone Babe!" I said I walked out of the shower leaving him to finish up without me. Grabbing the bags from the day before, I started to unpack. For the baby shower today, I picked one of the cute short and blazer set with a pair of heels and a handbag. As I was hanging up the new dresses, Babe came out and moved about in a foul mood. Now I was angry and wanted to give him a dig. "You want start with seeing my new shoes?"

Snapping at me, he acted as if I was the sidepiece of ass all of the sudden. "Shut up! What's your fucking schedule today, exactly?"

I wasn't use to this side to him at all. I glared giving him a sideways look; I answered him as coldly as I could. "HEY lose the fucking attitude! I'm going to the shower from one until four, then I'm coming home to change and we have to be at the El Carpe by seven."

"Be home by four thirty, I don't wanna be late! No stops either, come right home!" He said without looking at me, clearly getting more pissed by the moment.

I didn't answer him as I started to put on my makeup. My silence was making him crazier by the second. He slammed the cabinets and eventually went into his office, slamming the door behind him.

Was he pissed because I mentioned the shoes? Or was he protecting that girl? I sat in front of the mirror thinking about what was behind all the anger. When I was done, I walked to his door and knocked gently. He didn't answer, so I knocked louder; the door whipped open in a flash, and he was staring at me like a different person than I'd ever met before holding the phone, "What the fuck do you want?"

Stunned, I stuttered, "Ah, um, I wanted to say goodbye, I'm leaving." I started to walk out as I grabbed my bag and the presents. I opened the door without looking at him, but just asked quietly, "I know you're talking to her now"

"I'm a one woman, man! Everybody knows that! You're nuts and a victim of your own conscience! I want you to be the mother of my kids doesn't that say enough?" He shouted as I walked out.

Shaking my head, I walked towards the car. *Does he really think I could be that type of blind girl? The face of the family to take out in the light, the mom, the trophy wife, the "it" girl he won, while he bangs her in the dark? His response told me volumes, he was still with her and trying to shift the guilt towards me. She must have called him again complaining and got under his skin. Why would James show up at the store? Why would Babe be so mad at me?*

Popping the trunk, I put the boxes in and realized I forgot one. Looking up I saw him approach carrying the box. One look at my face and he could see I was upset.

Leaning into the trunk, he handed me the present, "Hey you forgot one."

I wasn't sure what to do or say, I could barely mumble thanks. I lowered my sunglasses, as so not to make eye contact. Trying to close the trunk, he put his hand on mine and turned me towards him. Before he could say anything, I asked, "Why are you in such a bad mood?"

Like a different person completely and thinking he was funny he said, "What are you talking about? I'm in a good mood. Sounds like you're not having a good day, is it that time? If so, I'll see you in seven to ten days."

"Are you kidding me? No, I do not have my period asshole! You're getting pissed because I mentioned shoes?"

"You're nuts, I'm not mad," he said grinning. "But stop already with the fucking shoes though!"

Totally hurt, I choked my words out, "Why would you say I'm nuts and a victim of your own conscience? That's pretty mean to say to me. Busting my chops is one thing, but busting nuts is another! I want to know, are you still with that girl?"

Avoiding my eyes, he spit out words with so much venom I was surprised, "I don't know where this conversation is going or what you're talking about. So maybe I should stop talking to you, because I have no idea what's happening here. Is this a game you're playing or what?"

Now I raised my voice repeating the question. "Are you still with JUSTINE? Answer the fucking question?"

"You're reading into this too much! Stop! You're just rotten; it's none of your bu..." He said as he tried to hug me, but stopped short when he realized he was going to say it wasn't my business.

Rotten? Me? He never once gave a direct answer. My eyes flashed wide and now I was crying, I could feel he was cheating on me. I slapped him across the face, open palmed so he knew I meant it disrespectfully. He never moved out of the way, or touched his cheek; Babe took it like a man and just stared me down. I was so fucking done, I turned and walked away from Babe, I knew it ended just as quickly as it started. I was going to leave him; it was just a matter of when and how to get away.

I closed the car door as he stood there watching, and by the look in his eyes, it quickly dawned on him that I was done with this nonsense. I picked up my glasses and stared at him for a moment before I pulled out. I could tell, he knew that I knew.

It didn't take long to get to the shower. It was like a mini wedding, only filled with a hundred and fifty girls, a DJ and endless banquet tables filled with presents. Walking in, I was greeted by so many friends, wives and girlfriends, all happy to be together socializing. Everyone was admiring all the beautiful presents. Finding my way to the table, I was surprised to see one empty seat left, right next to his sister. Jo-Anne welcomed me and made small talk throughout the party. I was fully composed and couldn't let anyone see me upset or I would have set the tongues wagging.

The food parade started. Food was a huge part of the life; every item looked more delicious than the next. If I actually ate everything at every event I went to I would become a fat fuck and today I just couldn't eat anything. I lost my appetite completely. In fact, the food was making me sick. I chatted through the pasta course, turning away everything put in front of me. Jo-Anne asked about where I went to school, grew up and what my likes and dislikes were.

I was evasive, but as friendly as I thought I could manage, without throwing up or crying. I hid my sorrow from everyone, it was nobody's business what went on between us and, soon enough, people would know I left him anyway.

Now the present portion of the party started. There's a system of opening presents, the grandparents' presents are opened first, and then the rest, in order of importance. All the bosses, skippers, made guys, associates go in order, then the regular people. When it was my turn- my pile was impressive. Babe's sister wrapped each item so beautifully; they received the right amount of oohs and ahh. Cake and coffee was served and I knew I was almost home free. Just then I looked around the room and spotted Justine. *How could this fucking girl be everywhere?*

She was at a table way across the room with a bunch of girls I didn't know; the B rated tables. I wanted to ask who knew her and why she was there, but I didn't want to tip my hand. This was definitely an arresting development to see her here as a guest. I ate two bites of the cake and pushed it away, downed my coffee and went outside to smoke. I needed to get some air, before anyone would see my anger brewing. Two cigarettes later, I returned back into the hall and found Justine sitting in my seat talking to everyone. *The fucking nerve of this girl!*

Totally thrown off guard, I said, "Oh Jesus fucking Christ!" Everyone turned and looked at me like I was crazy. I was done with this stupidity so I grabbed my things. "I'm sorry to interrupt. I just wanted to say goodbye, I'm leaving."

I kissed his sister as she tried to persuade me to stay. Not once did Justine get out of my seat or even make an offer. Jo-Anne added, "Oh I'm sorry I didn't introduce you, this is Justine, an old friend of the family. This is my brother's girlfriend, Dannie." She smiled wide for me and extended her hand. I looked at it like it was a filthy rag in front of me, and didn't touch it. Everyone at the table looked at each other unsure of what was happening.

I smiled at Jo-Anne and said, "Oh we've met a few times, and none of them were pleasant experiences." Moving my attention to Justine I said, "You can't possibly think I'm going to be polite, just because we're in public. Do you? You don't know me; I don't give a fuck about anyone or where I am. I'll kick your fucking ass right here, right now…again! By the way you look pretty good after I kicked your ass yesterday!"

"Oh, I had no idea. I'm sorry…" Jo-Anne said as she stood up and walked towards me.

I put up my hand cutting her off. "No problem, you didn't know. It's not like she told you exactly how we met." I turned my attention to Justine again and said, "Did you? No, I don't think so. I have to run, by the way Justine I hardly recognized you with fucking clothes on!" Everyone's face turned red, as she buried her face in her hands; I knew I went a little too far but I didn't care. *Fuck everybody!*

I tossed another bomb before walking out. "Oh let me ask you a question, so how was my boyfriend? Good?" Turning around I walked out leaving them all staring at me. Fuming, I jumped in my car the car. *This was becoming a terrible weekend.* I made it home a little earlier than planned, and jumped into bed. Burying my face in the pillows, I just laid there miserable, feeling sick. I heard the alarms chime and jumped up. I ran into the bathroom, locking the door behind me. Running the water, I sat there just listening to him call my name.

He turned the handle, but the door was locked. Knocking he shouted to open the door repeatedly, but I didn't respond; I just didn't want to hear his voice or deal with him. Babe was persistent, making me wish I were home back in my own apartment and far away from him. After, a few minutes, he gave up and left me alone. I shut the water off, quietly unlocked the door and walked into the bedroom. He must have gone inside the other room, because the bedroom was empty. I closed the bedroom door and locked it from the inside. I had enough time to close my eyes before getting dressed, because my head was swimming. While I lay there with my eyes closed, I heard him try to open the door.

He knocked on it, and then he banged shouting, "Hey what's the term? How long do I get locked out? Answer me! Don't make me take it off the fucking hinge!" Again I sat still and didn't answer; my silence was killing him and I was so glad! Feeling overwhelmed, I fell a sleep.

While in a dead sleep alone, I felt something next to me and jumped up screaming flipping out. He grabbed me trying to calm me down. "Hey, shush, calm down, stop screaming, it's me!"

"Get off of me! Don't touch me! Don't you ever touch me," I screamed until I realized it was Babe. Breathing hard, I was pushed up against the wall holding my hands against it. "How did you get in here? I locked the door."

"I have a key! Calm down, what's wrong with you?" He said looking totally confused.

"Leave me alone, there's nothing wrong with me! You can't sneak up on me! Are you fucking kidding me? After locking the door I fell asleep ALONE, and the next thing I know you is scaring the shit out of me!" I roared.

"Okay, okay calm down. Come here next to me," he said motioning for me.

I didn't move a muscle; "You're in a good mood now? You're trying to talk to me all nice, even though I'M rotten? Or are you in some crazy fucked up mood and once I come near you, you'll become a fucking psycho again?" Backing up towards the door I said, "So why didn't you tell me Justine knew your family and would be there today?"

Babe ran his fingers through his hair and started to look thuggish. He sneered titling his head as if he was about to jump on me. "Stop, this is your final warning! She's just a old friend. What do I have to do to get that through your thick head?"

"FUCK YOU! YOU DON'T SCARE ME! AND I DON'T FUCK MY OLD FRIENDS, but you do! You're cheating on me. I want out!" And then the first wave came over me, making me want to hurl.

Babe changed right before my eyes from a psycho to offended and a shocked man. "First, I'm not a cheater, 'Do unto others that you want done unto you!' is my motto! Second, I'm sorry I was having a bad morning, but that doesn't give you the right say stuff like that in front of my sister. Third, you better apologize to my sister!"

I flipped screaming at him, shoving him over and over again. Babe could have pummeled me. "Talk to your sister huh? You should have told me she would be there. I go smoke and when I come back she's in my fucking seat!"

"Stop!" He said as he put his hand up, signaling he had it with our conversation.

"No, fuck you! She's always going to be a haunt; you didn't talk to her, because you're still fucking her! So I'm done!" I said pulling my bag out from the closet; I pulled random items out of the drawers tossing them in. "You're a lying scumbag, just like all the others!"

He bolted up and grabbed my hand, "Hey, I said stop! We have to leave for a wedding; they're expecting us. You can't be a no show!"

As I was standing there, staring at him. The waves were fast and furious, but then a huge wave of nausea hit me and I bolted into the bathroom just making it in time to throw up. Babe followed me looking confused and tried to put his hands on my shoulders.

Recoiling, I jerked away from him and hissed, "Don't touch me! I wouldn't walk across the street with you, let alone go to a wedding!"

In his icy, I'm the boss voice he barked at me, "You don't want to be with me fine, but you can't NOT go tonight! But if you're pregnant you're going to have to get over this, because you're not going anywhere got that!" Babe stormed back in the bedroom, ripping mad, grabbing his clothes. "I'm going to get dressed, you do the same NOW! We leave in half an hour, that's final!"

I cleaned myself up and brushing my teeth, I dressed in the champagne beaded dress with the very delicate four-inch heels. My hair was jacked up to Jesus, adding my eyelashes and reapplying my makeup. I looked in the mirror and thought to myself that I really looked beautiful with his diamonds; I sprayed perfume as the final touch and felt I was ready. I walked into the living room and found him walking around on the phone talking to someone. He spotted me; his face said it all, as he hung up and stared at me. Walking over, he gently touched my elbow and kissed my cheek. "You really are beautiful!"

Coldly, I responded with a look of complete hatred, "You have about five hours tops left with me so let's get this over with." What I wanted to say was get a good look, because for the rest of your miserable fucking life, I hope you look back at me with tremendous regret on how you wasted this opportunity. The entire blame of this failed relationship rested squarely on his shoulders. Without another word, I walked out and waited inside the car. A minute later, Babe jumped in and we drove in silence.

Pulling up, the valet opened my door and I stepped out. Babe grabbed my elbow and kissed my cheek. He whispered, "I'm glad you're here with me. You're gonna rethink leaving tonight." I tried to pull away, but he firmly pulled back more. "We can work it all out." I didn't say a word; I just smiled coldly. Babe guided me into the hall and proceeded to say hello to everyone.

The cocktail hour was amazing. Italian weddings are outrageous to begin with, but Mafia weddings are over the top completely. There had to be over 500 people there. The wine and champagne was all top shelf along with the caviar, jumbo shrimp, lobster tails and every other delicacy imaginable. Babe kept me close on his arm during the whole cocktail hour, showering me with attention.

Once the lights were dimmed, we moved into the hall for the dinner and were seated at an A-list table. Babe made me sit so close; I was under his arm all night. We were with his crew and their wives and girls. I knew them all, so it was easy to forget I hated him. Once the couple was announced and danced their first dance, Babe grabbed my hand and led me to the dance floor, holding me tight against him; he looked into my eyes as we moved to Etta James, "When a Man Loves a Woman." He tried to be as charming as he was handsome. Babe was on fire, and I knew I was getting burned badly. He asked me, "You still mad?"

I said, sounding defeated, "Mad? Come on, don't treat me like a jerk off you know I'm more than mad."

"What can I do to make this up to you? What do you want? Whatever it is I'll get it for you." He leaned in, kissing me gently.

Trying not to kiss him back, because truly I wanted to throw up, I mumbled, "Nothing, not a thing, I don't trust you anymore. This can't be fixed, we're done."

"Stop, anything can be fixed." Again, he pulled me even closer and planted a big kiss on me. "Let me try, I can fix anything!" I didn't say anything. I just looked into his eyes with complete contempt and disappointment.

Once the song ended, he held my hand and walked me toward the table, but then diverted me in another direction. It was so crowded I couldn't see where he was taking me, but before I knew it, I was in the back near a table of girls. He had my hand in a vice grip and swung me along side of him. As soon as I saw where he took me I tried to get my hand out, but he wouldn't let me go. He cleared his throat and said, "Excuse me ladies," as he grabbed Justine's elbow roughly. "You need to come outside to the lobby; WE have to talk."

Dragging both of us to the lobby, he held me with one hand and her with the other, until we were finally facing each other. "Okay, Justine, this is my girl. What happened that one night is over. Don't approach her, don't talk to her, stop creating drama and leave my family alone. You know you're busting balls and I can't have that. You and me go back a long way and if we're gonna remain friendly you have to cut the shit. You understand?" Not waiting for an answer, he turned to me and said, "You're the one with the ring, are you satisfied now? I don't want to have this conversation again; this is it. You understand?" I shook my head and held his hand back. She was crying holding her elbow after his he released his mighty grip. Without another look at her, we walked back into the hall. He held my waist as we walked through the crowd, leaning in, kissing my hair.

Once we made our way back to our group, the rest of the night was wonderful. All the guys laughed and cheered the bride and groom. They walked over to thank everyone for coming and Babe pulled out an envelope that was so full it had packing tape on it. The boys give big wedding presents, depending on rank. As the night went on, the boys were more at ease; Babe pulled me to sit on his lap smoking a cigar. I think he was having a great time and I enjoyed the attention. He tickled my hips as they asked me questions about the car, and I turned around and just kissed him in front of everyone.

Just then, Phil came up with a brandy and a cigar and started to roar, "Hey look at the happy couple over here! You must have finally eaten the lobster with him!"

I jumped up and kissed Phil on the cheek and told him I adored him. Babe hugged him as they slapped each other on the back and made small talk. I saw they were slipping into a boy's conversation, so I went to dance with the other wives. His eyes never left me, I felt like a princess. *Maybe we could work things out, if Justine was out of the picture. Maybe, just maybe, except when it happens again. Why should I think it won't? Really they all cheat, why would my guy be the exception to the rule? Could I turn a blind eye and let him fuck another girl?* I had more questions than answers swirling around my head. The only thing I knew was that I was so in love, I couldn't think straight.

Returning to the table to take a sip of some water, Babe noticed for the first time I wasn't drinking alcohol. Leaning in he asked, "You want me to get you a drink? You feel okay?"

"I think I am, but I'm not sure. I can't eat and the thought of alcohol is making me nauseous."

He grinned wickedly at me, moved to kiss me standing up and started to dance with me. His guys went nuts and all jumped up joining in. There was a big mix of old school and new club guys, so it was quite a sight. He was all over me on the dance floor. Man, not only was he great lover, but he loved public displays of affection. It was his way of reasserting his claim on me in front of everyone, while making me feel a sense of security, even if it was fleeting.

The boys lay claim to their women, and depending on how you look at it, she's either the luckiest woman on the face of the earth, or saddest one on the face of the earth. He danced a few more times with me, but mostly stayed with his friends as the ringleader. There were so many toasts, even Babe spoke and wished the couple well.

Each table around us was part of the pointy collar group, if they weren't wearing a tuxedo. I could only imagine what the one regular guest sitting in the worst seat next to the kitchen was thinking. As the night came to a close, we walked out with his friends, and there were cop cars pulling up. They were setting up a DWI checkpoint. Luckily, I wasn't drinking, so I could drive.

"Babe give me the keys, I didn't have a drink tonight," I said holding my hand out.

This was blowing his head and good mood. "Okay, but this is bullshit, they're busting our balls."

"It doesn't matter, I'm fine and can drive," I said as I slid in the driver's seat and waited in line to get past the police roadblock. Inching up, I put the windows down and waited to be addressed.

A police officer pointed his flashlight in my face and said, "Have you been drinking tonight?"

Smiling, "No officer I haven't."

"Not one drink? You're leaving a wedding and you're telling me you didn't have one drink?" He asked.

Looking him the eye sounding very sober I stated clearly, "That's correct officer, not one, because I'm pregnant."

"Oh okay, you can pass. Have a safe night." He said as he flicked off the light and waved me through. Babe grabbed my hand, but I gave him a look.

"You know I just said that," I said as I moved my hand to shift.

"You might be, you don't know. You never took your pills before you threw them out anyway," he said with a big grin. "Did you have fun tonight?"

"It's your fault, you always make me wake up late and I forget to take them. I haven't really taken them for two months." Shooting him a sideways look, I asked, "I had a better time than I thought I would. Did you?" What I didn't tell him was that I had been waking up throwing up for the last three weeks, and I was always tired and starving, but couldn't really eat.

"Two months? Why didn't you tell me?" He saw I was turning red, so he changed the subject. "I did! It was good to see everybody out and together. You look so good in that dress, I wanted to toss you on the table all night," he said as he started to fondle me while I drove. Getting closer to the house, I spotted a CVS and stopped. He looked at me, "You want me to get something?"

"No, I'm good. Give me two seconds- do you want a pack of cigarettes?"

"Sure, wait, let me give you money," he said as he took money out of his pocket and handed me a twenty. "Need more?"

"No, I'm good." I said as I grabbed my purse and his money. As soon as I got inside, I went to the feminine hygiene isle and grabbed three pregnancy tests. I purchased our cigarettes separately, because I didn't want to tell him what I was buying. Opening the car door, I tossed the plastic bag in the back seat and gave him his pack of Marlboro and my Camels. "Hey light one for me please."

"You should think about quitting," he said as he handed me mine.

"Yeah, you should too. I can't quit while you smoke," I said as I pulled out of the spot, heading over the bridge to Breezy.

Holding my leg, tapping, he couldn't stop smiling at me. "Give me a reason and I will!" Pulling into our spot, I grabbed the bag and walked into the house with Babe. Tossing the keys on the island, he grabbed the bag and tried to look inside.

"Hey! Give me that bag right now!" I said as I tried to snatch it out of his hands. He held it higher and higher over my head until he looked up in it and saw what was in it through the plastic. He dropped the bag on the counter and picked me up placing me on the island. Placing his hands on the side of my face, he kissed me passionately. "This is the beginning of everything for us. Don't look back anymore, everything is different now...I promise you."

I tried to respond but he put his fingers on my lips and shook his head no. "Now tell me about tomorrow."

I don't believe you, but I want to. I know what you are and I'm a moron, but I love you so bad it hurts. "We're going to your sister's at 1 o'clock for dinner and then we have Phil's fundraiser at 7PM." I put my hand up and held his chest, "Tell me, are you able to stay home with me again?"

Kissing me lightly, Babe moved my hair away from my face. "We'll see I have to take it one day at a time." I leaned my head on his shoulder and hugged him. He noticed I was incredibly tired all of the sudden. "You okay?"

"All of the sudden, I'm so tired, I can't keep my eyes open anymore. Take me to bed, the room is spinning."

Not skipping a beat, he picked me up and carried me to bed and laid me down. He peeled off my dress, changed out of his own clothes and jumped in next to me. Putting his arm under my head, I started to drift off immediately as he whispered in my ear, "Marry me?"

Was I hearing things? I looked up, almost afraid to ask, "What did you say?"

Cradling me, he repeated the question, "I said, marry me."

He caught me off guard. "Are you serious?"

Babe spoke slowly and deliberately, "Very! Marry me?"

Shaking my head really unsure of what I heard I joked, "I must be delirious!"

Pressing even closer he asked again, "That's not an answer, Danielle will you marry me?"

No, I'd be a fool to marry you, because you're a lying, cheating scumbag! You'll never change, you're going to make me into a baby factory and lock me up so I can't go out, and just so you can do what you want without being caught! Hey heart you better hear me! I could barely keep my eyes open even though I was so excited. I whispered, "Are you kidding me? Yes! Yes, yes, yes! Did you hear that?"

Gently laughing, he whispered in my ear, "I did!"

"Good, it's yes again, just in case you didn't hear it correctly the first fifty times." I drifted off to sleep all night in his arms just skin-to-skin dreaming about our soon to be family, with the biggest smile on my face. *I must be completely insane! One minute I want to kill you, the next I'm marrying you!*

It was almost 10AM when I finally woke up. I could smell something, I wasn't sure if was delicious or going to make me sick. I got out of bed and grabbed his shirt slipping it on. I found Babe in the kitchen having a cup of coffee. He looked up and smiled, "Hey, come here." He said tapping his knee. "I ran out last night after you fell asleep and picked up some eggs, milk and coffee. Do you want a cup?"

"I'm not sure, I don't feel well," I said moving closer to him. I put my arms around his neck and spotted his breakfast. That was it- I started to gag. Running into the bathroom, I doubled over the toilet retching. He was right behind me, holding back my hair while he rubbed my back. After a few minutes, I was able to pick my head up. I wiped my mouth and looked up at him, "Oh my god, I'm so sorry! I feel so fucking sick!" I held my hand up and asked, "Help me up, I need to pee NOW."

"Wait you need to pee on that stick thing." Completely flustered he searched for the pregnancy test, but I couldn't wait. He came rushing in just as I was done and about to toss my cookies again. "Oh honey, what can I do for you?"

Not sure I could even answer; I just kept throwing up until I had nothing left. I felt like a mess. "I need to brush my teeth badly and take a shower, but wait! You know you proposed to me, right?"

"You're a nut! I know I did," he said laughing at me.

"Good, I just want to make sure I wasn't dreaming!"

He was so good to me, putting the toothpaste on my toothbrush and handed it me. While I brushed my teeth, he turned on the water, trying to do every little thing he could think of. He was right there with me helping as I took the fastest shower, washing every part of me gently. He even helped me out of the shower, dried and wrapped me in a robe. Babe bent down and carried me back to bed. Once I was horizontal, I started to feel much better.

"You look better, how do you feel?" He said gently moving my hair away from my face.

"I must have the flu, I have no idea what came over me," I said as he grinned at me.

"I don't think you have the flu, I think..." He stopped and kissed me tenderly. "I think we're going to have a baby."

"You think?" I asked unsure.

"I do! You have that sexy green look!" He said laughing.

"Come on!" I looked into his eyes and felt so tired all of the sudden. "Hey Babe I need to close my eyes, I'm so tired, let me sleep a little while longer." With that, I fell back. When I woke up, I felt like I'd been dragged through the streets. I walked into the living room again and Babe was on the couch talking to his sister, telling her we would be a little late. He saw me, rushed off, and jumped up with a mixture nervousness and excitement, "Hey how do you feel?"

"Hungry, I think," I said, laughing at him. I was standing there with a white fluffy robe, running my hands through my hair squinting in the sunlight that was pouring in through the windows.

Babe held my head in his hands and looked at me in the eyes and kissed me hard before mumbling, "Eat later." He scooped me up and carried me to the bedroom, opening my robe; he started to kiss my stomach and ran his hands all over me. Babe climbed on top of me and made the most intense passionate love to me. He was so loving and gentle; I had an urge to cry. I never wanted the moment to end.

He devoured me and held me afterward for the longest time. Babe had his hand on my stomach and as he was tracing my belly button with his finger, he gently kissed my head and finally asked, "Do you feel well enough to go to my sister's?"

"Sure, I think so. Lets get dressed, before I keep YOU in bed all day."

Getting ready was easy; he reached for everything and helped me. I looked at him, and he looked taller, bigger, and prouder. I was elated that I could make him feel that way. He had given me so much unconditionally, now I was giving him the ultimate gift, his biggest dream and desire was going to come true. Today was going to be a great day!

CHAPTER 32

Exhale

We decided to take my car, because it was a smoother ride, hoping I would be less inclined to throw up. Stopping for pastries and the newspaper, we started to drive away, excited to get to his family's house. I looked down at the paper on my lap, turning white. Babe pulled over concerned. "What's wrong?"

Stunned into complete silence, I finally stuttered. "Look...look at the headlines. There was a murder last night."

"Who cares unless you know them?" Babe asked as easily as he would if he wanted me to pass the salt.

"Yeah, I do...it's..." Continuing to stutter, I looked up at him and started to cry. "It's the guy!"

"What guy? What are you talking about?" He asked nonchalantly.

Whispering through my tears I choked out the words. "The GUY! The one that attacked me."

"Hmm, what's it say?" He asked with a bit of curiosity.

I stammered, "Oh my God it says they think he was car jacked!"

"Well, he either had hot wheels or he must of messed with the wrong person! I'm sure you weren't the only girl he attacked, that fucking piece of shit!" He leaned over and moved my hair away as I sat crying staring at the paper. "I guess now you can finally sleep without having nightmares."

WHAT? Calm down don't overreact! I turned my head away and mumbled, "I think I can exhale too. I feel like I've been holding my breath since it happened."

Very upbeat, he smiled as said, "You good? Ready to go?"

"I don't know. But who would." I was about to ask, but stopped short. *Idiot, don't speak, shut up!*

"Don't know, don't care! Fuck him!" He responded in gangster mode.

That comment was a like another bolt of lightening! I started to shake more and just couldn't keep my mouth shut as I held the paper. "Hey did you go out last night?"

Trying to brush me off, he tapped my leg as he answered, "I told you I did, and we needed milk and stuff. Why?"

Afraid to look at him, I mumbled, "Where else did you go?"

Babe gently turned my face towards him to look me square in the eyes. "Why?"

Looking at him with my big eyes, I asked what I already knew, "I want to know, where were you?"

Babe touched my jaw with his fingertip and asked, "Why? I told you I had a few stops to make, and some things to take care of."

"I, I, I don't know it's just..." I stuttered staring into his icy eyes.

"Hey, I want you to put this out of your head. Stop thinking about this guy, I'm here and NO ONE will ever bother you again. I gave you a new life, enjoy it." Babe leaned in and kissed my cheek.

You gave me a new life? What did you really give me last night? Did I really want to know? No, no not at all, I knew the truth in my soul and that was enough. I've wished that bastard was dead a million times a day for most of my life and now its done. I'm at peace, all is right in the world. Thank you!

Words were no longer needed; I was just relieved it was finally over. I flung myself over the armrest, on him, and buried my face in his neck, choking on my tears. He held me as I just lost it completely, until I didn't have a tear left. Rubbing my back, he kissed my hair, enveloping me in his protective way. "Babe, I love you, really love you!"

"Hey, no more crying! I love you too, more than you'll ever realize, so stop thinking about this. Come on, its over. You ready to go?" He said wiping the last of my tears away. He kissed me softly and slowly I moved back into my own seat.

Pulling up outside his sister's backyard, we made it in time just before dinner started; and found his mother and family. Babe introduced me to his nieces and nephews and we all talked for a while outside. Everyone was staring at my ring, but no one would bring it up. His brother offered me some wine, which I politely refused. Then he offered to cut it with cream soda and I still declined.

Babe came up behind me grinning and put his arms around me kissing me. They all started to stare at me and his brother asked if I wanted to sit down. I accepted the seat in the shade, hoping everyone would stop staring at me.

Babe's beeper went off and never stopped. I could see his facial expression change from being elated to stormy every time he looked at it. Before we were about to go inside, a car pulled up and one his closest friends got out; Babe walked outside of the gate and they spoke very quietly. My hair on my neck stood up, something had happened, I just knew it. He came back in and walked over to me. I stood up as he leaned in and said, "I gotta go."

I pulled away and looked at him as my arms were wrapped around his neck. *Please don't go! Don't answer the call, don't leave me, just don't!* I said what was in my heart, without the pleas, because I knew they would fall on deaf ears, "I don't think you know how much I really love you! Thank you for giving me such a beautiful life, really for everything! You've spoiled me with all the material things you think I could ever want, but all I really want is you. I can't imagine not being with you. Do you know that?"

"I always knew that. Money is nothing but dirty paper to you. I want you to know that from the day I met you, I knew you would be mine." Babe whispered to me looking both astonished and pained.

"And I always will be so remember you have two people to come home to! Hurry back, because we need you!" I said as I put his hand on my stomach.

He gave me a monster kiss in front of his family, keeping his hand over mine, protectively. "I love you!" Then he moved to his mother and sister, kissing them before he was about to leave, looking back one more time he grinned and dropped the bomb. "Hey Ma, by the way, we're getting married!" Babe was the happiest man on earth for one single moment before he took off towards the gate to hell.

I ran and called to him one last time. "Hey Babe, I KNOW what you did for me, I DO thank you!" I shouted as I hung over the fence in enough time for him to hear me before he closed the door as his friend drove away. He never broke eye contact with me the whole time until they turned the corner. I was left alone in the yard surrounded by his family all stunned. They were used him and his wild personality along with all the comings and goings, but I still wasn't, this was startling for me.

"Congratulations! Welcome to the family!" His mother said, as she gave me the biggest hug. Everyone came over, congratulated me, asking me a million questions, and finally one of the kids broke the tension of having the spot light on me, and said it was time to eat. We all went inside and enjoyed a Sunday Italian feast. For the first time in weeks, I ate like I'd never seen food before, devouring everything in front of me. After coffee we all started to leave because we all had the same gut feeling he wasn't coming back. No one mentioned it, but we all were lost in our own thoughts.

"You don't have to leave, stay a while longer," his mother said as she patted my arm.

"No thank you, I can't we have an event with Phil tonight. Everything was so good, thank you for having me." Saying my goodbyes, I jumped in my car and, before heading home, swung by the avenue, walked in the bar, which was empty, except for some locals. They must have thought I was checking up on Babe, so I used the rest room. When I came out I saw the breaking news; people were being arrested all day, but the names weren't released yet.

Checking my watch, I thought I should go home and rest before the fundraiser later on. Saying goodbye, I jumped in the car and drove by the club around the corner, before leaving the neighborhood. It was closed- not a good sign.

Go home and stay home. None of this has anything to do with us! Pulling up in my spot, I saw a lot of official cars around. I got out slowly and walked to the house. Federal agents met me at the door, asked for my ID, and directed me to sit down on the ground. I handed them my license and waited. They were ripping the house apart and removing boxes. I saw everything I took for granted everyday being carted out.

I'm sure there was something I was supposed to do, but I couldn't think of what it was. Finally, I stood up and asked to use the rest room, but was told no and to sit down. Fighting back tears, I sat there wringing the handles of my handbag, angry that I felt so helpless.

An hour or so later, an agent asked me to follow him inside and take a seat. Quietly, I followed and sat at the island. Agent

Murphy introduced himself and started right in with a million questions. "What is your relationship to the owner of this house?"

"He's my boyfriend. Excuse me, but I really need to use the bathroom."

"Let's just talk first, I have some serious questions I have to ask you. Where do you work?"

The only thing I would say was that I needed to use the bathroom over and over for two hours, until I thought I would have an accident. He saw my discomfort and seemed to enjoy it. On the verge of bursting a kidney I stood up and cried out, "No I don't think you understand, I need to use the restroom, NOW, before I have an accident. I'm pregnant." I said feeling desperate. I walked towards the bedroom, but was grabbed by an agent who shoved me back towards my seat.

I smashed into the chair arm and fell on the hard tile. I was shocked he touched me so roughly; gripping my stomach, I started to cry as I got up. Now I was in complete agony when I sat down again. They tore apart everything, smashed things, and threw the contents of the fridge in the sink. I wanted to scream, what did the fucking butter and eggs do to deserve this but held my tongue. The bag with the baby blanket was tossed on the floor and the tissue paper went flying.

Reaching forward, I grabbed the blanket off the floor, but lost my balance and fell face forward hard on the tile again. Totally embarrassed, I picked myself up and sat down again clutching the blanket fiercely. The pain was coming on fast and furious, but I mustered up the strength to ask a question. "I'm sure you have one, but may I see your warrant?" Murphy handed me a bunch of papers folded up. I looked at them, but I didn't know what they were; I had never seen any before. "Where are you taking my belongings? Will I get a receipt?"

He kept rambling, but I didn't really focus on anything he had to say to me. "Listen, we wouldn't be here if we weren't looking for specific items. Do you know where he keeps...?"

Breaking in, "I need to call a lawyer."

"Do you know your boyfriend's real

name?" Insulted, I said, "Yes, of course I

do!"

"Good, what other names does he use with you?"

I repeated the same line so many times, "I'm sorry, I need a lawyer before I can speak with you."

Trying to rattle my cage, and make me so nervous I would say anything, he continued his assault, "You don't understand he's facing a lot of time. Violating his parole is serious. Being a convicted felon, he'll have to serve the rest of his sentence besides all the new charges. This is a RICO case, which means a lot of time ahead. You could make it easier for him, if you just answered some of our questions. So let's start with..."

FUCK YOU, I'M NOT ANSWERING DICK! "I'm so sorry to waste your time, but I need to call a lawyer in order to speak with you and that's final," I said bluffing; I didn't have a lawyer.

Leering and trying to intimidate me he slowly, deliberately he said, "You're making a mistake."

Cutting him off I said, "Thank you but I'll need the receipts."

I had watched enough police TV shows to at least try and ask. *What's the worst he could do, say no?* Agent Murphy walked away and busied himself elsewhere. When he returned, he handed me more papers.

"You could be charged as an accessory. If not, don't think he will be coming home soon, if ever." Trying to frighten me, he continued. "Have your lawyer call me, we want you to come down for questioning," he said as he handed me his business card.

"Thank you." was all I would say. I was thanking him for destroying my life. I watched them all pack up and leave. I sat there looking at the shambles left behind. They went through everything. Glancing over, I saw Babe's office door open taunting me to peak inside at the world behind the curtain. I walked in and looked around for the first time.

There was a desk, phone, bookcase, couch and some chairs. The walls had some framed movie posters, but there wasn't anything of interest left there, except the photo I gave him months earlier, of me in a Halloween costume framed on the desk. I walked to the closet; it was empty. Whatever was in there was gone now. Our bedroom was a disaster, every drawer was open, the closet was empty; the agents threw the contents on the floor.

I picked up his white tuxedo shirt from yesterday and held it to my face. It still had his smell on it. I just wanted him in the shirt and nothing more.

My mind went crazy with fear and insecurity. Our life was over! I knew he wasn't going to encourage me to wait; otherwise he would have married me while he had the chance. What he doesn't realize is that one way or another I'll be there in some shape or form. *Where are you? I hope you're safe!*

I looked around the room and for the first time, I thought I could hang myself here. *No one would know no one would miss me.* This was all too much for me; I started to get such bad abdominal pains, because I was beyond having to pee now. Blood was already pouring down my legs as I ran to the bathroom. I was hemorrhaging; I was losing my little Babe.

After it was all over, I walked in the living room to lie down on the couch, holding his shirt, trying to find a shred of hope and hold on to it. I could only find one; he was alive. I was so grateful that at least he hadn't been shot to death like so many others. I couldn't bear it if he would have been killed. So many people lost, so many lives damaged beyond comprehension for what? Money? Power? I would never begin to understand or accept the reasons, because I never really knew them to begin with. I'm sure I wasn't the only girl with her head down praying.

Tremendous loss and prison were something very common in this life of ours. I closed my eyes on the couch gripping his shirt breathing in his smell hoping against hope this was a nightmare and I would wake up soon. But my life was just starting. I was going to have a beautiful baby with my nose and his eyes, he was going to marry me, we were going to have a big wedding and raise the roof on the house, I was going to quickly have another baby and we were going to have everything. All I had to do was wake up.

The End

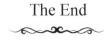

Coming Soon

- ***When We Owned New York***

- ***You Just Can't Help Yourself***

- ***Things***

47009844R00336

Made in the USA
Middletown, DE
05 June 2019